MW00929247

The Quest for Asian Sin

The Quest for Asian Sin

To Jewel,

Thank you for everything

Hope you enjoy the story.

Monty Lemley

Copyright © 2016 by Monty Lemley.

Library of Congress Control Number:		2016911412
ISBN:	Hardcover	978-1-5245-2568-2
	Softcover	978-1-5245-2567-5
	eBook	978-1-5245-2566-8

All rights reserved. No part of this book may be reproduced or transmitted in any form or by any means, electronic or mechanical, including photocopying, recording, or by any information storage and retrieval system, without permission in writing from the copyright owner.

This is a work of fiction. Names, characters, places and incidents either are the product of the author's imagination or are used fictitiously, and any resemblance to any actual persons, living or dead, events, or locales is entirely coincidental.

Any people depicted in stock imagery provided by Thinkstock are models, and such images are being used for illustrative purposes only.
Certain stock imagery © Thinkstock.

Print information available on the last page.

Rev. date: 08/05/2016

To order additional copies of this book, contact:
Xlibris
1-888-795-4274
www.Xlibris.com
Orders@Xlibris.com
733232

To my parents:

Donald A. and Louise Lemley

Acknowledgments

Like Jack Conner, I have no real way to express my thanks to the people who worked very hard to help me make this story what it has become. I can only say it wouldn't have been possible if it were not for their efforts.

Sheila Lemley Terrell
Mary Schwartz
Dean Brown
Kannika Lemley
Nancy (Hui Ying) Chen
Karen (Jie) Lin
Jeff Ramos
Donna Pylypczuk
Michael Hawkins, Graphic Designer
Cheri M.

Chapter 1

I wasn't looking for work or adventure; Lieutenant Jack Conner, retired, had had plenty of that in the last twenty-five years. I'd had a life filled with some adventure and some drama, but mostly boredom and occasionally sheer terror, probably the life of most police officers or deputy sheriffs. I was the latter. A 75 percent retirement with a generous severance package made it easy to accept the sheriff office's offer for an early out.

It started with a short newspaper article. I was in San Diego for the Mardi Gras celebration. I'm not sure why it caught my attention—maybe because "porn star" was in the headline. The paper was a week old, and the article was on page two. It was only a couple of paragraphs. Maybe it was because the story lacked page one lead attention that it caught my consideration. The television news failed to report it—locally, regionally, or nationally. It's possible I had missed it in the report since I don't watch much TV, but I seem to always have it on as background.

Maybe I just wasn't wise to what makes a good story. Stories need to make money. The free press once was considered the fourth branch of government—watchdogs for a free society—but now it exists only for money and entertainment. Regardless of what self-deluded sanctimony reporters have convinced themselves of, they are there to make money for their bosses and entertain the masses—nothing more.

The story started with a bold-type font, probably two or three font sizes larger than the text. In my opinion, it should have at least been four or five sizes bigger. "Retired porn star missing."

Apparently she went for her daily ritual of running along the beach and never came home. Her older daughter, a student at Berkeley, reported her mother's disappearance. The initial police investigation found no evidence of foul play, and the case was assigned to detectives to continue the inquiry.

The second paragraph described her career, with a slight hint of some self-righteous disapproval by the reporter. I checked the byline. My hunch was right; the reporter was a female.

I pushed my chair back from the table to enjoy the cool breeze and took another sip of my coffee and reflected. Maybe that was all a porn star should rate: a second-page, two-paragraph newspaper article. After all, we live in a paradoxical, judgmental society, at least on the surface.

After I stood up and dropped a couple of dollars on the table, it was time to start my day. The first thing on my agenda was a visit to the tall ship the *Star of India*. I strolled along the boardwalk and scanned the bay to see if some naval ships were anchored at the base. My attraction to large ships started as a child. I love them. Anytime I got an opportunity to travel, my choice was always to a place where there was a chance to tour a large ship.

As I approached the *Star*, my gaze went to her uncanvassed masts reaching toward the sky. The breeze rocked her slightly in the mooring. I wondered about my attraction to big ships as the American flag slow-danced on her stern. It didn't matter whether it was a tall ship or a modern battleship; ships attracted me, and I wasn't sure why. After all, I was raised a thousand miles from any ocean and five hundred miles from any sizable river.

At the same time, my mind continued to return to the article about the missing porn star. I wanted to forget it, forget her, but it wasn't that easy to let go. Maybe it wasn't her at all, but rather my memory of Xiu Tang, a young Chinese medical student I once knew. Actually, I loved her, or at least I thought I did. It was the summer after my high school graduation. I had tried to forget this girl, this young woman from another world so far away, but I never did. Maybe it was my past that wouldn't let it go. Perhaps a nap would rid me of this madness, so I decided to go back to my hotel near the Gaslamp Quarter before heading over to the aircraft carrier *Midway*.

My fast pace surprised me. I usually walked slowly, taking in everything around me, formulating words and sentences to describe my observations. With my brisk steps, I quickly made the mile walk to the hotel. A modest place, but it was close to the upcoming Fat Tuesday events. I headed straight for my room and then to the computer on the writing desk near the balcony doors. I typed in her name, or at least the name she was known by: "Asian Sin."

In less than a thousandth of a second, hits came on the screen. I scrolled down the list to a biography of the porn star. It seemed strange that there were only a couple of links to her being missing. I passed them for the time being and clicked on the bio page.

The page opened to a picture of a petite woman in a bikini. She was a stunning beauty with dark, enchanting eyes and a wicked, captivating smile. Her eyes and smile brought an uncomfortable familiarity to me.

The bio described her as Chinese. She had been adopted by an American couple who worked in the American Embassy in Bangkok, Thailand. Her American parents had named her Sara—Sara Jones. She was born in the late sixties or early seventies. Whoever dropped her at the Catholic orphanage left her without any information. With no verifiable birth date, her new parents used Sara's adoption date for a month and day and estimated the year for her birth. She would be in her mid- to late forties now, which meant her bio photo was at least twenty years, maybe thirty years old.

This bio link impressed me. It was straight-up facts. It wasn't selling anything and wasn't judgmental. Just the facts or truths somebody wrote without hyperbole for commercial purposes.

She attended private schools in Thailand from grade school to high school. Her first trip to the States was for college. She earned a couple of scholarships into Berkeley on a business major and a minor in modern American literature. She excelled in school, but in the second half of her freshman year, she began dancing in strip clubs. The biography didn't really explain why she selected stripping for a part-time job. I speculated money, thrills, or defiance—the three principal motivators of youth.

During her sophomore year, she'd become pregnant with the first of her two daughters. The web page did not disclose the names of her children; this added to the bio's credibility. I figured the writer must have had some ethics because he had not dragged her kids into the story, victimizing them as well—not a typical tabloid tactic. There was also no mention of the father or fathers in the article. Perhaps the fathers were unknown, even to Asian Sin herself.

She started porn under another alias in her junior year. She did not become known as Asian Sin until she had graduated with her bachelor's degree. She earned a master's in business and a second bachelor's in theater.

During her porn career, she was credited with eighty feature films and some three hundred compilations. She retired at the age of forty after accumulating a small fortune, which, with her education and drive, turned into a rather large fortune.

I read several more biographies that were consistent with the first, with the exception of her heritage. That differed somewhat depending on the article. Some stated that she was Thai, and others said she was Taiwanese. I failed to see the importance of defining her ethnicity or giving her more than one ethnic background.

I then opened one of the porn sites. Being in the police business for over twenty years, I was no stranger to porn. No, I hadn't heard of her, but on reflection, I didn't know the names of any porn stars. Other than a mild curiosity, I found pornography rather boring.

Her movies were typical porn, but I found her atypical. Beyond her beauty, she filled the screen with a seductive intensity I had never seen in this venue or in any other venue. Again, those magic eyes and smile captivated me. Her eyes took me back to that other time, in that other world.

Several hours passed, and it was only when hunger got the best of me that I realized how long I had been at my computer. With the press of a button, the screen went black. I pushed it to the wall and stretched my arms over my shoulders. I yawned as I stood. It was time for a walk. I grabbed my wallet, checked it for my key card, and headed to the door.

I walked down the hall and pressed the elevator button. The door opened to a car filled with laughter and conversation. The laughter was silenced as I, the interloper, stepped into the car. The two couples moved against the back wall as I turned to face the door. Behind me came the snickers of the four and the odor of alcohol. I felt their eyes directed at my back. Perhaps it was my boots or hat that attracted their stares. Perhaps they were practicing for Tuesday's festivities, and they were just attempting politeness, at least as polite as drunks could be.

They followed me out of the car and into the lobby. I didn't look back. I nodded at the stately clerk standing behind the counter and at the bellhop. The bellhop opened the door for me, and I responded with a thank you just above a whisper and walked out the door.

I met the coolness outside with a welcome breath. The fresh scent of ocean saturated the air as the evening welcomed the sunset. Dark shadows slowly crawled across the street. I noticed a convenience store during my wait for the light. While the street was not filled with people, there were a few bizarre human oddities walking past. I was invisible to most of them as they passed without recognizing that I was even standing there.

One strange couple clad in black leather and covered in tattoos caused me to stop and stare. They strolled by me, completely oblivious to my gaze. I turned to watch them walk. She had a silver metal collar with long spikes evenly divided along the circumference. A large silver-linked chain connected her collar to a silver-spiked cuff on his left arm.

"Huh," I said to myself with a grin and raised eyebrows. Before they could discover me staring at them, I turned and continued my walk. It was disappointing that my afternoon was wasted with something as stupid as thinking about a missing porn star. It was probably some publicity stunt, I rationalized. I discovered early in my career that rationalization is the cornerstone of laziness and procrastination. Cops use it all the time to get out of work and to avoid responsibility, and in this case, it was supposed to get me off the hook without any guilt or consequences.

But my mind just wouldn't let her go, so a silent argument persisted inside my head in an attempt to justify my inaction. Frankly, not only was it stupid but it wasn't my business. The local police were investigating.

The changing traffic light interrupted my thoughts. I crossed the street but stopped short of entering the small store. It was easier to pretend to study the goods through the windows than to dismiss or go forward with my decision. I knew that by entering the store and buying legal pads, pens, and other small things to document and organize a criminal investigation would commit me to this inquiry.

To avoid a decision or commitment, I directed my thoughts down the street to look for a place to eat. I grabbed a hamburger and a tap beer at one of the many local eateries and sat at an outside table to watch the people on the street.

The hamburger was okay, but the beer was great. I ordered a second one. The young woman serving me was both attentive and thoughtful. She stepped away swiftly to retrieve my request and returned almost immediately, placing the frosty mug on the table, and with a smile, left to tend to the other customers. With a sip of my second beer, I sighed with the knowledge I would forget this idiotic thing and go about my vacation, unhindered with the thoughts of a missing porn star. A sense of pride came over me for keeping my suspicious nature and imagination in check.

After my fourth celebratory beer, I paid my tab and gathered up my uneaten French fries to share with the birds on the waterfront. On my walk back down to the water, I broke up the fries in thirds and tossed them toward the smaller birds. It was still an almost impossible task for the little birds to catch or keep the food against the skill and determination of the quicker seagulls.

I sat down facing the bow of the *Star of India,* perhaps to seek an answer from the wisdom of the old vessel's years. Beyond her and on the bay, outlined by their lights, yachts and other boats cruised up the channel. They sounded lonely horns that echoed off the buildings behind me. I closed my eyes. There she was … Xiu Tang … or was it Asian Sin? I jumped to my feet and cursed myself. "Goddamn it, Jack, when are you going to grow up? She is not the person you knew. You're not a teenager at a county fair. This is not your problem." I walked on.

It was late when I returned to the hotel. The lateness required me to show my ID and key card to the security guard stalking the lobby. He was there to discourage any unruly guests or professional girls from hanging around the lobby or going up to the rooms; after all, this was the weekend before Mardi Gras.

I struggled to return my ID back into my wallet while trying to hold the sack filled with pens, a stapler, some legal pads, and a folder. My willpower had succumbed to my suspicious nature, and I had bought supplies at the convenience store as I returned to my room. I pressed the number 17 on the elevator and waited for the doors to close.

I like upper-level floors. I had read in some travel magazine they were cheaper than the lower floors. But I had also read—I think, in the same magazine sometime after that—that they were actually higher priced. The elevator car was empty and quiet.

The silence wasn't welcome. It made me think. For the moment on the vertical ride, I returned to my past to that first time I saw her … Xiu Tang.

When I got back to my room, I put my legal pads beside my computer and went to the bathroom for a shower. During my shower, I developed a strategy. I dressed quickly and went directly from the bathroom to the writer's desk and opened my computer.

I typed in Asian Sin's name again and had instant results: porn sites. I shook my head, went back to the search page, and typed in "disappearance" behind her name and got four results. I opened and read each one. The longest included her biography, which I copied and pasted and then sent to my e-mail.

I went back to the porn sites, opened several of them, and watched her for a short time. I wanted to know who I was looking for and why. I closed the last site and typed in the search "porn business" and began reading about the industry. I learned most successful stars sign with one of many companies that control the filming, editing, processing, and distribution. Those companies also develop websites for their stars, set up fan clubs, and arrange personal appearances at different venues, such as strip joints and private clubs.

Asian Sin was signed with Naked Triple X Videos and Films. She also served as an officer in the parent corporation, the Pacific Rim Entertainment Corporation. In addition to porn, they had a division that dubbed in English or added subtitles in movies from all over Asia. They also made movies in the Far East and managed minor Asian stars for mainstream movies made in the United States.

I started a list of people that needed to be interviewed, such as Asian Sin's costars, but my first stop would be the corporate headquarters for Naked Triple X Videos and Films. It was very late—or early, depending on your perspective. My mind was running too fast to sleep, so I went out in the hall for some ice. I returned to my room and dumped some ice in a glass and poured whiskey over the cubes. Along with the office supplies that I had purchased at the mini–mart, I had bought a bottle of whiskey as well. After my third drink, I fell asleep in front of the TV.

The morning was almost over by the time I got up. My decision was to wait until after Mardi Gras before I began my investigation on what I considered a very foolish venture. I didn't understand why I was doing it, nor why I couldn't let go. Waiting wouldn't spoil my Mardi Gras vacation, and it would allow more time for the police to finish their investigation.

The morning news was still on while I got ready. The weathergirl reported snow and cold in my home state of Colorado. It would be in the low seventies here. A call to the airline, and my ticket was changed for Los Angeles instead of going home. I wasn't really ready for subzero weather. One advantage of being unemployed is the ability to change destinations on a whim. That afternoon, I went to the aircraft carrier *Midway* to relax. However, there wasn't much relaxing. I walked the halls and decks of the old ship, spending most of my time formulating my investigation.

I did manage to keep my commitment to not do anything until Mardi Gras was over. The rest of my days in San Diego went fast, including the celebration. I probably drank too much, but I had fun. Every morning started the same, with opening the computer and searching for any new or additional information about Asian Sin. That never took long; there was none, not even a follow-up from the paper where I read the original article.

With the help of the computer and a couple of search engines, I found the jurisdiction of the disappearance: Wayfarer, California, incorporated 1995. I made several calls to the Wayfarer Police Department and found that for a smaller department, they were well entrenched in bureaucracy. An annoyed secretary told me that I would have to wait until the detective called me back. She also informed me that the detective sergeant, detective lieutenant, and detective captain were not available.

The only thing I hadn't done was call my daughters and tell them I was staying in California for an indeterminate time. I did not like talking to my girls. After fifteen years they still blamed me for my wife's and my divorce, even though she was the one that packed up the kids and moved to Colorado Springs. Within a year she was remarried. Perhaps my judgmental daughters were right. I was so involved with my work, I ignored my family. My ex-wife got a new husband and the allegiance of my children; I got the guilt.

Kathleen's phone rang several times before she answered. She was almost apathetic when I told her I was going up to Los Angeles for another couple weeks. She didn't ask why, or when I was coming home. She just told me to be careful and that she loved me as she hung up the telephone.

Margaret was polite enough to ask how long I was staying and if I needed anything. She was pragmatic in her tone. She volunteered her husband, Bill, to go check on my place and informed me that it was bitter cold and snowing in Colorado. She thought it was a good deal that I was extending my vacation. Then she was gone.

Chapter 2

Once in Los Angeles, I checked into a hotel within walking distance of the corporate headquarters for Naked Triple X Videos and Films, which was located in an area of Los Angles known as Little Tokyo. My hotel was just outside Little Tokyo. The hotels in Little Tokyo were better but more expensive.

I am far from rich, but with my retirement and a few investments, I was doing fine. There was enough money for me to travel and do what I wanted to do. My residence is on eighteen acres between Colorado Springs and Pueblo, along the river. It is a small piece of a much larger farm and ranch, which has been in my family for generations. I was lucky; I never had a house payment. During the spring, summer, and fall, my time is spent working on antique cars and farm tractors. In the winter, I travel, or at least since I retired a couple of years ago. But I still watch my money and expenses closely.

It was still early afternoon by the time I got settled. I relaxed some before reviewing my notes, which covered about thirty pages divided among the three legal pads. My folder contained about twenty documents and articles that the staff at the hotel in San Diego printed for me before I left.

I called the corporate office for Naked Triple X Videos and Films and got bounced around to several voice mails and secretaries. I disliked dealing with corporations. The staff was overly friendly as they avoided me and pawned me off to other staff or yet another electronic message system.

After they figured out I wasn't going away, they finally connected me to Spencer Manning, the vice president in charge of marketing. His voice was cold and suspicious. He asked me some questions, but I held firm that I would not answer any questions over the phone. Reluctantly, he agreed to see me later today after 3:00.

He said he was leaving soon and wanted to meet at a restaurant between my hotel and his office. I agreed. My suspicion was that the powers at the corporation didn't want me at their place of business, but they were curious about either my knowledge of the incident or what I was after. My best guess would be the former.

I had some time, so I tried the detective again at the police department. Unfortunately, the same secretary took my call. She stopped just short of telling me not to call again and assured me that the detective had the message and would call.

I arrived early at the restaurant and ordered an iced tea; I had finished my second glass when Manning arrived. I stood to meet him; he wasn't alone.

"Hello, Jack Conner?"

"Yes," I answered, looking past him at the stunning Asian female in a business suit at his side. Her jacket failed to hide her thin but athletic frame. She was tall for an Asian, and her skirt covered her long legs to her knees.

He turned slightly and with an open hand introduced the woman. "This is Keeley Nu."

"Glad to meet you." She presented her hand. I took her hand with a slight nod.

He added, "I hope you don't mind me inviting her; she is one of our lawyers."

I directed them to sit, "Please."

There was an awkward pause as we looked at one another. The vice president of marketing, Spencer Manning, wasn't what I expected. He didn't look like a pimp in loud colors and covered in jewelry. He was dressed in a moderate but expensive suit. I could tell by the way it fit him that it was tailored. He was in his late twenties or early thirties, clean-shaven, with light hair in a military cut. I suddenly felt very underdressed in my black denim jeans and light gray polo shirt.

He broke the ice with a curt, "May I see some ID, please?"

My driver's license, weapon concealment and carry permit, retired sheriff's ID, and private investigator ID with the license number were all ready for his inspection.

When I retired, I had started doing some civil process for a couple of law firms in Denver and Colorado Springs. Because they only gave me hard cases that required some investigation, the attorneys felt it necessary that I get a private investigator's license—lawyers.

Manning studied each card and then handed them to his female companion. She then examined them with even greater attention. As he passed the last one, he spoke again. "So why is a retired sheriff, slash, private investigator from Colorado looking into the disappearance of one of our retired stars?"

His eyes met mine as I formulated an answer. I glanced over at the attorney; she was also looking at me. I bit down on my lip. The truth was, I didn't know why, but I wasn't going to tell them that. It sounded crazy even to me.

"Are you some love-starved fan?" he asked harshly. "Are you a freak?"

"No." My answer came with a cold stare. "I'm just doing some preliminary work to see if there is even a case here. I haven't committed to anything yet. I don't want to waste my client's money if there is nothing here."

The lawyer asked, "Who is your client?"

"I would rather not say. They requested anonymity." I paused. "I hope you understand." What else was I going to say? My client was me? They'd know I was crazy. Keeley Nu's dark eyes reflected disapproval, but she remained silent.

"Look," I said. It was time I took control of this. "I have not officially taken this case. I hope she turns up. I am not seeking any confidential information, nor do I want you to answer anything that makes you feel uncomfortable. I will not ask any personal information. Those are my rules."

"What do you want to know?" Keeley asked. There was no emotion in her voice.

I smiled. "Well, for starters, is this a habit of hers, disappearing without a trace? Not contacting anyone?"

"No." Manning shook his head as he raised his Coke to his lips. He took a drink and continued, "She was very dependable and responsible. She never missed a day of work, and she was never late. This is very out of character for her."

"Work?" I asked.

Manning looked over at his partner and back at me with a glare. I knew he didn't trust me. I understood him. I wouldn't trust me either if our roles were opposite.

"What?" I asked.

He didn't want to answer. With reluctance he spoke. "She missed a board meeting, and we haven't been able to reach her since. We have tried everything: phone, cell, text, e-mail." He took another drink.

"Have you or anyone else had any ransom demands?"

Keeley and Manning looked at each other, and both shook their heads no.

Keeley asked me, "Have you contacted the police? Have they told you anything?"

"I've tried. I think they are stonewalling me. Not even a return call."

They looked at each other again. I could tell they had had the same experience with the police.

"Any idea why they haven't contacted you?" I asked.

"No, you were a cop. You think like them. Any ideas?" Keeley asked.

"No … and I don't think like these guys." I asked again in disbelief, "No one from the PD has contacted your company? Done any interviews? Done anything?"

"Not a word. They haven't returned any of our calls, either," Manning replied.

"Frankly, that surprises me, but it isn't my investigation." I sighed. "Maybe they are overwhelmed with prank calls and false leads. Maybe they have control of the situation and don't need any information." I felt awkward defending this department, especially after the way they had treated me.

We talked for a couple of hours. They taught me some things about their businesses and what they knew of Asian Sin. Neither had actually worked with her. They saw her only in passing, as neither of them was high enough on the corporate ladder to attend the meetings she attended.

Keeley defrosted some and even laughed some. Manning remained polite, but still I failed to gain his trust. Before they left I asked them, "Did she have an agent? I heard that actors and actresses have agents."

They both grinned. Apparently the term "actress" is archaic.

Manning finally volunteered, "Sort of. She did most of her own contract work and negotiations, but she had an agent for screening scripts, costars, things like that. He is …"

I stopped him. I put my room number and the hotel's phone number on the back of my business cards. I gave him three of them. I said, "You contact him and ask him if he would speak to me. All my contact information is on the card. I don't want to compromise anyone. It might seem like a silly thing, but I want people to know I am legitimate."

Manning smiled and nodded. I stood, and they shook my hand and walked out together.

Before I left, I ordered some food and wrote down some notes. She hadn't been threatened. There had been no strangers hanging around the office. Neither had heard of her having any problems with stalkers or strangers hanging around her house. Basically, our meeting was just another dead end, other than gaining some additional background information.

I finished my meal, gathered my stuff, and headed out on the street. Traffic was heavy, and the sidewalks were filled with daily workers likely heading home. I was about a block away from the hotel when I got a text message. It was from Keeley. "*Check the news.*"

I hate texting and would have been happier with a phone call. I didn't reply. I hurried up to my room, opened my laptop, and typed in "Asian Sin news." It was an article from the San Diego paper. "Porn Star Heads to Cabo San Lucas on Yacht with Lover."

I read the article. It was basically a standard police press release with some added background information. The police said they received a telephone call from a woman claiming to be Asian Sin, and she explained she was on a private yacht and wasn't aware that she had been reported missing. They added the case would not be closed until she returned to the United States. This meant the police weren't obligated to release additional information.

I called Keeley, but she didn't answer. I tried Spencer Manning. He answered that he had gotten the same text, but hadn't got home. I gave him the news.

"So, I guess you're done then?" he asked.

"No, not yet. I hope they're right, but I would like a little more."

Manning told me that he had contacted Asian's agent, who said he would be happy to talk with me. He would be calling. I thanked Manning and hung up. As I looked out my window, the streetlights began flickering in the setting sun. The dinner crowd started to fill the street.

I spotted a bar across the street. It looked inviting. I showered and decided to go over and have a drink. I sort of worried about drinking too much, but what the hell? A couple of drinks, and my concerns would go away … far, far away.

The next morning was rough. My head throbbed in pain. I'm not sure how much I ended up drinking or why the shower was running or where

the woman's clothing on the floor came from. Slowly, it started coming back to me, especially when I recognized the clothes. They were Keeley's.

She had called, and I had invited her over to the bar to talk. She wanted to know my perspective on the police's revelation. I probably talked too much, but I wasn't awake enough yet for self-castigation. Besides, I was more concerned about what I was going to do when the water stopped in the bathroom.

My cell rang. I looked down at the screen. It displayed a California number. I suspected it was the agent. "Hello?"

"Jack Conner?" a too energetic male voice asked.

"Yes," I managed before I yawned into the phone.

"This is Franklin Berry, Asian's agent."

I pulled myself up in the bed and covered myself with the sheets. I could never get comfortable talking to a guy without being dressed. I know it was on the phone, but that was just me.

"Yes, Mr. Berry, I am glad you called."

"I understand you want to talk to me."

I was distracted with the shower stopping. "Yes … yes, can we meet?"

"Can't we do this on the phone?" He sounded somewhat annoyed.

"No," I answered. I thought briefly about adding "sorry," but I wasn't. I was taking steps to protect Asian Sin and her family.

"Okay, how about your hotel's restaurant?" He paused. "How about one o'clock?"

I checked my watch. It was almost noon. I was stunned. "Yes … that would be fine." He hung up. I rolled on my back and stared at the ceiling, trying to get my senses back. "Christ," I said under my breath.

Keeley stepped out of the bathroom and began to gather her clothes. She made no attempt to cover her nude body. I rose back up in the bed, resting on one elbow. She was beautiful. I think she liked me staring at her, but it made me rather uncomfortable.

She must have known by the confused expression on my face that I was looking for some explanation. She dropped the bundle of clothes on the chair by the writing desk. Her pace slowed as she walked toward me.

She sat down, gathered my hand into hers, and placed my hand on the inside of her leg. She smiled. Her almond eyes danced. I was about to say something, but I really didn't know what. She leaned over and kissed me on the lips. It was a long kiss, full of desire and passion. It felt like the first time I had ever been kissed. She withdrew her lips and gently pressed her index finger on my lips to silence me.

She smiled as she spoke. "Look, it was just a thing. Okay? I'm not looking for any explanation or any valiant, romantic gestures on your part. It was my choice." She stood with a smile, grabbed her clothes, and returned to the bathroom.

I flopped back down. Oddly, my first thought was how reckless she was with her clothes. I am far from being an expert on women, but she was the first woman that I had seen who discarded her clothes as she did. And then gathered them up without care. Expensive clothes even.

It then dawned on me that, for a few hours at least, my mind was no longer on Asian Sin. Keeley had given me an escape for some time and some much needed, very deep sleep. I wanted to thank her, but for some reason, it seemed that would have trivialized the moment, the evening.

Keeley emerged from the bathroom fully dressed. She looked as sharp and professional as when we first met. I stood, pulled the sheet off the bed, and wrapped it around me.

She laughed as she came toward me. "You're such a little boy." She gave me a quick kiss, pulled away from me, and stepped to the door. She opened it and turned back to look at me. She sighed with a gentle smile as she spoke. "Good luck and be careful. I am not sure what you're getting yourself into. Call me if you need anything." She slipped through the door.

I stood for a moment looking at the closed door. A bit bewildered, I sat back down on the edge of the bed and filled my lungs with the air around me. The room was filled with her scent … her perfume. I stood again and stretched. I headed to the bathroom, the bedsheet in tow.

Franklin Berry wasn't what I'd imagined. I was expecting a bald man with a plaid suit and black-rimmed glasses, with gold rings on every finger and a large gold chain plainly visible, outlined by a bright-colored silk shirt with the buttons opened to his navel. So much for stereotypes.

Instead, there sat a well-dressed and groomed young man. He looked like a regular young businessman, who probably surfed on the weekends. His hair was bleached from the sun, and his tan was deep. His eyes were genuine and trustworthy. He stood as I approached.

We shook hands, and he invited me to sit. I slid in the booth, and before I could speak, a waitress put a glass of water in front of me and, with a commercial smile, asked if I would like something else to drink. I ordered coffee, and she deposited a menu in front of me and hurried away. I looked at Berry.

He shrugged. "Forgive me; I already ordered."

I pulled my IDs from my shirt pocket and handed them to Berry. He took them and glanced at each one.

"Please forgive me, Franklin, but do you have some ID?" I asked in a polite tone.

"Of course." He slid forward to pull his wallet from the rear pocket of his trousers. "That is why you wanted to meet. You wanted to make sure who you were talking to, right?"

I smiled. We started to talk. He first apologized for being short on the telephone with me. He talked some about himself, and he told me he had about twenty clients, all women. About half of them were in the porn industry, and the other half did bit parts and commercials. He said he had a couple that showed real promise. I didn't ask which genre.

For the first hour, he talked about everything except Asian Sin. He was conducting his own investigation of sorts and trying to establish some trust. Then, without me asking a single question, he started. He had been her agent for about twelve years. He reiterated that he only handled her preliminary inquiries; she handled her own contracts.

I asked him if he had been contacted by the police. He shook his head no and asked in an aggravated tone, "Do you believe that bullshit they're saying now about her being in Mexico?"

"Do you?" I returned the question.

"Hell, no!" He realized he'd become loud and looked around to see if anyone noticed. "She is the most reliable person I know. She would have never left without telling someone. She would have never left without telling me." He paused for reflection and a sip of coffee. "She was a true professional."

A joke about being a true professional came to mind, but I remained silent. In over an hour of conversation, "hell" was the first swear word he had used.

The conversation became more direct and almost a whisper. He asked, "Mr. Conner, who hired you?"

"I can't say." It made me uneasy that I was getting used to the lie.

He nodded in understanding. "What do you need from me?"

"Anything. What do you think happened?"

He sighed. "I don't know. I am sure she didn't go off with some guy on a fling. She didn't really date." He paused. "I think she is in trouble."

My heart sank. I hate being right. "Have you taken your concerns to the police?"

His voice rose slightly. "I would … I tried. The police aren't interested in her," he almost yelled. "They're not interested in this case."

I looked down at my untouched food. Sometimes the people in my chosen profession disgust me.

"What is next?" he asked.

My eyes moved up to meet his eyes. "I need to see where she disappeared. Did she live alone? Can you arrange for me to see the house?"

His eyes didn't move. "I wish you would tell me who hired you." He was still working on trust.

"I haven't been hired yet. I haven't agreed to take on the case. This is just a preliminary investigation to see if there is a case. I am not going to waste my time or someone's money until I am sure."

"I'm sure! What are your rates? I'll hire you."

"Thank you, but no. Not yet." I looked down again.

"Why?"

I could feel the coldness in my eyes when I answered, "Because I haven't cleared you as a suspect yet."

At first, he was shocked, but with a nervous laugh, he nodded. "Fair enough." He started to play with his food and got lost in his thoughts for a moment. "I'll call and get you on the property, and you can talk with her caretakers. They were in the porn industry for a while. They got out, got married, and she took them in."

"Can they be trusted?"

He shrugged. "She trusted them."

Before he could say more, I interrupted him. "I don't want any names or an address until you get them to agree … okay?"

"Sure. I think while you are in town, you should speak to her lawyer. I'll call when I get to the office." He checked his watch. "Speaking of which, I need to get to work."

He slid out of the booth. I did the same. We shook hands. He leaned over and grabbed the bill. "Will it prejudice you if I pick up the check?"

I smiled and shook my head no.

"I suspect you will hear from her lawyer sometime today," he said as he turned away and headed for the cashier.

I sat back down at the table and studied my food. It was cold, and I wasn't sure I was hungry. The waitress put my food in a wax paper box. I dropped the tip on the table and left.

Same routine: check e-mails, check the news on the Internet, turn on the TV, and flop back in the bed. I checked my cell phone to make sure it was working and that I had service. With slight disappointment, I put the phone down. I guess I was hoping Keeley would call. Sometimes I forget what a lonely life I lead.

I watched three different local news channels, but there were no news reports on Asian Sin. I didn't really figure on any, but I still hoped. I was bored, but I didn't really want to go out.

It was almost five when Asian Sin's lawyer called, or rather her lawyer's office called.

"Mr. Conner?" The voice was female, and she spoke with an accent. Asian, I suspected.

"Yes."

"Dallas Xiao Xu would like to meet with you tomorrow at two o'clock p.m.," she said—no doubt Asian. She added, "A car will pick you up around one thirty at your hotel. Is this acceptable?"

I asked if we could make it a morning meeting.

The girl answered, "No, two o'clock. Is that acceptable?" she asked with a slight edge to her voice.

I sighed. "Sure, two o'clock … one thirty … in front of the hotel, a car."

"Thank you, Mr. Conner. I am glad the times are acceptable." She hung up.

"I am glad the times are acceptable," I repeated under my breath with some aggravation. I was trying to figure out what choice there was.

It was dark again before I made it back down to the streets. I decided to walk to the park and back around to the hotel. Maybe hunger would hit me by then. I checked my telephone again. I guess Keeley really meant it when she said it was just a thing.

I actually didn't hear the roar of the traffic or watch the masses stride on the concrete sidewalks. My mind was too busy bouncing thoughts between Asian Sin and Keeley. I went over each interview in my mind. I went over each article, each story. I was missing something.

I decided on fast food for supper or dinner, depending on how removed you are from an agrarian background. I passed a newsstand on the sidewalk, where it widened to about the width of a single highway lane. Dozens of vendors were scattered on the concrete slab for a quarter mile or so. Each stand had some individualized specialty. One Asian lady sold T-shirts, and with a smile, she presented one for me to examine like a merchant of the past showing a rare and valuable Persian rug. Another woman sold silk scarves with oriental patterns. Although each had his or her specific items to sell, they shared common trinkets, like small animals carved from green jade or some hard green rock since I didn't have the skill or knowledge to know the difference. I passed them all and stood in the center of a three-sided newsstand. Newspapers from the entire world hung on the first partition, while the middle section held magazines. Books, maps, and odd periodicals filled the last section.

A gray-haired man sat behind a wooden TV tray. His arms were folded, and he rocked back in a wooden folding chair. His change purse hung from the back of the chair. He studied me closely as I browsed with my hands clasped together behind my back, a yielding demonstration of no ill intent on my part.

My selection consisted of three city newspapers: Denver, Los Angeles, and San Diego. I also grabbed up an underground paper, the *Adult-Only Free Press.* I gave the old man a ten dollar bill and motioned for him to keep the change as a tip. He smiled, leaned forward in his chair, and bowed in a gesture of thanks.

I folded the papers under my arm and headed toward the diner. I ordered the meal option with a double hamburger from the overhead menu by just giving the uniformed girl behind the cash register a number. She took my order with a tired smile and asked what I wanted to drink.

I told her, and she gave me a small plastic numbered tent and an empty cup. I took it over to the drink machine, poured my own drink, and sat down at a table. I unfolded the papers and put a straw in my drink. I wondered why she had asked me what I wanted to drink and then handed me an empty cup to serve myself.

The uniformed girl appeared with my order. I looked up, smiled, and pushed the tray to the side. I began to flip through my papers, starting with the Denver paper. I thumbed over to the weather section. The high was twenty degrees in Denver. I smiled. Los Angeles's current temperature reached in the high sixties at the moment.

I browsed the headlines in each paper between the bites of hamburger and French fries. As meals go, it wasn't very good. I skimmed several articles where the headlines caught my attention. There was nothing about Asian Sin. Asian Sin had already been forgotten by the mainstream, if there had been anything there in the first place. I doubted it. Porn stars are expendable and easily replaceable here.

I retrieved another drink and sat back down. I pushed back the conventional papers and began to examine the *Adult-Only Free Press.* I didn't even know this type of paper existed anymore. A person could get anything on the Internet these days.

Between the marijuana and hookah ads were articles about local underground bands and offbeat restaurants. Deeper in the paper, the articles attacked all levels of the government. The contributing writers spared no local, state, or federal entities from their wrath.

When I turned the page, I sat straight up in my booth. I read the headline several times: "No One Cries for Asian Sin."

The article started with the report of her disappearance, and then it gave a brief biography. The paragraphs after that really stirred my interest.

The writer started by condemning police and their investigation. According to the reporter, the police didn't interview anyone in the neighborhood, nor did they dive the waters near the beach where Asian Sin was last seen.

I went back to the headline and checked the byline. The reporter called himself Veritatis Inquisitor, a pseudonym no doubt. I checked the front of the weekly and then the back, looking for the rag's address.

I turned back to the article. Veritatis continued his diatribe against the police and their lack of an investigation. After my numerous attempts to get someone at the department to call me and being completely ignored, I had to wonder if he was right. He then wrote some vague accusations in the "why" question format.

Why won't the police release any reports concerning the investigation?

Why didn't the police interview any of the people around Asian Sin?

And his list continued, almost a recapitulation of the previous paragraphs. That is, until the last three whys:

Why wasn't Rock Hard interviewed?

Where was Rock Hard when Asian Sin disappeared?

Why did Rock Hard leave the city for an unknown location after the disappearance?

Leaving the other three papers, I finished my flat cola, gathered up the weekly, and stepped back out on the street.

Chapter 3

Several taxis ignored my wave, the drivers intentionally looking away, before one stopped, a bright orange minivan with white lettering. It reminded me of a large M&M's Peanut. I slid the door open and got in. I reached over the seat and handed the driver the paper and pointed to the address. He nodded. He typed the address in his GPS and pulled into traffic.

I leaned back in the seat and watched the city pass by the cab's window. My thoughts bounced around the text of the article. "What the hell is a Rock Hard?" I asked myself under my breath. Rock Hard must be a stage name for a male porn star that Asian worked with during her career. I didn't remember his name on my list. I surely would have remembered something as trite as Rock Hard.

The driver took me from a well-lit city, with streetlights on each corner and lights shining in every parking lot and from business windows, to a darker city. An old city that very few, other than the ones who lived there, ever crossed the imaginary line to visit. This area was a place where the residents lived and played by different rules. He glanced in his mirror looking for conversation. I had none.

It was time for reflection and doubt. I'd never considered myself naïve, but I felt it now. How could anyone with thirty years of experience dealing with the worst of society be naïve? This industry, these people, they seemed normal for the most part. However sordid the product, they were professionals in a business. It was a paradox to my preconceived ideals.

The taxi stopped in front of an old movie theater. The marquee was worn and faded. Only a few of the border lights provided any illumination. It was flanked on the right side by an all-night pawnshop; on the left stood a former convenience store, which now housed a massage parlor. The three buildings were separated by shared parking lots on both sides. The sidewalk was dirty and cracked, and trash filled the street along the gutter. There were only a few cars parked on the sides of the theater. A red flashing neon sign advertised, "All nude dancing." In addition to the dancing, the old building supported an adult book and novelty store. On the other side of the street was a host of liquor stores and small diners with dirty doors. Layers of old playbills and other trade advertisements covered their sides. Several young men and women stood under the one streetlight. They traded stories between puffs on cigarettes.

The cabby's face filled with concern and confusion as I opened the door. He double-checked the address on his GPS. In broken English he asked if I were sure. I leaned in the cab's window and assured him I would be fine. I stepped back onto the street and entered the lobby of the dank theater.

The hall was dark and smelled musty. Stripper music spilled into the darkness. Within a few steps sat a weary man in a black T-shirt with Marilyn Monroe's silhouette printed in white on the front. His dirty-blond hair was gathered into a ponytail. I smiled, showed him the paper, and pointed at the address. He looked aggravated. Without returning my smile, he pointed at the double doors, and then he pointed up. I thanked him and proceeded to the doors. He put his open hand out to stop me and pointed at the sign on the wall. There was a ten dollar cover charge. I paid him and walked through the doors.

It took a couple of blinks to adjust to the light as I entered the adult bookstore. Plastic genitals of both sexes and all colors hung from rotating racks. Costumes, CDs, and magazines lined the walls.

Behind a glass counter, a tattooed woman with multicolored hair carefully watched me as I approached. Her ear and nose piercings were sparkling in the light. She smiled and exposed diamond-studded teeth. "How can I help you?" she asked as she closed the magazine she was holding.

I showed her the paper. She answered with another smile, "The door is there in the back and up the stairs." She directed me with a wave and added, "It's late, but I'm sure they're still there. Nobody has come down."

I thanked her and walked through the door and up the stairs. The open stairs were lit with small dim lights along the treads and risers. Darkness filled the openness, and techno-rhythms echoed in my ears. Three nude dancers moved to the beat on three different stages below me.

The old theater was a ghost of itself. The screen was still covered by velvet curtains, but the old stage was now divided with chromed rails and three vertical poles. The stairs went to two balconies. The second balcony was now a VIP lounge. The third was the office for this weekly paper. I was finally here.

I opened the door, and a young woman sat at a computer, typing from notes on a yellow pad to her right. She looked at me as if I were an intruder. Leaning back in her chair, she took several moments to study me. I remained silent. I again figured it was my hat and boots, but she was more perceptive than that. She spoke with a suspicious tone. "What do you want, cop?"

I smiled, "Retired cop, but I admire your insight." In spite of her condescending tone, she was a very attractive young woman.

"What do you want?" she growled again.

I took the newspaper article out of my pocket and unfolded it. "I want to talk to the reporter who wrote this," I said, pointing at the title.

"Why?"

"I am investigating the disappearance."

"You sure you're not a cop?" She stared into my eyes.

"Like I said, retired." I sighed.

She broke her stare and picked up her phone. She whispered into the receiver. I couldn't hear what she was saying, and I didn't try. I even stepped back and turned away from her to ensure her privacy.

My eyes scanned her work area. It was small. I figured it was one of the projection rooms from the past. It was now a reception area and office. In the corner sat two easy chairs as well as a small table and a dimly lit lamp. The lamp had a cloth shade, and at the foot of the lamp lay a stack of past issues of the weekly. One wall with French doors overlooked the lower balcony and the stage. The doors opened out on a railed ledge that ran the full length of the third balcony. I thought about going out on the ledge so I could study the antique structure. I didn't.

"Sir"—she palmed the phone—"what is your name?" Her tone softened slightly.

I replied over my shoulder, "Jack, Jack Conner."

After what sounded like an argument, she hung up the phone and reluctantly murmured, "You may go in."

I knocked before I opened the door. Just below eye level, an engraved gold-colored *Editor* sign hung on the door. An unassuming voice answered my knock. "Come in."

I walked through the door and saw a man I guessed to be sixty, sitting at a desk stacked with piles of paper. He stood. His belly hung over his beltline, and red suspenders held his slacks up and supported his extra fifty pounds.

He reached over his desk with his large, highly detailed tattooed arm to shake my hand. The top of his head was bald, but below his timberline grew long gray hair that covered his ears and cascaded down his back. A well-trimmed goatee encompassed a cynical smile. He grabbed my hand with a firm grip.

"At last," I thought to myself, "a person who looked just like I imagined."

"William Parker." He released his grasp. "My friends call me Bill; you can call me Mr. Parker." He returned to his seat. "You have some ID?"

I pulled my IDs from my shirt and handed them to him.

"Please sit," he said as he began to study my credentials. I followed his instructions.

A small, ugly, fat-bodied, short-legged bulldog looked up at me. He studied me for a moment. He stood, stretched, and made a circle before flopping back down to sleep with a wheezing snore.

Mr. Parker slid my IDs to my side of the desk through the maze of papers. "So, how did a retired sheriff/private investigator from Colorado get involved in a missing porn star case?"

"Lucky … I guess." I kept my eyes on his.

"Who employed your services? How did they find you? There are thousands of private investigators in California." His tone was friendly, but guarded as well.

"I'm not telling you who I'm working for, but I think you know that. As far as how I was chosen for this, I didn't ask," I answered. He didn't say anything. He waited for me to give him more information. I remained silent. I recognized his old reporter trick: don't say anything to see if the subject volunteers any further information. The silence hung in the room like rancid cigar smoke.

I broke the stalemate with a question. "So why isn't this a big story or at least a bigger story with the media? Why haven't the police been more forthcoming with information?"

Mr. Parker sat up in his seat. "All good questions. I don't know. I should say I don't have any evidence to support any conclusions at this time."

"I would like to talk to the person who wrote this." I handed him the article. I didn't attempt to pronounce Veritatis Inquisitor.

Mr. Parker didn't look at the article. He already knew why I was there. "Veritatis Inquisitor, do you know what it means?"

"Virtue Investigator?"

"Close." He smiled. "It's Latin. Truth Seeker."

"Wouldn't that be Veritatis Cupitor?" I stumbled through the pronunciation.

My statement surprised him. "So, you are an educated man?"

"Hardly; no, I had a very strict eighth-grade Latin teacher. Latin was a required subject to enter high school a hundred years ago," I explained and added, "I'm not sure how I even remembered that."

"Education is a thing of the past, you know?"

"Well, other than being able to read the script on statue pedestals and on government buildings, I am not sure Latin would be my first choice of a second language." Silence again. "Mr. Parker"—I paused to take in a breath—"it is getting late; can we just move on and cut the BS? First, I think you wrote this. Second, I agree with you and some of the points you made. I am looking for help. I don't have the insight in this business."

He stood up and sauntered to large windows, the same type as the reception area had. He gazed out for several minutes, the king overlooking his subjects and kingdom. He turned and leaned back against the windowed wall.

"You know, this isn't the life I planned," he sighed. "This isn't the life my grandfather had envisioned when he built this. In the 1930s, this wasn't even the city. It was an oasis in the middle of orchards, and then the city grew and surrounded us. Still, it was a magnificent place, small high-class restaurants and nightclubs where you had to wait weeks for a reservation. This theater was once the centerpiece of the block, the anchor. The stories my father and grandfather would tell about the grand openings and the people all dressed in their finest clothes. In the sixties my grandfather remodeled the theater to accommodate Panorama. The people came. They dined on fine foods and went to the most modern movie technology Hollywood could offer. It was truly something. Then the city abandoned us. Its resources went to the suburbs and other parts of the city that were deemed more important."

I held my boredom in check while he talked; my mind wanted to wander off, but I stayed with him. There must be a point to this somewhere.

He continued, "My block then became a demilitarized zone. It was like the city drew a line between the people who count and those that society wanted to ignore or just forget about." The tone in his voice changed and filled with defeat. "My last attempt in the mainstream was a monthly tourist-type magazine. It covered the current, past, and future of Hollywood and LA. I think I sold three copies." He pointed at two magazines matted and framed that hung above his desk, the first and last editions.

"The diners closed; people stopped coming to the theater. So … I got into the adult entertainment business … a one-stop adult fantasy store. I started my underground paper in a futile attempt to save some part of my soul."

To my relief, he began his story of Asian Sin. "She started dancing for me some twenty, twenty-five years ago. You should have seen her. She was so young, so beautiful. When she danced she created magic; the customers loved her. She had something."

I interrupted. "Innocence?"

He retreated to his desk and took his seat. He looked directly at me. "Innocence? That girl was never innocent. No, it was something else."

He paused and looked up at the ceiling. He sighed. He seemed to be lost in a world that was long gone. He straightened up to speak. "You know, I tried to talk her out of this before she ever started, but she loved it. The same with the films."

I watched his face as he finished reminiscing. His fondness for her was real … maybe love. He looked at me again, and with a sigh of reality, he conceded, "Yes … I wrote the article. I'm Veritatis Inquisitor."

I pulled the article back off the desk. "So, who is Rock Hard?"

"Rock Hard," he repeated in a scowl. "Rock Hard is a no-talent piece of shit. He thinks he's a great porn star, but he is far from it. He gets some bit parts here and there, but that's about it. He enjoys roughing up the girls. He is really into that."

"I don't remember his name being mentioned in any of her movies."

"That is because you won't. She refused to work with him. She was a star. She only worked with a few men, and she could name her price. He wanted her, but it wasn't going to happen. She couldn't stand him. But he had a real thing for her. He followed her. He stalked her. He attacked her, but her bodyguard finished that," Parker explained as he searched his desk drawer for a cigar. He took his find and put it in his mouth to moisten it.

He carefully lit it, with very deliberate puffs to draw the fire into the cigar's end. He blew a small cloud of smoke into the air. "Rock Hard threatened to kill her, you know. Once word of the attack hit the streets, no one would work with him. He believes if it wasn't for her, he would be a big star. Not a two-bit extra."

"So how do you know he wasn't interviewed by the police?"

He laughed a fake laugh and blew more smoke. "I have a source in that poor excuse for a police department. He is a lousy source, but how does that cliché go about blind squirrels and acorns?"

"Okay." I pushed to keep him on track.

Parker's intensity grew. "The word is that the police got an anonymous call. The caller said he saw Asian get in a car on the beach. He supposedly saw her do a couple of lines of coke with the driver, a man. They then drank some beers and sped off laughing. Since then, the cops have purportedly received two phone calls from her. Allegedly, she told them she is yachting in Mexico." He continued, "Another rumor was word came down from Sacramento to the chief that this problem needed to go away. These convenient phone calls made it easy for the police to dump the case."

"So, could there be any truth in the calls?" I asked. "It does sound plausible."

"Of course it does if you don't know her. First, Asian never did drugs. She doesn't drink either. Asian would never have gone anywhere without letting her people know, and she would have briefed her people as to how to contact her. She is a businesswoman. She has like three or four cell phones, including a sat phone, plus her computer and iPad."

"Did the police ever verify these calls? Did they do a voice analysis?"

"According to my source … no."

"So again, could there be any truth in the calls?" I asked.

"Not from her. No, I refuse to believe that."

"You still haven't told me who this Rock Hard character is."

"Ahh …" Parker smiled and drew another puff from the cigar. "The Sacramento connection."

"Sacramento connection?"

"Rock Hard's real name is Dewayne McCormick." Parker continued his explanation, "Not to be an embarrassment to the family, McCormick is actually his maternal grandmother's maiden name. Before Dewayne's porn career, he was a Harrison, like John Bradley Harrison."

I opened my hands, palms up. "I don't know John Bradley Harrison. The name does nothing for me."

"Of course." Parker tapped his cigar on the edge of a crystal ashtray. "I forgot you're from Colorado. John Bradley Harrison is a state legislator. He is a right-wing fundamentalist. His son, John Bradley Harrison the second, is a wheel in a couple of unions in this part of the state. He also owns a truck company. He hauls newspapers and paper stock. He basically controls both the roll of paper stock before the newspaper is printed and the newspaper after it is printed. In other words, he controls the production and distribution of the printed news."

"A right-wing fundamentalist and a union leader …" I was confused by the contrast.

"It gets more interesting. John Bradley Harrison the third is Dewayne's older brother and is being groomed for something big: governor, US Senator. He graduated from West Point and Harvard Law. He serves as a reserve in the US Army Judge Advocate General's Corps. He hasn't even declared a party yet."

I filled in the rest. "Then, there is Dewayne."

"Exactly."

"Where is he?" I asked.

Parker thought before he spoke; he remembered he was talking to a possible adversary. He spoke slowly. "So, what are your politics, Mr. Conner? What do you stand for?"

"I don't know. I guess an unconventional conservative. I don't trust government. I trust government less when the liberals are in charge," I answered. "I believe in God, if that is what you're asking, but I'm pretty skeptical about organized religion."

He studied me for several seconds again. He jumped back to my original question. "My source said he went to Belize or Jamaica, but I think he is still here in LA."

"Why?"

"I think my source was fed this information to stop people from looking for him. I couldn't verify or confirm any of the information. I do know a bondsman, and his two bounty hunters are looking for him. Apparently Mr. Hard failed to show for court on a drug charge. With a warrant he would take a big chance trying to fly out, and I couldn't find where he bought a plane ticket. None of the family's corporate jets have been in Central or South America, at least not recently."

"He could have gone south to Mexico and either sailed or flew from there," I speculated. "Have you talked to Asian's girls?"

"No." His tone turned defensive. "I don't want to drag them into this, and I don't want you contacting them either, understand?"

I smiled. "A reporter with ethics—now that's something I haven't seen in a while."

"I could say the same about cops," he interrupted.

"Don't worry, Mr. Parker. I have no desire or need to talk to them at this point. If that changes and I think I need to, I'll call you. You can review my material and my questions. It's obvious you care very much for Asian Sin and her family."

"You're still a cop," he stated.

"Retired," I reiterated. "I'm not from California; I was a cow cop from Colorado. Besides, I don't know the girls' names; I don't know where they live or where they go to school. I haven't asked, and I don't want to know."

Mr. Parker nodded.

"Mr. Parker"—my voice softened—"I know how to investigate a crime. I am very good at my job, but this industry is out of my expertise. If I need help, may I call on you again?"

He looked at me for moment before he answered, "Sure, and in return, if you can throw me something I can write about, I would be appreciative."

I stood. He stood. We shook hands. "Mr. Parker, thank you."

He replied with a slight grin, "You can call me Bill. How did you get here? Drive?"

I answered, "Taxi."

He chuckled. "You'll never get a cab in this neighborhood. Not at this hour. I'll have someone drive you to your hotel."

"Thank you."

His car and driver met me on the street. The driver was a very beautiful woman. I guessed she was about twenty. She opened the right rear door. I asked if I could sit up front. She hesitated before agreeing and then opened the front passenger door.

While there was very little traffic in this part of town, it began to pick up as we drove through Thai Town. The trip was almost twice as fast as my trip going there. Parker's driver concentrated on driving and was very quiet. She didn't say a word. I didn't either; I was done talking. With her well-trimmed blond hair and stage makeup, I suspected she was one of his strippers. We arrived at the hotel. Before she could get my door, I had it opened and was on the street. She declined my offer of a twenty dollar tip, so I dropped it on the seat.

Chapter 4

I stood on the curb and watched the car disappear in traffic. My interest turned to the bars across the street and the consideration of a drink. I elected to go to my room.

I turned around to face three large men standing shoulder to shoulder. Before I could react, the two on the outside of me grabbed my arms and my hands. The one in the middle stuck a .357 Smith and Wesson revolver in my face. His thumb cocked the hammer. With a wave of his gun, they escorted me into the alley to a large metal dumpster parked in a cutaway on the hotel's wall. They were all taller than me, and I guessed them all to be in their twenties.

The men that flanked me shoved me up against the wall. The third stuck the Smith's muzzle hard into my forehead.

"Mr. Conner, glad to meet you," he sneered arrogantly.

My mind raced through all my possibilities and hypothetical options. Three strong young men, taller, heavier, at least thirty years younger than I and in better shape than I and in better shape than I, versus me; it seemed like a fair fight. I stomped down on the instep of the guy holding me on the right. He let go, and I hit the one on the left in the face with my forearm. Blood ran from his mouth and nose. I grabbed for the gun, but he stepped back, and the other two recovered enough to regain control of my hands and arms again. Once I was pinned up against the wall again, the guy with the gun stepped into my space.

My defiance earned me a very hard stomach punch. I tried to bend, but they held me up for a second punch. I recovered as I felt the gunman's breath on my face. "Mr. Conner, I came to deliver a message. Go home. Forget this case. The next visit may turn violent. Do you understand?"

I remained silent. He hit me across the face with the gun's muzzle; the front sight torn into my cheek and, with a return swipe, cut into my forehead. His voice rose. "Do you understand?" I nodded yes. He raised his gun above his head and slammed it into the back of my head.

I felt a bright light burn through my eyelids, and the strong smell of antiseptic filled my nose. My head throbbed. I opened my eyes and tried to jump up. Two nurses in light blue scrubs pushed me back down. A young woman in a white coat and latex gloves spoke. "Mr. Conner, glad to have you back in the land of consciousness!" Her voice was soft and reassuring. She instructed me, "Follow the light."

"Is this heaven? Are you God?" I asked.

She laughed as she moved the penlight back and forth and up and down. "Close! I am a doctor, and you are in the ER."

I was nauseated, dizzy, and confused. I motioned that I was going to throw up. The nurse released her grip and grabbed a bedpan.

After a short series of dry heaves, I heard a familiar voice talking to the doctor. The voice was Keeley's. The nurse put a plastic cup of water in front of me with the instruction to rinse. I did.

"Mr. Conner, you have a minor concussion, eleven stitches on your right cheek, and about that many on your forehead. The nausea is normal in these types of head injuries. It should pass in a few hours, maybe a day. We did a CAT scan and an MRI, and you have no internal bleeding or skull fracture. You are a very lucky man, Mr. Conner. If Miss Nu hadn't found you, you could have died."

I felt disconnected from my brain. Keeley took my hand and squeezed. Her eyes teared. Pain filled my body, and confusion filled my mind. I hurt too much to explore what was going on between Keeley and me.

The doctor spoke again. "Mr. Conner, I'm holding you at least overnight, maybe longer. You need to stay awake for a while." I attempted to shake my head "no" in protest. Intense pain stopped me. Keeley told the doctor that I would be staying even if she had to wake a judge and get a court order. I surrendered.

The first twenty-four hours consisted of sleep deprivation; the doctor explained this was a routine procedure with head injuries. The team that kept me awake consisted of the doctor, two nurses, and Keeley. Keeley appeared to be in charge. She only allowed me to doze.

Finally, I was allowed to fall asleep. Hours later I was startled awake. My eyes bounced around the room, a hospital room. I had forgotten where I was. "What the hell happened?" I said aloud. I tried to pull myself into a sitting position. A pair of familiar hands gently pressed down on my shoulders.

Keeley smiled. "Good afternoon, cowboy. You need to stay down until the doctor sees you … understand?"

"Doctor?" Things started to come back as pain tugged the stitches on my forehead and cheek. I examined the wounds with my fingertips. I wasn't sure all of this was necessary. I've suffered a lot worse injuries with less attention.

Keeley asked, "Do you remember anything?"

"I remember getting a ride from William Parker's theater to the hotel, but that's about it," I answered, "Look, I have to go. I have an appointment with Asian's attorney this afternoon." I tried sitting up again. Keeley pushed me back down.

"Relax. That was two days ago." Keeley laughed. "I called and rescheduled for Monday."

"Monday? Two days ago?" I couldn't believe it. "How did you know about the appointment?" She only smiled.

I looked around the room. Four bouquets of flowers lined the window. Keeley handed me several envelopes; they were get-well cards. I hadn't realized I had made so many friends here in Los Angeles. My guess was the senders were positioning themselves to be taken off my suspect list. She began to explain what she knew and what I had said in the last forty-eight hours.

"How did you know where to look for me?" I asked, trying to regain the last few days.

"Your hat," she answered with a trace of pride. "I saw your hat on the sidewalk. I walked down the alley and found you. The rest, as some say, is history." She added, "The police want to reinterview you."

"I don't remember them interviewing me the first time."

She told me what I had said to them. Then she asked me, "Did you really attack those three guys?"

I was trying to remember. "Maybe. Probably?"

She got angry. "What are you trying to do? Get yourself killed?"

"Killed?" I argued. "They weren't going to kill me. They were sent to give me a message."

"A message?"

"Yeah, to stop looking into the disappearance of Asian Sin." I twisted my neck to stretch.

Keeley sat back down on the bed. "I guess you really do have a case, but are you sure you want it?"

This would have been a great time to tell her I didn't have a client, but I still couldn't explain the attraction … the draw. How could I explain it to her when I couldn't explain it to myself? Keeley stood up and began straightening up the room. Every time I opened my eyes, she was there. I didn't understand this either. Was I in a relationship? Or was it what she said that first morning—just a thing?

Bill Parker surprised me by showing up to check on my well-being. Keeley was doubling as a nurse and a door guard. She knew Bill, and with my permission she allowed him in the room.

Bill brought me a couple of hot rod magazines and some chocolate. He told me that he had ears on the street but hadn't turned up anything yet. He asked me several questions before Keeley interrupted, "He doesn't remember anything." She then reminded both of us in a rather harsh tone that I needed rest, and Bill excused himself.

The next morning, the doctor released me from the hospital after one final check over. Keeley picked up my clothes, and she led the nurse who was wheeling me through the hospital. I wanted to walk out on my own, but it just became another lost argument.

On the way to the hotel, I had formulated a plan to start interviewing Asian Sin's costars, but Keeley changed my plans. We spent the weekend together. She took me around to different parks, to the Chinatown Central Plaza, and around Little Tokyo. She showed me things that I had never noticed on the same streets that I had explored earlier. We talked about everything, except those things that I considered important.

She refused to say anything about herself and dodged my questions. She never told me where she lived or invited me over to see her place. She didn't want to know anything about me. Keeley wanted the now, not the then, not the when … just the now.

CHAPTER 5

Monday morning came with Keeley's announcement that she needed to go into the office. I could see the concern in her face. She didn't want to leave me. I wasn't sure why. Was it the attack the other night, or was it us? I didn't ask. I didn't want to know. I assured her that I would be all right. My plans were to stay in the room until the attorney's car picked me up.

At one thirty promptly, I stepped onto the sidewalk to await my ride. Over the weekend, Keeley had purchased a couple of new suits for me. In spite of my protest, she had insisted. I had picked out the light gray suit for the day; it matched my gray felt hat almost perfectly. Even so, I was in a contradiction. I felt like I looked great, but at the same time, I was uncomfortable with the cut of the clothes. I had worn blue jeans and polo shirts for the last thirty years. I never wore a suit; it was always a western-cut sport jacket with my blue jeans.

A Chinese man, somewhere between thirty and forty, stood at the sliding door of an older minivan. He wore a light brown porkpie hat with a dark leather hatband and a Hawaiian-style shirt. He stepped on the curb and introduced himself as the attorney's driver and showed me his identification, a precaution set in place because of my recent attack. I had anticipated the arrival of a long black Cadillac or Lincoln, not a wood-paneled minivan. He motioned me toward the back, but I requested my traditional front passenger seat. He complied.

My anxiety grew as my driver dodged traffic and swore in Chinese at the slower drivers. Besides the NASCAR-style driving, lawyers make me nervous, including the one I'd spent the weekend with and who had bought me this suit. I pulled my cell phone out of my jacket pocket and called the Wayfarer PD … again. I was told the detective was very busy and would call me when he had the chance … again.

I barely got a glance of the office building as my driver made a dive down into the underground parking and slid into a numbered space marked "Private." He bounced from his seat, trotted to the passenger side, and opened the door for me. I smiled and followed my quick-paced escort to the elevator. He slipped a key card down through the card reader. The door of a private elevator opened, and we stepped across the threshold into another world.

My driver remained silent as the elevator car raced up to the fortieth floor. The door opened. Two gold-colored Imperial Guard statues stood sentry. Guardian lions sat at their feet on an ocean of red carpet.

The driver led me past the stone guards down a long hallway. The hallway was gold and red, trimmed in Chinese walnut. Six Buddhas, three on each side, maintained the guard to the reception area. My driver led me up to the receptionist, passing me on to her after he shook my hand and said he would see me later.

The receptionist stood to greet me; she was a very attractive, young, Asian woman. Her desk was immaculate, with nothing out of place and nothing extra. She asked, "How was the drive?"

"Interesting."

"Good, then?" she replied. I recognized her voice. She was the one that I first talked to, who made my original appointment.

With a sigh, I answered her, "Good, yes."

"Please come with me." She walked around her desk, and I followed her to a corner office. Large windows made up the corner. At the height of forty stories, the view took in a large part of the city. As any non-Californian would do, I checked to see if I could see the ocean. I couldn't.

She asked me to wait, and she left. I was glad for the moment to look around the office. The traditional diplomas hung on a well-organized wall. A person couldn't help but be impressed with this incredible pedigree: Harvard Law, Chinese University of Hong Kong, Faculty of Law, and a Lindsay Fellowship. Commendations, citations, and awards from all over the world circled the diplomas.

A very striking Asian woman entered the room. I assumed she was the attorney's private secretary. She had several documents in her hands. She smiled. "Mr. Conner?"

"Yes." I returned her smile.

"I'm Sara's attorney, Dallas Xiao Xu." She put her papers down and extended her hand.

"Sara?"

"Sara Jones."

For the moment, I had forgotten Asian Sin's given name. "Of course, Sara Jones."

I must have looked confused or slightly startled. She smiled; her voice held a slight tone of contempt. "You were expecting a man, weren't you?"

I felt my face turn red; I looked down for a moment. I then met her eyes and said, "Please forgive me. Dallas is predominately a man's name where I come from."

She replied, "Colorado? I'm guessing the attorneys are predominately males as well?"

"Sorry. Lately my reliance on stereotypes has been failing me greatly," I stuttered.

"That combined with years of gender bias, I'm sure," she answered condescendingly. Her thoughts trailed away before she invited me to take a chair. I waited for her invitation before I sat.

I started the conversation. "So, did I check out?"

"Check out?"

"Your background investigation on me. You did check me out, right? That is why you wanted to wait until the other afternoon to meet." I touched the stitches on my cheek. "My unfortunate accident gave you more time to see if I was legitimate."

"Yes, Mr. Conner." Her attention heightened. "I did have you checked out. Your old department described you as a bit of a rebel and loner, but had very high regard for you. By chance, I know a couple of attorneys you worked for, and they also have a great deal of respect for you as well." She pushed a couple of documents toward me. "Would you look at these, please."

The documents surprised me. I looked at her and began to shuffle them. She began to explain the papers to me. "Mr. Conner, I would like to be your attorney of record in California. I would also like you to sign an employment agreement with my firm as well."

"Why?" I asked.

"Mr. Conner, who hired you?"

"You haven't answered my question, counselor. Why?"

"Mr. Conner, if you are a client, I cannot disclose anything we discuss. If you work for me, you cannot disclose anything we talk about. You understand?"

"So, are you trying to protect Sara or control the investigation?" I was immediately defensive.

"Both."

"I'm sorry, Ms. Xiao Xu. I think I have wasted your time," I said as I stood and put her documents back on her desk.

"Wait." She stopped for a minute. "Are you familiar with the Chinese culture … with Asian culture?"

"I know enough to know I don't know anything … why?"

"The way you pronounced my name; you pronounced it correctly. Most Westerners try to pronounce it with an X sound. Like X-ray or something," she explained. "If I insulted you, I am sorry."

"I'm not sure an apology is warranted, but I don't want to give up my control of my investigation."

"The rebel," she interjected.

"Perhaps."

"I could get a restraining order," she quietly threatened.

"You could. These days, you can get a restraining order to prevent someone from eating a hamburger. But you would have a tough time proving a violation." I paused. "Why are we doing this? We are on the same side. I wasn't sure there was even a case until I was attacked. Besides, I couldn't afford one minute of your time."

She chuckled. "Money? Read the contract. Under this contract the firm's services are *pro bono* ... free."

"I know what *pro bono* means." I defended my intelligence.

"Who is your client, Mr. Conner?"

I took the papers back and signed them. I saw a Chinese flag framed and matted on the wall. I walked over to it and asked, "A protest flag?" The flag was blue with violet stars, the opposites of red and yellow.

She walked into my space and looked at the flag. Her delicate perfume mixed with the sweetness of her breath. I detected a slight hint of scotch or bourbon. She explained, "My parents were both distinguished doctors in China when Mao initiated 'The Great Leap.' Their small house was stripped from them; their families slaughtered. So, to escape famine, torture, or outright execution, they fled to Taiwan. With a great deal of help from many, they were smuggled to the island, along with my grandmother and one of my father's brothers. His other brother was killed in Vietnam after he defected. In my opinion, he was assassinated. My father lived in fear that he was being hunted by communist spies from the mainland. And it would only be a matter of time before they were killed. At the same time, Jiang Jieshi, known to you Westerners as Chiang Kai-shek, had his secret police track my father because they thought him to be a communist spy.

"He took his family and fled again. First, they boarded an old steam freighter and sailed dangerous waters to Hong Kong, then to the Philippines, Hawaii, and then to mainland America. His second cousin smuggled them to Houston, Texas. There they lived in Houston's Chinatown.

"My father worked in fish canneries at night. He went to school during the day to regain his ability to practice medicine. Both he and my mother treated the sick in Chinatown, in secret, all the time in fear of being discovered and returned to China. My mother had three children to take care of by this time.

"My father regained his medical license, and they moved to Dallas, where I was born. That is how I got my name. My parents refused to teach us Chinese; we were American. My grandmother, however, taught us Chinese and the Chinese traditional ways.

"Yes, Mr. Conner, it is a flag of protest. I fail to see why your history has been so kind to Mao Zedong and Chiang Kai-shek, both murderous criminals." Her eyes left the flag. Pain filled her eyes as she studied mine. Sadness covered her face. Her eyes searched my soul. She quietly repeated her original question: "Mr. Conner, who is your client?"

I stepped out of her space and walked over to one of the large windows overlooking the city. I guess it was my turn to reflect. "When I was eighteen, I was at a rodeo in a very small town just outside Colorado Springs. It was a county fair and rodeo." I turned toward her, "Do you know what a rodeo is?"

"You're kidding, right?" She leaned back on the flag wall and folded her arms. "I was raised in Dallas, remember."

"Of course," I continued. "I was tending to my horse when a Chinese girl approached me. She introduced herself as Xiu Tang. She explained that she was from China and had always wanted to meet a real western cowboy. Her spoken English sounded educated and refined. Her English was better than mine. I still can remember how beautiful she was. She was an exchange student studying in an eastern university. She was older than I, a college girl—the dream of every high school boy."

I hesitated, remembering with a half smile on my face. It was a sweet but poignant memory.

"We spent the summer together. I took her to the ranch where I worked. I taught her to ride, to shoot. It was probably the best time of my life." I paused to gather my thoughts. "I was so in love with her, but she was very honest. She was there for the summer … no more. She was going to complete her studies and return to China to be a doctor.

"Because of her family's influence, she was given a student visa out of Hong Kong. It was an odd time for her to be in America. The Vietnam War was going strong. I didn't know anything and really had no interest in learning anything. But she … she taught me a lot. She taught me about her country and her family. That fall she returned to school, and I never heard from her again. I suppose there isn't a day that goes by without me thinking of her. Sometimes I would imagine that when I got home from work, she would be there, cooking dinner, with a smile on her face as she greeted me with open arms." I stopped. I caught myself rambling. "Sorry. The truth is, I have no client. I am my client."

Dallas Xiao Xu returned to her desk and sat down. "So, why Sara?" she asked. Her voice had no emotion. "Are you a fan, an admirer?"

"No," I answered, "not really. I didn't even know who she was until I read an article about her missing in some week-old newspaper, and then I researched her on the computer. I don't really even like porn. I can't explain it. I flew to San Diego for vacation, and now I'm here."

"Mr. Conner, please have a seat," she requested softly. She remained silent until I was sitting. "Mr. Conner, my grandmother told me many years ago that sometimes we must take a path that we don't choose."

I looked at her cynically. "I figured you to be way too educated and refined to go for that Confucius stuff."

"I'm actually Buddhist," she confessed, "much to the dismay of my Catholic father and mother."

I understood now. I understood why her father and mother were forced from their home and country … educated and Christian. Her revelation should have been obvious to me. Numerous Buddhas decorated her office, all except one of the shelves behind her desk. There stood a statue of Christ, a cross, and several saints. This shelf served as a tribute to her parents.

"Mr. Conner, you seem like a good man. I frankly feel better that you are your own client. I was apprehensive that you'd been hired by some unscrupulous person or group to investigate this. Even though you are a good man, you are very naïve. By accepting this case for some of these people, you could have caused great harm without being aware of it." Her frankness was somewhat unnerving.

She continued, "Years ago, Sara assigned me the task of handling her affairs, both professional and private, in her absence. I am also the executor of her estate. So, for the time being, her estate will become your client. This is the best way to protect her and you."

I said nothing. She asked, "Are you all right?"

"Yes, thank you, but …" I trailed off.

"But what?"

"Well." I attempted to select my words carefully. "With all due respect, I have to ask how a civil rights attorney who owns an international law firm with branches all over the world takes on a porn star as a client. Please understand, I am not trying to be judgmental or sanctimonious. It just seems private or family practice is way beneath your organization."

She snickered like she had a private joke. "Thirty years ago, I was just a private attorney in a small office. I had many porn stars as clients then. The industry was filled with criminals and scum. It still is, but overall, the business has improved. At the time, most girls were lucky if they got enough money for bus fare. If the producers tried to violate her contract or failed to pay her, I stepped in with the threat of a lawsuit. We quickly figured out the legitimate filmmakers. Still, very few made it to the status of Sara. But she never used drugs, never partied with producers, and never got caught up in the idea it was going to last forever. She never spent a dime."

"I understand." I followed with an observation. "Of the few people I have interviewed, you're the first who has addressed her as Sara, not Asian Sin."

"I have only known her as Sara. She was ending her freshman year when we met. That had to be at least twenty or twenty-five years ago or more. Oddly, when we first met, it was over a sexual harassment and paternity suit. She had been referred by another dancer and adult film actor."

"Paternity suit?" I repeated. "What happened?"

"It was settled," she answered and added, "out of court, no public records."

"Should I add this person and incident to my suspect list?"

"I don't think so. They were in a big hurry to keep it quiet, and it has never been an issue since then."

"All right, then. Don't tell me any more unless my investigation heads that way. I don't want any names." I looked at her as I spoke. "Counselor, why me? In addition to your own investigators, I know your office hires at least two large private investigation firms … prestigious firms. Why not them instead of an unknown from Colorado?"

She looked at me questioningly.

"You see, counselor, you aren't the only one who does background checks. So, why me?"

"Because I like your style. I was impressed that you insisted on no names. You protect people and let them come to you. You have no hidden agenda," she replied with a slight smile.

"Thank you, but I do not extend that courtesy to everyone in an investigation."

The smile left her face. Her voice was cold. "I know. I was informed you could be ruthless and a man to be feared if you are crossed."

"I think the person you talked to was being a bit melodramatic."

"Maybe." She stood and walked over to the window. "But I think they were right. I can sense a very dark side to you."

"Now I think *you* are being a bit dramatic."

"My instincts are very solid."

"Forgive me, but I am not convinced. I think you have another reason."

"Well, Mr. Conner, perhaps it is a little self-serving." She turned to look at me and then said, "You see, this arrangement allows me to keep an eye on the guy fucking my daughter."

I froze. I gave no reaction.

She smiled. "Not even a blink! You see, you didn't deny it, nor did you confirm it."

I remained motionless, shocked by her bluntness.

"Oh, relax, Jack!" She sat back down. "Keeley told me. You said you're a true gentleman, and you just proved it. Surprised?"

"A little."

"Why?"

"Well …" I drifted off a minute, trying to figure out what I was going to say. "Well, frankly, I thought she was Korean."

She laughed. "Very perceptive. Her father was a Korean industrialist. She never knew him. She doesn't even know his name. He left me after he found out I was pregnant. He left and went back to his family in Korea. A family I knew nothing about. Nu was my first husband's name. He was killed in a car accident when she was four. Neither he nor she knew he wasn't her father."

I wasn't sure what to say. Why was she telling me this? Was this about her or her daughter? Did she want me to say my intentions were honorable? I didn't know my intentions. I remained silent.

She returned to business. "The estate will pay you five hundred a day plus expenses. I would like an update at least once a week. You will need receipts, when possible."

"That's a lot of money. Why are you willing to pay that much?"

"It's half of what I would pay one of the local firms. I will take care of your state and local licensing. You'll need to stop one floor down to get your picture and fingerprints taken." She reached in her desk and tossed two key cards in my direction. "We have furnished apartments a couple of floors up. I would like to move you to one of those. They are more secure, more comfortable, and cheaper. We own these." She paused. "What else can I do for you?"

"Any connections with the police where Asian disappeared?"

"Why?"

I explained Parker's theory to her and gave her the rundown on what I had done and what my next move would be. She took some notes as we talked.

"I don't know anyone down there, but I have friends with LAPD and the sheriff's office. I'll give them a call." She stopped for a moment to look over her notes. "As far as the Sacramento connection, I'll call the governor."

"Again, thank you."

"Is there anything else?"

"Can you get me a gun or two? I could send for mine, but that would take some time. I think it would be nice to have options next time someone sends me a message."

"Understandable. Sure; write down what you want. They will be delivered to your new room. I'll have your things moved from the hotel while you're getting your pictures done."

"Thank you." I stood to leave. "Thank you for everything."

"Jack?" She spoke with some vulnerability. "Keeley … she knows nothing of the Korean … Nu was the only father she has known."

I looked at her for a moment and nodded yes. Without a word she knew her secret was safe with me. I returned to the reception area.

Chapter 6

I took the elevator down to the next floor. They were expecting me. A young technician met me at the door. He was dressed in a white lab coat, white shirt, and black tie. His well-worn canvas tennis shoes were out of place. As everyone else I had met in this building, he was also of Chinese heritage.

I was amazed. I walked into a private, full-service forensic lab. My old department could only dream of such a lab.

The technician said, "We do work for police departments and private attorneys from all over the world. Not only the lab work and computer investigation; we also have a department for forensic accounting and documents."

I just followed him without a word as he proudly explained the facility. We stopped at the entry to a lounge. He continued, "Please accept my apologies; I must have you wait a few minutes before we can photograph you." He directed me to sit in one of two couches or overstuffed chairs, each divided by very elegant end tables stacked with ample reading material. There was a TV on the wall and below it a full refreshment center, including fresh coffee, tea, and assorted fruits.

I poured myself a coffee and sat down in one of the chairs. I glanced at some magazines. My mind was too busy thinking about my meeting with Dallas Xiao Xu to flip through the periodicals. I had thought I couldn't get any more confused until I met her. I found it interesting that she had disclosed something that I doubted she had ever told anyone before, but never asked me to address her by her first name. I wondered why. I didn't have an answer.

Not only that, but then she told me her family history, including, for better or worse, the fact that Keeley was her daughter. Damn! It would have been nice if Keeley would have shared that with me. But it did explain the insistence on a new suit.

Another thing I found very strange was that Asian, rather Sara, had never returned to the East. She never even went back to Bangkok to see her parents. Sara and her girls traveled to Europe, Australia, even South America. Her parents would often meet her at these different destinations. Sometimes they would stay for a couple of months. She traveled the world, but never back to the East.

By the time they completed my fingerprints and photos, the back of my head throbbed in pain. So I headed for the elevator to find my new room. I slid the key card, and the door opened. Keeley startled me as she stepped into the doorway of the five-room suite.

"Conner!" she reached out for me with open arms. She closed her arms around me in a strong hug. Kissing me, she then asked, "How are you doing?"

"Fine." I forgot about my throbbing head. She took my hand and led me into the apartment. The beauty and elegance were overwhelming. The walls were divided in half by carved walnut trim. Above the trim, fine framed and matted oriental prints hung on cream-color walls.

Keeley escorted me to a dark leather couch. "Here; rest." She walked over to the kitchenette to finish putting Chinese takeout on expensive dishes. "How did your meeting go with my mother?" she asked as she carefully placed equal portions of Chinese cuisine on the plates. I wanted to be angry at her for not disclosing that Dallas was her mother, but she made it very difficult. She wore a very short Chinese cheongsam. Her hair was up in a tight roll, and the dress's high collar complemented her natural beauty. Her blue eye shadow and red lipstick defined her mystic aura. Her dark eyeliner and long eyelashes accentuated the smoldering fire in her eyes. I said nothing.

Early morning found me on the couch so Keeley wouldn't be disturbed. The evening had ended more than spectacularly, but it had also left me even more perplexed. Nothing more had been said about her mother, her day, or my day.

I must have fallen back asleep. A knock on the door woke me. I found myself covered with a blanket. Keeley must have covered me before going off to work.

A second series of raps came from the door. I opened it to a uniformed deliveryman pulling a hand truck with several boxes. I signed the electronic receipt, and he disappeared down the hallway. By the weight and size of the packages, I knew my guns had arrived. I unpacked my two new 1911 .45 caliber handguns with shoulder holsters and several extra magazines. The second package was a semiauto shotgun with a sling, and in the third, a thousand rounds of ammunition.

I found a gun range on the Internet and made an appointment for the afternoon. I was busy fitting the holsters when my cell phone rang. It was Bill Parker.

"Jack, it's Bill." He sounded excited. "I think I got something on Rock Hard. He's holed up in an old penthouse apartment in North Hollywood."

"You got the address?"

"Not exactly, but I'll call you when I have it."

I hung up the phone. I left a note for Keeley and left her a message on her cell phone. In my short time with Keeley, I had learned she did not answer her phone, and I hated texting.

Dallas Xiao Xu had arranged a car and driver for me. I called for the car, and the receptionist told me to meet my driver in the basement.

I gathered up my new arsenal and headed downstairs. The elevator door opened, and there he was, my little Asian NASCAR driver with a colossal smile and his wood-paneled minivan. The van door was already open. With trepidation, I threw my shotgun in the backseat and crawled in the front passenger seat.

We ate a late lunch and went to the range. I learned my driver's name was Deng Toa, but he went by Dan. He had immigrated to the United States from Hong Kong. He liked to talk, and did he talk! Without prompting, I learned a great deal about his family, his wife, that he worked part time and was a full-time law student. During his monologue, he stopped and shyly asked if I would let him shoot. I agreed.

Dan and I practiced at the range while we waited to hear from Bill Parker. It was almost dark before he finally called. Bill was ready to meet. Dan thanked me several times on the drive to the old theater for letting him shoot. He was actually very good and handled a gun extremely well. We parked on the street, and I insisted that Dan go in with me. He was worried about what his wife would think. I solved the dilemma by suggesting to him he either not tell her or lie to her, but there was no way I wanted to leave him alone on the street.

Parker's blond-haired troll waved us past without a cover charge. I said hello to the tattooed girl with the multicolored hair as we headed for the stairs. Dan's head swung back and forth trying to take in everything the sex store had to offer. His face displayed disapproving shock. I guessed he had never been in a place like that before.

We headed up the stairs. We could hear voices below. The dancers, bouncers, and bartender were talking at the corner of the bar. The stage was empty and the music silent. There were no customers to drink or to watch. Maybe it was too early.

The young receptionist stood with a smile as we entered the door. "Mr. Conner, nice to see you again." Her greeting was pleasant and genuine. "You may go on in; the editor is expecting you."

Out of politeness I knocked on the closed door. I waited until I heard Bill's voice answer the knock with a "come in." Parker stood in front of his desk. An unlit cigar hung from his lips. He took the cigar into his teeth and said with a smile, "Good to see you, Jack." We shook hands, and I introduced him to Dan. He shook Dan's hand. Parker looked carefully at the flesh-colored tape that covered my stitches. "Well, it looks like you're healing."

Two short but very large men stood behind Bill. I figured they each weighed about 250 to 300 pounds. With their matching faces and their builds, I assumed them to be twins. Bill confirmed that in his introduction. "Jack," he said, putting his arms around their tree-trunk necks, "This is Darrell and David Nelson; they are bounty hunters for an acquaintance of mine, Retread Miller, a bondsman who rents an office from me." Both nodded and eagerly shook my hand.

"Retread?" I asked.

"Yeah," Parker explained. "It seems he ran into some trouble that earned him a prison sentence, but he got a retrial and was acquitted. So, he got his bond license back, thus Retread."

"Trouble? Acquitted?" I then added, "I didn't hear that he was innocent."

Bill left his center position between the two giant pandas. "I suppose he might have broken a rule or two."

"A rule or two."

"You're never going to get out of here if you continue to repeat everything I say," Bill huffed.

"Okay, so what's the deal with Bert and Ernie?"

"Darrell and David."

"Whatever."

Bill walked to his desk and picked up a folded paper. "Here is your address."

I reached out for the paper. He pulled it away and said, "There's one condition … well, actually two."

"What?"

"You have to take Darrell and David," Bill answered.

"What?"

"This could be very dangerous. I don't know how old Rock is going to react when you go knocking on his door." Bill rationalized his excuse.

"I can take care of myself. Besides, I've got Dan."

Bill rolled his eyes and brushed my scarred cheek. "Yeah, you've done so well so far. You never know. You might need them as nothing more than impartial witnesses. Besides, they have paper on him."

"Paper?"

"Remember, I told you about the bounty hunters. They're the ones who have the warrant for him."

"Yeah, I remember." I sighed. "Okay, what is the second?"

"The second?"

"You said you had two conditions."

Bill replied, "Oh, yes, the second. Bring me back a story."

"With the permission of my client."

"Of course." Parker smiled.

Dan, Darrell, David, and I headed for the address. Dan drove, and I sat up front in the twenty-year-old minivan, and Darrell and David squeezed into the bucket seats behind us. Our unwelcome backseat guests requested a quick stop at the nearest drive-through. After we agreed, an argument ensued on where the closest drive-through was and the choice between burritos or hamburgers.

I had to intervene when the dispute escalated to them calling each other names and pushing at each other. Dan looked at me with a rather cynical, disapproving glance. I warded off Dan's mutiny with a frustrated, openhanded shrug. "I know."

Darrell and David finally settled on hamburgers. A new fight started when David thought Darrell was taking too long to order. Another intervention was required, which included the threat of Dan and me throwing them out on the street.

I felt aggravation growing, but once I heard David and Darrell's plan, the irritation left. Their plan had credibility.

Finding Rock Hard's location was purely by accident. David and Darrell were hunting for a pimp who had also skipped bond. They found him in the same building where Rock Hard was staying. The pimp begged for a deal so he could get another bond. David and Darrell's boss agreed for any good information he could provide. Besides giving locations on a couple of other criminals on the run, the pimp had revealed to them that Rock Hard was residing in the penthouse apartment. Rock Hard was not at home when they were there earlier, but the pimp assured them that he would be home later.

The plan was they would grab Rock and let me interview him before they took him to jail. They knew him. They didn't believe he would be any problem and would cooperate. I agreed with the plan. I like smooth, quiet operations.

Dan pulled to the curb about four buildings down from our target building. One of the twins told us the building was owned by a porn director that specialized in homosexual movies. The old apartment building suffered from a serious lack of maintenance.

Weeds grew through piles of trash, old tires, and various car parts that filled the yard around the building. Broken plank steps led to the double doors in the front of the building. Forty or fifty years ago, the elegantly trimmed doors had provided a welcome into a very exclusive residence. Now covered in graffiti, they hung on loose hinges, with broken windows. The old building was also tagged by several spray can artists over several layers of chipped and faded paint.

Darrell and David's tactical moves impressed me. Both of them carried short-barreled pump shotguns. I kept wondering how they managed to keep them hidden until now. They moved carefully, quickly, and deliberately. Their silent approach went unnoticed by the drunk resting on the steps. They cleared the doorway and headed up the stairs. I followed, and Dan followed me.

We made it up to the second and third floors without any incident. On the fourth-floor landing, Darrell and David were confronted by three young prostitutes. Two wore very short miniskirts and high spiked heels. The other had shorts and knee-high boots. With their painted faces in angry scowls, all three hissed at the giant pandas through bright red lips.

By the profanity-filled diatribes, I gathered their boss was the pimp that Darrell and David had arrested earlier.

Darrell held the lead. David turned to the side and extended his open hand to stop me. Emotion got the best of one of the short-skirted girls, and she went after Darrell with her fingers curled, cutting into his face with her long, hard nails. She crawled up him like a squirrel up a tree. She wrapped her legs around his neck. Her weight threw him off balance, and he tried to catch himself by grabbing the handrail with his shotgun in hand. The shotgun discharged, and bird shot tore into the ceiling. The drywall exploded with thick white dust and chunks of spackling.

My eyes burned as they filled with drywall dust. I bent down and tried to blink. The shotgun blast had startled the hooker, and she released her grip on Darrell. He dropped to one knee and threw her over his shoulder. Her face was covered with white drywall dust.

I cleared my eyes enough to see her flying over David and down on me. Her red lips now in a scream and her powdered white face made her look like a mad banshee swooping in for a kill. It was too late to duck. She hit me, and I fell backward on top of Dan. She tumbled over the top of both of us, rolled down the stairs, and came to rest on the third-floor landing.

I crawled off Dan; his face was covered with blood spatter. It was to be determined later whose blood. Before I could ask him if he was okay, another gun shot rang out. A ragged hole appeared on the back wall of the third-floor landing. That shot was quickly followed by three or four more. Darrell and David returned fire. Dan helped me drag the half-crazed hooker around the corner out of the line of fire.

More shots came down the stairway. David fired three rounds at the wall that protected the shooter. The wall shattered. David had switched from bird shot to slugs. The slugs found their intended target, and a man fell into view from his cover. The grip on his gun relaxed when he hit the floor, dead. We heard hurried footsteps and glass breaking. David yelled down the stairs, "They're going down the fire escape!"

I scooped up my hat and followed Dan back down the stairs. Dan leaped, skipping four or five treads at a time. We ran out the door together.

I tripped over a small crumbled section of chain-link fence and fell into a pile of scrap metal. The metal's sharp edges tore through my trousers and ripped deep into my legs, burying itself in my thighs as I struggled to free myself. Dan disappeared around the building.

Once freed, I ran for the building and pasted myself against the wall. I peeked around the corner and saw three figures bunched together swiftly moving down the stairs. The lead figure came into enough light that I could see the gun in his hand. He fired. A brick burst at my chest level. I retreated behind the corner and pulled my guns. When I reappeared, I couldn't engage. Dan was in my line of fire. Somehow he had gotten behind them by crawling up the outside of the fire escape.

I left my brick sanctuary and ran toward a large pile of trash to distract the men trying to escape and to keep Dan from being discovered. Bullets screamed around me. I jumped for the back side of the trash but fell short and had to roll to safety. I looked over the top of the heap to see Dan slam both of his feet in the back of the last man's head. He fell forward into the backs of the other two men. They also began to fall. Dan grabbed the handrail with both hands and swung his legs to the outside, and his shoes met both of their faces before they hit the ground. Bending over each of the suspects, he patted them down. When he stood, he held up four handguns hanging on his fingers by their trigger guards.

I limped over to him, wiping blood from my eyes. The tumble down the stairs had torn my stitches out. It was my blood that covered Dan's face. Dan's smile covered his pride-filled and blood-spattered face.

Dan looked at me from head to toe. "Looks like you need a doctor again … and a new suit."

"Sure," I answered, trying not to groan. I asked, "Okay, how did you manage this? All of this?" I waved my hand over the three wounded bodies at our feet.

"Did I mention I was a black belt in four different martial arts disciplines?" he answered coyly. "I was a master instructor in two of them."

"No, no, you didn't mention that."

"Yeah, it was something I studied as a young child and as a Hong Kong police officer under the British."

"A police officer?"

"Did I forget that too?"

I nodded.

"When the Chinese reclaimed Hong Kong, I moved my family to California with the help of Ms. Xiao Xu."

"I see."

Before I could ask more, one of the twins yelled down from the top of the building, "Hey, you guys all right?"

Dan looked at me dripping blood down my face and legs. "For the most part, yeah!"

"You need to get up here now!" the giant panda yelled back.

"Handcuffs!" I shouted. "We need handcuffs!" Without a word, he immediately responded by throwing three pairs over the edge. They landed at my feet. Dan quickly grabbed them up. He rolled the three suspects over on their stomachs and snapped the cuffs on their wrists behind their backs.

Two of the thugs were barely conscious. The third thrashed in pain. He was the first one Dan had kicked. When he fell forward, he couldn't catch himself, and he hit his face on the steel handrail. The collision between mouth and steel sheared his front teeth off. Dan pushed him over on his back. The suspect gasped for air; he was drowning on his own blood.

I looked at him carefully; even with the blood bubbling from his mouth and nose, I recognized him. He was one of the three men that had led me down the alley by my hotel the other night. I examined the faces of the next two suspects on the ground, and there was another one of my attackers. I went back and knelt down by the suspect missing teeth and gasping for air. "Who sent you to attack me?"

He turned over on his side to clear his mouth and nose of blood, then rolled his head back into my view. Before I could ask the question again, he spit out the words mixed with blood, "Fuck off!"

I drove my knee hard into his chest, forcing him onto his back. I grabbed up an old discarded shirt lying on the ground and covered his mouth and nose. I pressed hard. He struggled. With both knees, I pushed my weight down on his chest, balancing myself with my toes. He gasped for air.

I knelt over to his ear and whispered, "You can drown, or you can tell me. I have two more I can ask, so I don't really need you. You just happen to be the only one awake at the time. Understand?"

I rolled him back over onto his side. He hesitated. I started to push him on his back again. He forced the words through the blood. "No, wait … It was Sky Lee."

"Who?" I wanted him to repeat it.

"Sky Lee," he panted.

"Who is Sky Lee?"

He stalled. I began to force him over. He began to talk again. "She's a high-stepping hooker … half black … half Chinese."

"Where can we find her?" Dan stepped into my interview. I looked at him. Intenseness filled Dan's voice.

"Man, fuck!" the suspect gasped. "She contacted us at a bar we hang out at. She gave each of us a hundred bucks to scare the cowboy. Really, I don't know any more. Please!"

Dan and I looked at each other. We nodded together. Dan stated, "He's telling the truth." I ripped the old shirt in half and tied it over my trouser leg to slow the bleeding.

The twins shouted down again, "Hurry up, damn it!"

"I think you're right," I answered Dan. "Are you going to be all right down here while I go see what is going on up there?" He rolled his eyes and sent me off with a head nod.

I began my way up the fire escape to the fourth-floor hall window. Each step filled my new injuries with pain, but I maintained a quick pace and skipped about every other tread. Darrell and David stood at the window. Both their faces twisted in a combination of fear and relief. The gunfight had ended, but now came the reckoning.

Neither said a word. They helped me through the window and motioned me to follow them. I followed them up another flight of stairs to the penthouse apartment. The penthouse was centered on the roof. The penthouse's condition made the lower floors look like the interior of a five-star hotel. Only two windows were intact; the rest were either broken or boarded up. Gray rotting wood, with scattered sections of chipped and faded paint, made up the outside walls.

We had to cross about twenty feet of roof before we made it to the planked walkway that led to the front door of the penthouse. The roof creaked under our feet. We looked at each other as the roof sagged with each step. With great care we made the perilous journey across the torn tar paper and heaps of trash to the wooden walk.

The twin pandas led me up to the door. It lay in the threshold torn from its hinges. Darrell, I think, pointed into the living room. There, slumped over in a recliner, was a man's body. From the wounds covering the pale corpse, it was obvious that he had been beaten badly. Blood seeped from some of the purple and red bruises. I walked closer. One of the twins said, "It is Rock Hard, or what's left of him." I nodded even though his injuries were so bad I could not recognize him from pictures I had seen.

I sighed in disappointment. I looked him over carefully. It appeared that the dreadful four had beaten him for some reason and then finished him with a couple of bullets in his knees and then a third in his right temple. His apartment appeared to be torn apart in a search, but I wasn't sure if it had been searched or if Rock Hard was that bad a housekeeper.

My gaze turned toward the twins. "The other guy … the one doing all the shooting?" They both shook their heads. "Well, darn." I sighed again and followed with another question, "You guys ever hear of a Sky Lee?"

They glanced at each other, and both said no and asked why. Before I could explain, the sounds of hurried sirens broke my concentration. Another sigh. "Well, this is going to be fun." I walked out and down the stairs. I went around the corner to look at the guy the twins had shot.

I knelt down to examine him closer; his body was almost cut in half. Only his shredded clothes held him together. The result of three twelve-gauge slugs in the torso. It was the third guy who had assaulted me.

The twins stood behind me. I turned around and told them to follow me. We went back down the stairs. The crazy hooker sat with her back against the wall. Her legs were crossed in front of her, and her face was buried in her hands. She took time to rise up and hiss at us when we walked past her.

"Look, the cops will need to talk to you, so you need to stay right here. Understand?" I ordered her with my best command voice.

Her first answer came through clenched teeth. "Fuck you!"

"Look, lady, it hasn't been the best of evenings, and I am in no mood to put up with your behavior. Either agree, or I am going to have these guys tie you to the stairs." I stood over her until she nodded in agreement.

We went down to the car. I got the keys from Dan, and we locked up our guns. I didn't really want to get shot by the police. Street cops get nervous about guys with guns and dead people scattered about. Darrell, David, and I met the two marked police cars at the curb. Dan stayed with our suspects. We kept our hands in view at all times.

Four uniformed cops rolled out of their two cars. They kept behind the doors, their guns drawn. Fortunately, two of the officers knew the twins. The one on the right asked as he holstered his gun, "David … Darrell? What the fuck?"

The other three officers lowered their guns at the lead of the first officer. They all shook hands, and then the twins introduced me. They separated us and took custody of the three suspects. I got a younger officer. He offered to get me an ambulance, but I declined. I told him I would go later.

More police arrived. Darrell took the latest arrivals on a tour of the crime scene. The sergeant arrived and took control. He assigned what appeared to be the youngest officer to me. He looked very young and very nervous. I asked, "Your first shooting? Homicide?" He nodded yes. "Don't worry," I told him, "the detectives will do the heavy lifting." He seemed to relax some, but I could tell from his expression that I still needed some trust-earning.

He invited me to sit down in his car to complete my preliminary statement. It took about a half hour to finish my declaration. Before he excused me, he took my credentials, and asked me to turn over my guns. The officer thanked me as we retrieved the weapons and told me a detective would meet me at the hospital.

I watched the officers and detectives come and go. Two plainclothes officers escorted the hooker to a car. Her hands were cuffed behind her back. The way she was struggling and cussing at the officers, I figured the interview didn't go well. Before they pushed her thrashing frame into the patrol car, she had one "Fuck you!" left for us.

Chapter 7

Dan opened the minivan's door for me, a simplistic gesture as he looked at me closer in the streetlight. "We are going to the hospital," he commanded.

I instructed him to find an overnight clinic, explaining that the cost would be cheaper. When he pulled into the hospital emergency room entrance, I glared at him. He glanced over when he sensed my irritation.

"Sorry, boss," he said. "This is where I told the cops we would be. It was either here or the police station." He looked down at my legs. "I don't think you have enough blood left to sit around a police station." I capitulated with a long sigh.

I limped into a fairly quiet ER waiting room and found a newer easy chair in front of the TV. The local news was on and reporting the shootout. I relived the battle. I felt guilty that I didn't even get a shot off. At the same time, I felt glad I hadn't. Dan left to get some assistance.

I sat there wondering if I should have confronted Dan. I suspected that Dan's job of driver concealed his real job as a private detective—Dallas Xiao Xu's private detective. She must have assigned him either to spy on me, to protect me, or a combination of both. The throbbing of my forehead and the deep sting from the newest cuts on my knees and legs distracted me. My decision on how to handle this would have to wait.

Dan returned with an admission clerk and a triage nurse. Both recognized me from my previous visit. The officious clerk asked if she could just use my information from before, and I nodded yes. Dan interrupted and instructed her to send both bills to the address on the card he presented to her: Dallas Xiao Xu's card.

The male nurse was not in scrubs, but a light blue jumpsuit. A dark blue stripe traveled up his legs, under his arms, and down the long sleeves covering his arms. Silver wings were embroidered over his right pocket. He doubled as a flight nurse.

He gently dabbed a wet disposable towel on my forehead and cheek to clean the dried blood from my face. He scrubbed white powder and small pieces of drywall out of my reopened wounds and hair. The pain magnified, and I flinched with each touch. And then came the familiar smell of the antiseptic. Dan took over as a spokesman and answered both the clerk's and nurse's questions.

Once the clerk completed her task, the nurse pushed a wheelchair up beside me and asked me if I could move over to the wheelchair. I nodded and pushed myself to a standing position with the help of the armrests on the chair in which I was sitting. The nurse steadied and guided me with his hands on my shoulders. Once he was convinced I was safely seated, he pushed me to a private room of glass and curtains.

He stopped the chair by a hospital bed and asked if I wanted to try to remove my pants or if he should cut them off. With a slight frown, I undid my belt and pulled it through the loops of my pants and empty holsters. The pants stuck to my cuts. I struggled to keep my face expressionless as I pulled the blood-glued cloth from the gashes. I slowly worked the trousers to the floor. Fresh blood began to flow again.

I sat down on the bed, and the nurse helped me get my legs up and in the bed. He began to clean the wounds. My injuries were deeper and longer than I thought.

A younger female nurse came in to obtain my vitals. Concern filled her face at the conclusion of her blood pressure test. "Your blood pressure is very high. Is that usual?"

"I was attacked by a flying hooker in the middle of a gunfight. Could that contribute to high blood pressure?" I grimaced with my explanation.

Her lack of expression made it clear she didn't appreciate my sense of humor.

With one hand she gave me a small plastic cup with a pill in it. In her other hand was a plastic water glass. "Doctor's orders."

I tried to focus on how the murder of Rock Hard was tied to the disappearance of Asian Sin to distract myself from the pain inflicted by the flight nurse cleaning out my cuts. It wasn't working. So, I switched to small talk. His single-word answers made it tough to engage in a conversation of any depth.

The doctor entered the room with a smile. It was the same female doctor as the other night. "Well, Mr. Conner, good morning. I see you came back to see us." Her smile changed to concern as she looked at my legs. She ordered another painkiller for me and ordered the nurse to start injecting my injuries with an anesthetic. Her face changed to a smile again. She asked, "Mr. Conner, are you planning to stay here for a while?"

"Why?" I questioned.

Her voice dripped with sarcasm. "Because if you are, I think I need to order some more thread and read up on gunshot wounds."

"So you heard."

"Oh, yes, I heard."

While the nurse filled my wounds with painkiller, I felt one of the two pills beginning to take effect. It still hurt, but it seemed distant. The doctor returned with her sewing equipment and a staple gun. She explained that she had to repair some tissue and muscle damage with disposable thread, and she was going to staple the cut. I shrugged. What else could I do?

She scrubbed the cuts for a third time. By now, I couldn't feel a thing. A short man about forty years old came in the room and showed the doctor and nurses his badge as they worked. His short hairline was an inch above his nylon jacket collar, the jacket he wore to cover his gun.

"Mr. Conner?" he asked as he looked around the doctor sewing my leg. "You Conner?"

"Yeah, I'm Conner, or at least what's left of him," I answered.

"Jim Collins, Detective Jim Collins, Los Angeles Sheriff's Department, homicide." He introduced himself and extended his hand. I shook it.

"Homicide?" I asked. "Aren't you a little early, or do you know more than I do?"

"Maybe," he joked back. "You might be very much alive, at least for the moment, but the shootout at the LA Corral left a couple not as lucky."

"Yeah, sorry."

"Do you mind answering a few questions?"

"No, but hurry. These drugs they gave me are kicking in," I answered.

He explained, "I read your statement and wanted to know if you had anything to add."

I thought a minute, and I shook my head no. "Not really."

He continued, "You have any idea who the suspects are?"

"Well, no, but they were the ones who attacked me the other day."

"I know," he answered. "They're here."

"What?"

"The suspects. They are here in the same hospital and under guard."

"By the way, I tried to interview one of them at the scene."

"Yeah, I know." He looked down in hesitation and then back up at me. A frown grew on his face. "He tells me you tried to drown him in his own blood." He paused. "Any idea what he's talking about?"

"Why?" I didn't want to lie to him.

"Just asking; I'm sure it was a misperception thing. You were probably trying to provide first aid," he filled in with a cynical voice.

"Sure." I smiled. He saved me from a lie.

He continued his explanation, "It looks like they went there to kill Rock Hard. They just didn't figure on you guys."

"They didn't happen to mention why they killed Rock Hard, did they?" I asked.

"They all lawyered up … all but the dead one." He sighed. "I was hoping you found that out when you were rendering aid."

"I didn't know Rock Hard was dead when I was rendering aid." I used the detective's term. "You guys showed up before I could render further aid."

"You find out anything?"

"Yeah, he told me that a high-class hooker by the name of Sky Lee hired them to rough me up." My words started to fade. The painkiller's influence grew. "You heard of her?" Before the detective could answer, I added, "You think this has something to do with the disappearance of Asian Sin?"

After a brief moment of thought, he answered, "I had never heard of Asian Sin until I read your statement, so, short answer, I don't know."

Surprised, I wanted to ask him if he was sure that he hadn't heard of Asian Sin. No teletypes, no flyers, nothing? It didn't make sense, but my mind was a drug-filled fog. I managed to ask one more question: "So did you know about Sky Lee?" I mummered groggily. If he answered, I never heard it.

It was late the next afternoon before I convinced the doctor to release me, and with some hesitation and a promise from Dan that he would take care of me and watch me, she agreed. Dan drove me home after he was given lengthy, detailed instructions regarding my care, including bed rest. Dan recited his instructions to me on the drive back to the apartment. I dozed and didn't listen.

He continued his oration on the way up in the elevator. I just nodded on the trip up and as he guided me into the suite and into the bedroom. With the painkillers, I was in no condition to argue.

"It's going to take you some time to heal," Dan said as he shut off the bedroom lights and closed the door behind him. I just rolled over and fell asleep.

I woke in the late morning, and it took a moment for me to gather my bearings and figure out I was back in the corporate apartment. Every part of me hurt with every move. I heard movement from the kitchenette and suspected it was Keeley. I hoped it was Keeley. It upset me that she hadn't come to the hospital last night.

I listened to footsteps as they approached from the kitchenette to the bedroom. A soft knock came from the other side of the bedroom door. I answered the knock with a simple, "yes," and managed to get up on one elbow. My smile disappeared.

Dan stood in the open door, not Keeley. I fell onto my back as he stepped in the room. "How are you doing?" His smile grew as he spoke, but then disappeared with my reaction to his arrival. I knew it upset him some, but I couldn't tell him I was expecting Keeley, not him.

I summoned a smile and tried to act happy. "Sorry; the pain got me for a moment."

He bought my excuse. "Do you need a pill? A painkiller?"

"No." I struggled back up to a sitting position. He went to the nightstand and dialed the phone.

He spoke over his shoulder. "I was given strict instructions to call Ms. Xiao Xu when you woke up." There was no point trying to listen as he spoke into the phone; the conversation was in Chinese. When he hung up, he spoke again. "Ms. Xiao Xu said she would be up in a little while."

I nodded and asked, "Anyone else call?" He shook his head no.

I found my cell phone by the reading lamp and checked it for any missed calls. None. I wanted to ask Dan if Keeley had stopped by or called, but I didn't. I didn't want anyone else that didn't already know about Keeley's and my relationship—or our nonrelationship—to find out about us.

Dan broke my thoughts of self-pity. "Are you hungry?"

"No," I answered.

"You know, Mr. Conner, you haven't eaten in two days."

"Sorry; I'm just not hungry. Would you mind getting my sweat suit from the closet?"

"You're not thinking about getting up, are you?" Dan asked and then added, "I promised the doctor."

"No, not really. Just moving to the couch."

"That is not bed rest."

"Sure it is. Besides, I refuse to go before the queen without wearing clothes and out of this bed."

Shrugging reluctantly, he pulled the sweat suit out of the closet and threw it on the bed.

He stood looking at me.

"Would you please excuse me, so I can dress?"

He shut the door behind him. Instantly, I felt my heart sink. Keeley's voice, her presence came to me in thought. Until then I really hadn't realized my feelings for Keeley. It was time to start lying to myself. I have always had the miserable habit of falling in love too quickly, and it never works out. Here I was again. I had to convince myself this was an infatuation and nothing more. After all, it was "just a thing."

I managed to get seated in the easy chair before Dallas arrived. Dan got the door. She didn't just walk into a room; she glided in on refined elegance, ability, and confidence.

I spoke as she found a seat on the sofa. "Forgive me for not standing."

"I understand. Are you going to be all right?" She crossed her legs at her ankles.

"Sure, just some scratches."

Dan interrupted. "He has deep lacerations to both legs below the knees, and one severe laceration above his right knee that cuts into the muscles. He required a total of twenty stitches and thirty staples." I glared at him. He responded to my disapproval, "What? She's going to find out what happened when she gets the bills." His uneasiness brought out a more pronounced accent.

I detailed the entire account of the shooting and the investigation to Dallas. She listened carefully; no questions. Dan added different aspects to the incident where I overlooked them or just didn't see them.

"Where are you going from here?" she asked at the conclusion of my narrative.

"Mr. Conner will require at least three weeks convalescing before he can do anything," Dan added. "Doctor's orders."

I again frowned at him, only this time with greater intensity. "Dan, would you excuse us for a minute?" I paused to see his reaction. "Please," I added. He made a short bow and left the apartment. I remained silent until the door closed. My attention turned to Dallas. "Why didn't you tell me Dan was your detective, your spy? Please don't try to deny it."

Her bottom lip rolled in with a breath. "I am not sure. I don't think it was to spy on you exactly." She stood, walked around, and leaned on the back of the sofa with her back to me. "Jack, you were too good to be true. You're too easy to talk to. For God's sakes, Jack, I told you about Keeley's real father. No one knew, not Keeley, not my husband. I am not sure why I even told you, a total stranger that just walked into my office." She added, "A total stranger that just walked into my office searching for a missing porn star."

I fought back the urge to ask her about Keeley. I waited for her to continue.

"You see! Think of what I just said." She turned around, her face angry. "Damn, I sound so much like a girl. I hate that. What I should have done was told you to go to hell. I'm not required to explain anything to you. After all, you work for me." She turned away. Her anger diminished, and her tone softened. "I hope you understand. He wasn't there to spy. I just wanted to know who you were. What would you do in my place? How would you protect your client—a client I am very fond of?" She faced me again. "Tell me, Jack, what would you have done?"

I thought of several answers, but remained quiet. I thought of accusing her of sending her daughter to spy on me until Dan could replace her. I didn't, but the thought still remained.

"Well, Jack, what would you do?" she asked again insistently as she returned to the sofa.

I wasn't ready to concede. I answered with a question. "What happened to your grandmother and 'we must take a path that we don't choose?'"

"I may be a granddaughter to my grandmother, but I'm still a skeptical jurist, a cynical attorney, and a rational businesswoman."

"I think I like you more as a granddaughter and a girl."

She almost smiled. A person of Dallas's stature wasn't going to go along with a harmless flirtation. It took less than a second for her to recompose herself. "Now what?" she asked. "You're out for a while."

"A couple days maybe," I replied.

"Three or four weeks," she retorted.

"Maybe a few days. If you have a place I could work, I thought I would go back to doing some more background interviews. You know, her costars and such. If it is all right with you, I'll have Dan do any legwork for the time being." I paused for a moment. "Please excuse the pun."

Suddenly my thoughts returned to Asian Sin, and my mood darkened. "We're running out of time. It already may be too late." My tone was sober. "This long … this late … and now this." I waved my hands over my legs. "I hope we're not just wasting everyone's time."

She looked intently at me, taking in my statement. She spoke dryly. "Her children need to know one way or the other. They deserve knowing. The investigation continues, understand?" She stood. "Now, get some rest."

"So I have your permission to let Dan do the legwork for me for the time being?"

She nodded. She walked out as Dan entered. He stood at the entry waiting to be invited into the living room area.

"Come here, Dan," I yelled over my back. He walked into my view. I saw the hurt on his face. I searched for words and decided to go with the undiplomatic truth. "I asked her if you were supposed to spy on me, to investigate me."

"She never told me to spy. She just wanted me to watch out for you. Once you were attacked, they worried you were going to get killed," Dan explained.

"They?" I asked.

"Dallas and Keeley."

"But you were to report back? To both of them?" I asked, afraid of the answer.

I could see Dan struggled with the answer. He finally spoke. "Both of them."

I pulled myself up. I limped over to the bar, poured some whiskey over some ice, and took a big drink. "You want a drink?"

"No, thank you, sir. I am not sure you should be mixing alcohol with your medicine."

I took another drink and filled the glass again. I made it back to the chair. Dan was still standing. He wouldn't sit until he was invited. I gestured him to sit. He followed my direction.

We sat there a moment looking at each other.

He finally asked me, "How did you know?"

"I knew."

"How?"

I smiled. "It was easy. Actually, I didn't, not at first. I just knew you were more than a law student and a driver."

He asked again, "How?"

"First, the way you drove a car. Second, the way you handled a gun and the way you shot. I suspected you had considerable formal training. When you laid waste to the three suspects at the apartment building with your self-defense tactics and the way you handcuffed those guys, you confirmed my suspicions. Then you told me you were a Hong Kong cop, everything came together. I should have figured it out the first day. I guess I'm slipping."

I wanted to talk. It took the pain away. Not the pain in my legs or face, but in my heart, as I questioned whether Keeley had been there with me just to protect her mother's company and the company's asset, Asian Sin. We traded police stories until I became weary. He offered food again and again, but I turned it down. We talked over some plans for the next few days. I drank one more glass of whiskey before retiring for the night.

I woke up early. The moon was still high in the western sky. I managed to get myself out on the balcony and listen to the city spring into the birth of a new day. Cars honking, light trucks finishing their early morning deliveries, readying the city for the rush of hordes of commuters finding their way to work.

I felt pretty good considering the amount I drank last night. I was tempted to start the morning with the remaining whiskey that was left, but settled on coffee with some real cream and sugar. I usually drink coffee black, but this morning I needed something different.

I studied the cell phone. My mind fought with the idea of calling Keeley or not calling. I checked missed calls for at least the tenth or twentieth time. I felt so foolish. I am not sure why I thought we were something. She never led me on, and in fact, it made sense that she didn't really want to talk about herself. She was protecting herself.

I had to get my mind back on the job. With my third cup of coffee, I retrieved my files and started from the beginning. I felt that I had missed something. I still hadn't found it by the time Dan showed up.

He pushed his way through the door. "Hey, how about a breakfast burrito and some green tea? The green tea will help you mend quicker."

I knew I needed to eat, so I didn't argue. The lack of food for the last few days left me trembling, but still, I played with my breakfast more than I ate. I might need food, but the desire to eat wasn't there. When Dan took away the plate, his face showed a mixture of aggravation and disappointment over the amount of food I had left. I followed him back off the balcony and into the kitchen. We laid out the paperwork to begin the day.

We made a list of people that Dan would make initial contact with and we would interview together here in Dallas's building. The list consisted of people who had worked with Asian Sin: actors, film crews, anyone we could think of that might have been involved with her in the industry and would talk to us.

Chapter 8

Dan left to start interviewing the contacts, and I reviewed the case again. My day was filled with interruptions and a parade of visitors. The first was Jim Collins, the detective. He showed up at the door with an unlit cigarette in his mouth.

"Come on; let's go out on the balcony so you can smoke that thing," I said, limping to the sliding doors.

He lit his cigarette with a metal lighter. I like the snap sound of the lid on a metal lighter. It takes me back to the many war movies in my youth, where heroes under fire and in the face of death took the time to pull their metal lighter from a waistband or shirt pocket and light their dying buddy's cigarette.

He took in a deep draw and blew the smoke over the ledge. "I haven't found out a thing that would connect Rock Hard's murder and the disappearance of Asian Sin. The best I can tell, it's just not there. But it's difficult. The only information I got about Asian Sin is from you and the Internet."

"Why?"

"I don't know. I can't get a bit of information out of the Wayfarer Police—not a missing person report, not a teletype, nothing."

"Been there," I sympathized.

"Hell, they won't even talk with me. I can't tell you how many times I call down there just to be blown off." His voice rose with a hint of frustration and confusion when he spoke of this other police department.

"Why should you be different?"

He lit his second cigarette. "I'm just not used to being treated that way, especially by other cops, is all."

"I know. So what about Rock Hard?"

"Word on the street is that Rock Hard stole a large amount of cocaine from a local gangster known as Joey Gunn."

"Joey Gunn?"

"Yeah, a real ghost. We have nothing on him. No picture, no prints. We aren't sure Joey Gunn is even a real name."

Jim looked tired. I knew the look very well. I had been there myself. He continued his story, now on his third cigarette. "It's hell at the office; the great Senator, John Bradley Harrison, paid a visit to the sheriff, and now we are required to have a formal briefing for him once a day."

I rolled my eyes. "Where are you going to find the time for that?"

"I don't know." He shrugged.

"What about the three from the shootout at Rock Hard's apartment building?"

"The only one of our three suspects talking is the one you 'rendered aid to.' He is still trying to make a criminal complaint against you for trying to kill him."

I jumped in with a short comment. "I wasn't trying to kill him. I know that because he is still alive."

"I am not sure that is the best defense."

"Find out anything about Sky Lee?"

The detective shook his head slowly. They had nothing. But they weren't finished.

My next visitors were the twins, Darrell and David. They told me their boss, Retread, had almost fired them, but since the judge released him from Rock Hard's bond, he was happy.

"Well, I'm glad your boss didn't fire you," I said. They both nodded, with big smiles. "So, did you guys find out anything about Sky Lee?"

Their smiles disappeared. They shook their heads in unison. "No, sir," they said together.

"I have another one for you. Have either of you heard of a Joey Gunn? He is supposed to be a real player, but the police have nothing—only a wicked reputation."

They again shook their heads. I don't know which one spoke, but the one on the right said, "We will work on it. Somebody that bad should be easy to find." They both walked over to my couch and shook my hand before they left. I thanked them.

Bill Parker showed up late in the afternoon. He came bearing gifts as before: scotch, candy, and a newspaper. We talked for at least a couple of hours. During our conversation, he made at least four apologies for almost getting me killed. When we spoke of Asian Sin, his voice softened, along with the expression on his face. I was sure he had a reverence for her … probably love. He didn't know anything about Joey Gunn, other than a reputation for being a ruthless killer and drug dealer. He used the same description as Jim Collins: "This guy is a ghost." He knew nothing of Sky Lee as well. He also reassured me he would look into it further.

My last visitor entered without a knock—Dallas Xiao Xu. "You're not going to do me any good if you land back in the hospital."

I wanted to tell her that work was the only way to keep my mind off her daughter. I didn't. I let her reprimand me and nodded in humbled capitulation.

"We need information on a guy by the name of Joey Gunn," I interjected.

"Who?"

"Joey Gunn. Both Jim Collins and Bill Parker have heard of him. However, it's only by reputation. He is supposed to be a dope-dealing gangster and a killer, but apparently no one has seen him or knows anything about him."

"Okay"—she paused—"but it comes at a price. You rest this weekend."

"Dallas, we are running out of time, I fear." I blanched when I realized I had called her by her first name uninvited.

"Look, I know your concern, but I need you healed."

"Sky Lee."

"What?"

"Sky Lee," I repeated. "We need to find her."

She sighed. "We will. Next week." I could tell she was getting aggravated with me. "Good night, Jack."

Darkness saturated the windows by the time she left. Although she had stopped by to chastise me, somehow we parted on a first-name basis. And now I was alone in the dark—quiet and dark, both powerful enemies to a man thinking of a woman. In my case, two women: Keeley and Asian Sin.

I retrieved my new bottle of scotch and took a drink from the bottle. After a couple more drinks, I surrendered my pride and decided to dial Keeley's number. It went directly to voice mail. I hung up and drank some more, a lot more. I finally left her a message, but only after I rehearsed my lines to avoid any words of pathetic desperation.

The next few days went fast. The next few nights went slow. Dan spent his time finding everyone he could that was connected to Asian Sin and brought them up to the apartment to interview. We did our best to hide our activities from Dallas, so she wouldn't have to take the time to yell at me again. I suspected she was well informed, but chose not to pursue it.

We interviewed some twenty actors, cameramen, and other support personnel. Other than enhancing my knowledge of moviemaking, we learned nothing. My education in the film industry grew with each interview. I learned that producers don't use their own money to make films; they find investors, moneymen. All that did for us was to add more people to the list of possible witnesses or suspects.

During the middle of these interviews, we had to take time out for a visit to the doctor, who had scheduled the appointment when I was at the hospital. A nurse's aide led me to a private room. After the regular routine of blood pressure and temperature, she left. It seemed forever before the doctor showed up.

After some pleasant exchange of hellos, she went right to work. She seemed pleased with her work as she studied my cuts. I didn't realize how beautiful my doctor was until now. Her blond hair was carefully trimmed and outlined the striking features of her face.

"Well, Mr. Conner, you're healing fine. I think we can pull these staples next week if you behave." She went to the sink to wash her hands.

"Behave?" I asked as I dressed.

She flicked the water from her hands into the sink and turned with a smile. "Yeah, you know. Avoid flying whores and bullets."

"Oh."

She left the room with instructions to make another appointment.

On the way back to Dallas's building, Dan and I strategized our next steps. We were running out of ideas as well as leads. My worry about the well-being of Asian Sin grew as Dan threaded the minivan through the afternoon traffic.

Nothing remarkable came of the investigation for the next couple of days. I told Dan to go home late in the afternoon and take a couple of days to recharge. My mood fell to a ragged edge. Between not being able to walk without pain or fear of tearing my staples and my sleepless, drunken nights pining over my affair or my nonaffair with Keeley, I felt like exploding and throwing furniture out the window. Add to this dark pool of self-pity the fact that we were stagnant on this case.

I left the piles of paper on the kitchen table to find my easy chair. I found the remote and clicked on the TV. I decided not to pour a drink and settled for cold coffee from the kitchen.

My phone woke me; it took a moment for me to gather my consciousness. What started with mindlessly watching TV last night had turned into a much-needed deep sleep. I checked my watch; it was well past one. The darkness told me it was well past one o'clock in the morning.

"Hello?" I stuttered into the phone.

"Jack? It's Bill, Bill Parker." He sounded excited and scared.

"Yes, Bill, how are you?" I knew I sounded disappointed; I was thinking it would be Keeley.

"Jack, I need to see you … I have something on Joey Gunn and Sky Lee."

I straightened in my chair. "What?"

"Not over the phone; we need to meet … now."

"Give me a few minutes. I'll grab a cab." I pushed myself out of the chair and onto my feet.

"Don't bother. I'm driving over now."

"Okay … I'll call security so you can get in." I yawned into the phone.

The next thirty minutes seemed to take forever. My mind raced with baseless scenarios concerning Sky Lee and Joey Gunn. The imaginary scenes stopped with Bill's knock on the door. I yelled for him to come in, and he entered with his hand full of papers. We shook hands without me having to stand again. Bill sat on the sofa across from me, and he spread the papers out on the coffee table. I took them up and began to read.

Bill remained silent while I studied the documents. They were advertisements for very high-class escorts, exotic escorts. There were thirty-some pages, each displaying a different woman. They varied in age from twenty-one to forty and from Bali to the Ukraine and all points in between. I pulled one out and set the others back on the table.

Besides the text on the paper, there were several photos of a stunning young black woman with very distinctive Southeast Asian features. Her bio reported she was half-African and half-Chinese and was twenty-six years old. She had a bachelor's degree in cultural studies, and the bio included other personal information. She called herself Hiean Nushen. I folded the paper down so I could see Bill over it. I took a breath and asked, "Hiean Nushen?"

"It's Chinese for Dark Goddess," Bill explained. "And there's more. You see the corporate name—Mount Tai Exotics Inc.?" I lacked understanding, and Bill picked up on it. "You see," Bill continued, "if you look carefully, each girl uses a deity term as a part of her name. Mount Tai is the southern gateway to heaven in China."

"Okay." I paused. "Clever, cute, maybe even romantic, but how is this important?"

"It isn't, but you gotta love the symbolism," Bill answered with some intellectual arrogance.

"Bill, it's two in the morning."

"Yes; sorry." He sounded slightly giddy. "But this took some doing." Bill pointed down at the stacks of paper on the coffee table. "And all of that paper and even more research, but we sifted through a quagmire of corporations to one name, Joshua Harvey. Joshua Harvey's real name is Jiang Lung. Lung is rumored to be high in the Triads. He may even be a Dragon or Mountain Master to the clan here in Chinatown. Look at the phrase at the bottom of the page."

I looked at the script and said, "It's in Chinese."

"I know. Mandarin to be exact," Bill interjected. "It means the Heaven and Earth Society, followed by the number 489. This society was a Triad organization in the eighteen hundreds. The 489 is a numbered code for the leader, the Dragon Master."

I was slow with my reply. "Bill, I see you guys put a lot of work into this, but it isn't exactly a smoking gun." I paused. "I can't believe a high-level gangster of such an elite or notorious organization would put his mark on the bottom of each ad for a girl."

"Arrogance."

"Do you have anything to prove this Hiean Nushen is Sky Lee?"

"Not yet, but we will. You see, he also runs another escort service, which features retired porn stars." Bill's voice now turned nervous. "You see, Joshua Harvey, Jiang Lung, and Joey Gun are the same person. He wanted Asian to work for him, and when she refused, he took her or killed her." He looked down in pain with the thought she might be dead.

"Do you have anything but supposition?"

"Not really, but it all fits. Don't you think?" His eyes met mine.

"I think if you are right, you need to be quiet about this. You'll be the next one missing if this gets out." He took note of my serious tone.

"I know." Bill's answer was grim and worried.

"Of course, you realize this is your second theory." I raised my eyebrows and spoke with a smirk. "And, if I recall, your first theory got me into a gunfight."

"A gunfight in which you did not fire a shot," he retorted with a half smile. "Too bad about Rock Hard. He was a great suspect until he got killed."

"Yeah; too bad he didn't kidnap her. This would be over."

Again he argued, "We don't know that yet."

"True."

I walked, or rather limped, Bill to the door. I warned him again: "Bill, we have to keep this secret. If you are right, these people can make you and your staff disappear."

He agreed. Before I closed the door behind him, I cautioned him a third time. "Please make sure the people you had working on this know they have to keep quiet. It could cost them their lives."

He nodded and left.

In order not to be caught by Dallas, I decided to head out now instead of returning to bed. I took up the ad for Hiean Nushen and left the apartment. When I finally made it to the street, my legs were throbbing. I waited on a bus stop bench until I finally hailed a cab. I asked him to take me to a convenience store that sold disposable cell phones. The cabby drove to a small store just a few blocks from Dallas's building. He offered to go in the store for me. I gladly accepted. In a few minutes he returned with the phone and asked, "Where to?"

I answered, "Back to the bus stop, please."

On the drive back to the bus stop, I plotted a way to approach or contact Hiean Nushen. I thought of using a fake name and getting a car to pick me up at the airport. I could even get a friend at my old office to set up a fake website for me. Somewhere in my thoughts, it dawned on me that she must already know who I am. How else would she know whom to send the Neanderthals after?

The driver pulled up to the curb, and I gave him a twenty over the meter. Before I left, he asked me if I wanted a cane. I looked confused until he explained that an older man had left one in the cab several months ago. He had kept it, hoping that someday he could return it to the old man. I took it and thanked him.

The cane made it considerably less painful to get around. I returned to my apartment and to my chair. I dug the ad out of my pocket and called the number. The woman answering the phone was too awake to be the girl in the ad. After all, it was now a little past six. I was right. It was an answering service. Ditching the cloak-and-dagger approach, I identified myself as Jack and told the girl I wanted a date with Hiean Nushen.

The operator asked when and where. I told her I only had a couple of days, so I wanted to meet as soon as possible and I wanted to meet her at her house or apartment. The ad offered the usual in-call or out-call service, or from the days of black-and-white movies, "Your place or mine." She told me that Hiean would be in touch. I thanked her and hung up.

I took a shower, ate a small snack, and went to bed. About three hours later, my new phone rang. Since I wasn't used to the ring, it took a moment to figure out what the noise was. It was her. Her sensual voice poured through the speaker like fine bourbon. I detected a slight accent, hidden by education and practice. We made some small talk, and she agreed to meet me; she instructed me to just give the cabdriver my phone, and she would give him the address, with driving instructions. We agreed to meet this afternoon and for a twenty-four-hour period. She closed by informing me that her charge was a thousand dollars an hour, but for a twenty-four-hour period, she would discount it to an even ten thousand. I agreed.

I slept a couple more hours before I got up and dressed. I decided not to tell anyone about my plan to confront Hiean Nushen. They would only try to figure out how to cover me, get the local cops involved, or talk me out of going altogether. I didn't need any of that. I dressed in one of the suits that Keeley and I had bought together. The suit was equally pain and pleasure.

I sat for a minute to rest my leg before heading to the street. I grabbed up the cane the taxicab driver had given me. It looked expensive—rich wood with a darker wood inlay. Ivory stars and half-moons stood out in the dark wood. My reflection shone in the highly polished wood. The titanium grip felt natural in my hand. Embedded red and white stones trimmed the grip, along with gold and silver inlays. I studied the grip and found a seam where the grip met the shaft. I twisted it slightly and found that it unscrewed. I turned the grip out of the shaft's threads and pulled. A very sharp double-edged sword emerged from the shaft. High-quality steel made up the blade, and its edges glowed like a razor. It impressed me. I felt for the unfortunate man who had forgotten this. It had to be a prized possession.

Saturday found Dallas's building almost empty. The dim hallways gave off an unnerving feeling. With the quiet, I could hear my own footsteps. Other than the guards at the doors, I saw no one. Before I summoned a cab, I limped to the bank in the center of the block. I remembered either reading or hearing they were open all day on Saturday. It took less than two minutes to draw ten thousand dollars out in cash. It only required an ID and a few clicks on the computer, and I was flush with cash. I had no intentions of spending my money on this girl. I would use it only as flash money if necessary.

I followed Hiean Nushen's instructions and gave the phone to the taxi driver. Once the instructions were relayed, the driver pulled out into traffic and stepped on the accelerator. I felt nervous without my guns. The police still had them, along with all my IDs except my driver's license. The driver never spoke a word during the drive. I welcomed the silence. I needed to think.

The drive took about forty minutes. Since I didn't know Los Angeles, I had no idea where we were. All the houses were set back from the street with manicured lawns and trees. Flower gardens with marble statues stood along the fenced driveways. The way the driver looked from side to side, taking in the residences, I wasn't sure he knew this neighborhood existed. This was a neighborhood of long limousines and Rolls Royces, not beat-up yellow Crown Vics.

He stopped at a bricked drive and waited as two wrought iron gates slowly opened. He pulled around the circle drive and stopped. I told him thanks, paid him, and sent him on his way. I walked up the three marble steps with the assistance of my new cane to the large oak doors and used the cast iron knocker to announce my presence on the step.

She opened the door. There she stood. A crimson silk robe clung to her body. I swallowed hard. "Please." She invited me in with an openhanded gesture. Her perfume filled my nose as I walked past her and stepped into the room.

"The escort business must be better than I thought," I said as I scanned the enormity of the room. My house would fit into this room. Stairs led up to a balcony that followed the wall around the second story. Sunlight shone from a glass dome centered in the ceiling at least three stories high. The sun's light reflected off the marble floor.

She laughed as she closed the door. "Please; I am watching this place for a client. He is in Europe or South America. He told me to make myself at home."

"How fortunate," I replied.

"Indeed." She paused and then added, "The staff is also on holiday; the house is mine, or should I say ours."

I pulled the money from my jacket and showed her.

"Later." She turned and walked around me. "Would you like a drink?"

"Sure; whiskey and ice."

She led me through a side double door and down a long hall to an outside bar near a large swimming pool. She walked behind the bar and poured my whiskey; then she poured herself something lighter, a wine or sherry. She was spectacular. Her photos didn't do her justice. I have never seen a high-fashion model in person, but she looked as I imagined one would appear. Not a hair out of place, perfect makeup, and meticulously choreographed moves encompassed in a perfect form that truly made her a stunning ebony goddess.

Her age, however, as reported was disingenuous. She would easily fool the average inexperienced occidental, but I was far from average and, for better or worse, experienced. I guessed her to be in her early thirties to midthirties. I took a drink and watched her sip from her glass. Her magenta lips caressed the edge of the crystal. The same shade shadowed her almond eyes. Her light charcoal skin shimmered in the late sun.

"So, you're the woman that hired the goons to beat me up." I thought I'd better confront her before her beauty got the best of me.

Shock replaced her sensuous expression. "What?"

I stepped around the bar and into her space. "You're Sky Lee, aren't you? Or at least sometimes?" Her face filled with fear—a reaction I questioned. *Was it real or not?* I asked myself.

"Please don't try to deny it. I don't want to waste my time with a lot of crying and denials." My harsh tone was cold and direct. She stepped back out of my space. I could see the fear in her eyes. She turned away to avoid eye contact. I continued, "I'm Jack Conner. You know, the guy you had three gorillas grab off the street and pistol-whip." I touched the cuts on my face for effect. She remained silent.

"Look," I said. My tone softened, but remained firm. "I just want to know why and for whom. Then I'm gone. Okay?"

She swallowed the rest of her drink in three large gulps; she poured a second. Gone was the alluring, seductive sip; her hands trembled as she poured whiskey, not wine, into her glass. She took another drink.

"Slow down. I need you to talk, not pass out." I uttered my warning quietly in an attempt to calm her.

She set the glass down. "They weren't supposed to hurt you. You know that. They were given very specific instructions not to touch you. Idiots! I should have known better. I'm surprised they are still alive after their blatant disobedience." She reached for her glass; I pulled it away.

"One isn't."

"I know; I heard. It was all over the news." She bit down on her lip, as if wondering her fate.

I touched my forehead and smiled. "Well, they could have been provoked some."

"It doesn't matter. One does not fail the people I work for."

I questioned sharply, "Who are these people?"

"These people…" She spoke in a scared chuckle. "These people do what they want, to whom they want, without mercy and without fear."

"Who?" I grabbed her wrist and pulled her to me.

She twisted out of my grasp. I didn't resist. "I don't know. I don't know his name. I was told if I didn't do it, I'd be dead." She paused. "I'm probably already dead."

"If you don't tell me what you know, I'll kill you," I threatened.

Another scared chuckle. "Mr. Conner, you won't kill me. You're a man of honor and rules. You cannot betray your ethics."

"What makes you so sure?"

She paused and studied me for a moment. Her eyes met mine. She had regained some of her guarded composure. "Because you're still alive." She retrieved her drink and took a sip. "You see, the men that wanted you warned told me a little about you. You're an honest man above reproach, they told me."

"So, who are these men, and why did they send a girl out to do a man's job?" I asked. "I assume they have their own goons to take care of such matters."

"Easy … separation. They knew if you didn't take the warning, you would attempt to find them. After all, their attacking you gave you your best lead, and using unknown contract help gave them more options without casting any suspicion toward them." Her soft tone and subtle accent strengthened.

"They told you that?" Cynicism saturated my tone.

"No, I figured that out." She turned away to avoid my eyes; she sensed her own vulnerability again. "Mr. Conner, why don't you just go home. You're into something way out of your league and way beyond your ability … Just go home."

I reached out and lightly touched her flawless face with my fingertips. With the slight pressure on her cheek, she looked up at me. "I can't," I whispered. "I'm trying to find someone."

"Asian Sin. I know."

"So, who sent you?" I asked again.

"I don't know." She fought back the fear in her voice. "I don't know, but when these people ask a favor, you do it."

"Was it your boss, Joshua Harvey?"

"Boss?" She looked baffled. "Joshua isn't my boss. Far from it."

"But, what about the website?" I joined her in being confused.

"We are all private contractors," she explained. "For a small fee the company updates our websites, takes care of credit card receipts, things like that. It's a phone call, not a person."

"Do you know Joshua?"

"Sure, but I couldn't tell you if he is connected to the website or not. I couldn't tell you if he were involved with anything. I've just heard things."

"Things?" I repeated.

"Things that would get me killed if I told you." Her firm answer rang sharp in my ears. She fought back real tears and real fear.

I sighed and thought for a minute. I hoped her overpowering beauty hadn't colored my judgment. "Look; I concede." I smiled. "I'm not going to ask. I have no desire to see you hurt … I'm leaving now." She smiled past her fear, but the fear didn't leave. "I'm sorry to have bothered you." I looked directly into her eyes. "Good-bye, ma'am."

"Wait; I'll take you." She relaxed some and led me back through the endless hallway.

I stopped to take in the palace one last time. I turned to her. "Ma'am, please forgive me, but what makes a woman like you worth ten thousand a night?"

Her smile dissipated. Her eyes filled with fire, and her lips opened slightly. She rolled her silk robe off her shoulders and let it fall at her feet. She took my hands and pulled me close. I felt her breath on my face.

I left the mansion late Sunday night. This mystic princess—Niean Nushen, the Dark Goddess, Sky Lee—walked me down the stone steps hand in hand. A light mist fell. The wet air was sharp against the skin. The warm southern winds had surrendered to a northern cold front over the weekend. Sky gave me one of the property owner's long coats. It was one of the many that hung in the cedar-lined closets. It was a welcome gift that would ward off the chill air. I was reluctant at first to take it, but she assured me he would never miss it.

We said our good-byes beside one of the marble statues. It stood where the driveway met the steps of her temporary castle. I held her tightly with my eyes closed. I didn't want to let go. She pushed away and caressed my face with her long fingers. "Wait; I need to give you the …"

She put her finger gently over my lips as a signal to remain silent. She stepped away from me to the waiting taxi and opened the cab door for me. I slid into the backseat. She said something in French and closed the door.

I had no idea what she said. I only understood one word, *amour*. I didn't want to leave. I was ready to propose to her, per my penchant for falling in love too quickly. From the rear window I watched her watch me until the cab turned out on the street. I straightened up in the seat and took my last look at the streets with the clean and painted curbs. I was faced with reality again, reality with trash in the gutters and broken curbs.

Chapter 9

As the taxi drove in the direction of Little Tokyo, I let my body slide down in the seat and stared at the car's ceiling. After my weekend in a spotless paradise, everything looked dirty; even the taxi smelled. I fought the idea of going back to the empty apartment with a mind swirling in thoughts and guilt. Somehow I convinced myself I had cheated on Keeley. Bizarre, I know, but that was my thought.

I had checked my phone several times while at the manor: no calls. I dialed Bill Parker. He answered. His voice was happy until I told him what I wanted. I needed to know where I could find Joshua Harvey. After rants of "What in hell are you doing?" and "Are you just trying to get killed?" he surrendered. He failed to find a home address for Harvey, so I had to settle for a business address. I gave it to the driver.

Among Harvey's illegitimate affairs, he also operated a wholesale food distribution center. His center specialized in delivering food to Asian restaurants all over southern California. If he was like most gangsters, he also ran numbers and took some off the top of each restaurant for protection.

The quick drive placed me in a market area just outside Chinatown. Refrigerated semis lined the docks. Another column of large trucks were parked on the curb waiting for their turn at the docks. Small trucks darted in and out of vacant spaces to load. Dockworkers on break smoked their cigarettes under the overhangs to keep dry. Across the street, homeless vagabonds huddled around a burning fifty-five-gallon barrel in front of an abandoned building. Later, when the trucks moved, the street people would scurry about gathering up what food was dropped from the docks or fell from the trucks. This was a regular routine for their meals and was repeated throughout the day.

The light rain increased to a steady shower. Being delivered in a taxi warranted some attention from the truck drivers as well as from the lumpers and forklift drivers.

My driver found a covered space so I avoided getting soaked due to my slow pace. It took several inquiries to naturally distrusting workers before I received directions to the right building. I learned quickly how to support most of the weight of my right leg with my cane, and as I did, my pace quickened. I worked myself across the wooden and cement docks and down the steps to the Harvey building's entrance, a brick facade with recessed double doors. Rain echoed off the rusted, corrugated tin sides. I stepped into the doorway and pushed one of the oak doors. It opened.

I stepped in only to meet two armed Chinese men. They stood in silence with their arms folded, towering over me by five or six inches. These guys were professionals, not like the thugs who had accosted me.

"Is Mr. Harvey around?" I asked. "I need to speak with him." I returned their glares with my own. The malevolent expressions on these massive predators remained, without flinching and without fear. I took a few paces back and carefully opened my coat to show them I was unarmed. They stood as if they were statues.

Before the two terra-cotta-like warriors could pick me up and throw me out like discarded trash, a well-dressed Chinese man stepped into view. I know nothing about clothes, but I guessed his suit cost somewhere in the range of four or five thousand dollars. He was tall for his heritage, and I guessed him to be in his early forties. He spoke with a friendly smile. "Gentlemen, let Mr. Conner pass."

They separated. "Please, follow me," he invited as he turned around and walked out of the reception area and into an open part of the warehouse that stored large cardboard boxes marked in Chinese. We entered his private office. Elegant fixtures decorated the large room.

It was well-organized. Leather-bound classic books lined two large bookcases divided by a large window behind a large desk. Red and gold curtains with oriental print bordered the window. Everything was in a deep red color with gold trim. Both oil and watercolor paintings of Chinese influence hung on one wall. The paintings, although painted in different styles by different artists, all portrayed the same subjects: mountains, dragons, and deities from the East. The opposite side was a devotional wall. A monument to the Buddha, and one for Christ mixed with some signs of Taoism and other symbols that I did not recognize.

He moved around the desk and sat down in a large brown leather chair with a high back. Two golden-colored dragons flanked the chair. Two matching small gold dragons sat on the mahogany desk. These dragons were perched on mountaintops; they looked ready to defend their mountains to the death with vigilant ruthlessness.

He looked at me carefully. "So, you're Mr. Jack Conner, our cowboy sheriff from Colorado. I am glad to finally meet you in person."

"Why's that?"

"I know a lot about you, Sheriff." He looked up at me to see my response.

"I know a lot about you as well, Joshua, Joey Gun, or Jiang Lung." I continued, "Or whatever you're calling yourself today."

"And?" His eyebrows rose.

"You're a drug-dealing, murderous gangster, a criminal, and a son of a bitch. Forgive me if I'm being redundant."

"Please sit." He motioned to one of two chairs that matched his. I sat down. It felt like the chair swallowed me. His face changed; a dark coldness poisoned his demeanor. "If you had any proof of this, you would have brought an army with you … Sheriff."

"Retired."

"You're the first person who has ever talked to me that way without immediate consequences. I haven't figured out if you are an idiot or just stupid." His expression warmed some. "So, why are you here?"

"Asian Sin. Did you take her, kill her?" I took the direct approach again. It worked so well for me in my last encounter.

He snorted. "Mr. Conner, please. Such foolish accusations. Do you always behave this way when you are a guest?"

"No, I am usually blunt instead of showing this respectful reverence."

"You are such a fool. I recommend you spend more time on your investigations before you start accusing people."

"So, are you telling me you did take her or kill her?"

He snapped with anger, "Of course I didn't, you fucking idiot!" He caught himself. "I have a great respect for her. Even after being raised by Americans, she held on to some of her traditional values."

"You mean she paid you homage or at least gave you money." I continued, "Or did you just screw her?"

"On the contrary, I financed several of her movies. Her movies made me money … a lot of money. As far as sex, I fail to see where that is any of your business, but no … I never touched her. She never slept with any of her producers or financiers. It was a strict rule of hers." He paused. "Mr. Conner, I am not your enemy here. I am also looking for her. I owe her."

"You financed her, you owe her, and you never slept with her?"

"No!" His open hand slapped the desk. He took a moment to control his anger. "Never. The idea is revolting."

"Because of her being a porn star?" I should have stopped there. "A little hypocritical for a moneyman behind the scenes, don't you think?"

He glared across the desk at me. "For someone who has a supposed reputation of being a brilliant investigator, you sure are stupid. No, Mr. Conner. I just find the idea of sleeping with my first cousin revolting."

"First cousin?" I sat back in the chair. His revelation stunned me. I searched the rug at my feet for answers. Then the printed bios and articles flashed in my mind. I knew. I knew what I had missed before. The majority of the bios stated she was Chinese. She knew her heritage; her family knew her heritage. I rubbed my forehead; I hunted for answers, conclusions, but nothing materialized. I realized I may have been unfairly rude. I finally spoke, my voice full of contrition. "She knows who she is. Is that why she was kidnapped?"

Joshua rose from his chair. "Maybe you do have some intelligence after all." He walked around the desk and stood over me. He deliberated for a moment. "Would you like a drink?" He moved toward his bar. The bar was built in the wall, and the rows and rows of all types of bottled alcohol from around the world sat on mirror shelves, the edges trimmed in dark walnut. A stainless steel coffeepot sat near the sink.

"Coffee with cream, if that would be possible." It had been a very long weekend.

"Sure; it will take a short time for it to brew." He poured water in the coffeepot. Then he poured himself a large whiskey, Irish whiskey. He waited for the coffee. I heard the trickle, and the aroma of brewing coffee overtook the smell of incense in the office. We said nothing. A thousand pieces of a complex landscape puzzle filled my head, but I had no picture to follow, to help me. I wished I knew what consumed Joshua's thoughts. The trickle changed to a few drops, and then I heard the pouring of the coffee in a cup. A spoon made the cup ring when he hit the side. He asked, "Cream and sugar?"

"Please." The arrogance had disappeared from my voice. A feeling of uneasiness crept through my soul. A man like me does not befriend a mobster. Yet now I was being served coffee by this ruthless outlaw instead of being dead.

He presented me the coffee in a fine oriental-etched crystal cup with gold trim.

"Thank you," I said sincerely and took a welcome sip of the creamy, aromatic brew.

He returned to the bar to refill his glass.

Once he sat back down firmly on his throne, he spoke. "It took a lot of nerve for you to come here and speak to me with such candor, especially unarmed. I don't recall ever being talked to in such an insulting manner, and yet, you haven't threatened me. I wonder what you would have done if I had said I killed her? What then?"

"I would like to think I would have killed you."

He laughed. His laugh was genuine. "Mr. Conner, you wouldn't have. You have rules … honor. No, Mr. Conner, I hate to disappoint you, but you wouldn't have killed me."

I forced a slight smile. He repeated Sky Lee's words. Did he just confirm that he was the one who had ordered my assault? But why? I wanted to ask, but decided to wait. I asked another question. "Do you know where Asian Sin is? Do you know who has her?"

"No, to both questions." He took a small drink. "I don't know, and there is nothing on the street."

"Do you think she is still alive?" My voice trembled slightly. His answer worried me.

"Yes," he answered confidently. "They can't kill her. They need something. She's bait."

"Okay … how about why?"

"Why?" He paused. "Forgive me; the why is difficult. I am not sure I am ready to trust you."

"If it helps, I certainly don't trust you."

"I do admire your honesty. Even if it is in very poor taste and crude, it is honest." I remained silent. He thought a minute before continuing, "Are you familiar with Chinese history?"

"No … maybe a little … not really." I thought of telling him of the medical student, but I reminded myself this was not a friend or someone to confide in.

Joshua studied me for a moment. He massaged his chin with his left hand; his left elbow rested on his desk. "What would you say if I told you Asian was next in line as the empress of China behind her mother, Lin Suen?"

I wasn't sure if he was joking or not. But why would he joke? He didn't appear to be the joking type. "Empress of China? You really expect me to believe that? A porn star, empress of China?"

"It's her lineage, perhaps her obligatory duty, so why not?" Joshua defended his statement.

"Forgive me, but the last time I knew, China was a communist country, not an imperial government."

"Do you know who Aisin-Gioro Puyi was?"

"No."

Joshua stood, left his drink on the desk, and walked to the window. He looked down upon his kingdom with a look of reverence. "I love the rain; it cleanses the world. It smells so fresh after a rain, don't you think?" He didn't let me answer. He only paused to gather his words. "Aisin-Gioro Puyi was better known as Emperor Puyi. Besides being the grandfather of Asian Sin, he was the last reigning emperor of China. He was crowned at the age of two and abdicated the throne when he was six. He later was put back into power by the Japanese during World War Two as a puppet ruler.

"That is the history we know. The history we were taught. But there is a secret history only known by a few. A history handed down by our families, families that longed for a free China.

"The war was a very dark time for the Chinese, and a dark time for many years after that. I was lucky my family escaped before I was born. I am a natural-born citizen of the United States of America. But even though I have never set foot in my homeland, I am still Chinese. My grandmother spent hours teaching me all things Chinese—the culture, the language, and the history … and the secret history.

"When the emperor was put back into power by the Japanese during the war, the Japanese controlled and manipulated him. I believe he consented to this not out of uncontrolled arrogance but in an attempt to save Chinese lives. Of course, most scholars would disagree.

"Puyi was a smart man. He had an affair with a Japanese woman during the war. Not just any woman, but a sister to the emperor of Japan, Hirohito. A sister lost to history because she also was a product of an affaire de coeur. They had a child together, a girl, Lin. Only a few knew of the secret. When it was thought the girl's existence was discovered by some in the new government of China, she was sent to French Indochina for her protection.

"There she met and married Chung Suen. He was a Chinese military officer who had defected and fled to French Indochina, modern-day Vietnam. Her husband, a traitor to the Chinese government, folk hero to a few, became a propaganda tool for both sides. The French left, and the Americans took over the conflict. Chung Suen was either killed at war or was assassinated, depending on who is telling the story. Pregnant and in great fear of being killed herself, Lin fled Vietnam with the help of the Americans. She found sanctuary in the American Embassy in Thailand. She gave birth to a daughter in 1975. To protect her and her newborn, the story was invented that her daughter was an orphan.

"And to give credibility to this fabrication, a high-level embassy employee, Kyle Jones, and his wife legally adopted this girl and named her Sara Jones. It fit well; the Joneses already had adopted several Asian children. Asian or Sara's mother, Lin Suen, the rightful empress of China, pretended to work for the Jones family as a housekeeper. It was her wish that Sara never know the truth of her real lineage, and reluctantly, the adoptive parents agreed. A bit ironic, wouldn't you say? The empress worked as a domestic servant, and her father, the emperor, served as a gardener until the end of his life."

"I would say it is a lot more ironic that the next in line for empress is a porn star."

Joshua asked, "Do you want some more coffee?"

"Yes." I stood. I told him I would get it. Slowly, I worked my way over to the bar. I poured myself a cup, mixed in the cream and sugar, and took hold of the bottle of Irish whiskey. I limped my way back to the chair. I filled Joshua's glass before I sat back down.

I took a sip. Joshua stood at the window. He only moved once to retrieve his drink. Thunder and lightning joined the rain, which had increased to a heavy storm. "It looks like this is going to settle in for a few days."

"It must have been very painful for Sara's mother, being so close to her, to watch her daughter being raised as an American." I wanted him to return to the topic.

"I suppose … maybe, but they were together, and she taught Sara to speak Chinese, both Mandarin and Cantonese. She taught her to be Chinese as well as American."

"I thought you told me she was raised as an American?"

"I did. I hadn't decided whether I was going to share this with you before. You can add liar to your list of dislikes of me. She was raised as an American, but she was encouraged to embrace her Chinese heritage."

"So, what happened?" I fought back a yawn. My body was surrendering to exhaustion.

"Certain powers that be in China discovered she existed. They knew her lineage, and worse, her father was a suspected traitor. However, even Chairman Mao Tse-tung was smart enough to know that he needed to use caution on how he dealt with the royalty because of the deeply ingrained traditions of the Chinese. He watched out for the imperial family, especially those that renounced imperialism for communism. He could have executed the emperor because of his collaboration with the Japanese, but instead, the emperor was jailed. Mao knew that the execution would have been very unpopular and might have resulted in another civil war.

"But others in the government would rather have followed the way of the Bolsheviks and how they dealt with the Russian czar and his family. These are powerful men, powerful men who couldn't allow this secret to be exposed. China is going through some extraordinary changes, but it is still a communist country." Joshua concluded, "I am not sure how long China can keep up this vigorous attempt at capitalism on the world market and survive under communist rule. If the threat grows too great, the hard-liners will never allow a free China … but the people have a taste of something better … civil war may be the final product."

"I've heard this before. But what does this have to do with Sara Jones-Asian Sin?" I asked.

"The Chinese people are entrenched in an old culture and a very traditional society. The harsh years of a tyrannical, totalitarian government couldn't erase their core values. An American-style government wouldn't be accepted by the masses, but a parliamentary monarchy might thrive." Joshua continued this explanation, "The hard-line communists would never allow this; they fear this. They will do anything to protect the status quo."

I frowned; my eyes narrowed. "The Chinese government declared war on Asian Sin?" My voice filled with a cynical bias.

"No, of course not," he replied. "I believe a few powerful people in the government, dangerous people, might think it would be better if she disappeared."

I found this whole thing incredible. "I'm sorry, Mr. Harvey, but this is way too convenient. A lover, who is the sister to the emperor of Japan and mother to the only child of the emperor to China unknown by history. Is this really what you want me to believe? Christ, I have an open mind, but this is a fairy tale."

Joshua turned away from the window to look at me. "Mr. Conner, do you know what a Keizu or a Jia Pu is?"

"No." I didn't even try to guess what they were.

"Keizu and Jia Pu are books of lineage. Japanese and Chinese books respectively. Some of these books or documents go back hundreds and hundreds of years. Mao had most of these books destroyed in China, but a few were saved. There are four documents that confirm what I just told you—four documents with the undisputed seals of two emperors and one king," he explained.

"So, you've seen these documents?"

"No, but they do exist. I think that these powers found copies or discovered the existence of these documents and will do anything to have them destroyed. There is one here … in the United States."

"Where?" I asked.

"I don't know, and frankly, if I did, I would be very reluctant to tell you … I probably wouldn't."

"I understand, but documents are very easy to forge."

"Perhaps, but it is almost impossible to forge the seal of kings or emperors, and it is impossible to forge DNA," he replied with confidence.

"DNA?"

"Yes, when all of this was disclosed to Sara, she had two different firms confirm the documents with DNA tests."

"How?"

"Surprisingly, it wasn't that difficult. Part of the Chinese emperor's family lives here in LA, and with some investigation and evidence, the DNA was collected without harm or suspicion, and the tests were confirmed by two independent organizations, while a third lab ratified the results."

"How did Sara react to this revelation?"

"Because of who she is, her first thoughts were for her children and how it would affect them. Especially her son."

"Her son!" I sat up in my chair. "She doesn't have a son."

"Oh?"

"I read everything I could about her, and all she has is two daughters." I wasn't sure if I was arguing with him or myself. "Nothing in any of the biographies mentioned anything about a third child … not even a hint."

"She had three children. Her son was born several years after her daughters were born. He is much younger than the girls."

"The documents and the boy, that's what they want, if I'm to believe this fantasy." It still seemed unreal.

"Very good." He returned to his seat. "You see, Sara took a hiatus from films for two years. I really don't know much, other than her original plan was to only take off for a few months. Her vacation lasted for two years."

I rubbed my forehead. I was too tired to comprehend all of this. I needed rest and sleep. I had a few more questions that needed answers, though. "Did you send me the warning, the guys that attacked me?"

"No, I didn't send them, and no, I don't know who did. But it turned out for the best."

"Turned out for the best?" My voice was sharp.

"Yes, for the best," he answered and then explained further, "We were concerned that if nothing broke in the case, you would just let it go and go home, especially after the news report about her being in Mexico. When you were assaulted, we knew you'd dig in hard. I'm sorry you were hurt, but since it wasn't serious, there was no real harm done."

"No real harm? Have you seen my face?"

"You'll live."

"Who is this 'we'?"

"My sister and niece."

"Who are your sister and niece?" I already suspected the answer, but I wanted him to say it.

"Dallas and Keeley. Dallas is my sister; thus, Keeley would be my niece." He smiled. "You know, she is quite fond of you."

"Which one?" I felt betrayed.

"Well, actually both of them, but Keeley has a particular fondness for you. Frankly, I don't see the attraction, but I'm not her. I should caution you concerning Keeley."

I interrupted, "I think that's over."

"Good." He gave a sarcastic glare. "I would hate the thought of you calling me uncle."

I gazed into space, and my eyelids dropped.

Joshua spoke again. "I'll have someone drive you. You need some sleep."

I fought back my exhaustion. "Wait … wait, just two more questions. Are you Joey Gunn, and did you kill Rock Hard?"

He shook his head. "I didn't kill Rock Hard or anyone else. I don't kill. Killing brings too many cops asking questions; I don't need that. Not in my business. Blood wars are expensive and attract too much attention. Rock Hard stole a large amount of cocaine from one of my supposed competitors. The idiot even tried to sell it to me."

"So you told your competitor. That's just like killing him yourself."

"I sent him back and told him to return it," Joshua snapped. "I don't know who this supposed competitor is—just rumors."

“Okay, what about Joey Gunn?”

Joshua laughed. “There is no Joey Gunn.”

“Huh?”

“He doesn’t exist. He is a figment of some cop’s imagination. Joey Gunn is an enigma. This evil, murderous figure was born of poor intelligence and has grown into this fearful monster. He doesn’t exist.” He took a swallow of his drink. “Of course, I propagate his escapades when it serves me, but other than that, he is literally no one. Now, go. We will talk again.”

I didn’t remember much of the ride back from Joshua’s warehouse. I must have slept the whole trip to Dallas’s building. Hobbling to the security office, I left word that I was not to be disturbed until I got some rest. “Tell anyone who wants me that I will contact them after I wake up.”

Chapter 10

It was late Tuesday afternoon before I woke up. I cleaned up and dressed in a fresh set of sweats and decided it would be tomorrow before I checked on who had bothered to check on me. With my notes gathered up and my spot in the easy chair, I once again started through the pile of paper, reading each page. I read the words again and again, but my cognitive thoughts failed me. The sentences refused to come together. My mind spun out of control. Flashes of faces shot into view. Sky Lee, Joshua, Dallas, Bill Parker … all rushed past my closed eyes. And one face returned over and over again: Keeley. I dropped the papers on the floor by my chair and buried my face in my hands.

With a deep breath, I got up from the chair, changed clothes, and headed for the street. I remembered a small shopping mall a couple of miles from Dallas's building. In the center of this shopping mall stood a steak house that looked intriguing, and I thought a steak sounded good.

My legs felt steady, so I thought the walk might bring the world back into perspective.

As I left, I asked the guard at the security desk if he knew of the steakhouse at the shopping mall. "Yeah, they grill up a pretty decent meal. Are you sure you feel like walking that far? I can call a car for you."

"No, I need the walk. Thanks, though."

Walking to the restaurant in the rain proved to be a mistake. About halfway there, pain began to surge through my legs with each step. Even though the rain had let up some, by the time I got to the restaurant, I was chilled, and my new coat was soaked. I engaged in a short conversation with the hostess. Apparently, I had slept through a torrential storm yesterday. I ordered a large steak, a coffee, and some whiskey.

The whiskey took the chill out of my bones, and the coffee kept it away. I ordered a second of both. The waitress took my request with a smile and commented on the weather. Armed with my self-confession of being from Colorado, she informed me that Denver's temperature reached the low seventies today, while forty-five degrees marked the top for Los Angeles—God's joke on me.

I felt a presence and caught the subtle scent of perfume, Keeley's perfume. I snapped around and looked up. It was her. She stood there with a face filled with apprehension. Her eyes welcomed my smile. I had rehearsed this moment in my mind a million times. My plan entailed a cold and reserved greeting without emotion. No happiness, no anger, just a polite, detached salutation. She beat me to the punch.

"Hi, Conner. The security desk told me you were headed here."

My passion betrayed me. I tried to stand. She saw the pain in my eyes and told me to sit. She slid across from me and took my hands in a tight grasp. She smiled, the fear still in her eyes. I saw vulnerability in her face for the first time. I said nothing. Words would only cheapen the moment.

The waitress brought my second round of drinks. I broke the silence by asking Keeley if she wanted a drink. She ordered wine. Silence again. I waited until the wine came before I took a drink. Keeley brought her wine to her lips and sipped.

"Conner, I owe you such an apology." She spoke with a broken voice. "I'm so sorry."

I remained silent. I knew what was coming, the final good-bye. I finished my whiskey and waited for her elegant "screw you."

After another sip she began, "Conner, I know you don't know this, but I was at the hospital the night of the shooting. It had been on the news, but I hadn't really thought much about it. After all, there are shootings here all the time, especially in that neighborhood. Even when they reported there were at least two fatalities, I actually had forgotten about it by the time I went to bed. Then Bill Parker called and told me that you were there. It was your gunfight. After hearing that, I caught a cab for the hospital." She laughed slightly through her tears. "You should have seen the poor cabdriver. I was screaming at him to drive faster. He kept saying, 'Yes, ma'am, yes, ma'am.'

"I ran into the emergency room, and there were two cops at the entry doors talking about the shooting. I overheard them say there were two dead at the scene. I asked them who had been killed. I asked them if you were all right. Both of them just shook their heads. They couldn't or wouldn't tell me, or maybe they just didn't know. But all of a sudden, I felt like I was four years old again and sitting alone watching my mother desperately trying to find out about my father." She paused. Tears trickled down her cheeks. She ignored the tears and continued, "I remember my mother, this strong woman whom I had never seen cry, just folded and sobbed while the doctors told us that my father had died. I didn't know what dead was. I didn't understand. I just knew my dad was gone. I couldn't believe it. I screamed and grabbed my mother.

"It hurt so bad … it all came back to me, only this time it was you. I thought it was you. I thought it was you that died in that trash heap. I couldn't take that again. I ran away. I freaked." She wiped tears and forced a smile. "Can you forgive me?"

I sat there in shock. I needed to say something profound, but what? I nodded. I spoke in confusion. "Soooo, you're not dumping me?" So much for being a smooth ladies' man with always the right thing to say.

Her almond eyes widened. She started to laugh. "Conner, what the hell? I'm not done with you yet." She asked again, "So, can you forgive me for my behavior?"

I whispered with the most genuine tone I could muster, "There is nothing to forgive. I'm just glad you're back."

"Careful! I might be back for a long while."

We touched glasses. For the next several hours, we talked. First, she explained everything. When she heard that I had called her office inquiring about Asian Sin, she had called her mother, and her mother started checking on me. Dallas instructed Keeley to see what she could find out by meeting me. After we met, both Dallas and she agreed, along with Joshua, that it would be beneficial for me to continue my quest.

I asked her why she had lied to me about knowing Asian Sin at our first meeting. She argued that she didn't lie; she repeated the question I had asked her that day. She stated that I had asked if she worked with Asian Sin, not if she knew her. I gave up.

She explained that a having an American, a westerner, on the case would avoid any barriers. I had to ask what barriers. Keeley believed that being Asian would be a deterrent because of biases, and she gave examples of such acts of prejudice. I was disappointed; I thought such things were long gone.

We changed the conversation. I listened as she told me about her childhood. She reminisced about high school, college, and law school. She relished talking about this part of her past, and I loved it. However, she stopped short of revealing anything intimate. If she had secrets, she kept them. The conversation switched when she asked, "Conner, have you ever killed anyone?"

Her face turned somber. The mood changed. The lighthearted conversation disappeared. She waited for my answer. I looked down at my empty whiskey glass. I wished it were full again. Another type of pain filled my eyes. "Why did you ask me that?"

She shrugged. I pressed her. "Don't you know? Your mother did a full background on me."

"She didn't tell me. No," she answered and then reasked, "Have you?"

"Yes, once."

"I see." She sounded disappointed.

"It was a very long time ago. It was in the line of duty … self-defense. He shot, and I returned fire."

"Conner, I was told you tried to smother one of those guys … drown him on his own blood."

"I convinced him to talk. He was never in any danger."

She studied my reaction to her questions. She asked another question. "So, do you ever think of the man you killed?"

"Every single day. It doesn't just go away." I paused. "Even when it was justified."

"So, what about the guy who was shot the other day? What about Rock Hard? Do you ever get used to it … all this death?"

"As anyone that has to deal with death, I learned to live with it. I know not all cops deal with it the same way, and we all try to convince ourselves we are immune from it. For me, it works until the nightmares come, or the nights when you're alone and have time to think. Then it comes back. I know some try to drink it away or take pills, but that just turns a nightmare into a reality. I never went that route. I just don't talk about it. Not to anyone." I smiled slightly. That was her cue to change the subject.

We left when the staff locked the doors and began cleaning. She drove us back to Dallas's building. We started a new type of conversation—one that needed few words. It continued in the apartment until daylight. The rain had stopped, and with the rising sun, the blue sky appeared through broken clouds. Keeley instructed me to enjoy it; there was another storm coming.

Keeley called into her office, and we went to sleep. We slept until late afternoon. I woke up first. When she did wake up, she found me in the easy chair drinking coffee and looking over my notes. She pulled the papers from my hands and let them fall to the floor. She sat down in my lap and kissed me.

"What's wrong, Conner?"

"Why don't you call me Jack?" I asked.

"I don't like Jack. Conner sounds stronger."

"Stronger, huh?" I answered. I was still struggling with her bluntness and candor.

"What's wrong?" she asked again.

"I'm back to square one." I sighed. "Your uncle was my last lead. I have to start all over. I'm not sure where to start. All these weeks, and I have nothing."

She procured my coffee from my hand and took a drink. She put the cup down and said, "It's only been a couple of weeks at best. Stop being so dramatic."

"It seems longer." I defended my exaggeration.

"We'll start tomorrow," she proclaimed.

"We? Tomorrow?" I asked.

"Yeah, you're going to be too tired to do anything today." Her tone and smile teased.

I woke up when Dan knocked. We were still in bed. I found my clothes and hurried to the door. Keeley grabbed her clothes and escaped to the bathroom. I opened the door and found Dan with his arms full of breakfast.

He laid out the food on the counter and pulled the plates out of the cupboard. Keeley entered the room fully dressed. I watched Dan for a surprised reaction. He had none. He and Keeley spoke in Chinese and then laughed. This annoyed me a bit, but I let it pass for the time being.

We planned our new strategy. I learned what the "we" from last night meant. Keeley had joined the team. I thought of objecting because of the danger, but I wanted her there. I could protect her.

We decided to finish the interviews with Asian Sin's coworkers and then go to her home and canvass the area. We discussed going to the police department, but Keeley insisted we let her mother deal with the local police. We agreed.

We finished the last of the interviews in two days. We learned nothing about her disappearance, but I learned a lot about Asian Sin. She loved fun and spent a lot of time making her coworkers laugh with pranks and jokes. She gave of herself as well; everyone spoke of her generosity. My inner questions about how a person would pull pranks at a porn filming distracted me. But I worked through it.

While Dan and Keeley reviewed the statements, I checked one of the websites to confirm what Joshua had said about Asian Sin's two-year vacation. Joshua's information was correct. In her list of movies, there were two years that she didn't release any new movies, only compilations. I'm sure it had some relevance, but I had no idea what it was.

During my search I discovered something else very strange; nowhere could I find any evidence that Joshua Harvey ever fronted money for one of her films. I found information and some evidence, including photographs, that all the producers of her films were actual people, so he couldn't have used an alias. My conclusion was that the named producers borrowed money from him to produce the films.

As much as Keeley had disclosed, she never spoke a word of Asian's son, the documents proving her heritage, or the DNA results. I was certain Dallas had at least one of the documents, if not all four, plus the DNA results proving this royal lineage. I didn't ask. I didn't really want to know for sure. Plausible denial can be a good thing for police interviews, grand juries, and bad guys trying to beat information out of a person. I also believed that the child was with Asian Sin's parents. That supposition I was keeping to myself.

The knock at the door went unnoticed by Dan and Keeley. They continued shuffling papers and conversing in Chinese. They were both talking at the same time, and I questioned if either of them was actually listening. I walked to the door and opened it. Detective Jim Collins stood in the doorway. He carried two aluminum cases and my shotgun slung over his shoulder. His exhaustion showed in his eyes; he needed sleep.

"Detective, please come in. You know you should get some sleep. You look like hell." I smiled.

He stepped past me, put the cases down on the coffee table, and propped the shotgun against the wall. He spoke as he straightened up. "Thanks."

"You're welcome."

Jim heard Dan and Keeley out in the kitchen. "Company?"

"Just ignore them," I replied. "So, you want anything to drink?"

"Sure, a beer."

"Please sit down."

He explained, "I'm off duty. I thought I'd drop your guns off on my way home."

I handed him his beer with a napkin and coaster. "Thanks." He took the beer. "There are some release forms you need to sign. Your IDs are there, too."

I looked at the hard-sided gun cases in which he had carried my weapons and said, "Nice."

"Keep them, courtesy of the sheriff's office."

"Thank you. So, how is your investigation going?"

"It's not. Well, I can't really say that. We are chasing some rumors right now. Rock Hard may have stolen some drugs from another drug dealer, and it cost him his life, but Joey Gun wasn't involved."

"I think you're on the right track. I heard the same thing, clearing Joey Gun."

Jim nodded but said nothing, possibly not to disclose any classified information. I wondered why he didn't ask more, like whom I had been talking to. I suspected he already knew I had learned my information from Joshua Harvey.

"So, I was right. Our investigations are only connected by coincidence," I stated.

He put his beer down and cleared his throat. "Maybe not," he said with some reluctance. "Can I trust you with a secret?"

"Sure, but I don't want to compromise you or your investigation."

"You won't. I am sure one of the Senator's enemies will leak it to the press before long, but I wanted you to know first. I think it might explain some of the stonewalling from the other agency."

"What?" I slid to the edge of my chair.

"We went back to that dump apartment building and executed another search warrant in the penthouse. We found a large stash of cocaine hidden under the floorboards." Collins spoke just above a whisper.

"Okay ..."

"Four kilos of top-of-the-line cocaine, probably Asian."

"How does this connect with Asian Sin?" I asked, trying to see a correlation other than her cousin Joshua Harvey.

Collins rubbed his forehead. He searched for words. "The kilos were packaged as evidence, police evidence, from the Wayfarer Police, the same jurisdiction you've been trying to deal with ... hell, the department I've been trying to deal with."

I slid back in my chair and stared at the ceiling. "So, if the Wayfarer cops are involved, how far up the chain of command does it go?"

"I don't know. I am not sure they even know it's missing from their evidence room; it could be a very brave burglar." He spoke in a ragged voice. I sat back up in my chair and looked him squarely in the face. Before I said anything, Keeley and Dan came into the living room.

Keeley smiled and said, "Conner, you didn't tell me we had company."

Collins stood to greet her. I introduced them, and they shook hands.

"Yes, I remember seeing you at the hospital," Keeley recalled and continued, "We would be happy if you stayed for dinner. We have plenty."

"Thank you, but no. I think my wife would like me home before midnight at least one day this week," he explained. "Jack, I'll call you when I get some more information."

Keeley walked him to the door. "Good night, Detective."

Chapter 11

I talked my partners into taking the coast highway to Asian Sin's residence. They protested, but I reminded them I was a tourist and technically still on vacation. Keeley conceded and offered to drive her convertible as a peace offering. However, she reserved the right to say, "I told you so," at every stoplight and every stretch of heavy traffic. I hated to think of the consequences if her prediction about the rain were correct.

The drive took a couple of hours. Keeley, scowling at her gold wristwatch, advised me of the extra time about every fifteen minutes. I made no apologies. I rode in the back, taking in all the scenery and enjoying the ride while Dan and she conversed in their energetic dialect. I was almost jealous. I watched the ocean, the structures, and the people as we drove.

For the moment, the road freed me. I should have been concentrating on the case, but there was too much to think about, too much to do. It would wait. I had the road with its sights, the ocean with its smells, and I had Keeley. Keeley's presence, her splendor, subjugated any sight the road or ocean offered.

Even in the open car, her scent blended with the freshness of the ocean, drifted to the backseat, and settled over me. Her compelling beauty made it difficult to watch anything else. She and Dan were so wrapped up in their friendly argument, she was unaware of my contemplation.

Wayfarer, California, the small town Asian Sin called home, was an unassuming community. The town was mainly made up of gated neighborhoods. The small neighborhoods were separated by stone walls, well-maintained parks, tennis courts, clubhouses, and golf courses. Scattered about these million-dollar neighborhoods were a few small strip malls, with every imaginable type of store one could desire. Noticeably absent were the type of shops found in North Hollywood, like massage parlors, strip joints, pawnshops, and liquor stores. This was a sanitized city. People in towns like this kept their private lives private. I wondered just what dark and lust-filled secrets lived behind the doors of these residences. I asked myself, "How did Asian Sin's neighbors react when they found out about her past and what she did for a living? Maybe they didn't know; maybe they didn't even know her. Or maybe it just didn't matter." I hoped it was the latter.

The town had become incorporated about a decade ago. The city fathers formed a complete government, including a police department. Unlike other towns in the area, which employed the services of the county sheriff, the founders of Wayfarer wanted local control. From my limited knowledge, it was a very poor choice. As Keeley drove through the winding streets looking for Asian's home, I pondered which house the kilos of cocaine had come from—the cocaine that the police had taken and lost.

Asian Sin's home was more than just a residence; it was a small estate. At the center of the estate stood the main house, surrounded by a well-groomed yard. The neatly trimmed vegetation, trees, and bushes gave the property an East-West charm. The backyard extended to the beach and stopped at a five-foot seawall.

The groundskeeper and housekeeper walked out of a smaller house, met us on the bricked walk between the two residences, and greeted us. They were expecting us. Keeley had contacted them the day before and made the arrangements. For retired porn stars, they looked like a normal couple, if there were such a thing in Southern California. The housekeeper introduced herself as Bree and then introduced her husband, Chase. They welcomed us with politeness and delight. They looked somewhat familiar.

Maybe I had seen them in one of the movies I had viewed as part of my research. Both were dressed very neatly and conservatively. Bree's blond hair lay on her tan shoulders. Lines gathered at the corners of her eyes showing her age; still, she was a good-looking woman. He looked at least fifty but fit. She did most of the talking.

They first gave us a tour of Asian's home. We entered through the side door. The house was immaculate. As we walked through each room, I looked for anything out of place, anything that didn't fit. Her family photos hung throughout the house. There was no evidence of her porn career. None of her awards or credits were displayed. Chinese and Japanese trinkets and pictures decorated the halls. The furniture was also oriental. She had several pictures of her American parents, her children, and her real mother on walls, shelves, and any other flat area she could use, like the top of dressers and her end tables. Included in the array of family photos hung several landscape photos, all framed and placed to create a balance of family and worldly beauty.

One end of the second story held the master bedroom. It shared the second floor with four other bedrooms. There were two bedrooms on each side of a long hallway. The master suite included a king-size bed, two large overstuffed chairs, and a loveseat. Through another archway was a very large open bathroom, with a double shower that stood in the corner of a marble-floored room; in the other corner was a three- or four-person bathtub with water jets. The master bedroom had two very large walk-in closets. One of them could have easily held my entire bedroom.

Nothing in the upstairs rooms looked out of place or disturbed. All her clothes and her children's clothes were organized by color, style, and fashion. I also learned from Bree, as she was our official tour guide, that Asian Sin had never had a date spend the night. She hosted a few parties and some neighborhood socials, but never a date. Once again, another contradiction of how a porn star lived her private life assailed my preconceptions of porn star life.

The living room was an open concept and connected to the formal sitting room and kitchen with wide doorless archways. Large dark walnut doors opened into the study and library. The living room hosted her deity shelf. Much like Dallas's shelf and Joshua's wall, it held Christian as well as Buddhist tributes, plus a few items of Taoism. Unlike Dallas's and Joshua's accolades, Asian added a Shinto to her religion shelf. Another difference was that Asian placed her shelf high on the wall. I would require a step stool to reach the small symbols of praise and worship. A wooden ladder leaned on the wall at the side of the unreachable mantelpiece. The carved ladder was made of the finest woods; the oriental etchings detailed mythological demon animals at the bottom of the ladder, and deities ruled the top. The top three rungs had been removed.

We checked the basement, each closet, even the kitchen cupboards, and found nothing that would assist our investigation. The last room we searched was her office. The office reflected the private Asian Sin. Her private library, her computer, her life, excluding the porn, was found in here. If she had kept anything of her life as a porn star, it must be stored or displayed elsewhere.

Her library contained classic books and books in Japanese and Chinese. Her hobby must have been photography, judging by the number of photography books on the shelves and the photos on her walls. Her subjects were a balance of old and new, Asian and Western. Her photo interests included sunsets, sunrises, and the ocean.

The search in the house produced no evidence, no clues, nothing to direct us or guide us. We walked the area where Asian Sin ran and exercised with the caretakers at our sides. As I expected, there was no evidence to find, just as in the house, there had been nothing to find. Dan and Keeley agreed to stay and interview the caretakers. I started going house to house to contact every neighbor willing to speak with me.

I finished canvassing the first block in an hour. By then, the painful reality of my injured legs was setting in. And for what? None of the neighbors had much to say. They were friendly enough, but they just didn't know anything. It disappointed me to learn they didn't even know that she was missing. Also a shock was that no one had been contacted by the police. It is such an elementary procedure. Her neighbors on the second block, like the first block, were very open and willing to talk, but none of them could tell me anything to aid our investigation.

I started to walk up to another of the calendar picture-perfect houses on the third block. I saw a guy in the backyard practicing putting and called to him for permission to enter. He waved me in. I waited for him to finish his putt before entering the property. He made the putt and stood proudly on his green. He tucked his putter under his left arm as he extended his right hand. "Hi. I am Jeffery Goodman."

"Bent grass, that's the ticket," he proclaimed.

"Excuse me?" I asked.

"Bent grass. It's the best putting green grass in the world," he explained. He ran his fingers through the front of his graying hair. "What can I do for you?"

"Sir, I am looking into the disappearance of your neighbor."

"Yes, the Asian woman. I heard," he answered.

The first one in the whole housing complex that reads a newspaper, I thought to myself.

"Are you the police?" he asked.

"No, private investigator. I am looking into it for the family," I explained. "I'm sorry. I should have introduced myself before starting with the questions. My name is Jack Conner. " I handed him my IDs.

He looked at them for a second and handed them back. "Okay, Mr. Conner, what can I do for you?"

"Thank you. Think back to the day your neighbor went missing." I purposely used "neighbor" instead of Asian Sin or Sara Jones. I wasn't sure which name he knew her as. "Remember anything strange or different around here?"

He explored his memory as we walked into his four-car garage. He leaned on the fender of a 1930 Lincoln to think. He finally answered, "Yes. I remember a gray blue limousine driving around here that day. Even at the time, I thought it was strange."

"Do you remember the make?" I asked. I was taken back a bit. I actually found someone with some information.

He patted the fender of his old car, "A Lincoln, by coincidence, a Lincoln."

"I don't suppose you know whose car?"

"I do. It's an airport courtesy car. It belongs to one of the jet centers at the Chino Airport. It's about seventy or eighty miles from here." His answer stunned me.

"How do you know that?" I questioned, still in disbelief of his answers.

"I have two old airplanes under restoration hangared there." He added, "You need one of these to get on the restricted side of the airport." He walked over and pointed in the windshield of a new Ford half-ton pickup. A red sticker with a numbered code in black letters was glued to the lower right-hand corner.

We spent another hour talking about airplanes and antique cars. I enjoyed talking to him and would probably still be there if it hadn't been for Keeley and Dan, who had been driving the neighborhood looking for me. I excused myself and got into the car. I saw immediately that both Keeley and Dan were aggravated. Keeley barked, "We have been driving around for an hour looking for you!"

"Have you guys ever heard of a cell phone?" I said.

Keeley tossed something over her shoulder. It barely missed hitting my head as it struck the back of my seat and fell to my side. It was my cell phone. I decided not to request a return drive back on the coast highway.

We left the land of gated neighborhoods, stone walls, and extravagant residences with their beautiful gardens and drove to the main road that connected to the interstate. A police car with a siren blasting and lights flashing darted in front of our car, and another patrol cruiser rushed in behind us. Keeley slammed on the brakes and squealed to a stop. The officers exited their vehicles with their handguns drawn and pointed at us.

"Raise your hands! Let me see your hands! Let me see your hands!" the uniformed officers screamed.

I spoke through gritted teeth to Keeley and Dan. "Just do want they want. Don't give them an excuse to shoot us."

"Fuck them!" Keeley spit back, but she complied with the cops' orders.

We sat in the car with our hands in the air waiting for the next instructions from the uniformed adversaries. I studied the two at the front of the car. I didn't dare look back. The young officers at the front looked very nervous and out of place. They glanced at each other, seeking approval. They knew they were on the edge of committing a criminal act.

Keeley yelled at the officer closest to her, "What's the charge?"

In a loud whisper, I told her, "Just let it go; this isn't the time or place."

She whispered back a "fuck them" but heeded my order.

I moved my head slightly to the side so I could see the rearview mirror. An unmarked car slid in behind the patrol car that was behind us. Two men dressed in street clothes got out of the car and approached the uniformed officers at the rear of our car. Both uniformed officers gave a quick nod to the plainclothesmen as a greeting. I assumed they were detectives. One wore a business suit; the other was dressed in a sports jacket with blue jeans. The business suit detective looked considerably younger than the one in jeans; he appeared uneasy, as if he didn't want to be there. It was clear the one in jeans was in charge. He gestured to the other officers to holster their weapons. They complied.

He walked up to the car and glared at me. A conceited smile covered his face. He didn't even bother to address my two partners. He spoke directly at me. "Mr. Conner."

"Yes?" I answered him, my hands still in the air.

"Put your hands down," he ordered.

"I'd rather not."

"Just do it!" His voice rose. He was a thin man about the same age as I. He used his arrogance to hide his failed ability to be a credible police officer. I knew the type well. Every police department has its share. He spoke again. "I should haul all of your asses to jail!"

"On what charge?" Keeley turned and looked up to yell at him.

"Tell your slant-eyed bitch to shut up, or you'll all be spending the night in jail."

Instant anger filled my entire being. I closed my hands into fists. I was ready to attack. With a deep breath and closed eyes, I calmed myself. If

I struck out, he would win. It was exactly what he wanted. Keeley turned away; she had never seen this side of me.

"I want to see your supervisor," I said slowly, with my best professional voice.

"Fuck you! The charges are imitating a police officer, interfering with a criminal investigation, and obstruction." He smirked with his answer. "Now, surrender your firearms and your reports, and I'll let you go."

He had shown no sign of fear or concern when I requested his supervisor—a telling tale: this corruption went higher. I thought I would test him again. "Sir, since you will not contact your supervisor, I can only assume he is as corrupt as everyone here. So, would you and the other officers give me your business cards?"

"Listen, fucker!" he said through clenched teeth. "Give me your reports and guns before I kick your cowboy ass!"

"Well, none of us are armed, so that would be very difficult," I retorted. I added, "What reports? We have nothing, only notes. See?" I held up a legal pad where I had jotted down a few things, so sparse and so poorly written they meant nothing to anyone but me.

He grabbed it out of my hands and flipped through the pages. He passed it to one of the uniforms. "Just what the fuck do you think you're doing?"

I just couldn't let it go. "Well, my first thought is, your job."

He jerked the car door open and ordered me out. I moved slowly, too slowly for him. He took hold of my shoulders and yanked until I was standing. He slammed my legs into the car's door post. Pain shot down my legs as the staples gave way. He grabbed my wrist and twisted hard. The uniformed officers moved closer. He spun me around, shoved me to the back of the car, pushed my face down on the trunk, and pressed down. He frisked me. Once he found out I was telling him the truth about not having guns, he let me stand. He handed me a document.

"This is a court order," he said. "It states you are required to turn over all your documents concerning the missing of Sara Jones, also known as Asian Sin, and includes a cease and desist order. You have twenty-four hours to surrender your documents to our department or face arrest. Do you understand?"

I nodded. "Yes."

"Good. Now get the fuck out of here!" he yelled, so agitated with me he was almost screaming.

I got back in the car, and in a very quiet voice, I cautioned Keeley not to speak. She nodded; both she and Dan wore faces of disbelief and fear. We waited in silence for the officers in front of our car to move their squad car so we could go. None of us said anything until we were well away from the town.

Once on the road, Keeley broke out in an angry rage, cursing in English and Chinese. Dan looked straight at the road, still in disbelief. To my surprise, Keeley took the coast highway. Maybe she needed the drive to gather her sanity. After several miles, she regained her composure. I suggested we stop for food. Dan and she looked at each other and agreed.

We stopped at a small blue diner trimmed with white shutters and a picket fence. While Dan and I studied the menu, Keeley reviewed the court order. I instructed her to order and tried to hand her a menu. She ignored me and continued reading the document.

Dan and I ordered from the menu. Keeley looked up from the papers and ordered a salad and some breaded chicken. The waitress nodded, and Keeley dropped her eyes back down to the black print.

She finished reading the documents, threw them down in front of her, and called her mother. The waitress brought the food; Dan and I waited politely for Keeley to finish. She motioned for us to go ahead. Dan and I ate while she talked on the phone. We were almost done eating when she got off the phone.

"This order is worthless, like I suspected," she said in a proud voice.

I slid her plate past the papers and requested that she eat. She picked up her fork and stabbed her salad. She explained that the papers were issued from the Wayfarer Municipal Court, which is not a court of record.

"We'll have this quashed in a minute in front of a real court," she said as she put a forkful of salad to her mouth. She used her knife and fork to slowly peel the breading and skin off one of the pieces of chicken. Her intensity and care were that of a surgeon with a scalpel.

I had to ask, "So, why didn't you just order grilled chicken instead of the breaded chicken?"

She stopped her operation for a moment, looked up at me, and glared. Well, that answered that.

I watched her consume her food without saying another word. My mind returned to the car stop and the insult the detective had shouted. I felt so guilty for not killing that SOB. He had no right to bring Keeley's heritage into this. He had wanted me to attack. I knew and understood it was a vain attempt to escalate the situation, a situation that could have ended with our deaths. I thought about Joshua telling me about needing a white guy to lead the investigation because of prejudices. He had proved to be right.

"I wish we had more to take to the courts. I would like to go after these guys with more," Keeley stated as she pushed back her plate.

Dan jumped into the conversation. "We didn't even get their names."

"We can get the SOB's name off the return of service on the paper when he files it. Not a problem." I wanted to tell them about the cocaine, but I didn't. I had given my word to Jim Collins. Besides, I had other pertinent information. "Would a digital recording and some cell phone pictures help?" I asked.

"Of course. Why?" She looked puzzled.

I dug out my digital recorder and played back part of the recording I made during the ordeal with the cops. She smiled. I then showed them the few pictures I had taken.

"How did you manage that?" Her surprise increased.

"When the patrol car first pulled in front of us, I turned on my recorder." I paused. "When he ordered me to put my hands down, I just started snapping pictures with my phone. I stuffed my phone under the seat when he slammed the door open. He didn't see a thing. He was so full of himself; I could have shot him while he was doing his tough cop thing."

"Why, Conner, you're a sneaky son of a bitch." Keeley sounded proud.

"There's more." I stopped talking for effect. Dan and Keeley slid closer to listen carefully. I remained silent. I savored the moment.

A few moments passed.

"God damn it, Conner, say something!" Keeley yelled.

I laughed a little. "Okay, we have a lead, a real lead." I stopped with a large smile.

"Conner! I'm gonna kick your ass!" she yelled again.

I laughed again and then explained to them about Jeffery Goodman and the courtesy car from the Chino Airport. "That has to be the car they used to snag up our girl."

"How do we find that out?" Dan asked.

"Does your mother have a business jet?" I asked Keeley as she sipped her iced tea. I had already started formulating a plan as we drove out of town.

"She owns one and leases another one or two," Keeley answered, looking slightly confused. "Why?"

"I have an idea, but we need to find a forensic team first."

"My mother has that also. Her lab technicians are top-of-the-line forensic scientists. Most of them retired from police departments from the area and are recognized as experts in several state courts, as well as in federal court."

"Good." I nodded. "In the morning we'll get with her if she is available."

"Why not tonight? It is still early," Keeley said.

"I have to go see Jim Collins, the LA detective." I sighed with a wave of guilt. I didn't like holding back the cocaine scandal, but I had to. I also wanted the time to figure out how all of this was connected. I wouldn't be surprised if the police weren't the ones who took Asian Sin and had Rock Hard killed. But why?

The rain Keeley promised finally started. With the first few sprinkles, Keeley made sure that we knew she had correctly predicted the weather. We paid our bill and ran out to the car, and with the press of a button, the top came down before the seats suffered more than a few drops.

The setting sun glowed bright orange on the clouds coming in off the ocean; Keeley pulled up on the coast highway and headed to Little Tokyo. The light traffic let her drive the speed limit.

CHAPTER 12

I called Jim, and he told me to meet him at a small Japanese restaurant called the Kyoto Inn, just a few blocks from Dallas's building. He asked if I needed a ride, and I told him Keeley would drop me off if he would give me a ride back. He happily accepted. Keeley approved, with some disappointment that she wasn't invited.

I thought of the coincidence of Jim's restaurant selection, the Kyoto Inn. Kyoto was the imperial capital of Japan for decades, a city of peace and tranquility. The United States had removed it from the A-bomb list because of its cultural importance to its citizens and the world.

I slid back in my seat to relax. Dan and Keeley remained quiet. Both of them looked tired. As I looked at the rain-distorted lights, I pondered my thoughts. For the moment I was no longer in the back of a convertible. Once again, my memory had taken me back many years to that hot day at the county fairgrounds, back to the days when I had thought I was in love but had never said it. Or at least I don't remember saying it. At the time, Xiu Tang had made it clear she was with me only for the summer, and it was too painful to say words that would never be said to me. Of all the many things she taught me, two lessons stand alone. Love was the first, and pain was the second. Even to this day, I wonder if I still love her.

My thoughts jumped from the past to the present: to Asian Sin, another Chinese beauty that had changed the course of my life. Awe filled me. I asked myself, why had she started in the flesh business? What was it in her past? Does a person's past, her childhood, make the person, or does her present? Damn if I knew. Everyone spoke of her genuine friendliness, generosity, and her fun-loving pranks.

From a porn star to a potential empress, how did she react to the news that she could be the ruler of 20 percent of the world's population? Had she told her children, her son? It seemed surreal. Of course, her reign would never be recognized, but how would the world react? Except for a few traditional loyalists hidden in the shadows of the consuming Red Chinese regime, I doubt the world would ever know or care.

Would her divine status as empress be suppressed by her career as a porn star? I saw neither a deified empress nor a porn star. I closed my eyes and saw that vehement intensity that showed in her eyes. I couldn't really say much about her movies and her sexual acts because I never got past her eyes and her sensual smile. I worried that I was feeling something for her as well, feelings for someone I had never met. I explored the stupidity in the idea that I might be in love with her as well and figured it had to be pretty high on the stupid scale.

Next, Sky Lee … Hiean Nushen, the Dark Goddess. My thoughts froze as recent memories of her flashed into my mind, and I faded into a daydream of her. Her touch, her sweet scent, and her smile all raced into my consciousness. I sometimes feared that Keeley knew my thoughts, although she had never asked. I wondered if she watched me when I was just looking into space with a subtle smile.

Dallas Xiao Xu, my boss, the woman who had confided in me a very deep secret. I didn't know why she told me and I didn't know if this was her darkest secret, but not telling her late husband who Keeley's real father was had to rate somewhere around the top. Was I attracted to her as well, or did I just admire her? This one was hard for me, but she did come into my thoughts from time to time. And there was a tension there. I didn't think it was passion or love. Also, there was the fact I was sleeping with her daughter. Even I'm not that weird! No, it was two people who shared something about themselves to the other without fear of condemnation or reprisal. After all, I also shared the story about Xiu Tang, the med student.

We were just two people held together by vulnerability and trust. I did trust her; I trusted her very much.

And the last, Keeley. I wanted to tell her I loved her. But other than her standard resume, she had not shared one intimate detail about herself. I didn't know her. Unfortunately, I very much believed she was there for the now and nothing else. She was unlike anyone I had ever met before. I had no idea what she saw in me. I would ask for more … commitment, even marriage, but I was sure of the answer.

I asked myself if there was a country song about a man who had lost his soul to mystic, dark-eyed princesses of the East. And more importantly, had he ever redeemed his soul? … Probably not.

The rain increased, and our drive slowed. It made me late to the restaurant by a few minutes. I entered the Kyoto Inn and scanned the interior. Jim Collins sat with a beer in front of him. A geisha with a painted face led me to his table. I ordered before I sat, and I shook hands with Jim while I slid into the booth. Jim appeared to be in good spirits and rested. The booth was private but still had a good view of the surroundings. Shirabyoshi dancers huddled in the corner preparing for their next set on the bamboo-decorated stage.

My expression turned sober after a few friendly exchanges. "Jim, I need your permission to let my colleagues know about the cocaine. Short of that, at least let me tell Dallas Xiao Xu. She is my attorney of record. She couldn't tell anyone without a violation of the attorney-client relationship."

"How about her mobster brother?" he asked.

The geisha brought me my drink, and Jim ordered another. I whispered my answer. "You know about Joshua Harvey? Is this LA's worst-kept secret?"

"I know a little."

"What can you tell me about him?"

"Nothing, another damn ghost. We have nothing. The feds have nothing. The feds have had a tap on his business for months, maybe years … nothing but rumors. All I can tell you is he visits the Taiwanese Consulate a couple times a month. We think he has someone on the inside." Jim brought us back to the original subject. "Why do you need to tell your people about the coke?"

"You have someone inside his organization?" It was time for me to prove my theory.

"No." Jim shook his head. "Feds may have, but I think it is all electronic."

"We got stopped and shook down today just outside Wayfarer."

"By whom?"

"The cops," I answered. I slid the court order over to him. He took it up and started to read between sips of beer. I continued with my story. I played him the recording and showed him the pictures on my phone.

He took my phone and had a closer look at the pictures. He asked, "Can I have copies of these?"

"Sure. I'll have some made for you once I figure out how to get them off my phone."

"Really? Watch." He pressed a couple numbers on my phone, entered his e-mail, and within seconds he had the pictures on his phone. He looked at me in disbelief.

I defended myself. "How was I supposed to know that?"

He ignored the question and asked if he could have a copy of the digital recording. I said yes, and he pushed a thumb drive into the side of my recorder. I did know that.

"Can your colleagues be trusted?" Jim asked while he pocketed the thumb drive.

"With my life."

"Okay? How about my career?"

I nodded. "Yeah."

"All right, then. Tell them."

"Thanks," I replied and went to the next question. "Do you have any more information on the cocaine stolen from the Wayfarer Police evidence?"

"Nothing, really. The 'nothing' really bothers me." He continued, "There are no records in the San Bernardino courts, district courts, or at the state or federal level. A bust that scored that much coke should have had arrests or search warrants … some sort of legal paper trail, but there's nothing."

"Maybe it wasn't the police after all," I speculated. "Think about it. If a group of drug dealers got some uniforms, some badges, and some counterfeit evidence bags, they could work in the open. Dummy up some paperwork, and you could haul this stuff anywhere without fear." I paused for a moment to let Jim collect his thoughts. I spoke again. "If I stopped a truckload of dope being escorted or driven by uniformed officers with official-looking paperwork, I would never question it."

Jim took another swallow of his fourth beer. "Or the cops are getting the dope themselves from the source. Then they packaged it as evidence. It would be simple to stage a raid or inspection, and no one would think anything about it. You could off-load a plane or boat in front of the world. Who would think any different? All you would have to do is notify customs or the Coast Guard and tell them you were working a case. Hell, you could probably get them to help unload it."

"I like my noncop scenario better, but after today, I agree with you." I paused and looked the detective straight in his eyes. "Jim, how high up would this have to go to make that work? I'm guessing at least up to a captain. It would be too much for a street sergeant, so how high up the police administration ladder would it have to go?"

"High, and who the hell knows who else is involved: harbormaster, other guys from other departments … hell, the cops might even have someone in the Coast Guard on the hook. An officer working off a drunk-driving rap to save his career. A couple seamen caught with some weed. Hell, the list is endless."

"Where does our missing porn star come into our scenario?"

"I'm not sure. Maybe she knows them. Maybe she fronts the money, or maybe she just saw something," he reasoned.

"Or maybe she took pictures!" My heart leaped. "Damn it! We searched her house today. There were photos everywhere and books on photography. She loves it."

Jim looked confused. "So?"

"Not one camera. No cameras, no printers ... nothing."

Jim ordered another beer. "Guess we're taking cabs home tonight."

I smiled. He finished the beer in front of him and asked, "So, where do we go from here?"

I told him about my plan for tomorrow, and he gave his approval with, "Good luck. Happy hunting." We touched our glasses together in a silent toast.

I insisted that Jim take the first taxi. I was in no hurry. I enjoyed the rain and the freshness it brought. The short wait for a cab gave me time to reflect. I was pleased with my meeting with Jim. The theory we had formulated made a lot more sense than Asian Sin being stolen away by loyal Communist patriots. Manufacturing a case against ruthless smugglers and crooked cops fitted my conventional beliefs much better. It was convenient as well. But it also meant that Asian Sin was dead, probably in an ocean grave, never to be found. My happiness departed. I found holes in my own theory about the cameras as well. She might have kept her cameras in her car or her work office—things to check.

The cab dropped me off a little after midnight. Keeley was waiting for me. I informed her about the cocaine and my plan. She told me she had talked to her mother, and Dallas would be here in the morning. A day walking on my leg took its toll. It started to throb. I thought Keeley would be angry with me for not telling her about the cocaine, but she understood. She told me forsaking Jim Collins's trust would have been a betrayal hard to forgive. The image of Sky Lee dropping her robe caused a wave of guilt to roll right over the top of me.

A little after sunrise, Dan and Dallas knocked at the door. The hammering at the door woke me, and I jumped out of bed and quickly stood. Pain immediately shot up both legs. The first mistake of the day: I had forgotten my injuries. Getting dragged out of the car yesterday didn't help my healing. The assault had resulted in a few staples being removed early. I found my shirt, trousers, and cane and headed for the door.

"It's very simple," I said while everyone was finishing breakfast. It was time to share my plans. "Dallas has agreed to let us use one of her business jets. We need two people for this part of the operation: one person to be the rich, difficult traveler and the other one to be the combination attentive assistant and chauffeur. It will land at Chino, and our person, along with the pretend chauffeur, will go into the office and request a courtesy car."

Dallas immediately spoke. "I'll find someone for both parts. I already have an idea."

"Remember, they need to walk straight into that office like they own the place, tell some story about their car breaking down, and request the courtesy car," I instructed her. "If you want, I can brief whoever you find."

"No, I know what to tell them. Does this company have more than one courtesy car?"

"The company has four courtesy cars: two Cadillacs, a Lincoln, and a Ford," I answered. "Based on what I was told by one of Asian's neighbors, we're after the Lincoln."

"So, how do we make sure that that is the car they give us?" Keeley asked.

"That is why our undercover person must act as if they are the most important person in the world and demand the Lincoln."

"Why?" Dan asked.

"Why what?" I answered Dan with a question.

"Why would our people only drive Lincolns?"

I was a bit aggravated at the question but refrained from showing it. "I don't know. Maybe they like the looks of the Lincoln, or his or her ex drives a Cadillac. They can think of something!"

Keeley picked up on my dwindling patience and interrupted, "I think we should use one of our forensic team members for one of the parts. That way, we could establish control and a very clear chain of evidence right from the start." We all nodded in agreement. By the expression on Keeley's face, I could tell she was pleased with her contribution.

I continued with my plan. "Okay, we have the Lincoln, and they drive off to the shop or garage where the forensic team can search it. And once they leave, we need the pilots to go into the jet center and try to dig up information on the jets that had landed and taken off the day that Asian disappeared."

Dan raised his hand. I didn't want to acknowledge him after his last question, but I did. "Where are you taking the car to be searched? We should already have the forensic team and their equipment set up and ready to go."

"I don't know," I answered. I didn't have a place to search the car.

"Don't worry." Dallas made the day. With two phone calls, she secured a shop about ten miles from the airport, and her forensic team would drive out early and meet the car. We were prepared. We just had to wait until the weather cooperated.

By the next day the weather lifted enough to go on with the plans. Dan and I drove the old minivan to Chino. We left behind schedule, but the light I-10 traffic put us within ten minutes of the original timetable. I began to worry the weather had moved back in because it was raining by the time we got to Chino. Keeley and an attorney from her mother's firm went to San Bernardino to get the bogus court order quashed. They took two armed private detectives with them as well.

We turned in the drive guarded by the majestic B-17 on static display and drove around the rows of hangars to get a view of the jet center. I had taped an all-entry sticker in the corner of the windshield of our well-worn ride. Jeffery Goodman had loaned me the sticker and a key for his hangar during our meeting in Wayfarer. I didn't plan on using the key unless it was absolutely necessary. It impressed Dan that I gotten a key from a perfect stranger, a key that opened a door to over a million dollars' worth of antique aircraft. I just had to remind Dan that he and Keeley had been angry with me because they couldn't find me while I was developing this relationship. He shrugged.

Another hour passed before the weather lifted enough to clear airplanes to land. Two prop-driven Cessnas and a cargo plane set down on the runway before Dallas's plane landed. To my surprise, Dallas made her way down the steps of the aircraft, and, as planned, one of the forensic technicians accompanied her. Within a few minutes, they drove off in the target car. From all our perspectives, the plan was working. We waited a few minutes before heading over to watch the forensic team work.

If somewhere there is a list of all the boring things a person could spend his or her time doing, watching a forensic team work must rate in the top ten, especially a fastidious forensic team. They meticulously searched every square inch of the car and then searched it again. Dressed in white lab coats, coveralls, and surgical gloves, the team swabbed, fingerprinted, and photographed every speck of suspicious-looking material they found.

Dallas spent her time on her cell phone and scribbling notes on a pad. She had dressed the part of a rich jet-setter very well. She looked powerful and entrancing at the same time. I would have given her the jet center, let alone a car, if she had walked into my business. I was a little disappointed she was too busy to visit.

About halfway through the search, Jim Collins called and asked if we could meet. I asked him when, and he said as soon as possible. I told him it would be later, and I updated him on our operation. We agreed on a time later in the evening, and he agreed to let me bring Keeley.

Dan left and returned with some food for everyone. I ate alone, pondering my next move. I guessed it would be four or five days before the lab returned some results. I hoped the pilot had learned something that required some follow-up if nothing else. Keeley called. I barely understood her story. She talked so fast she needed to repeat it several times. She had successfully had a district court judge quash the Wayfarer court order. The judge was so upset with her story that he was going to request a judicial review of and an ethics violation on the city attorney and municipal judge who signed the order. I congratulated her on her win and told her about the meeting with Jim Collins.

I hung up the phone, and a cold, hard feeling of fear and dread struck me. I knew the Wayfarer Police Department wouldn't let this loss go; they couldn't. They would try something else. I thought a moment. A search warrant popped into my mind. They would attempt to execute a search warrant. I wadded up the remainder of my meal, threw it away, and headed off to find Dallas.

Dallas hadn't touched her sack of hamburgers and French fries. She spoke into a Bluetooth as she texted on another phone. I waved at her to get her attention and mouthed the words, "We need to talk." She nodded in understanding and changed her conversation to close the call.

"What?" Her short tone both aggravated and surprised me.

I wanted to tell her to forget it, but I swallowed my emotion and said, "Keeley got the order quashed."

"I know that. Who do you think I was texting?" Her voice bit into me.

"They're not going to stop, but if what you're doing is more important, I'll handle it myself." My rude return stunned her. She wasn't used to employees snapping back at her.

Fire filled her eyes, and she asked sharply, "Explain to me just what the hell you're talking about."

"The police. They lost this round, but they will come back only harder. I think they'll go for a search warrant and seize all our work, including what we're doing here."

"They couldn't," she said as she absorbed my statement.

"Depends what they put in the warrant," I retorted. "If these people are willing to kill and kidnap, perjury is nothing."

"It's a different jurisdiction; it would be difficult."

"Difficult, not impossible."

"Yes, of course. Suggestions?" she asked, her hand at her chin.

"We hide everything—the reports, documents, and anything your team finds here—somewhere it can't be found," I answered. "But we need to do it now. They're going to find out about Keeley's victory very soon, and there will be consequences."

"Can't be found or can't be touched? I know a place where everything will be safe." She pressed a number on her cell and began speaking in Chinese. "What is wrong with English?" I asked myself. After three calls, she looked up at me with a satisfied smile. "It's being handled."

"How?"

She chuckled when she answered, "I sent Keeley shopping."

Before I could inquire further, the head of the forensic team approached us and announced they were done.

Dallas answered, "Good," and instructed him to make sure he took the potential evidence to Keeley. He nodded and turned away. She told me she would tell me everything back on the airplane. She got into the car and waved for me.

The same technician drove the car as before. Dallas and I rode in the back. He told us they found several prints, some hair, some bills and papers. Before we left, I met with Dan and told him I was going back with Dallas and would meet him back at Dallas's building.

"Will you pick up the forensic technician from the airport before coming back?"

"Sure," Dan answered. "Would it be all right if I looked around before going back?"

I nodded. "Be careful," I urged as I headed toward the plane.

Dallas sighed. "I had hoped we would be able to start on the forensics today. But now … how sure are you about this police corruption theory of yours?" She turned to look at me.

I returned her gaze with sober reality. "Am I sure? No, I actually hope I'm wrong."

Two young pilots sat at the controls doing a preflight check as we entered the plane. I found a seat and looked around the cabin in amazement at the luxury. Dallas smiled as she watched me caress the soft leather seat and take in the lavish grandeur. I held my cane with care and wrapped it with my coat corner so as not to scratch the trim or décor. Unlike her law building, the plane had no oriental ornamentation; the interior was ethnic neutral, but it was not status neutral. It radiated wealth.

"So, you've never been in a private jet before?" she asked. I shook my head no. She added, "For a leased plane, this one's acceptable, but I prefer my private plane."

It was only the two of us. Dallas sat across from me with her back to the cockpit. A fine inlaid wood table divided us. The plane's new smell filled my nostrils. She asked me if I wanted a drink. I replied no. The chief pilot walked back, sat down to the right of me, and said, "Ma'am, with your permission, we are ready to depart." Even seated, the captain looked tall and fit. He wore a traditional white shirt with captain's epaulettes on the shoulders and gold wings above the pocket.

Without standing, Dallas introduced me to him as Brian Green. I pressed down on the armrest to stand. The captain stopped me and extended his hand across the aisle. Then Dallas asked him if he had found out anything.

He started his story. "I found out a lot. I told the guy at the counter that my boss was interested in buying a long-range jet. I told him we wanted a jet that would fly to Southeast Asia nonstop. We talked about the Bombardier and Gulfstream—which is better. Did you know Cessna has a new long-range Citation that can fly to Europe?"

Impatiently, Dallas interrupted, "What did you find out?"

"Oh, he told me about three jets that land here nonstop from that area. He said they land here about once or twice a month."

"Are they owned by the same company … person?" I asked.

The captain looked proud of himself as he reached into his shirt pocket. "I got the company name, addresses (both foreign and local), and the crews' names for all three planes." He handed the paper to Dallas.

His answer impressed both of us. She looked over the paper and asked, "How?"

"I just asked the guy if he thought I could contact the people who own these planes to see how good an experience they had with them," Captain Green answered. "He just wrote them down for me and gave me the paper. He also told me that he didn't think they would give me much. He said they're kinda weird."

"Weird?" Dallas repeated.

"Yeah," he replied. "He said they never come in or visit. They land, fuel, go to their hangar, change crews, and leave. Everything is paid for in cash on the spot."

"Three different company planes use the same hangar?" Dallas asked.

"All of them do the exact same thing?" I added.

"Yes, ma'am … and sir." The captain bounced his answer between us.

Dallas and I looked at each other before I asked, "Did you get the name of the company that owns this hangar?"

"He didn't know." The captain looked toward the cockpit. We sat in silence for a moment.

With a sigh, Dallas asked in lieu of a command, "Shall we go?"

"Yes, ma'am." The young captain stood and headed for the cockpit.

"Brian," Dallas said, and the captain stopped and turned back. "Good job!" He smiled, nodded, and made his way to the cockpit.

I waited a minute before I spoke. "It will be easy to find out whose name is on the lease or owns the hangar. Finding out who really owns it will be more of a challenge. If you don't mind, I would like to give that task to Bill Parker. He'll figure it out. He is very good at research."

Dallas pondered my statement as the engines spooled up and we started to creep across the wet tarmac. The captain asked if we were buckled, and Dallas waved over her shoulder. We took the active runway before she answered, "I'm sure you're right … If they don't kill him while he is figuring it out."

I nodded with a somber expression. She was right. The plane gathered speed and effortlessly leaped into the air. I looked out at the rain streaming off the windows and wings. The engines settled into a quiet drone, which was almost unnoticeable. It floated as it ascended into the heavens. The captain's voice announced over a speaker that we would be on the ground at Van Nuys in fifteen minutes if the weather held.

I'm not sure Dallas even heard the announcement. Her head was down in concentration as she read and replied to her e-mails. I watched her study the small screen and type her responses. Her long fingers with bright red-painted nails moved speedily and skillfully over the display. I admired the highly detailed Chinese markings in black and gold on her fingernails. She clearly was proud of her heritage.

Her dark eyes moved from left to right as she absorbed the electronic words appearing on her magic device. I wondered what it would be like to be in her place. A person who had started her life with humble means, to become the head of an international business with offices all over the world. A person who had the governor of California's private number, a person the governor would take a call from any time day or night.

I thought of the enormity of her organization. She must employ thousands. Her personal staff exceeded thirty employees. And, of course, there was her office complex that covered two city blocks. It must take several hundred people just to keep up the maintenance on the gigantic building. She was truly an amazing person. What type of drive did it take to build this empire? Was it drive, desire, ambition, dedication, or blood? After all, her great uncle was an emperor. She was a world power, all of five feet-plus and a hundred pounds.

We circled twice waiting for the weather to clear enough to land. Even with a clearance, we descended through rain and heavy clouds before reaching the security of land. We taxied across the tarmac and to Dallas's private hangar. The ground person, dressed in white coveralls, waited at the open door to marshal the jet into its dry shelter.

Dallas looked out the window as the plane turned about and the engines slowed. "Good. My car," she announced. "I was afraid he would be late. He had to run it over to the garage after he brought me here this morning."

It wasn't Dan's old wood-sided minivan. Dallas's classic Rolls waited in the hangar with the rear passenger door open. Her uniformed driver stood attentively at the door. The 1930s vintage Rolls Royce Phantom was deep silver with black fenders. It looked new inside and out. British-style license plates from Hong Kong were displayed on both front and rear, highly polished, chrome bumper rails.

Dallas could see I was enthralled with the car. "I found it in Hong Kong and had it shipped here before the People's Republic of China took over. They probably would have had it destroyed because it embodies the evils of capitalism." The antique Rolls was another one of Dallas's subtle protests against the PRC and a demonstration of the virtues of hard work and capitalism.

I followed Dallas into the car, and the driver closed the door. The Rolls's interior had a delicate oriental flavor. I, again, sat facing forward. I don't like riding backward. A soft leather-covered wall separated the driver from the passenger cabin. The old car hummed as it pulled onto the street and accelerated. I tried to hide my excitement, but failed. It was a magnificent car and ride.

Dallas's attention turned to me. "What did you mean when you said you hoped you were wrong?"

"What?" I replied, disappointed that I couldn't just sit and enjoy the drive.

"When I asked you about the search warrant and if you were sure, you said you hoped not," she explained.

"The potential for injurious actions would be unlimited if this group of police used the courts to support or cover up their crimes. They would be virtually unrestrained in their destruction of a person or persons. Think of the power; I would be surprised if they didn't have an arrest warrant for Keeley and me right now along with the search warrant." I paused for a minute. "Once this gets out about their order being vacated by a higher court, they won't make that mistake again. They'll go to a district court."

"I'll stop it." Dallas spoke in a defiant tone. "I've taken on bigger … corporations, governments … even the IRS and won."

"Yeah … maybe … if you know who signed it before we are killed resisting arrest or trying to escape."

"I'll go to the chief justice; I know him," she said as she explored the options.

"We can't … not yet; we don't know where this is going to lead or who is involved. We have to wait for a while."

"I will vouch for the chief justice. He is above reproach."

"I don't doubt it, but how many judges are under him? What if the cops go after sealed warrants? He wouldn't even know until after it was served."

"I don't want you or Keeley to stay at the office; I'll get you into a hotel for the time being. The last thing I need is for you or her to get shot refusing to cooperate with a search warrant," she stated, her voice filled with concern. She waited a full minute and added, "Jack, I hope you're wrong."

"Where are the reports, our notes, and evidence?"

She answered with a clever smirk, "A diplomatic courier is delivering them to the Taiwan Consulate as we speak. It is considered to be an extension of their embassy. The courier can't be stopped or held once he identifies himself. Everything is or will be on foreign soil and untouchable. My technicians even have permission to process the evidence in their building."

"You dragged another country into this mess? Wasn't China, Japan, and the United States enough?" I shook my head in wonderment.

CHAPTER 13

I called Jim Collins and Bill Parker from our suite in the Beachwood Arms Hotel, a new, very high-end hotel in Koreatown just a few minutes west of Little Tokyo. I figured it had to be a bad omen that I could see the Robert F. Kennedy Community School from our twentieth-floor balcony. The school had replaced the Ambassador Hotel, where Robert Kennedy was assassinated, a fact shared with me by Keeley.

Bill was happy to hear from me. It had been a few days. I explained to him about the hangar and figured its true owner was buried under a magnitude of fake corporations and false titles. He agreed to do the research but reminded me, "You owe me a story."

"I don't have much, or I would tell you."

"What about Joshua Harvey?"

We hadn't talked since I had met with Joshua. I wanted to tell him about the royalty conspiracy, but thought better of it. First, it was too unbelievable even for me; second, I now had a solid theory. I told him I'd give him a rundown in the next few days. Bill said he'd call when he had something about the hangar and hung up.

Jim agreed to meet in our suite. Dallas had booked the room under a corporation name that couldn't be traced back to any of us or any of her businesses. Keeley met Jim at the door and led him into the living room. He looked around in awe; he was obviously taken in by the enormity of the suite. I had done the same thing when I pushed the door open and stepped into this multilevel retreat. I didn't know such places existed. Keeley was less impressed.

She asked Jim to join us for dinner. He politely declined. It took some doing, but Keeley finally wore him into submission. We ordered and made small talk until our room service arrived. A uniformed server pushed the cart into the dining room and set the table for us. Keeley tipped the server, escorted him to the door, and then joined us at the table. We kept the conversation light during the meal. Keeley did most of the talking.

Jim pushed the empty serving cart into the hall, and we settled in the living room to talk business. He looked tired, but anxious to talk. Keeley served drinks while I told Jim everything that we had accomplished today. He seemed impressed and said, "Good job."

Our guest took a drink of his cola and started to talk. He had sworn off alcohol for the time being after last night. "I contacted a guy I know in the Coast Guard. He did some checking and found that over the last six months, the Wayfarer Marine Police assisted four tramp steamers just out of territorial waters during this time frame. All the ships reported mechanical problems, and Wayfarer Police jumped in to help them. Each one of them anchored off shore for several days to make repairs before steaming to Long Beach to clear customs and off-load and load."

"Why didn't the Coast Guard suspect anything?" I asked.

"I asked the same question," Jim replied. "With the hundreds of ships coming and going along a thousand miles of coastline and a thousand ports, along with shift changes and different people, four ships would be easy to forget about, especially if the local police filed an inspection report. All these ships sailed from Southeast Asia, such as Hong Kong, Vietnam, and Thailand, and returned to the same region."

"Tramp steamers? Is there such a thing these days with all the container ships?" I asked.

"Surprisingly, there are quite a few. From what I could find out, these are older vessels; one is still powered by steam. They all fly flags of convenience: Panama, Liberia, and the Marshall Islands. The best I can find out, they are all owned by a couple of companies that have branches in the same ports they call home: Vietnam, Philippines, Thailand, any Oriental country or region that has a dock."

"Do you have the names of the companies and the other ships?" I asked.

He handed me the list. "Some ship names and register information. I'm guessing the registries are false. I tried to track them, but it was a dead end. I couldn't find out anything locally. The Coast Guard wasn't any help; maybe you'll have better luck with one of the contacts."

"Well, it all fits." I stretched and interlaced my fingers behind my neck. "They anchor offshore; Wayfarer's Marine Division takes the distress calls and off-loads the drugs, probably already packaged in evidence bags, and brings them ashore."

Keeley asked, "Why not pull into a dock?"

"Wayfarer doesn't have a slip or dock that could handle the draft or the size of these ships. They're small compared to the freighters of today, but they're not boats—they're ships," Jim answered. He discounted my supposition. "They wouldn't package the dope on the ship. What if they got discovered or questioned by the Coast Guard or state? They'd have to make it look like a real bust … probably up to arresting the crew. No, they would have to package it somewhere else. Hell, I bet they're doing it at the PD."

"The ships? Were any of them here when Asian disappeared?" I yawned my question.

"Yes, the *Yuan Liang*."

"The *Yuan Liang*?" I repeated.

"The *Forgiven*," Keeley chimed in. "It's Chinese."

"Yeah, she's about four hundred foot, fifty to sixty foot at the beam, and displaces around ten thousand tons." Jim checked his notes for accuracy. "She made her distress call the last week of January and weighed anchor on the first of February. She laid in Long Beach for a week to off-load and load. Her cargo wasn't anything unusual. She put to sea the second week of February to answer a call in Hong Kong the middle of March."

"A month to make the crossing?"

"Sure. I doubt if she could make three hundred knots a day," Jim answered. "It's a long trip making ten knots an hour."

"She would still be at sea," I speculated.

"Yeah, especially if she had to deal with weather." Jim supported my statement.

Actually the "she" I referred to was Asian Sin, not the ship, but I let it go. "Well, that gives us four scenarios: Asian was loaded on a plane, a boat, or she is still here somewhere." I stopped.

"What's the fourth?" Keeley asked as she sipped her wine.

"She's dead," Jim answered in a cold voice before I could. I nodded in agreement.

"Is the Coast Guard going to let us know if one of these ships shows up?" I asked while thinking how to work this part of the investigation.

"They are supposed to. That is, if my contact gets the information," Jim answered, searching his shirt pocket for a cigarette.

"I'm not sure where to go or what to do," I sighed.

"Join the crowd," Jim retorted sarcastically. "I still have the investigation into the murder of a state senator's son to work as well."

"You have the killers in jail," I reminded him with equal sarcasm.

"Yeah, okay, now, who hired them?"

"I'm betting on the Wayfarer Police." I shrugged.

"And you have evidence to support that?" Jim smiled. He enjoyed the banter. "You know, that thing called proof and beyond reasonable doubt? I know you guys in Colorado still hang people from trees without a lot of details."

"Not yet, but I will." My smile left, and I rubbed my forehead as I recapped the enormity of this case in my mind. Jim saw my expression change.

"Well, before you drown yourself, I've got more." Jim smiled, trying to rescue my initiative. He explained that he had found out the name of the Wayfarer detective that had shoved me around: Charles William Easton. I was surprised to hear he had started his police career in Denver. The best Jim could find out was that Easton had resigned due to some accusations before he could be fired. The case lacked enough evidence to pursue criminal charges. Easton's attorney managed to get the whole thing sealed. Jim only found out what he did by calling in a favor from an old Denver investigator he knew. Easton had bounced around some small agencies from Nevada to California. Then, when Wayfarer incorporated, he was hired in the first phase.

I asked Jim if he had any idea what the accusations were, and he told me that Easton had been assigned to an undercover multijurisdictional task force. Drugs came up missing. Rumors started that he had gotten chummy with some drug dealers, dealers with Asian connections.

Jim checked his wristwatch and stood. "I gotta go. I haven't been home before ten since your shoot-out. Going home drunk in the cab last night didn't help, especially when my wife had to get up early to drive me to my car."

I struggled out of my chair and walked Jim to the door. He stepped into the hall and turned. "What next?" he asked.

I held up the paper. "Joshua Harvey. He'll know who owns the ships."

"Be careful … Good night." Jim managed a tired smile.

I sent Dan and one of his associates to Chino to wait for one of the mysterious jets from the East to land and to watch their movements. This could be a long wait, a wait that could take a couple of months. Asian Sin didn't have a couple of months. I needed answers.

I called Joshua and gave him the names of the ships. He agreed to ask around.

"You do realize that you have now asked a man with an unscrupulous reputation for a favor, a favor that will need to be repaid," he said in a not too joking manner. "We need to meet again."

"Anytime, but it will have to be here at the hotel." It didn't surprise me that he didn't ask why when I told him I was confined to the hotel for a time. Men like him don't have much use for the whys.

Dallas arrived at Keeley's and my suite early. She and Keeley talked over coffee in the dining room while I was on the phone. She was visibly annoyed even with her victory. At two this morning, the Wayfarer Police detectives, supported by a twelve-member SWAT team, hit my room in Dallas's office building. She had the head of her security and her top criminal attorney there to meet them, along with a professional video photographer. The police were quite surprised. They got a second surprise when they opened forty boxes of Chinese New Year's napkins.

I asked, "Napkins?"

"Yes," she answered. "You remember the shopping trip I sent Keeley on?" Keeley and she laughed together. They sounded the same. They looked more like sisters than mother and daughter.

"Yeah." Keeley spoke through her laughter. "I bought four hundred boxes of napkins and other trinkets and had them delivered to the room and distributed throughout Los Angeles, ten lots per delivery. Mother wanted to divide any surveillance teams the police might have had on the place. The attaché picked up your materials in identical boxes. We kept forty boxes there so the cops would have something to find."

The desire to laugh with them entered my mind, but fear quickly replaced it. I spoke. "I appreciate the humor, but these are dangerous men. I wouldn't recommend toying with them."

"Jack," Dallas said with a smile, "relax some. Enjoy our small victory. I now have the judge's name. I just have to wait for you to give the go-ahead, and I'll have a meeting with the chief justice … And, yes, the cops, they were angry. According to my people, they were furious. I think they would have trashed the place if my staff hadn't been there."

I asked myself in silent thought, was that a search team or a third-world death squad? Keeley's cell phone rang, and she excused herself to answer the call. Dallas waited for Keeley to leave before she asked me what I thought the Wayfarer Police would do next.

"Issue arrest warrants for Keeley and me?"

She nodded.

I spoke in a whisper. "We need to get Keeley out of here. As much as I enjoy her company and her sharp mind, I don't think she understands the gravity of our situation. This is going to end in a gunfight. It's not a game, and I don't want her here when that happens." I directed Dallas's eyes to my legs. "I'm not sure I'll be ready when it comes, but it will come."

"Maybe not," Dallas answered. "I hope not. I find your prediction disturbing. Modern men don't handle problems this way."

"Maybe some modern men don't; criminals do … especially criminals with guns. Dallas, listen to me! I don't want her to get hurt." It was the second time I had called her by her first name.

She stared at the floor; she nodded and spoke. "You're right. I will work on it." Her eyes snapped up to mine. "Anything else?"

"Contact your judge." I explored the consequences as I spoke. "What is the chance of taking someone from the attorney general's office with you?"

"Good." Reluctance filled her voice. "Are you sure this is the time?"

"No, I'm far from being sure, but I can't sit around here for too long." I added, "I don't need to be looking over my shoulder for the cops to shoot me or have an accident in their jail."

"So that I am perfectly clear, do you want me to attempt to stop the Wayfarer Police by going to the judge?" Dallas asked.

"No. We don't have enough evidence for any type of criminal case against them. Just brief your judge. Make him aware of what's happening and see if you can find out anything on the judge who signed the search warrant.

"I know judges don't like to look at other judges, but we need to find out. Honestly, I don't think the judge is involved. He probably just signed whatever the police handed him, but I don't want an arrest warrant hanging over me. So help out your judge. Come up with something, like the chief justice wants to audit arrest warrant requests … something."

"I agree with you," Dallas replied thoughtfully. "I'm guessing the judge was probably random. If it is the same there as here in LA, when the police or DA need any court order, they would just be sent to any available judge.

So if their policies are similar and they applied for another warrant, they would be sent to whomever."

"It's the same where I came from … unless I had a judge that was already familiar with my case. I might request the same judge then. So even if they requested the same judge, that wouldn't make him necessarily involved."

"Okay?" Dallas smiled nervously. "I'll think of something." She thought a moment. "Jack, I think we need to bring the sheriff into this. She needs to know what is going on in her county."

"She?"

"You have a problem with a woman sheriff?"

"No, just wondering if she were a relative."

"No." Resolve filled her voice. "Just a friend." Her confidence returned.

"I'll see if Jim Collins can go with you as well."

Keeley entered the room before I could say more. She looked upset. I hoped she hadn't heard her mother and me plotting against her. Dallas and Keeley excused themselves and went back to the dining room for some coffee and to talk … in Chinese. I hate that.

I poured myself a cup of coffee and found a seat in the living room. The chair rocked. I sipped as I pitched back and forth. An argument battled silently in my head. Was she taken by jet or by ship? If I were doing the kidnapping, it would definitely be by air. Quick, clean, and out of the country before the locals closed in or the feds got interested. But since the locals are in this at some level, there are considerably more options. I wouldn't be surprised if the Wayfarer Police had stuffed Asian Sin in a basement cell at their station. Still, a fast-moving private jet would be the best.

I closed my eyes and imagined Asian Sin … Sara Jones, sweltering in the cruel, humid heat as she sat in a dark, damp corner of a cargo hold. I couldn't conjure her as being afraid. Like her cousin Dallas or her niece Keeley, nothing scared these women.

My thoughts returned to the ship. How would I find an antiquated ship steaming between here and the prime meridian, flanked by the equator and the Tropic of Cancer? If she were taken, I hoped it was by airplane. It would be considerably better for her to be on an airplane for ten or twelve hours than bouncing across the Pacific in an old rat-infested ship. My thoughts were not totally altruistic. Selfishly, I hoped she was on a plane. How would I ever find a ship in the Pacific Ocean or the South China Sea? If I found it at sea, how could I rescue Asian Sin without getting her killed? Boarding and assaulting ships are jobs for Navy SEAL teams or Somalian pirates … not me. I would wait until the ship docked and take her back then. I didn't have the resources, knowledge, or time for any other operation. I whispered aloud, "Hold on, girl … hold on."

Three days passed, and my mood had darkened considerably. My case had stalled. We made very little progress, and frustration built. My personal life was worse; however, I am not sure exactly where my personal life started and professional life ended. My professional and personal lives were so interwoven, I couldn't find the lines. Throughout my life, I had sought these lines and had wanted to live by the rules that separated professional and personal boundaries. It seemed that no matter how hard I had tried, I failed to stay within those borders.

Keeley announced with tear-filled eyes that she had to go because of some contract issues that had just come up. I suspected Dallas had manipulated the contract emergencies that required immediate attention. I would thank her later. Dallas insisted that Keeley take a bodyguard and use her private jet for travel. I stopped Keeley from disclosing her destination. I didn't want to know. Knowing could be dangerous for both Keeley and me.

I rode to the airport with Keeley. It was a painful trip. We had spent a great night together, but both of us stopped sort of using the "L" word, which left me in great doubt about the future of this relationship. Yes, it was my desire to send her away, but it was to protect her, to keep her safe.

I sat beside her on the drive. We held hands, and I glanced in her direction, looking for a sign of commitment from her. As much as I wanted to, I avoided telling Keeley I loved her and we should consider marriage. I feared that to say "I love you" would scare her away. I knew she loved her freedom and herself as she was. She even said a long-term relationship didn't fit in her lifestyle. I wondered who she was trying to convince the most, her or me. She had kissed me and held me tightly. Her tears fell against my cheek.

"I already miss you, Conner." She smiled through her tears. "I will hurry home."

"You know, we don't have a home, remember?" I reminded her.

Her reply was quick and to the point. "Home is anywhere you are."

I felt a little better on the drive back to the hotel. Did I dare try to interpret what those words might mean when this investigation was all settled?

Chapter 14

On the second night without Keeley, I sipped from my second glass of a rare whiskey. After another day under house arrest, my pure intention was to get drunk and rock myself into a lugubrious pit of self-pity. My disposable cell rang. I knew who it was without looking, but it still was a surprise. "Hello, Sky," I said with another sip.

"Jack?" She spoke in a whisper. "Jack, I need to see you. I think I have something. It's important."

I told her where I was staying. She interrupted as I tried to give her the address. She knew it. I didn't ask. Within the hour, she arrived at the door. She looked both ways down the hall with a nervous glance. She almost jumped through the threshold. Without asking, I poured her some whiskey out of my new bottle of vintage bourbon. She took the glass in both hands and swallowed without any appreciation of the quality of my offering. I poured her a second and invited her to sit.

"Jack"—her voice trembled—"I need to tell you I think I found out something about Asian Sin."

"So, tell." My answer was cold to defend myself from getting drawn into her beauty.

"Yes." She was taken aback by my response. "I am not sure where to start." She paused to find the correct words. I struggled with my feelings for this person. I was afraid she was a siren drawing me toward moral rocks in a ragged sea.

With a gentle smile, I spoke, steering my integrity closer to the reef. "From the beginning."

"The night before last, I entertained a new client." She looked for a judgmental reaction from me. She got none, but I did wonder why the confession. She continued, "I'm sure he was Chinese."

"Chinese?" She had my attention. "Excuse me," I said. "I heard or read somewhere that Asian men prefer pasty white American blondes. Is that true?"

"I've heard the same thing. I don't really know," she answered and added, "Why?"

"If there is any merit to that overgeneralization about Asian men, why you? I'm just wondering if this was some sort of setup. So, how was he?"

"He was a horrible man—very demanding. He controlled everything. He took a phone call and spoke to the person very openly in Chinese. Consumed with his own arrogance, he never suspected that I speak Chinese and understood his every word."

In my ignorance, I never suspected that she could either. "What did they talk about?" I asked.

She continued, "About a cargo that was supposed to be delivered by air, but because of the US Customs and the Treasury being at the airport, they were forced to load the cargo on a ship … Jack, during the conversation. I heard him say something about the police had to load the cargo, and the cargo was a woman."

"Are you sure?"

"Yes." Her dark eyes drew me into a dark abyss. "I was very careful not to react; I was afraid he might kill me."

"Question is, was it a mistake, or was it on purpose?"

"On purpose?" She was surprised by my question.

"Yeah. I am a bit concerned that just out of the blue, he selected you. I just wonder if he knew who you were and that you spoke Chinese. Maybe he is trying to send a message or throw me off. That is, if he even knows who I am. Did he say anything or ask anything that would make you think he knows of me or the investigation?"

"No, not that I can think of."

I sought to reassure her. "Then maybe my paranoia is getting to me. Where can I find him?"

"He told me he was returning to the East. That would have been yesterday morning."

"Write down his name. I'll check into it."

She wrote down the name and carefully placed the paper on the end table. She caught me admiring her. I didn't even attempt to hide my desire or my vulnerability. With a seductive expression on her face, she sauntered slowly and deliberately to my chair and slid down on my lap. Her kiss was slow and forceful. My virtue crashed upon the coral.

Just a little over forty-eight hours ago, I was lying in bed looking at the beautiful face of Keeley. Now the Dark Goddess slept in her place. Sky's splendor filled me with desire, but not the same passion I felt for Keeley. It was just as intense, but it was easier, without pain or fear. Sky Lee, Hiean Nushen, the Dark Goddess was a moment in time, without any consideration of a future. No, she would never be mine.

Suddenly the phone interrupted my thoughts. Dallas was calling. "Jack, I have some great news. I had a meeting with the chief justice. The sheriff and Jim Collins, along with a host of others, were there as well. The chief justice gave me his word there would be no arrest warrants issued for Keeley and you."

"That is great!"

"Jack, you may proceed with your investigation, but be careful and keep me informed."

"Sure."

"Oh, I almost forgot. The lab techs confirmed the hair they had retrieved from the courtesy car was consistent with being Asian, but they had not finished the DNA comparison."

"Looks like we are on the right track." I knew I sounded worried, worried for Asian Sin. "Dallas, I need a couple more people. I need Dan here working with me, not on the surveillance of the Chino Airport."

"I agree. By the way, the sheriff had suspected something was going on out there at the airport for a while but had nothing but rumors."

I replied with a question, "Which is better, supposition or rumors?" She laughed.

It was late when Sky Lee left. I had hoped she would spend another night with me, but I was just as glad when she politely declined. This would leave me plenty of time to feel remorse for my infidelity. Whiskey would supply the strength to let me sleep without guilt. She said good-bye with the same French phrase as our last encounter.

Before I got started with an evening of self-castigation, a knock came at the door, and there stood Joshua Harvey. One of his two giant bodyguards entered my suite first. With steely eyes, the guard checked the room. He stopped his visual search and listened for anyone else in the suite. I stood silently. Once the guard had convinced himself the room was safe, he waved to Joshua. Joshua entered. The guard exited to join his partner, where they stood guard at each side of the door.

"Mr. Harvey, what a surprise. I thought you were going to call first." My salutation sounded suspicious.

"Sheriff Conner, where is the fun in being predictable?" His voice also carried suspicion. "You'd be shocked at what you can find if you come unannounced, but I am sure you've utilized the same techniques as an investigator."

"I didn't know I needed to be investigated."

"Everyone is watched by someone."

He was correct. But he was the type of man that would just accuse someone straight up. Why bother with such tricks? Speaking in vague accusations might lend to a confession in some people, but I wasn't ready for absolution of my recent indiscretions by a mobster; nor was I ready for his retribution if he lacked the ability to forgive my dalliance with Sky.

"So, are you watching me? If you have something to say or ask, just do it." I stared directly into his eyes. He studied me, looking for some fear or doubt. I had none for him: guilt maybe, but that wasn't for him. I spoke again. "Did you find out anything about the ships?"

"Do you have anything to drink?" he asked. His narrowed eyes opened, and he smiled.

"Whiskey all right?"

He watched me walk. "You're walking better … good."

"Yeah, I get the staples out next week. I don't need the cane that much, but I like carrying it," I said over my shoulder as I poured drinks.

He settled on the couch across from my rocking chair. He took up his drink in his left hand. "Your ships all belong to an organization headed by a gentleman who refers to himself as Zhang-Fei." He paused so I could ask who Zhang-Fei was. I didn't. He continued, "Zhang-Fei, the God of Butchers from the Chinese novel *Romance of the Three Kingdoms*, a fourteenth-century book. The real Zhang-Fei, unlike this contemporary namesake, was one of three heroic brothers: Guan-Yu, Liu-Bei, and Zhang-Fei. The three excelled in combat. Many past and current Chinese leaders associate or compare themselves to these mythical champions."

"So, I'm guessing from what you are telling me, this is a bad guy?"

"About as bad as they get. He is the leader of a group, the Mimi Shenghou Mogwai or MSM." He paused again.

This time I asked, "The MSM?" I didn't even try to pronounce Mimi Shenghou Mogwai.

Joshua pronounced it for me as he explained, "The Mimi Shenghou Mogwai, translated loosely, means the Secret Life of Demons."

"Let me guess. This Zhang-Fei and his group are loyal to the empire and will do anything to rebuild it." I tried hard to hold back my sarcasm.

"On the contrary, Zhang-Fei pretends to be a hard-core traditional communist. Rumors have it that he had connections with Fusako Shigenobu, the leader of the Japanese Red Army, before she was jailed. But it's hype. All of his dogma and his trying to spread his beliefs all over Southeast Asia are a front. He is really nothing more than a ruthless criminal looking for a buck."

I was going to say it takes one to know one, but decided to forgo the cliché. "Do you know this guy's real name?"

"No, he has dozens of aliases. I cannot even get a picture of him."

"Another Joey Gunn?" I asked this time, adding a sarcastic smirk.

Joshua seriously deliberated my question. "I'm not sure, but I don't think so. I think this is a real person."

"Where do I find him?"

"Asia."

"Can you narrow it down some?"

He smiled. "Sure, Southeast Asia." I rolled my eyes. He added, "Look, he has connections all over—Laos, Cambodia, Thailand, and south China. He also has friends in governments and business, as well as the underworld."

"Did you ever do business with him?"

"No, never. At least not intentionally."

"Did you find out anything specific about the *Yuan Liang*?"

"Not much more than you already know. She is registered in Panama to a shipping company in Hong Kong, the Far East Shipping and Holding Company. It goes through several layers, but the company is Zhang-Fei's. The ships may be under different corporate names, but he owns them all."

"Anything else?"

"Another rumor: the *Yuan Liang* was diverted from her original destination of Hong Kong to Bangkok. I couldn't find out why, but I suspect the port wasn't clear … probably police."

"When will she make land?"

"Ten days, couple weeks … it all depends on currents and weather, but I did find out another one of his ships is headed this way and should land in a few days … Her name is the *Yuan Gui* … ghost with a grievance."

I cut him off before he could explain further. "Ghost with a grievance? How do you get superstitious sailors to sail such a vessel with ghost in its name?"

"Perhaps it is actually good luck. The quest for justice for those who were killed wrongly, redemption for those that cannot rest." Joshua finished his drink.

I grabbed a piece of paper and copied down the name that Sky Lee had given me. I carefully folded up the note from Joshua's sight. I thought he might recognize the writing. When I finished, I handed him the name. "Can you find out about this guy?"

His face filled with anxiety. He attempted to hide it. "Where did you get this?"

"You know this guy." I didn't give him the chance to deny it. "Who is he?"

"A very dangerous man." He finally gave up an answer after some hesitation.

"Who?"

Joshua stood, leaving his glass on the end table. "Walk away from this one. Forget you ever heard the name."

"What makes him more dangerous than Zhang-Fei? You didn't warn me off Zhang-Fei. He sounds about as notorious as they come."

"Leave it."

"You know I can't do that."

He nodded in understanding and walked to the door. "Do this for me: put him on the bottom of your list. You have plenty to do for now. If the time comes, I will tell you more. Will you promise?"

"Okay for now." I closed the door behind him. I stood there looking at the closed door. What was going on? Why should I trust Joshua, a mobster himself?

I went to the couch and flopped down … a mistake. I was still not that healed. I called Dallas and asked her to come over. She agreed, but she would be a while, and she volunteered to bring some pizza. I told her to bring two pizzas. I informed her I had seen the type of pizza her kin favored—fish and other critters. I ordered an all-meat pizza … American meats. She laughed.

She entered carrying two pizza boxes. I already had the table set, and I quickly poured wine for her and a whiskey for me. We ate and laughed. I enjoyed her company. It was nice to talk about something besides the case. I wished the conversation would last the night. It didn't.

"So, what is so important?" she asked, working on her third or fourth glass of wine—I had lost count. I was on my second whiskey at that point.

I handed her the name that Sky Lee had given me on the folded note. "Do you know who this is?"

She unfolded the note. Her face registered shock. She trembled as she put her glass down. Her actions scared me. I had never seen her like this. This headstrong woman with the world at her feet was now fighting back tears.

"Who is he?"

She forced herself to speak. "How is he involved?"

"He might be involved. A friend told me about overhearing him talking about putting a woman on a ship because they couldn't load her on a plane as planned." I paused a moment to study her reaction. "Of course, this is all unconfirmed. I just started working on this lead."

She took a breath. "The name is not Chinese; it's Korean. He is Keeley's real father."

Now I have spent a considerable amount of time training myself not to swear, cuss, or use vulgar language, but I found nothing to respond with except, "Aw, fuck!"

"Indeed," she responded, wiping her tears.

Chapter 15

Morning found another woman on Keeley's pillow. Her mother, in all of her elegance, slept a deep sleep. The sun crept through a small gap in the curtains and illuminated her perfect face. Under different circumstances, I would have been enthralled. I rolled onto my back and swore under my breath. I had become a womanizing son of a bitch. I looked at her again … I was enthralled—so much for character. God, what a bastard.

Before I could even start with evaluating what I'd done, my cell phone rang. It was Dan. I answered with meekness and uncertainty in my voice. "Hello."

"Boss, we have a problem!" He sounded worried.

"You wouldn't even begin to know," I answered, glancing over at my bed partner.

"What?"

"Never mind. What's up?"

"I need you to come to the airport … now!" His worry grew to borderline panic.

"Airport? Which airport? Why?" The sleepy fog enveloping my consciousness made me struggle to remember what was going on. Dallas had that effect on me. "What are you doing still at the airport? I thought your replacement had that covered."

"Chino! The airport in Chino, please! I need you, now!" His voice pierced my half-asleep brain and had me worried now.

"What happened?"

"I don't want to talk over the phone … just get here."

"Okay, give me thirty minutes plus driving time."

"Good, just get here." Dan had some relief in his voice. "Meet me at Jeffery Goodman's hangar."

I woke Dallas with a kiss. I confirmed in my mind that I was a soulless SOB. "Dan called with an emergency, and I have to go."

"Dan? What? What emergency?" She sat up in bed and pulled the cover up to her chin. "What is going on?"

"I don't know. He wouldn't tell me over the phone. All I know is that I have to go to Chino." I stopped to look at her. "This is not how I planned our morning." I actually didn't have a plan and was almost thankful I could avoid this whole situation until later. Add cowardice to my resume.

"I know." She gave me an understanding smile. She didn't push or ask again. She was too disciplined for that. She knew if I said I didn't know, I didn't know. "We have to talk when you get back," she whispered.

"Yep."

I called down to the front desk and arranged for a car before I showered and dressed. On my way through the lobby, I grabbed some sweet rolls, a banana, and two covered cups of coffee under the annoyed scrutiny of a very pretty uniformed hostess. I hurried past the doorman and into the back of the waiting car. I started stuffing food into my mouth.

Ideally, my strategy was to keep my mouth full and chewing to keep my mind off Dallas, Sky Lee, and Keeley. I wasn't ready for self-examination concerning my recent decisions. Fortunately, the ride passed quickly, and I had enough food for the trip to keep my mind occupied. The car stopped in front of the Goodman hangar, and Dan was waiting at the walk-through door. He waved for me to hurry.

I stepped through the door, and in less than twelve hours, I used the phrase "aw, fuck" for the second time, a phrase I had managed to avoid saying for at least three or four years. Between a partially assembled P-51 Mustang and an old Corsair sat four rolling office chairs. On these four chairs sat four individuals dressed in dark tactical-style clothes. They were securely duct-taped to the chairs with what appeared to be more than an ample amount of tape. The silver tape went around their waists and chests and around the back of the chairs many times. Their arms were stuck to the chair with several layers of tape, and their legs were immobilized to the center riser between the base and seat of their chairs. Behind them stood three very proud private detectives; they displayed their captives as if they were big-game hunters posing with their trophies.

I looked over at Dan, and beside him stood a formidable and intimidating man. He had to be at least six and a half feet tall and must have weighed a muscular three hundred pounds. His head was shaved but sported a well-trimmed goatee.

"Mr. Conner, this is Chewy Huang, my second-in-command," Dan said as he formally introduced me to his lieutenant. "Chewy, this is Mr. Conner. Mr. Conner is in charge of our operation." Chewy reached out to shake my hand, but I was so angry, I ignored his gesture. For the moment, I didn't feel like I was in charge of anything. I felt like I was just going to be the person to blame for this mess.

Dan continued, trying to calm my anger, "His mother was a Mexican woman. His father met her while he was traveling in the southern part of Mexico. She taught both him and his father Spanish. Chewy can speak Spanish, Chinese, and English."

"What the hell, Dan? Just why in the world would you think that I need to hear Chewy's family history or his resume? I need to know this!" I pointed at the captives. "I want to know what happened here—now and why!" I asked Dan, trying hard not to yell. Chewy left Dan's side to secure the door.

Dan began his explanation. "With what you had learned from Ms. Xiao Xu's pilots, a plane landed last night and did just what we were told they would do. The plane taxied to the private hangar, took on fuel, and changed crews. At the same time, this van drove in the hangar." He pointed at a white utility van with no windows beyond the front doors. "Once inside and when the doors closed, these guys went to work." He looked back down at the individuals strapped to the office chairs. "They unloaded several boxes, put them into waterproof containers, and then loaded them into the plane.

"Chewy couldn't get hold of me or you, so he improvised. His guys stopped the van, grabbed these suspects, and taped them to the chairs."

"And for what crime? For all we know, they loaded fortune cookies on that plane," I huffed as I folded my arms.

Dan reached down, pulled a heavy duffel bag to my feet, and opened it. He pulled out one of four fully loaded and fully automatic, short-barreled AK-47s. "How about this?"

I took the rifle from Dan's grip and examined it. The markings were all Chinese. It lacked the required American serial numbers for legal sale in the United States. "Okay, that helps. That may keep us out of jail … maybe."

I set the carbine back in the bag and walked over to the captives. I found the one with the most fear in his eyes and ripped the tape off his mouth. "Where's the girl?" He looked up at me in fear and responded in Chinese.

Dan repeated my question to him in Chinese. After an exchange between the terrified prisoner and Dan, he shook his head and said, "He doesn't know."

I continued my interrogation. I asked him, through Dan, if they boarded a Chinese woman a couple of weeks ago. I pulled one of my .45s and waved it in the direction of the captives for effect. He continued to ramble in Chinese. I looked at Dan.

Dan spoke over the diatribe. "He says he doesn't know. He claims he doesn't know what I was talking about. He doesn't know anything about a woman. He just helps the flight crews and handles the money shipments." Dan interjected his opinion, "Frankly, boss, I believe him. Look at these guys. They don't look like high-caliber criminals to me."

I nodded. "Ask him about the money shipments."

He told Dan that the boxes they unloaded from the van and put in the watertight containers were filled with money … lots of money. Once the money was transferred, it was loaded back on the plane. They completed a shipment about once a month. I asked for the address where they picked up the money. He said he didn't know the address, but would direct us to the location.

"Who do they work for?" I asked. Dan repeated the question in Chinese.

Dan waited for him to finish and gave me the captive's answer. "He doesn't know. But, boss, these guys are all MSM."

"MSM?" I repeated. "A minute ago they were just low-level thugs."

Dan shrugged. "I didn't say they were great MSM members." He looked at me for my next order.

"All right." I holstered my gun. "Load them in the van … chairs and all."

"Their van?" he asked.

"Sure," I answered. "Why not? We might as well add motor vehicle theft on top of kidnapping charges, don't you think?"

Dan reluctantly repeated my order in Chinese, and his crew began rolling the captives to the rear of the van. Dan turned back to me for an explanation.

"Well, now that we have 'em, we can't just let them go."

I pulled my cell phone out of my jacket and pressed in Joshua's number. When he answered, I lowered my voice. "Joshua, I need another favor … yeah, yeah, yeah … I know."

Dan drove, and I sat in the passenger seat contemplating my next move. Dan's crew rode silently in back with their game. In a short time, somebody was going to miss their people and van, I thought as we made our way to the warehouse district outside of Chinatown. I wanted to hurry and get to the warehouse, but Dan drove with great care and vigilance—a move I appreciated. I am not sure how I would explain four hoods taped to office chairs in the back of a stolen van. When we arrived at Joshua's warehouse, we parked inside, and Joshua's people secured the large doors behind us.

Joshua watched as the detectives unloaded our captives. He smiled as he watched me. "Well, Sheriff, congratulations on your first crime. I am not sure I would have started with kidnapping, but what the hell."

Not only was I a kidnapper, but I had allied myself with a mobster. A mobster to whom I now owed another favor, another favor that would have to be repaid. I didn't say a word. Joshua assured me that he would take very good care of his new guests until he heard from me. I asked if he could run down the owner of the van.

He answered, "Sure."

"Can we not share the kidnapping and stolen van with your sister?"

He agreed with a wry smile. "Yet another favor, huh, Sheriff?"

Dan arranged for Chewy and his detectives to return to the Chino Airport since I wanted to continue the surveillance. We took a cab back to my hotel. Neither Dan nor I spoke during the ride. I found myself checking my cell phone for calls from Keeley, the first step to start feeling sorry for myself and pining over her. I left her a message.

On the way up to the suite, Dan appeared anxious to talk. I didn't ask. I lacked preparation for a lecture or a request for ideas on how to make four hostages wrapped to office chairs disappear. I had no ideas. I was not sure if I were the kidnapper or an accomplice. Either way, it was a felony, and I was involved.

The timing of an incoming call spared me from insulting Dan. A phone call I felt compelled to answer. It was Jim Collins. "Hello."

"Jack, how are you doing?" Jim spoke with a polite greeting.

"I have had better days," I sighed into the phone.

"You want to tell me about it?"

"No." I looked over at Dan. "Not really."

"Well, cheer up. I have some good news for you. My guy from the Coast Guard called today and told me one of their helicopters on an unrelated mission saw an old tramp steamer headed east just a couple days off the coast. She was still in international waters."

I asked, "Did you get a name?"

"No, but she was flying Panama colors."

"Jim, would you check to see if DEA or Treasury was involved with something at the Chino Airport the night Asian Sin disappeared?"

He agreed. I updated him on the investigation, except for kidnapping the four bagmen. I asked him for another favor: "If Asian Sin was being chased, she probably made a 9-1-1 call."

"Makes sense."

"I was told that all 9-1-1 calls go through operators at the county dispatch center. In turn, the operators transfer the calls to the appropriate jurisdictions."

"That's right," Jim confirmed.

"If such a call exists, do you think you could get the 9-1-1 tape of that call without it getting back to the Wayfarer Police?"

"I think so."

"Good; thanks."

Another call followed Jim's. Dallas wanted to meet, but I explained to her I needed to go to Wayfarer. I sent Dan out to retrieve a car for our trip. I wanted to see the Wayfarer Police Marina and the beach around it before dark. I knew he questioned my wisdom. So did I. As a general rule, I don't like traversing enemy grounds.

Once he left, I called Dallas back. I wasn't sure whether I would be talking to the impeccable lawyer and tough businesswoman, or to the scared girl I had seen last night. It was hard to believe they were one and the same. I asked her to excuse my shortness on the previous call. I hadn't wanted to talk in front of Dan. She understood.

I stuttered the words, "I don't know what to say."

She answered with a warm whisper. "Say nothing right now." I was talking to the girl.

"I don't know what happened last night." I was searching for words, along with an explanation to justify my behavior.

"Stop. Sometimes we must take a path that we don't choose." She repeated her grandmother's phrase; it was the same phrase she had quoted me when first we met.

I shared with her Jim Collins's information concerning the tramp steamer. Even though I had very little, I suspected this might be one of the ships we were looking for. I wanted to wait and watch for her when she made land or called in distress. I warned Dallas that this might take some time, maybe two or three days. Dallas agreed and told me not to worry about her, that I had too many other things to think about.

"Jack?"

"I'm still here," I answered.

"Jack, I'm not a starry-eyed college student. I'm a fully grown woman. I know what I am doing."

Her soft voice filled my mind with memories of last night. I pressed the end button on the phone and stared at it. I said to myself, "Well, that makes one of us."

Dan picked me up in the old minivan. I had hoped for more, but it was safe and I was getting used to it. Dan's old driving habits returned. He raced down the road dodging traffic, earning honking horns, and cursing drivers along his path.

I attempted to use the drive time to encourage Dan not to worry about the four guys his detectives had kidnapped. My logic failed to relax Dan's fears, but I tried. I told him they were money smugglers, probably working for the Wayfarer cops and some big-time dope smugglers. The legitimate cops would never learn about the kidnapping; however, everyone else involved would probably try to kill us. Dan still wasn't happy … go figure.

Dan didn't speak for the rest of the drive. He didn't even look my direction until he pulled into the parking lot. We were there, the public beaches maintained by the city of Wayfarer.

The city of Wayfarer controls about three miles of beach and shoreline. At the far north end of the beach, a small canal about fifty feet wide was dug in about two hundred yards. The police marina rested at the end of the canal. The marina on the land side was protected by high chain-link fence and topped with a running coil of concertina wire. There were four small, military-style, inflatable fast boats and one large fifty- or sixty-foot patrol boat. Traditional police markings ran along the sides of each boat, with red and blue lights mounted on overhead bars. I wondered how they turned the large boat around in the narrow canal.

Just to the south of the police marina and closer to the shoreline was an abandoned lifeguard tower built on top of a shower and restroom facility. Faded county logos decorated the cinder block sides along with colorful territorial graffiti. The doors were gone, and most of the glass had been shattered away.

I decided to challenge fate even more and walk the full length of the beach in Wayfarer's jurisdiction. Low clouds filled the sky, and cold mist filled the air. I sent Dan down to the south end of the beach with the van so I wouldn't have to walk back. I watched the waves crash on the sand. Small crabs found new hiding places when the water returned to the ocean. Seagulls floated in the breeze above the sand hunting for food. One would occasionally dive down on a fish or something, only to have it stolen away by an endless swarm of competing birds. The birds were my only company.

With the winds and angry ocean, I found myself talking aloud without the fear of anyone thinking I was crazy, even though my conversation was on the brink of insanity. But the last few weeks had been far from sane. I asked myself, if you are involved in a nonrelationship with a noncommittal female, is it cheating when you stray? I appreciated the simplicity of my solution—never tell her, and it will never be an issue, much like the hypothetical question "If a tree falls in the forest …" and all that.

I stopped thinking about my guilt for the time being and went back to work. I finished my walk and, in police terms, my recon. I had known several cops and investigators who would be out taking pictures of every detail. I refrained. I used photography for evidence only. It was cumbersome to carry around a camera, and it made it easier to be identified as a cop.

At the end of the beach sat the faded minivan. Dan carefully watched every step I made. I smiled as I crawled in the van and closed the door. It was warm in the box-shaped vehicle. It felt good, and I mocked a shiver to seek Dan's sympathy. It didn't work. I told him to go back to the lifeguard tower. "Okay," he replied and pulled the van into gear.

The restrooms' entries both faced the ocean. The entries never had doors; instead, discretion depended upon an eleven- or twelve-foot hall and a hard right angle into the inner facilities. I was surprised that there was very little trash along the walls, mostly cigarette butts and small bits of paper. The police must keep the vagabonds expelled, probably to keep their own nefarious acts from being discovered. Layers of graffiti of all types and styles painted the walls. Small pools of seawater filled the lower spots on the broken tile floor. In between the male and female entries was an open stairway that led up to the roof and gave access to the old wooden tower. The entire structure smelled old and damp, but lacked the nauseating smell of most public restrooms. It must have been abandoned when the town first incorporated.

Dan and I climbed the stairs to the roof. I climbed the ladder onto the lifeguard platform, testing the wooden floor by carefully adding weight with my first step. Since it didn't break through, I used both feet and bounced. The floor was solid except in one corner that gathered moisture. The tower had four-foot wooden walls and provided great concealment; however, the thin, tattered wood would never stop a bullet. The tower roof sloped toward the beach. The tin roof rattled in the wind. I studied the marina for a few minutes. The boats bounced in the protected water. We were alone. The cold was keeping everyone else away.

I turned to Dan and motioned him to go. On our way to the van, I told him I would be returning to wait for the approaching tramp steamer. He volunteered to come along as well. He was shivering for real.

"Come on before you freeze," I said. "We need to get some supplies and a coat for you. Let's go so we can get back before dark."

"Are you going to use the watchtower?" Dan asked.

"No; maybe later. I'm sure the cops are going to search the place before they get started. They might even put a sniper and spotter in the tower. If I were them, I would."

Dan nodded.

I pointed at some very large boulders several yards to the south of the old facility. "There. There is where we will watch this operation unfold."

Chapter 16

We ate a late lunch, found a Walmart, and bought everything I thought we might need, including two large backpacks, road flares, and flashlights. On the way back to the beach, Dan broke the silence with a request. "What do you think about me going back to LA to get my rifle and shotgun?"

I smiled. "Actually that sounds like a great idea."

"So you approve?"

"Yes, I approve. Are they in watertight cases?" I asked. "With all the sand, you don't need a malfunction."

"They are."

"Good; then go!"

Back at the beach, Dan dropped me off after we made sure no one was around. I made my way to the boulders. It wasn't until I was standing at the base of these rocks that I realized how huge they really were. There were five boulders that had to be over fifteen feet tall and twice that wide. Scattered around and against the larger stones were several smaller rocks. The rocks were situated in an oval. I squeezed between the largest boulders and into a small open center.

The wind had died down as the daylight gave way to the night. I managed to find my way up to the top of the tallest of the boulders after sliding back down the damp rock and into the sand three or four times. Two functioning legs would have made the climb easier. Once on my perch, I confirmed that I could see the marina and the canal's outlet.

The boulders were about a hundred yards from the shoreline and were at least the same distance to the south of the old lifeguard tower. The lifeguard shack blocked part of my view of the canal. I could also see the marina parking lot and the public lot beside it. I discovered a problem with my location. My rock fortress was too far away for a pistol shot. I had no plans to take on well-armed political militants, dope smugglers, or crooked cops—I'd lose. Regardless of my strategy to not engage, I would feel a lot better when Dan returned with his long guns.

I slid back down the rock, my choice this time, and settled in for a long night. The trouble with this, besides the cold and wet, was being alone again. Alone with time, time to think; Dallas's last words haunted me. I wondered, when she stated, "I'm not a starry-eyed college student," if she was referring to Xiu Tang, the graduate student I met when I was in high school. I regretted telling Dallas about her. It made me vulnerable. Dallas must have known that and how the affair changed my life. I have never forgotten this girl and still spend many hours pondering her. Sometimes when I close my eyes, I can still feel her breath on my face and smell her perfume. Of all the things to say, Xiu Tang found my very young soul and touched it … touched me forever.

In many ways, Dallas reminded me of her. Dallas and she were very open with me, and neither was afraid to share their most intimate thoughts with me. I knew more things about Dallas in one night than I had learned in weeks with her daughter. I knew more about Sky Lee than I did about Keeley. Keeley carried her emotional intimacy behind an iron curtain. If I was to ever have a true relationship with her, I would have to find a way around it or through it.

I pulled some canned meat and crackers out of my pack and opened the meat. Before I could cut a slice, I heard Dan calling out my name in a loud whisper. From within the rock fortress, I answered quietly. He pushed his gear in front of him as he crawled through the narrow passage. I took his gear as he struggled into the rocks. He stood to brush himself off. I looked up at him after setting his gear by mine and started to laugh. He was wearing a fur-lined parka with the hood over his head. He looked like an Eskimo on a seal hunt.

"What?" Dan sounded embarrassed. "I don't like being cold."

"It has to be in the high forties or fifties. You're dressed for a NOVA episode in the Antarctic." I laughed my reply. Before I could say something else, my cell rang … Jim Collins.

"Hey, Jack, my guy with the Coast Guard called. He said a tramp steamer just radioed in about an hour ago. Her radioman reported trouble, and she was going to anchor in international waters just west of the city of Wayfarer." Jim sounded excited. Or at least as excited as an experienced LA sheriff could sound. "Wayfarer answered the distress call and told the Coast Guard they would provide assistance."

"Let me guess. The ship's name is the *Yuan Gui*," I answered with some arrogance.

"Yeah, that's it. How did you know?"

"I have sources." I chuckled.

"Of course, you do! Are you headed down there?"

"Already here."

"You want me to come down?" Jim sounded concerned.

"No, I have Dan with me; and besides, I have no intentions of doing anything but watching and maybe following. Any hero stuff will have to come from you guys with the badges."

"Good." He hung up.

Dan and I climbed the rock and watched the marina. Dan pulled his rifle case up by a rope, and with the care of a mother lifting a baby from the cradle, a bolt-action Mark V Weatherby emerged from the hard-sided case. Dan sat the bipod and worked the adjustment knobs on the large scope.

"Hunting for polar bear?" I snickered. Dan just glared at me.

The chill made the time interminable, but only an hour passed before a standard unmarked police car pulled into the secure parking lot. The ocean and wind had calmed so that we could hear their voices as the cops exited the car. From what we could see and hear, there were at least four police officers dressed in tactical gear, all black, with black, gray, and white patches on their shoulders. They immediately began work preparing the fast boats. Another unmarked police car arrived and parked in the marina parking lot, and two more men dressed the same got out and headed for the boats. We couldn't make out their conversation, but the tone was jovial. I pulled on Dan's coat to get his attention and pointed. Two of the uniformed men were walking toward the old tower. One carried a rifle case, and the other carried a large scope on a tripod.

"There's the sniper and spotter," I whispered to Dan. He nodded.

The other four boarded their boats and headed down the canal, both their engines at a low idle. Once at the end of the canal, they opened up the engines and disappeared in the low-lying fog that clung to the beach's edge.

Between the small waves crawling to shore, we could hear the fast boats' engines running at full throttle. I calculated if they made thirty or forty knots, they'd reach the ship within a few minutes. The sound faded in the waves. I rolled over onto my back and looked into the darkness. I welcomed the ocean air into my lungs. I closed my eyes.

Within the hour the engines' roar returned, and the louder they got, the more they slowed. They were searching for the shore in the fog without any lights. Dan tapped me on the shoulder and pointed. Another plain police car, lights off, pulled into the parking lot and backed onto the dock in the secured police marina. The two occupants jumped out of the car, opened the trunk, and stood waiting. Dan switched from his rifle to a high-powered camera he kept in the same case. He snapped away.

Shortly, the first fast boat entered the canal and idled up to the dock. The two on the boat threw plastic packages up to the men standing by the car. Each package was about the size of a wrapped kilo. Dan continued taking digital images as the four worked. The second boat entered the canal as the first one headed back out to sea. They off-loaded the second, and it sped back out into the murky darkness. The two on the dock leaned up against the car. One lit up a cigarette. I turned to Dan, and with a smile,

I whispered, "We've got them. Now all we have to prove is that there is cocaine in those kilo packages."

"How do we do that?" Dan whispered back.

I rolled onto my back again. "I don't know."

Another hour passed, and the first boat returned to shore and off-loaded. They tied up the boat and pulled the car out of the fenced area and backed another one in its place. They all got in the loaded car and left. Resting my chin on my clasped hands, I watched them drive off. I wondered what to do now.

We could hear the engines of the second boat, but its sound was different. The boat wasn't heading to the marina; it was heading directly at us. A bullet hit our rocky perch at the same time as I heard a rifle's report; then a second shot rang out. The sky filled with white. Dan and I slid off the rock and onto the sand. The white followed us down. Snow? I yelled at Dan, "Are you all right?" He nodded. I grabbed at the white falling on top of us. I caught one piece and looked at it. Feathers! What in the world?

"Feathers?" I showed it to my confused partner. Then I looked at Dan again, still wrapped in his arctic parka. "Dan, turn around." He did. The back of his parka was split open from the neck to the tail. It was duck down falling on us. "Are you sure you're all right?"

"Fine; why?" Dan checked himself by patting his front.

"Your parka's dead, Nanook," I said in a make-believe somber tone.

Before he could ask, the speedboat slid up onshore at high speed, both occupants firing at the rocks as the boat slowed to a stop. Dan took his rifle, crawled to the edge of the boulder, and took aim. He squeezed the trigger, and the tower sniper jerked backward over the half wall.

I climbed back up on the smaller rock and engaged the two on the boat. My second shot found its mark, and one fell sideways out of the boat. I heard the squealing of accelerating tires as a car escaped. It must have been the spotter. Dan never got a second shot at the tower.

The second shooter dropped out of sight in the boat. I yelled at Dan to join me with his rifle. I pointed at the boat and whispered, "Cover me."

"What?" Dan asked as I slipped down the rock and squeezed through the entrance of our natural fortress.

I walked toward the boat with both my .45s drawn. I knelt at the lifeless body between me and the tactical watercraft. I rolled him over. It was the reluctant young detective who had stepped back when the older detective assaulted me at the traffic stop the other day. I winced. I always thought he was an unwilling partner.

I stood and shouted, "You in the boat, stand up slowly with your hands up." No response. I stepped closer and gave the same command. Still no response. I was so close I didn't have to yell again. I spoke in a firm voice. "Peek up at the rocks. You see the guy with the rifle? In a minute I am going to have him open up on this rubber toy. He has a big-game Weatherby. If he shoots, he'll blow you in two. If you don't believe me, just look up on the roof of the guard tower. Your sniper's head is gone."

I heard a familiar voice from the boat. "Don't shoot!" It was the detective that attacked me, Detective Charles William Easton.

"C. W., is that you?" I smiled over my gunsights. "Just throw your guns overboard." I wasn't sure that was the correct thing to say, now that the boat was on dry land, but since I had always wanted to say it, I used the phrase.

"Dan!" I yelled over my shoulder. The Weatherby's bolt slammed closed and locked on his rifle.

"Okay, okay, just don't shoot!" A desperate voice came from the boat.

"The guns!" I yelled.

One at a time, three carbines and a handgun hit the sand about twenty feet from the boat.

"Stand up slowly." I pulled the hammer back with my thumb on my right gun. The outlaw detective slowly came to his feet, his hands extended over his head. "Now step out and turn around."

"So you can shoot me in the back," he spit.

"That's your style, not mine," I retorted. "Now do it!"

He turned. I yelled for Dan to come down. Dan slung his rifle over his shoulder, slid down the rocks, and ran toward me. He held a large-magnum revolver in his right hand as he approached.

"Search him," I ordered Dan. He holstered the magnum and grabbed Easton's hands. He pulled Easton back to throw Easton's balance off. Dan methodically swept the detective's clothing as he searched him from head to toe. When he finished, he gave a satisfactory nod and stepped back to my side. His gun was now trained back on target. I looked at his gun and asked, "Do you have any guns not capable of bringing down a charging grizzly?"

He smiled sheepishly and shrugged.

I instructed Easton to turn back toward me. He complied, his hands still over his head. He spoke in anger. His words were full of hate. "I should have killed you the other day!"

I heard a rustle and whimper from the rubber craft. I holstered my left gun, pulled out a flashlight from my rear pocket, and shone it in the boat. Stacks of square packages and three duffel bags occupied the boat's interior. The duffel bags moved.

There are some things in life so horrific that your conscious or unconscious mind cannot comprehend them. It protects your sanity. I holstered my right gun and cut open the first bag. I pushed the bag down, and a small girl about six years old appeared out of the opening. She was an Asian girl, with dirt and blood smeared on her face. Her hands and feet were tied with plastic zip ties. Carefully I cut the ties. I then did the same with the second and third bags, each of which also contained a little girl. The sight dazed me. I stepped back in disbelief, trying to piece together what was happening. I looked at Dan. Anger filled his face. Still confused, I looked at Easton. "What the fuck?"

Easton's lips turned to a smirk. "These are spoken for, but I can get you one or two for free. Just let me walk. I was supposed to get a couple more, but they got sick so the crew had to pitch them."

My daze turned to anger. My mind put it together. I gave Dan a look of reassurance and glared hatefully at Easton. My knife slipped out of my fingers and hit the sand. I drew my gun and fired. The bullet shattered Easton's ankle as it passed through, and a puff of sand flew around his foot. Easton collapsed to the sand and grabbed his ankle, screaming. Dan jumped with the shot and then stood in shock.

I stood over Easton, my gun aimed at his head. "Asian Sin, where is she?" I demanded.

"Fuck you!"

I fired again. The bullet ripped into his thigh. He thrashed in horrendous pain. He cried in agony.

"Where is she?" I repeated. I felt nothing for him.

"No! No more!" He panted between shrieks. "We were paid to snag her and put her on a plane." He rolled again with another scream. I aimed for his other leg. "No! Wait! The fucking feds were at the airport, so we loaded her on a ship." He gasped as he spoke.

"Who hired you?"

"Dear god! Dear god!" he pleaded.

"He's not here! Who hired you?" I asked again.

"I don't know! Oh god, I don't know! One of the guys we buy the dope from. You'll have to ask the chief."

I fired a third time, hitting him in the throat. He grabbed at his throat. Blood squeezed through his fingers as he thrashed. Terror consumed his eyes. I just stood and watched until he stopped breathing and the involuntary muscle contractions started.

Dan was at the boat caring for the children. He had pushed them to the bottom of the hull to spare them from witnessing my barbaric act. When it was over, he helped the children up and started assessing the remaining cargo. He said, "Look!" and held up one of the packages. It looked like money, mixed currency from all over the world, bundled in a tight plastic wrap. Dan said, "It appears to be about half drugs and half cash."

Before I could evaluate the situation, I heard boat engines coming to shore very fast. "He must have radioed the ship when he was pinned down. He was stalling for time," I yelled. "Dan, get these kids out of here and take a couple of those packages! I'll do what I can." He nodded. He pulled each child from the boat with considerable care and sent them running up toward the parking lots and away from the beach.

I took up Dan's rifle and headed for the rocks. I gathered our backpacks and ran over to the guard shack. Pain shot up my legs with every stride. Because my arms were full, I dropped my cane between the rocks and shack. I searched Dan's pack for more ammunition and found a few rounds. I threw the bags on top of the restrooms and returned for my cane, but in my haste dropped it again at the threshold of one of the restrooms. The engines stopped. They were going to use the waves to bring them to ground. I retreated up the stairs to the roof. I dropped to a prone position and crawled to the ocean side. I reloaded Dan's rifle and waited.

I counted ten sailors emerging from the darkness onto the beach. All of them carried AK-47s. They spoke in Chinese. I remained motionless. They commenced a sweep of the area after examining Easton's and his partner's bodies. Three of them approached the shack. I could get them easy enough, but that left seven with automatic carbines to deal with me. I slid back to the center of the roof and grabbed up several road flares. I listened and waited for them to enter the restroom from the hallway. I heard them whisper as their steps echoed on the rotten tile. I lit the fuses and dropped them through the holes in the roof. They started to yell and cough. The hot burning fuses blinded them. They screamed in panic. They slapped the inside walls to find the hall. I swung down from the roof and fired blindly down the corridor. Screams of pain permeated the cinder block cavern. All three fell. Silence replaced the cries. I turned to see the others running toward the commotion. I reloaded and pulled my second gun. Shots rang out, but not from the charging sailors. They came from the direction of the street.

The advancing sailors fell to the ground dead. I stepped out of cover to see where the shots had come from; before I took a second step, someone slammed me in the back. One of the sailors in the restroom was only wounded and still could fight. The force of his hit caused me to lose the grip on my guns as I fell, dropping them into the dark void. I looked over my shoulder as I felt in the darkness for my guns. He fired, but his gun failed. He tried again. I rolled onto my back to see my bleeding foe fumble with his rifle's bolt and action. Failing to resolve the malfunction, he unfolded the bayonet from under the barrel of his rifle. I saw my cane in the sand by the doorway, and I grabbed it, twisting the handle, and pulled the blade so that it cleared the wood as he charged. I stuck it out, and he ran right into it. I thrust it deeper into his chest. He fell at my feet.

I heard footsteps. I searched for my guns, but I was too slow. A medium-size man stood over me and commanded me to stop with only a hand gesture. He held a small automatic pistol. Unlike the sailors, he was neatly dressed in an unmarked black utility uniform. His face was covered with a black pullover.

"Mr. Conner, just stay there. It's over. Now, let us do our jobs." His voice was calm and polite.

"Who are you?"

"That's not important. Now please just rest."

I rolled onto my side. There must have been at least twenty of them. They gathered the bodies in body bags and carried them away in the darkness. They worked furiously. They cleaned the dead sniper's blood off the tower and roof, as well as the restroom where the two sailors met their demise. They even shoveled up the blood-soaked sand. In a few minutes, the place looked like nothing had happened. They drug the police fast boat off the beach and back out to sea, and as quickly as they came, they were gone. My guns, cane, and all my other equipment left with them. Before they left, the one who had spoken to me told me not to worry.

I remained on the sand looking up. My hands started to tremble. I was wired. I get this way after the fact, never during the fight. I felt almost in a panic. I dug in my pocket and found my phone. I called Dan.

"Dan, you and the kids all right?" My voice broke as I spoke.

"We're fine. You?" he asked.

"I'll live."

"I called Dallas. She is going to meet me and pick up the kids." He paused, then asked, "What are we going to do now?"

"Nothing." I sighed in disbelief of what had just happened.

"Nothing? Nothing? We both just killed. Men died. We can't sweep that under a rug and forget about it."

"Well, I am not sure anything happened." I pulled myself up to a sitting position and leaned back on the cinder blocks. "Just drop the kids with Dallas and get back, okay?" I surveyed the sanitized beach. My right leg was bleeding again; it soaked through my trousers. I sat staring at the fog and ocean. The cold crept through my body and limbs. The only thing good about freezing was it kept the pain in my leg from throbbing. The fog succumbed to a soft rain.

I wanted to doze, but the cold forbade it. After an hour or so, headlights cut through the rain and fog, and by the clicking noise of the engine, I knew Dan had returned. Dan walked down to me. He looked over the area with the same confusion I had. He slid to a sitting position beside me.

"What happened? How?" he asked, staring forward in a curious state of surprise. "Where did everyone go?"

"Damned if I know," I said. I faked a lighthearted tone. "The crew off the boat came to shore. We got into a firefight, and these guys dressed in black showed up, killed everyone but me … packed the bodies off … cleaned the place up … and disappeared … with our guns."

"Really?" Dan turned his head toward me. "Took my guns?"

"Yep," I replied.

"Weird." His voice was full of amazement and tinged with sadness. "Took my guns …"

"Yeah. The one guy even called me by name."

"Huh?"

"Yep."

Dan stood and extended his hand to help me up. "Come on; let's get out of here before you freeze to death."

CHAPTER 17

I welcomed the warmth inside the old minivan. I shivered as I warmed.

"If you had a parka like mine, you wouldn't be shivering," Dan said, remembering my earlier laughter at his expense.

"If I had one like yours, the guys in black would still be picking up duck feathers!" I joked, trying to lighten the deadly pall that was threatening us.

"Those were prime goose down, mind you." Evidently my efforts were working.

Dan requested to hear my story again. I repeated it. He still didn't believe it. And even with me giving the anecdotal recap, I had trouble believing it. Dan pulled up a package that was jammed between his seat and the center console and threw it on my lap. We stopped at a red light, and with illumination from the streetlight, I saw the neatly wrapped, individual bundles of cash. They appeared to be bills from all over the world. I only recognized the US currency.

Dan spoke as he squinted at oncoming headlights. "There must have been one or two hundred of those packages, along with drugs."

"Why would these guys bring cash in by sea and then ship it by airplane back to the Orient?" I didn't know if I was asking Dan or myself.

"Maybe the cash is going to South America?"

"Then just sail there. Why risk a transfer here?"

Dan shared another on-the-spot-theory. "Maybe it's not real?"

His theory hit me like a bolt of electricity. "Of course, counterfeit. Why not? These guys are into everything else! We'll have to get this stuff verified by someone."

For the next several minutes, we drove in silence. I know Dan wanted to talk more about the gunfight, but I was not ready to accept the reality of my actions, let alone talk about it. After all, I killed five men tonight. To avoid thinking of the gunfight, I changed subjects in my mind. I thought of cigars. I regretted I had stopped smoking cigars. This would be a great time for a cigar. I weighed the pros and cons of starting the habit again. Then an emotional coldness built inside me. I remembered my last cigar. It shocked me I had forgotten. The last time I smoked a cigar was when I was being intensely interviewed by a sheriff's captain, two sergeants, and two investigators. They comprised an investigation team known as a shooting board. The last time I smoked a cigar was when I shot and killed a man about twenty years ago.

Dan broke the silence. "What do we tell Dallas now?"

"What?"

"I told Dallas about the gunfight."

"Everything?"

"No, I left out …"

"Thanks, Dan, but you don't have to protect me."

Dan slammed on the brakes and slid into the curb. He sat, staring forward, watching the windshield wipers pass his line of sight. "Mr. Conner"—his voice was soft and filled with genuine sincerity—how could you justify letting that man live? He was evil, pure evil. You should have heard the atrocities those children shared with me. I'll never forget—or forgive. Your people, Christian people, have a hell … I hope this is the fate of that man's soul. You did right tonight, Mr. Conner."

"No … Dan, I didn't … I killed him in cold blood. Frankly this scares the hell out of me. I saw those kids, and I just lost it. And I don't feel anything but regret."

"Regret would be normal," Dan interjected.

"No, Dan. The regret I feel is there is no way I could kill that monster enough to make this right again … After tonight, I'm not sure anything could be right again. Call Dallas and tell her we'll talk in the morning. I'm exhausted. This whole mess can wait until the morning." Dan nodded and pulled back on the street.

"Dan?" He turned. I worked up a smile. "Thank you." He returned the smile.

Dan dropped me off at the lobby door. I waved good night, limped into the lobby, and headed for the elevators. I missed my cane. I avoided eye contact with the few people I met as I made my way through the lobby. They stared at my torn, blood-soaked pant legs and the sand stuck on my face and clothes.

I stepped into my suite, closed the door, and started to undress only a few feet from the threshold. I didn't want to spread sand all over this executive apartment. Dallas stepped out of the dining room and stared at my condition. Her casual clothing failed to hide her beauty. She wore a faded cotton shirt with a flowered pattern on a blue background and tight blue jeans. Her canvas shoes matched the light shade of the blue in her shirt. Her hair was pinned up in a bun with traditional Chinese hairpins.

She smiled. "Jack, you look like hell."

"Well, frankly, I feel like hell. It was a hell of a night."

"I heard. I'm surprised the sheriffs let you go so soon."

"I didn't call the sheriff. I didn't call anyone."

"You just left? That's not going to look good. I should call our criminal division, get you back to the scene, and get the sheriff involved."

"Why?"

"Why? Jack, you can't just walk away from three dead policemen and not have consequences. You of all people should know that!"

"Things changed since you talked to Dan. There is no scene. There are no bodies. There is nothing."

"Jack, you can't do that," she interrupted.

"I didn't. I don't know who did, but there is nothing. You are going to have to trust me on this. As incredible as it sounds, there is nothing left to tell a story." I rolled my coat off my right shoulder and let it fall. Attempting to change the focus, I asked, "How are the kids?"

"Fine. They're at my house, in new clothes, and I would guess they are on their second or third bowl of fish and rice. I have been appointed as their temporary guardian ad litem. I also obtained a court order to protect them from deportation or seizure until I can get their visas."

"In two or three hours in the middle of the night? I'm impressed." I struggled with the buttons on my shirt, which were caked with mud and sand.

"Here; let me help you." She stepped into my space. I made a half step back. She glared at me, her black eyes flashing. "Get back here! Have you forgotten that my father was a doctor?"

"No." I looked down to watch her unbutton my shirt. The scent of her hair was sweet and drew my eyes to the traditional Chinese butterfly-shaped ornament centered on the bun. Its gold and silver wings were outlined in diamonds and other precious gems. Four smaller and ornate matching butterfly hairpins held the centerpiece in place. With a gentle squeeze and pull, I removed one of the smaller pins and held it up. "I have one of these."

"From the girl in your past, no doubt?"

A trace of sadness crossed my face. "Yes, she gave me one before she left. I still have it."

"When a Chinese girl reaches fifteen, she is given her first hairpins. She is forbidden to wear her hair in a bun or wear hairpins before that. It is her rite of passage from a girl to a woman. When she meets her love … her future husband, she gives the pin to him as a symbol of engagement and commitment."

I leaned against the wall. "I didn't know that."

"She loved you, Jack," Dallas whispered. "She probably never married."

"I would have married her. She left. I didn't. I was here. I would have followed her."

"For Christ's sake, Jack! She couldn't stay, and you couldn't go there. She knew that! Stop and think of the times. Then, let her live in your heart! Don't trivialize her gift. She would have never wanted that." Small tears gathered in the corners of her eyes. She turned so I wouldn't see them. "Now, should we get those pants off and you in the shower?"

My pants stuck to my legs with blood. Dallas decided on the quick ripping technique over my slow and deliberate pulling a quarter inch at a time. Her rapid action took my breath away with a wince. Dallas scolded me, "Don't be such a baby, and don't lean on my wall!"

"Your wall?"

"You know, this should be seen by a doctor. This is badly torn." She studied the blood-seeping wound.

"You said your wall."

"Oh. Did I forget to mention I own this place?"

"I don't recall you mentioning that. I thought you picked this hotel because there was no way to connect you with it. I would say owning it makes a connection, wouldn't you, counselor?"

"I should say I own the controlling stocks since it went public. I don't really get involved in the day-to-day operation." Her answer was coy.

"Now, come on. Let's get you in the shower." She raised my arm over her head and around to her shoulder. Her hundred-pound frame steadied my limp on the trek to the shower.

The hot shower felt good on my face and stung my legs. My eyes grew heavy. I needed sleep before I started thinking about the night. If I started thinking, it could be hours.

I entered the bedroom with a towel around my waist. Dallas had laid towels on the bed and an array of bandages and a bottle of antiseptic on the night table. She instructed me to lie down.

I watched her as she dabbed at my wound. "You should really go to the doctor."

"No." My last desire was to end up in the ER to listen to the sarcasm of the cute emergency doctor as she repaired her previous work. "Dallas, we need to talk."

"I know. I thought you were just going to observe and not get involved."

"I wasn't. They started it."

"So, how many men did you guys shoot? If it was self-defense, why didn't you call the sheriff? She knew of the situation."

She continued to clean as she talked. "You know, if you don't quit screwing around with this leg, you're going to get an infection."

"Can we talk about just one thing at a time?"

"Okay, tell me about the shooting."

"No, I want to talk about Keeley."

"Keeley? Why?"

"Why?"

"I know you think you love her, and I think she loves you."

"But …"

"But what?" She bent over me, and with open hands pressed against both my cheeks, she brought my guilt-filled stare to her glare. She leaned closer and whispered in a fake, monosyllabic Chinese accent, her warm breath against my face with each sarcastic word, "We fuck to gedder. Dat all. Okay, GI?" She sat back up and poured the antiseptic in the deepest cut.

"Dallas! Damn it! Ouch!" I yelled as she wiped my leg.

Completely ignoring my exaggerated agony, she dabbed again. "I like you, Jack. But you have a weakness. You love too much, and not every act of intercourse is a gift of the gods. God! You remind me of my parents. We had sex. Maybe we will again. So?"

"You do remember Keeley? You know … your daughter. What would she think?"

"If you decide in some fleeting moment of self-preserving morality to confess to her, she will see you as weak. You're not a weak man, Jack."

"So don't tell her? That is your solution? And what of us?" I sounded shocked, but it was the same conclusion I had reached. I felt like I was in a remake of the movie *The Graduate*, and although I don't remember for sure, I think he lost everything or everyone.

"I am fond of you, Jack, but my hairpin is not yours." She started taping.

I slept until the early afternoon. I heard voices beyond the bedroom, but I went to the shower before greeting my guest. Dallas had my clothes laid out in the bathroom. It was difficult for me to see such a powerful woman behaving as a normal human. Maybe it wasn't at the level of a Nobel Peace Prize, but it was an act of genuine kindness, a paradox of my established beliefs and my reality. I wasn't ready to reflect. It was an unnerving feeling to have no remorse or guilt in killing Easton. It terrified me to actually discover what I was capable of without considering the results. It violated my self-conceived sanctimony. After all, I was a man of rules and procedures.

I felt anger building deep in my subconscious. I already found myself swearing I would kill everyone involved in taking Asian Sin or those little girls. An impossible task—I was only one man. These men could buy police departments and governments like houses and hotels on a *Monopoly* board. No ... anger and false promises, even promises I had made to myself, would not help Asian Sin. I needed to concentrate on what I was going to do next.

I cleaned up and dressed in my Dallas-selected clothes. My leg felt warm and was bright red around the cut. I wasn't sure if this was the result of Dallas feeding my mind with ideas of infections or something real. I took the former over the latter. I followed the voices to the dining room.

Dan and Dallas were talking over iced tea. Both gave their hellos, and I sat at the end of the table. When Dan wasn't looking, Dallas gave me a smile, the type of smile that held secrets. She then transformed into an astute litigator. Dan had told her everything from beginning to end, except the part where I killed Easton after he surrendered. He had changed that to Easton suffered a mortal wound during our exchanged gunfire.

She requested I repeat the story. I complied. To save Dan face, my account was the same as Dan's concerning the demise of Detective Easton. Dallas listened to each word I spoke with great attentiveness. I looked for a reaction. Her face remained emotionless. She only took her eyes off me to write notes on a legal pad. She, as Dan and I, couldn't believe or understand the part about the men who assisted me and then sanitized the crime scene. All I knew for sure was that I owed them my life.

Dallas dropped her pen on her yellow tablet. "We need to take this to the sheriff. These guys need to be taken down."

"With what? We have nothing. It's normal for police departments and sheriff's offices to have drugs in their evidence room," I argued. "These guys are untouchable." I had never realized the power that could be abused.

"A DEA audit against the cases they filed, maybe?" Dallas searched for solutions.

"Fake suspects, fake arrest reports. Hell, just file it that the suspects are unknown or just file charges on somebody they want or have. Keep in mind they would only have to pull the reports if someone got suspicious. All they would have to do is keep it electronically and fill in the dates if the time comes." I felt discouraged.

"There has to be someone in that place that is honest," she retorted.

I sat up in my chair. "William Parker … Parker told me he had an informant inside. I dismissed it. I figured they knew about the informant and were feeding him false information. But how is this going to help me find Asian Sin … Sara? If we're not careful, we could get her killed. I do think she is still alive."

Dallas and Dan sat there, pondering my last statement.

"Look, I want these guys, but I am not sure it is going to help … not now. Give me some time." After a pause, I spoke again. "Let me call Parker. Maybe he will give up his informant. Can we give him something to write?"

"Sure, I'll work on it." Dallas sounded upbeat. Her "I'll work on it" meant she would give it to an intern to write up something. She stood, and

I followed. She gestured for me to stop and sit back down. "Please." She didn't like the polite gesture. She looked at me. "I'll call you later."

Dan and I waited for her to leave before saying anything. I looked over at Dan. He either sensed something, or my guilt was coming to my conscience.

"Dan, see what you can find out about the chief of Wayfarer and the rest of the brass down there. Be careful; don't go down there. After all, they have to explain away three missing cops. You might make a good explanation."

Dan nodded and asked, "What are you going to do?"

"I'm going to call Bill Parker and see if he will meet with me."

He nodded and stood.

"Dan … really … be careful." Dan left, and I found some coffee. A knock came with my first sip. It was Jim Collins. He held three newspapers.

I invited him in; he spoke as he stepped into the apartment. "You didn't call last night. I was getting worried."

"Please sit. You want anything to drink?"

"I think I need a drink." He sat down and tossed the papers on the coffee table. "You know anything about this?"

I served him a whiskey and sat down with my coffee. I took up the papers. The first headline read, "Police boat found capsized, three policemen missing, feared dead." Well, I thought, they found a way to explain it.

I read as Jim asked again, "Do you know anything about this?"

"I do," I said, looking over the paper at him.

"So, are you going to tell me about it?"

"No," I answered as I started reading the second paper.

"Okay, why?" He took another sip and waited for my answer.

"Because I don't want to lie to you, and even I don't believe the truth."

He thought a moment. "Interesting."

"Tell me about it."

"So, when?"

"Soon," I answered in a sheepish tone. He nodded.

"Oh, I almost forgot. Asian Sin did use her phone to call 9-1-1 that night."

"Did you get the recordings?"

"I have them, but only what the call center received before they transferred the call to Wayfarer. I had them transcribed. You were right. Before the call was transferred, she was in the process of telling the dispatcher where she was. After the transfer, she ended up leading her captors right to her."

"We can only guess what happened after that," I interrupted.

"Yeah." Jim gave a sober sigh. We sat in silence. Finally Jim spoke. "The feds did have something going on at Chino, but they're pretty tight-lipped about it." He addressed the floor. He never looked up.

"Who can blame them?"

"Jack." He stopped. "Jack, you'd tell me if this had anything to do with the Rock Hard homicide?"

"I would, and I'm sure it does. I just don't know how. I'm sure they ordered the hit on your victim. But …"

"Proving it …" We said together.

Jim stayed almost until dark. He stopped with the first drink so he didn't have to explain to his wife why he took a cab again. Once Jim left, I called Parker. After a scolding for not calling him, he told me what he found out about the lease on the hangar at Chino. He gave details of his search. I only wanted the results, but I listened.

He found out, after peeling off several layers, the lease was controlled by a company out of Taipei by the name of MSM Exports. He couldn't find out anything about the corporate officers or who was in charge, but they supposedly had offices throughout Southeast Asia. He called a friend in Manila, an ex-pat that ran a bar there, and asked him to check around.

"Great. Another country dragged into the fray," I thought to myself. I felt guilty I didn't disclose my knowledge of the MSM, the Mimi Shenghou Mogwai, the Secret Life of Demons, to Parker. I thanked him and told him I would be getting him a story soon. He closed by telling me not to worry about the story—just find Asian Sin. I should have asked him about his informant, but I wanted to do that face-to-face. It would be harder for him to say no.

I read the two articles again and then took up the last paper. It was a West Coast mariner paper filled with shipping news and ads looking for everything from boat parts to able seamen. The front page had the AP report on the capsized police boat. Nothing new there, but the second article reported that during the search, the Coast Guard found a ship adrift, an old freighter called the *Yuan Gui*. The news story reported that the abandoned freighter was a mystery. The ship's crew was gone. The cargo was still intact, as well as provisions for the sailors. None of the lifeboats were missing. The Coast Guard towed her to their base for further investigation and to be claimed.

Dan returned. His worried voice instructed me to turn on the TV. I did. There on cable news was the chief of the Wayfarer Police Department, Blaine Harris. On TV, he didn't look like a head of an international smuggling ring. Perhaps it was my bias, but he didn't look much like a police chief either. He had thin gray hair and a narrow face with a large nose. He looked like a weasel to me. His fake sobs stirred the reporters' emotions as he told of the search for his noble colleagues continuing into the night.

I rolled my eyes at Dan. I threw him the mariner paper and remained quiet as he read. He finished the story and returned the paper to the coffee table. "The *Yuan Gui*."

"Well, I know of two spirits that will rest," he added. I made a nod for him to finish his thought. "The two girls they pitched overboard."

I nodded. "Did you have time to find out anything yet?"

Dan shook his head. "No, not really; I heard the news on the radio and thought you should know."

"Thanks," I replied. "I'll see you tomorrow." He waved as he shut the door behind him.

Dallas's phone call prevented me wandering down a lonesome trail of pining over Keeley. She sounded excited. She told me she had the lab results from the courtesy car and was heading over. I asked her what they were, and she said, "I want to give the results to you in person!"

I wondered who was on the phone, the girl or the attorney.

I felt I had something. I had no hard evidence that the MSM on the hangar lease was, in fact, the Secret Demons that Joshua had talked about. However, there was enough to be more than a coincidence. MSM must be an initialization that stood for something other than the Secret Life of Demons. The MSM was the name of my enemy. I had a name for their leader … Zhang-Fei. I had a name to villainize. Not an imperialist, a hard-line communist, or a capitalist, Zhang-Fei was nothing but a greed-consumed criminal.

I sat there contemplating whether continuing the fight against the Wayfarer Police Department would benefit my investigation. I argued both sides internally. The easy route and probably the most logical was, the case needed to be transferred to the county or the feds. Just pick some letters out of the alphabet, and you'd have a federal agency that had jurisdiction to investigate these guys for something. These horrendous people had done just about everything bad a person could do. The only problem: I had not one shred of evidence to give any agency.

The door opened. I didn't need to look. Dallas had a master key card. I stood and turned to greet her with a smile and a hello. Her left hand held a rich brown leather briefcase. She walked past me, set the briefcase on the coffee table, and opened it. She took a manila file out and threw it at me. I caught it and waited for her to sit before I took my seat.

I opened the file, but my eyes remained on her. "You know, in a polite society, when a person greets another with a hello, the custom suggests that the addressed party return a salutation of equal or greater pleasantries."

Her black eyes attacked. "Unless the addressed party chooses to be a bitch."

I surrendered to the file. "Why don't you just tell me what's in this report?" I held up a twenty-page report stapled in the upper left-hand corner. “Please spare me from deciphering this technical periphrastic paper.”

Her eyes changed to a smile. “Periphrastic? I am impressed.”

“It’s one of three big words I know.” I returned the smile. “Give me a break.”

“The hair is a match. Sara was in the car. Actually, her hair was found both in the rear seat and trunk,” she answered.

“Well, that proves she was in the car. It does nothing to prove how she got there.”

“In the trunk?” Dallas asked.

“It came off the luggage. Maybe she bent over to get something.”

She nodded. I pulled the next report. It concerned the cash that Dan had taken from the police boat. The report confirmed what Dan and I first thought. It was counterfeit. It was a world of fake money: Euro, American, Yuan, Yen, and almost every country within Southeast Asia.

“We need to turn it over to the Secret Service,” I said as I closed the file and threw it back in her briefcase.

“Exactly how do we explain our coming into the possession of this money?”

“I don’t know … say we found it along the beach.” I saw the perplexity of her question.

“We found it and then did a full-fledged forensic workup to confirm it was counterfeit?”

“I see your point. But we can’t keep it … It’s a felony.”

“Maybe we should give it back.” Dallas chuckled at her own joke.

I didn’t laugh or answer at first. I thought about her statement. “Maybe we should.”

“What?”

“What do you say we call up good old Chief Blaine Harris and ask him if he wants his money and drugs back for a few million dollars?” I was plotting the plan as I spoke.

“A sting!” Dallas followed my thoughts.

I nodded in confirmation. I decided to go back to another subject. "So, who saddled you with a burr under your blanket this afternoon?"

"What do you mean?" She failed to understand my colloquialism.

"Your attitude when you stomped in here."

Dallas's face dropped to a somber expression. She struggled with her reply. "Jack, there's another file." She reached down to her briefcase and pulled out another manila file.

"What's in it?"

"If you had a choice to know or not know about someone you cared about, would you want to know or not?" she asked.

"Keeley! Is she all right?"

"Yes, she's fine. Answer the question, Jack."

"To know … I guess … If Keeley is all right, then who?"

She handed me the folder. I opened it. It was an article scripted in Chinese. I immediately recognized the attached picture. I looked back at Dallas. Her eyes grieved for me. "I had it translated for you," she said.

I turned the page. The article was over thirty years old:

> *Tuesday, May 4*
>
> *Young Doctor Killed in Plane Crash. Doctor Xiu Tang succumbed to injuries she received in a plane crash in the Gansu Province about 10 kilometers south of the Mongolian border. Doctor Tang was working as part of a rescue team in the area when the accident happened. She led a triage team in many remote locations as well as providing medical care in her home village.*

Tears started to well up in my eyes. I quickly wiped them away to avoid detection. I looked up at Dallas and gave a slight smile as camouflage. It failed. I let the folder drop to my lap. Dallas finished the story for me.

> *Dr. Tang loved the American West and loved the romance stories of the Old West. She collected western art and literature. She even*

owned a horse. Doctor Xiu Tang was loved and respected by everyone she knew and met.

"Where did you get this?"

"I contacted my office in Beijing. I asked them to look for her."

"Why?" I asked, trying to keep the tears back.

"For you," Dallas answered softly with a faint smile. "I hoped it would give you the chance to decide on your life and what you want."

"You mean decide between Xiu Tang, the doctor, and Keeley Nu, the lawyer."

"Maybe. I think I did it for you," Dallas replied. "Jack, I had no idea."

"Of course not. Who would? … After my divorce, I tried to find her." My tone was soft and withdrawn. "I am not sure why … maybe for resolution … I don't really know."

Dallas left the couch and sat down on the arm of my chair. She took my hands into hers. "I am sorry, Jack. I should have left it alone."

"No, I'm glad you did this. I never imagined she would be gone. I still think of her every day. Do you remember what I said when we first met? I used to think when I got home from work, she would be there, cooking dinner. She would greet me at the door every night with open arms."

Dallas squeezed my hands and extended a sympathetic smile. I sat, feeling stunned. Pain filled my chest. What was I going to do now? The memory of this girl had carried me through some of the hardest times of my life. I can even remember times pretending to have conversations with her. Gone.

I excused myself, and Dallas stood so I could get up. I walked out on the balcony to look out over the city. Maybe among the thousands of lights was a light that twinkled redemption? Dallas left me alone for some time. She sensed I needed to be alone. I sobbed.

After some time passed, Dallas asked me if I wanted a drink. I asked her for coffee. She brought the coffee out on the deck, along with a wineglass full of whiskey and ice. She informed me that I was out of wine. She sat sipping her whiskey as wine and watched me survey the city below us. I blew across the rim of my coffee cup. The steam quickly blended with the night's heavy humidity. I liked her being there.

Dallas cleared her throat to speak. "There is a Chinese legend about a young couple who went to school together. Because of the times, the girl had to disguise herself as a boy. They became best friends as they studied together. Eventually she was discovered by the boy, and they fell in love, a great love."

I interrupted and finished the story from the deck rail. "The girl was promised to another for marriage, and the boy died heartbroken. The day of her wedding, she flung herself into the boy's grave and died. Later they were seen as butterflies, never to part again." I turned around to face Dallas. "Right? … The Butterfly Lovers."

"Close … How did you know?"

"She told me that story the day she left," I said with a ragged smile.

"Well, I fucked that." Dallas sighed. She took a large swallow.

"Not really. How would you know? Dallas, did you do this for me or for your daughter?"

"For you … and her."

I nodded. "You know I love her … your daughter."

"I know … you also loved Xiu Tang. You still love her."

"Yes." Unwelcome tears assembled again in the corners of my eyes. I turned away.

"Jack, it's been over thirty years! Let her go! She's gone! Tell me, Jack, how would you have felt if the article told of a woman who was happily married with children and a loving husband?"

"I don't know. I hope I would be very happy for her. Maybe I would even have sent her a card or something. At least, she would've lived and had a fulfilled life."

Dallas thought a moment. "Unselfish love. You did love her, but you have to let her go. She would have never wanted you to pine your life away for her. It's time to let her go."

"Why?"

"So you can move on with your life. Jack, a woman knows when your heart is not hers. Why do you think your marriage failed? Your wife could never get past the memory of this girl. How could she? You deified Xiu Tang. How could you really love anyone else with her on your mind and in your heart?"

"I never told my wife anything about her … the same with Keeley."

"You didn't have to; they already knew. Maybe not by name, but they knew."

"Did you tell Keeley anything about Xiu Tang?" I asked.

"No; why would I?"

"I don't know. Maybe I thought you would try to save her."

"Come on; you need some sleep." Dallas gathered my hand into hers, and we walked together back into the apartment.

Chapter 18

Over breakfast the next morning, Dan reported his findings concerning the police chief, Blaine Harris. I didn't want to be there; I was trying to wrap my mind around the news of Xiu Tang's death. I wanted to be alone. I wanted time to think. I wanted to relive my life. I should have followed her. All I could do now is apologize for being young and ignorant. Damn the consequences and for everything I've done in the past and now. Damn me.

Dan's report was full of information. At first, it was hard to listen with my thoughts in another world, but Dan's professional dissertation brought me back to the current priority. I was impressed. Dan had valuable resources and knew how to use them. He knew how to disseminate information. From his presentation, I knew Dan's experience was more than a Hong Kong street cop. He either served in an intelligence bureau or a high-level investigation detail.

Wayfarer Police Chief Blaine Harris was educated as a journalist and served as a correspondent in Southeast Asia after college. He worked for a travel magazine. From Asia he traveled to northern China, Mongolia, and then into Russia. He traveled for years. He returned to the Far East several times during his writing career. After his return to the United States, he worked for a public relations firm until he started his own company that did research and analysis.

Dan found several contradictions in Harris's career. For being a writer, he didn't produce many articles for his employers during an employment that spanned several years. Sometimes he traveled on a diplomatic passport. The diplomatic passport allowed him numerous advantages. In some countries he would have been given a rubber-stamped visa without application or waiting. Other special privileges included being able to make multiple entries into countries that restricted the number of entries allowed within a certain time frame.

Dan discovered another detail that he thought was unusual. Harris had never held a police job or worked in law enforcement. Also, his past editor and publisher were currently serving as councilmen on the Wayfarer City Board. The mayor was Harris's partner in the research company. They had all been in their current positions since the city filed for incorporation.

Dallas was the first to comment. "They created a town to cover up their smuggling operation?"

"Worse. They are spooks," I answered. Dallas questioned my answer with her expression. I added, "Spies."

"Spies? Spies for whom?" Dallas asked.

Dan interjected, "I don't think it matters. I think they've been out of the business for a long time … at least ten years."

"Unless they still have friends around," I added. "Harris and his buddies must have developed relationships with the dope suppliers while they were over there."

Dallas worked her words. "First, it was a few crooked cops. Then it was a police department. Now it is a city?"

"Yep," I said.

"What are we going to do?" Dan asked.

"Dan, I need you to go get two disposable phones. Enter the number of one of them into one phone and give the other to me. I need to test it to make sure my recorder picks up both voices. Make sure the one you give to me doesn't have a GPS." Dan carefully listened to my instructions. I turned to Dallas. "Counselor, can your lab do voice recognition?"

"Of course."

"Good. Would you check with them and see if they can get a copy of Easton's voice when he was talking to the press and if they can use that as an independent voice sample for comparison?"

"Sure … why?"

I smiled and looked at Dan and Dallas individually. "Why? Because we're going to take them down, and then I'm going to go and find Asian Sin."

Dan left to buy phones. Dallas and I worked over the details to my plan as it developed. About three hours into the formation of the operation, Dallas needed to go to her office. Her phone was filling with unanswered e-mails with each buzz. I continued to plan.

Dan returned with the phones, and we went over the operation. He took in the information with great attentiveness and approval. I finished up, and Dan was getting ready to go home when a knock on the door interrupted us. He answered the door for a delivery driver, who had several packages on a hand truck. Dan directed him to a place he could unload. We watched the driver unload his cart, and Dan let him back into the hallway.

I asked the driver if he knew where the packages came from; he didn't know. Once he left, we opened all the packages. With some apprehension and caution, I opened the longest of the packages. It was Dan's Weatherby. The mystery defenders had returned all of our guns and equipment.

I checked my .45s. Their actions had been replaced, along with new barrels. The used barrels were probably either pitched in very deep water or smashed and melted. Dan's Weatherby had been worked on as well.

They returned my cane cleaned and polished. If by some slim chance a body were recovered, none of these weapons could be traced to the incident on the beach. Not a spot of blood, a fingerprint, or DNA could be found on our equipment or guns. I thought of calling Dallas to see about processing the packages, but I knew it would be in vain and worthless.

Dan asked, "Why didn't they just destroy our guns and replace them?"

I explained, "The serial numbers had to match. Because of the gunfight at that rattrap apartment, the police already have the serial numbers to some of these weapons. So, to avoid a lot of new questions if we ever have to turn over our guns again, the serial numbers need to match our first incident. How would we explain guns that didn't match without casting a whole bunch of new suspicion?" He understood. Dan packed up his rifle and equipment and left for the day.

I sipped some coffee as I rocked in the soft chair. I used the excuse I was too tired to turn on the TV, even though the remote was on the end table. Maybe I just needed the quiet. No distraction, no conversation, just an occasional creak from the chair. I tried to call Keeley … three times, with no answer. As much as I welcomed the peace, I hated being alone.

Dallas brought in a heavy cardboard box with her evening visit. It contained several bottles of wine. Another surprise—a person of her resources could have easily had it delivered. I was glad to see her. She saved me from drifting into another melancholic recollection about my relationships, past or present. But I was worried. My plan was large and filled with the chance of error. I wished I knew the entirety of the Wayfarer operation. Dallas sensed my anxiety. To avoid the question, I asked her if she had heard from Keeley. She hadn't.

She poured herself a glass of wine and sat down across from me. She studied me very carefully. She stole her statement right out of my mind. Her intuition frightened me. "Jack, you're not getting rid of me. I am not sending myself away to work on 'actors' contracts.'"

Once I got over the shock of her statement, I answered, "I'm afraid you're getting too involved in the investigation. Remember, we sent Keeley away for the same thing."

"You miss her, don't you?" Her voice was coy.

"Dallas, don't try to change the subject. This is serious stuff."

"Answer the question."

"Of course, I do. Don't do this. You know this is going to get worse before it gets better. I hate dealing with you bigger-than-life people."

"Bigger than life? Huh? Look, I know this could go south, but I am not going away, and unlike Keeley, I am not going out in the field. I'm allergic to small townships and grass. I hate the suburbs. I'll be fine." I gave her a skeptical glare. Amused, she gave in to my concerns with a concession, "Okay, I'll expand my security and take a couple of armed guards with me for the time being." I agreed with a nod. I smiled at her.

With a curious look, she asked, "What?"

"You know that sometimes when you're speaking, you have a Texas accent?" My smile grew. "I know you, with your refined demeanor and education; you do well hiding it, but you have it. Your daughter has it too. Slight, but it is there in both of you. It's cute."

"Screw you, Jack," she drawled in a coquettish voice. "You can call me just about anything but cute." She exaggerated the accent. Her next question caught me off guard. "What about Keeley? Are you thinking about marrying her or what?"

I cleared my throat. "I'm guessing on the 'or what.' Would I like to have a long-term relationship? Sure, but she guards herself very well. She won't share her thoughts, her plans. She refuses to discuss anything about commitment."

"Not a surprise."

"Why?"

"Jack, you know, for a very smart person, you're pretty stupid."

"I already heard that … from your brother actually," I answered dryly.

"Her father, the father she knew, died." She got up and went into the kitchen. She poured herself another drink, brought the coffeepot out, and filled my cup. "Just like you, she too has to let go. Give her time."

"Maybe it's me. Maybe I'm not ready."

"Why do you say that?"

"How can I be so in love, and yet it is so easy for me to sleep with others? You know, I never cheated on my wife."

"Sure you did, only worse. You cheated with your heart. You loved a woman ten thousand miles away. Even now, I am not sure you're ready to let go of this infatuation. In fact, if I hadn't showed up, you'd be thinking of this Xiu Tang and wondering, if you had done something different, would she still be alive." She paused. I looked down to avoid her eyes. "Well, tell me, Jack, am I wrong?" I slowly shook my head.

"So, what about us?" I asked without looking up.

"Nothing we've done has been with love." One thing about Dallas: she doesn't sugarcoat her opinions.

I raised my eyes to hers. "So, have you ever been in love?"

"The Korean, perhaps, or maybe just enamored. He was such a powerful man. I was so very young myself." She paused. "And of course my first husband. He was a wonderful man … and such a good father."

"You married again after he died?"

"For a short time—a lawyer. Never marry a lawyer."

"Really?"

"Oh, yeah, sorry; I forgot whom I was talking to!"

Chapter 19

I actually have never cared much for undercover or any clandestine investigation. It takes an enormous amount of manpower to keep the operatives safe, and things never seem to work out as they are planned. This type of operation can turn dangerous, and the results, for the most part, are minimal at best.

Although he wore the uniform and drove a panel truck, he really wasn't a delivery driver. He was one of Dallas's investigators and process servers. Being occidental made Jeffery Hart an oddity in Dallas's firm, but his experience and his reputation of never giving up and never taking no for an answer made him perfect for the role. Dan and I carefully briefed him in detail on what we needed.

Dan pulled on some latex gloves and instructed Hart to do the same. He then handed Hart a large white envelope. We took special care to make sure it was void of any of our fingerprints. To give credibility to the deception, we had the package marked that it had been shipped from Oakland to a delivery company in San Diego. With Dallas's talent for acquiring things we needed, she obtained the delivery truck and uniform without any questions.

Hart turned the package in his hands. The package contained a sample bundle of the counterfeit bills we took the other night and one of the cell phones Dan bought yesterday. Hart didn't ask about the contents. Dan gave him very specific instructions not to give the package to anyone but

Chief Harris. Hart understood. Before Hart left, he was wired with two different body microphones, and he met with two of the four detectives that would be covering him.

Dan, Dallas, and I, along with a radio technician, waited in one of the meeting rooms for Hart to arrive in Wayfarer. I paced while Dan and Dallas watched. None of us spoke. It seemed to take forever. Then the technician raised his hand to get our attention. Hart was on the air. He had arrived and was giving us a narrative as he entered the police building at Wayfarer.

Hart's experience made it easy for him to get through the first couple layers of security. His first real point of resistance came upon meeting Harris's private secretary. It took Hart a great deal of convincing, but the obstinate secretary finally agreed to have him wait on a couch outside of Harris's office.

Hart waited, still whispering his status in the hidden mics. He seemed very calm and professional. Either he really didn't realize how much danger he was in, or he was really good. He waited about half an hour before Chief Blaine Harris entered.

Harris walked past his secretary without a hello or good morning. She never had a chance to introduce him to our deliveryman. Hart passively stood to be noticed but not block the chief's way. "Chief Harris, good to meet you. I have a package for you. Please." Hart continued, "You look tired, Chief."

"Yes, well, if you have heard the news, there hasn't been much sleep."

"No, I haven't, but I hope everything will be all right. Please, I need you to sign. Here. Thank you." Hart watched the chief walk into his office with the package and close the door. "I am out of here," Hart closed.

I could breathe again. I looked over at Dan and Dallas. "Well, the trap's been baited. Now we wait again."

I figured Harris would have the phone, the money, and even the envelope checked out before he attempted to call the only number on the cell phone. The number was for the second disposable phone. Only it was no longer a disposable phone. Dallas's lab cloned it, and now it was integrated into a very smart computer. To prevent a trace from the Wayfarer Police, Dallas's computer experts would bounce the call over three continents and at least twenty countries before returning it to Dallas's lab.

Deep within the halls of Dallas's building and on the opposite side of the hall from the forensic lab was the computer and technical department. It was a large area with a clean room, a soundproof room, and at least a dozen technicians. Computers and digital screens lined the workbench and every cubicle.

Under Dallas's instructions, I was given a private room, and three computer experts were assigned to assist me. The techs had set up the computer for voice to text, or we could use a keyboard. I liked the idea of the keyboard. It gave me a few seconds to think of my responses, and I could see them before sending them out in the form of an electronic voice. One of the techs volunteered to operate the keyboard. I gladly accepted the offer. Typing was not one of my strong suits.

With coffee and pacing, I waited with the techs. They conversed within their small group, not inviting me to join them. I was an outsider. I didn't mind. I lacked the necessary background to engage in anything more than idle small talk. Dallas dropped in and out throughout the day. Her presence made her employees notably nervous. This was probably the first time they had actually ever seen her.

My pacing continued. I counted every minute and every second. Then, after eleven hours, twenty-six minutes, and sixteen seconds, the call came. After a few seconds, I spoke as the tech typed. "Chief Harris, I almost gave up on you."

"Chief Harris? I don't know a Chief Harris," was the response.

I reached over the tech and pressed the disconnect button. The tech and Dallas shared expressions of disapproval. "Don't worry," I answered with a quick glance at each of them. "He'll call back in a minute."

Two hours, eleven minutes, and five seconds later, Harris called back. "Harris, if you hang up again or deny anything, I'll kill one of your buddies I've got here."

"What the fuck do you want?" Harris was cold and calm. His professional training overrode our first encounter. He checked his emotions, and his fear disappeared. I suspected he was no longer alone and had called in support. I felt he was in the embryo stages of a counterattack.

"A meeting."

"Where?" he asked.

"I'll get back to you." I disconnected again. Sixteen hours of work and waiting for the exchange of forty or fifty words. We were ready for the next day.

The next day, we had a real carrier service deliver another envelope to Harris. The package was smaller and shipped from Bakersfield. It wasn't nearly as important as the first package, which carried the counterfeit bills. It was a plane ticket to Las Vegas that we could get replaced easily enough.

I waited for over an hour after we had the delivery confirmation before I called. He answered. I dictated to the tech, "I know who you are. I know what you look like. I'll see you on the plane. You will wear a T-shirt, no jacket, no carry-on, no cell phone or iPod. You'd better hurry. You've got a plane to catch."

"What do you want?" Harris asked. He remained detached with his words. I would have felt better if he had threatened me. Men like him don't make threats; they act.

"I'll tell you on the plane. Now, tell me you understand," I answered with as much frost as I could deliver. I doubted the computer was smart enough to put my tone in the delivery, but I did it for my own satisfaction. And … it impressed the computer tech.

Dallas forgot her promise. She rode to LAX with me. She spent her time reminding me of everything that could go wrong with this operation. I already was well aware of the majority of her concerns. I had thought of them myself. However, I never considered the MSM blowing up the plane, as Dallas suggested. I dismissed it. That would bring too much heat.

The United States would go to war over such misdeeds. I also didn't think Harris would go outside his own organization for assistance. He would appear weak.

Los Angeles International Airport has some of the tightest security I could think of for this type of meeting. Dallas bought all the available seats so we could fill them with our own people. With the airline policy of overselling seats, we figured Harris would have allies on the flight. We would have more.

Dan had already set up a surveillance team at the airport. He and his team of half a dozen would board the flight in different sections and seats. They were all dressed differently and appeared to be from different walks of life. Dan and another investigator, unknown to me, took the seats behind those seats assigned to Harris and me.

Dan and his team shared one commonality. They each wore a mandala that hung from a thin, gold-colored necklace. The gold-clad wire was actually a stainless steel garrote. It was very thin and very strong. Dan had told me that he could behead a man between the victim's heartbeats with this wire. I wondered, but I did not ask how or why he knew this.

I boarded first. I only gave Harris a 50 percent chance of showing up. He might be ruthless, but he was a behind-the-scenes operator. He directed others to do the dirty work … a coward. If anyone showed up, it would be a subordinate. I had one advantage. We purchased the ticket in his name. Unless they used their law enforcement influence, it could not be switched. However, I didn't think they would risk the attention of the LA police or the TSA.

I pulled the safety card out and studied the airplane's layout. Thanks to Dallas, I couldn't get the image out of my mind of an airplane exploding at thirty-five thousand feet. I'm not sure what the safety card would do for me in that case, but I read it anyway. I stretched my legs out to settle down for the flight.

I was just about convinced that Harris was not going to show up when there, standing over me, was the rat-faced weasel. I pondered if mixing rodents was as incorrect as mixing metaphors. He sat down without any acknowledgment and buckled the safety belt. I gave a quick glance to confirm it was him. It was.

Neither of us spoke until the flight was off the ground and at cruising altitude. He spoke first. "Well, I'm here. Now, what do you want?"

I said nothing. I pulled three fake confessions out of a file folder and handed them to him. The confessions explained the smuggling, the kidnappings and murders, an overview of the whole operation as we saw it. The confessions were in typed print; however, the hand-signed signatures were forged by Dallas's experts. They researched court documents that the dead Wayfarer officers had signed to provide credible examples.

I watched him study the documents before I handed him a fourth sheet of paper, a memorandum. The memo stated that if something happened to me or any of the people they thought were connected to me, the confessions, his kilos of drugs, the money, and his three men would be delivered to the state attorney general of California. Also, copies of the confession, a sample of the money, and a detailed report would be sent to five different attorneys across the United States, as well as to the Associated Press. None of the documents mentioned the children we rescued. Just the thought of using them in any manner sickened me. Even if it was for the good or they never knew, there was no way these children would be exploited again for any reason.

"Okay, what do you want?" Harris asked again.

I passed another document to him. It was the numbers for an offshore, untraceable bank account. "Transfer five million to this account, and you can have it all back: the confessions, the dope, the money, and the cops." I spoke at a near whisper.

He chuckled quietly. "What makes me believe I can trust you? How do I know any of this is real?" He raised the handful of documents into my view.

"I thought being fellow kidnappers would earn me some respect"—I paused—"and trust."

"Kidnappers?"

"The porn star?" I jogged his memory.

"Oh, yeah, that bitch."

"Where is she?"

"What makes you think we took her?" He spit his words. "And why do you want to know?"

"I never met one, that's all." I smirked.

"Forget about it. You have any proof my guys are still alive?"

"And give you evidence to use against me? No thanks, cop. You might be low-life scum and a smuggler, but you're still a cop," I answered; he just glared at me, saying nothing. I wanted to press him about Asian Sin, but didn't. It wouldn't have done any good and might have caused more harm. "So, do you want to finish this, or just sit there looking at me?"

He thought some. "Okay, I'll play along. Tell me the rest of your plan."

I handed him a map. "It's very easy; there's an abandoned truck stop on the road I have marked. The local farmers still use the bulk plant for fuel and fertilizer. I will have your property and people in a van. Once I verify the transfer of the money, I will get in a car with some of my associates and drive away. You can get in the van and drive away."

"That's it?"

"Oh." I spoke again. "I will have a couple pounds of C-4 attached to the van, and I will have a remote dead man's switch. If something goes wrong or seems out of place, I let go of the button. If I see a helicopter, an airplane, or a cotton farmer I think is one of your men, I let go. Oh—one more thing. Each of your guys will be wearing a vest with the same type of explosive. If they try to remove the vest, they will explode. If for some reason I am unable to remotely deactivate the switch, they will detonate in two hours. This gives me two hours to get away if you are thinking about trying something."

"You will never get away with this. You realize that, don't you?" he whispered. He never lost his composure, but I saw the hate in his expression.

"Do you want the time and date?" I replied dryly.

"Yeah."

"Five days from now, four thirty in the morning. Don't lose the map."

Neither of us looked at each other nor spoke for the remainder of the flight. I thought of trying to engage him in conversation, but didn't. If he was a trained spy, the attempt would be futile. Once the plane landed, I waited in my seat until the plane was empty. Harris remained as well, a stalemate. He finally left when the cleaning crew boarded.

Dallas insisted I stay in Las Vegas for the weekend. She arranged for an executive suite at her expense. I argued, but lost. She had offered Dan and his crew the same. Dan's crew stayed, but Dan returned to his wife.

Dallas took care of every detail. Some of it was a bit too cloak-and-dagger for me. There were no names, only confirmation numbers. Dallas required the trip from the airport to the hotel to include three car switches with armed drivers. I felt like a rock star. The last car stopped in a basement, where the driver handed me off to a pair of armed chaperones. They escorted me to a penthouse suite via a freight elevator.

I understood the security when I stepped inside another luxury suite well beyond anything I could afford. There, in a white robe, stood Keeley. Now I understood the intense security. It was to protect her. I failed to find words. Her eyes held mine in sensual enchantment.

"Conner, damn you! Don't ever do that again!" She spoke half angry, half teasing.

"What?"

"Send me away."

"I didn ..."

"Don't lie!" she snapped.

"Okay, I did, but ..."

"But what?" she interrupted.

"Damn it, girl; I love you. Can't you see? I love you. How could I let you get hurt?" I looked away. It wasn't my plan to disclose my feelings.

"It should have been my decision, don't you think? At least a decision we should have made together."

"I understand. But this is life-and-death stuff. I was thinking of you, Dan, and his people." I defended my decision. "If I was worried about you, I might make a mistake. I hope you understand as well."

"I do understand. Don't you think I'm grown-up enough to understand? To be trusted to make the right decision?" I didn't answer fast enough. She continued, "Then to go to my mother? Damn you, Conner!"

"Well, you are a spoiled little rich girl." Before the fire in those dark eyes could explode, I weakened. "You're right," I conceded. "My decision was blinded by love."

"God, Conner, that's the best you can do? A cliché?" She stepped closer and embraced me. She kissed me, and then she tipped her head back to look up at me. "You know, Conner, for a smart man, you're really stupid sometimes."

For the next three mornings we watched the sunrise over the city. An emergence of red and orange colors rose in the east, delivering a new day to the desert city. When the cool yielded to heat, we retreated into the suite to escape the heat. We slept until late afternoon.

Our fervency for each other consumed us. We talked very little about the investigation. Keeley asked a few questions, which I avoided answering in detail. I didn't say anything about the sting operation. She never asked, but I knew she wanted to be involved. I felt selfish. Feeling guilty, I thought several times about confessing to her about what I had done with her mother and also Sky Lee. In the end, I followed both my own and Dallas's advice and said nothing.

As perfect as things seemed, Keeley kept her feelings well-guarded. I told her again I loved her. She acknowledged with a simple, "I know." Perhaps I pushed too hard or dug too deep. It was our last morning together before I was to return to California. Keeley seemed distant. I knew something was going on, and I dogged her for an explanation.

She finally gave in to my pestering. "Conner." Her voice was broken, and she spoke with trembling lips. My heart began to sink. "Conner," she repeated, "I care for you so much. But I can't do this. I thought I could, but I can't."

"Do what? You can't what? Wait!" I tried to stop her from saying more.

"I can't stand the thought of someone I care so much for getting killed. I thought I could handle it, but I was wrong!" Her words came with tears she tried so hard to prevent. Dallas was right again. Keeley was far from letting her father's death go.

"For God's sake! Nothing is going to happen to me."

"I'm sorry, Conner. I should have stayed away the first time. I'm so sorry to lead you on like this."

"This is it. My last. After this case, I am through chasing after criminals!" I pleaded.

"You can't quit. You left all of it once. Remember, you were going to travel and work on old cars, but look where you are. Look at what you are doing! No, Conner, you can't quit, and I can't ask you to."

"I can! Just watch!" I argued.

"Then quit," she snapped back. "Just walk away from this one."

"What?"

"You know! Your hunt—no, your quest for Asian Sin."

"Huh?" I was startled and confused.

"Call my mother right now and tell her you're done," she shouted.

"You know I can't do that. I can't do that! Keeley, you know the people involved. I can't just up and walk away! You know that." I stuttered through my retort.

She forced a smile through her tears. "Yeah, Conner, I do—and now you do as well."

The fear I feared the most had happened: another good-bye. I fought back the tears; we desperately held each other at the door. It was the combined pain of this moment and my past. I had lived this before. I walked into the hall and turned. She stood there with her own tears. Her eyes filled with apprehension. She ran to me and kissed me hard. I felt her angst in her strong embrace. She gave me one last look, let me go and left, shutting the door behind her.

The next day, I woke up in my suite in California. I wasn't sure how I got there. I explored a hungover mind for any trace of recent memory. The only things I remembered for sure were that I had gulped a considerable amount of the complimentary whiskey in the limousine on the drive to the airport, Keeley was gone, and I was alone. Maybe that was what I deserved. I remember not wanting to be alone. I suppose being alone was and is my greatest fear. However, in contrast, the only time I remember truly never feeling alone was the summer I spent with Xiu Tang.

I contemplated pouring myself a whiskey and starting again from where I had left off, but decided on coffee. I hated losing my sense of time, but I had. I was on my third cup of coffee when Dallas called and told me that she was en route to my location for a meeting.

I was ready when she arrived. She brought two of her top criminal attorneys with her. Both had years of experience as prosecutors. Dan arrived with his second-in-command, Chewy Huang. With Dan being short and lightweight and Chewy a massive, towering man, they made quite a pair to look at, but as detectives they complemented each other. Both men were very intelligent and diversified in cultures and police work.

The dining table became the improvised conference table. I gave a detailed briefing and played the recording from the airplane. The two ex-prosecutors' combined conclusion was the same as mine. We didn't have enough for an arrest, let alone a case that could be tried.

Dallas snapped at me, "Why didn't you ask more questions? Why didn't you try to get him to open up?"

"What? Should I have invited him to the buffet line at the Flamingo? Or bought him a hooker?"

The older of the two criminal lawyers defended me with some diplomacy. "If Harris is the trained professional we suspect, we are lucky we got this much."

"All right." She calmed some. "What do we do now?"

"We finish it." I spoke with determination. "We make the deal, and I'll get it out of him." Dan winced. He had observed my last interrogation. I turned to Dallas. "You just have the sheriff's team armed with guns and search warrants ready to hit the Wayfarer Police Department the moment I call from the desert."

"You haven't forgotten the fact you truly don't have the money, the drugs, or the men?" Dallas went on the offense. She didn't like retreat, however slight, and especially not in front of her subordinates.

"A small problem, but don't worry; it'll work," I replied with some defiance.

Dallas and her law team left with the recording and their notes to meet with the sheriff at the Taiwan Consulate. She still didn't trust any other place to store the evidence. Dallas and her colleagues would lay out everything we had to the sheriff.

Dan and Chewy remained with me, and we continued to examine photos, maps, and sketches of our chosen rendezvous. We established the exchange point at a vacant truck stop that sat at the intersection of two old major highways. Before the interstates made these roads obsolete, they carried a considerable volume of commercial and recreational traffic. The old routes, now all but abandoned, were still used by the local farmers and the few occasional curious travelers who liked exploring and steering away from four-lane highways.

Dan and Chewy, looking for areas that had potential for an ambush, had driven to the location and checked it inside and out. They noted a couple stretches of road that could be very vulnerable for us, so the plans were modified to have those areas manned before the exchange.

The abandoned truck stop was antiquated by today's standards and lacked the size to accommodate modern trucks. Surrounded by sand and sparse desert vegetation, the small building contained an office, a diner, and a garage. A single concrete island that once supported three gas pumps was situated at the front of the station. Two islands were at the south side of the structure. Farther to the south was a fuel and fertilizer tank farm still utilized by a local farmer cooperative. To the north were foundations where a small hotel and a private residence had once stood. Dan posted round-the-clock guards to watch over the old buildings, ensuring the integrity and safety of the exchange point.

We covered every detail we could think of over a four-hour period. Dan had already obtained the necessary props for the exchange. The fake drugs, wrapped in kilo-size bricks, were a combination of flour and sugars, both white and brown. The fake money came from a print shop that had thousands of dollar-size expired coupons that a customer never claimed. They were loaded in a van identical to the van we had stolen—I preferred the word borrowed—from the money smugglers. I was hoping Harris or one of his men might mistakenly identify our van as the MSM van. The plan was to aggravate the situation to get the admission we wanted.

To avoid an ambush by the Wayfarer Police department, we decided to drive the van for the exchange out to the truck stop area two days early. It would be hidden under heavy guard until the time for the exchange. At that time, I would be the one to actually drive it to the exchange point.

It was a simple plan. Once at the exchange point and after Harris showed up, I would open the van for Harris to inspect. The idea was not to let Harris or his men get too close to see they were being scammed. To make even a more credible distraction, I would argue for a larger cut or for them to let me join their organization. I hoped badgering them in this manner would trick them into an admission or confession. The sheriffs could take the information and raid the police department. All that was left was the wait.

CHAPTER 20

I was asleep when my very first disposable phone rang. It was the one the cabdriver bought for me. Only one person knew the number … Sky Lee. "What in the world?" I said under my breath. "Hello?" I answered.

"Jack?" She sounded panicked. "Jack, I need your help! Please!"

"Sky, what's up?"

"I need your help," she sobbed.

"What is going on?"

"It's bad, really bad."

"What's bad?" I said, trying not to sound aggravated. "Please tell me what is going on."

"Can we do it in person?"

It took a moment to gather my thoughts. "Sure, come to my hotel." She told me she would be there within the hour.

I was dressed and drinking coffee when she arrived. She was dressed in black sweats; a paisley scarf held her hair. She wasn't the calm, cool sophisticate I had first met. Her hair was wadded under the scarf, and her eye makeup streamed down her face with her continuous tears. She looked exhausted and defeated. She managed to compose herself somewhat as she entered the living room. I asked her, "What happened?"

She began her story between sobs. "My sister is missing. She called a couple of days ago and told me things at work were spinning out of control."

"Out of control?"

"You know, out of control! Numerous closed-door meetings and whispers were the prevalent mode of conversation. She suspected that her employers were into something very illegal and that something big was coming. She had thought that for a long time."

"What do you mean big? Do you know what?"

"No, but she told me that she thought her employers suspected that she was an informant."

I asked her, "Who does your sister work for?"

She looked at me, her eyes red from tears, and she sobbed the answer. "She's a secretary at a police station down south. She told me that she did tell a reporter from some underground newspaper about some things, but that's all."

"Ahh, fuck." I'm not sure if I said it or thought it. "What's her name?"

"Jia Lee … she goes by Jay," she answered.

"I always thought your name was made up."

"Not my last—only my first. Far is my real name."

She looked lost, so I insisted she stay in the suite. I didn't want to worry about her, and I needed her someplace safe so I could think.

"I haven't counted all the bedrooms yet," I joked, trying to get her to relax some. "Take the one next to mine," I suggested and followed her into the room. I helped her into bed and waited in an overstuffed chair by her bed until she fell asleep. I then returned downstairs to consider how this new wrinkle figured into the picture.

After I gathered my thoughts, I called Bill Parker. "You need to get over here ASAP."

"These late-hour meetings are getting to be a habit." I could tell from his voice that, for once, he had been asleep when I called.

"Yeah, but you really need to get here, like an hour ago."

My next call was to Dan and Chewy, and I made the same request. After I hung up from Dan, I went to the kitchen and made some coffee. The coffee was to replace sleep, and within a few minutes, I was sipping a fresh cup while I waited for everyone to arrive.

And there I was, alone with my thoughts … again. What a mess I had made of things. How was I going to explain this? Secrets are lies without words. Omissions of fact, whether for self-preservation or altruism, are disingenuous acts of misdirection through silence. I couldn't remember what I had told whom and what I had not told whom. I had no plans of disclosing anything, but I did switch from coffee to whiskey.

Bill Parker was the first to arrive. "So, what is the big deal you couldn't tell me about over the phone?"

"I just found out your informant Jay Lee is missing," I said with as much calmness as I could muster.

"What?" He became crazy furious and turned back toward the door. "I am going to Wayfarer, and those sons of bitches better tell me where she is!" His face had turned red with rage, and his hands had rolled up into fists.

I grabbed his shirt with both hands below his collar and shoved him up against the wall. "Just what the hell are you going to do?" I screamed in his face. "These men aren't just professional, well-trained men! They are coldhearted, ruthless killers. They will kill you and kill her! And maybe in the process get Asian Sin killed! No! We don't even know where she is for sure!"

His eyes sought to kill me, but somewhere in his angry mind, he knew I was right. I understood his blaming himself, but it was they, not he, who owned the blame.

"It would have been nice to have known who your informant in the Wayfarer Police Department was," I told him as he sat down.

I wished I had pressed Parker to identify his informant. But if I were to be honest with myself, I probably wouldn't have put it together, even if I had had her name. And from what I remember in a past conversation, Parker used the male pronoun to describe his informant. However, I should have known that Sky Lee was never just randomly picked to send those goons after me when I first started my investigation. They knew exactly what they were doing, and Sky was just another unknowing pawn following orders out of fear.

Even if I had known, I am not sure if it would have made a difference, but I would like to think—no, I'm sure I would have had her removed from danger. But that might have required explaining Sky Lee to my boss, Dallas, and her daughter, Keeley. I'm pretty sure out of self-survival, I failed to mention to either Dallas or Keeley that I had befriended a very expensive hooker. And then there was that omission that I had slept with her on more than one occasion.

Once Dan and Chewy showed up, I explained, "Gentlemen, we have another problem. The woman that gave Bill Parker information about the Wayfarer Police Department is missing and is in big trouble. Big trouble like being killed trouble. I am going after her, and I need your help. Will you help me?"

Dan asked, "What's your plan?"

I buried my hands in my pockets and admitted, "I don't have one. We are going to have to make this up as we go. Are you gentlemen okay with that … for now?"

Dan looked over at Chewy and Bill Parker. They both nodded in agreement. "Let's do this." Chewy voiced their agreement.

I smiled my gratitude for their esprit de corps and said gravely, "All right then. Do I need to remind anyone that we have less than thirty-six hours to solve this? Remember, we have a previous engagement in the desert. I have already decided to forgo delivering the van early. We are just going to have to drive it there on the day of the exchange."

Chewy spoke out. "Let me go down to the Wayfarer Police and see what I can find out. I wasn't on the plane the other day, so they won't know who I am."

"Okay," I replied with a bit of fear. "Dan, brief him on what you can."

Dan nodded.

"Bill, I need you to promise you will not go to Wayfarer."

"Okay, I promise, but you don't expect me to just sit around and do nothing, do you?"

"No, I don't expect you to do nothing." I answered him sharply to display the importance of what I wanted to assign him. "I need you to contact your street sources for intelligence."

"Okay, I'll do it. What are you going to do?"

I sighed and looked at Dan. "I'm going to have to tell Joshua Harvey that I am going to owe him another favor."

Chewy and Dan went to the kitchen for some coffee and to make their plans. Bill Parker stood, walked over, and shook my hand. "Good luck," he offered as he left.

I took a moment for me and sat down. I felt a little guilty that I hadn't told them about Sky Lee. Even though Bill Parker knew a little about Sky, he was either kind enough not to say anything or just didn't think of it. And, of course, I never disclosed she was sleeping upstairs.

Even though he eventually complied with my request, Joshua's irritation with me showed. He had become angry and nervous with his assignment as caretaker of the four kidnapped deliverymen. I understood his position. It might be one thing to be a gangster for your own benefit, but to be a gangster for another without compensation was a lot to ask. I think Joshua would have dumped me days ago if it weren't for his cousin Asian Sin.

He and three of his men delivered one of the kidnapped suspects, or victims depending on your perspective, to Joshua's warehouse for questioning. I entered the warehouse with Dan, and I recognized our captive. At the Chino Airport, he was the one who had volunteered to direct us to their building where they would pick up and drop off the cash.

Joshua's men held the captive up against a stack of fifty-pound rice sacks in the middle of the warehouse. Joshua spoke. "We have a problem. He won't talk or help you."

"What? Why?" I asked. "He said he would."

"That was days ago; he thinks if he talks, we will just kill him," Joshua answered.

"Tell him to quit screwing with me and talk, or I *will* kill him. Maybe one of the others will be more apt to talk if he is dead on the floor. Remind him I have three more. I'm sure if I start piling them up, one will talk."

Joshua repeated my threat. We waited for the man to answer.

He spat his words at Joshua as if his mouth was full of poison. Joshua looked up at me and said, "He's not buying it. He thinks you're bluffing."

Without hesitation or flinching, I pulled my gun and fired. It hit a rice sack just above the captive's head—right where I had wanted it to hit. Joshua's men released him and, in less than a second, had their guns trained on me. Joshua waved his open hand down. With some reluctance, his men followed the silent order. Joshua glared at me with a half smile as rice showered the reluctant captive like snow sliding off a tree.

"You're paying for that." Joshua, looking at me, spoke over the man who was yelling in Chinese.

I shrugged. "What's he saying?"

"It seems he has changed his mind. He is ready to direct you to their stash house." Joshua turned to walk away. "Why don't you go with us?" I invited him.

He shook his head and waved as he continued to walk away. "Maybe later."

We secured the captive with tape and a blindfold before we loaded him. I drove without a destination. I made several turns during the several-mile drive before we took the blindfold off our imprisoned guest. Once he got his bearings, he directed us through the city and into another forsaken section of town.

The MSM gang building was an old four-story brick structure that sat at the end of the block at the northwest corner of a T intersection. The lots were empty on the south and west sides of the old building. It appeared from the fresh-turned and leveled dirt, saturated with small broken pieces of rock, concrete, and brick, that several buildings had once stood on the lots around our target building. The next building being demolished was a few hundred feet away to the south. A huge excavator track hoe sat waiting silently and patiently to finish devouring the aging walls of brick and mortar. The entire west side of the street was being systematically destroyed. There were three buildings still standing farther south than the one being torn down, blocked off by chain-link fencing.

The buildings across the street remained unharmed, and some still seemed to have inhabitants. After securing our hostage, Dan and I walked down the narrow alley between two buildings facing our target building. The smell of rot and urine filled the dark, narrow corridor, along with trash and cardboard shelters thrown together by homeless wanderers. We stepped carefully to avoid waking any of the homeless street residents. Dan touched my shoulder and pointed up. Two armed sentries held rooftop positions at the front corners of the MSM building.

The night grew cool and humid as Dan and I studied the fortress of our adversaries. The main entry doors were three steps above the sidewalk. To the right of the main entrance was a ten-by-ten-foot white garage door at street level. It was considerably newer than the rest of the building and looked out of place.

I whispered to Dan, "This is the place. Jay Lee is here."

"How do you know?" Dan asked, still in a whisper.

"I just do. A hunch."

"A hunch? You are going to lay siege on a hunch?" Dan shook his head in disbelief.

On our trip back to Joshua's warehouse to return our captive, Dan's cell phone rang. Dan for the most part just listened, only adding a "yes" or an occasional "okay" to the conversation. Finally, Dan put his phone up to his chest to cover the mouthpiece and spoke. "Chewy is driving back up from Wayfarer and has some great news. He said he needs to meet with us."

I was about to ask why, but I didn't. It would only be logical for him to request a debrief after a recon mission, so I asked, "What's the good news?"

"He wants to wait," Dan said. Then he asked, "What do you want me to tell him?"

"Just have him meet us at Joshua's warehouse," I answered.

I blamed myself. There was no one else to blame. Pacing nervously, I looked down again in disbelief at what I saw in the open trunk of Chewy's Cadillac. Twice, I walked away, hoping my latest problem would just disappear. It didn't. On the third pass, I stopped. In the trunk was a uniformed Wayfarer police officer. Well-secured by several wrapped layers of silver-colored duct tape, he lay in a fetal position. Chewy had been so kind as to put a pillow under the officer's head, like that was going to help the situation.

I really should have known better than to send Chewy. It was Chewy that came up with idea of taking the four hostages at the Chino Airport. I know I had reiterated to Dan there was to be no more kidnapping, and I knew Dan had given Chewy specific instructions not to kidnap anyone from Wayfarer. Dan and Chewy knew I was furious. I refrained from speaking until I gathered my composure. Dan started to speak, and I stopped him with an open hand. My mind was racing, as was my pulse.

I took a few steps away from the car and took in a deep breath. Dan sat on the edge of the open trunk. Chewy leaned on the driver's side front fender with his arms folded, staring down at the empty street like a scolded child. I walked back to Dan with an angry glare. "So why?" I asked Dan with a frown added to my glare.

"He thought you might want to interview someone from there?"

"Really? Where did you say Chewy was a cop?" I asked shortly, but my voice remained calm.

"Tijuana."

"Tijuana?" I yelled. I rubbed my forehead under my hat with hard fingertips. "Well, that explains a hell of a lot. Does he understand that in this country you don't just grab people off the streets? Especially cops!"

"He's learning, boss."

My glare remained. I reached over and ripped the tape off the officer's mouth and removed his blindfold. Removing the tape and blindfold exposed the man's youth. He looked about twenty-five or thirty, fit and well-groomed, in spite of tape restraints and the ride in a car trunk. He started begging for his family's life.

"Please," he pleaded, "I didn't tell anyone. I didn't tell the feds. Please let my family go. Leave them. Take me!"

The words in his plea caught me by surprise. "Take it easy, son." I touched his shoulders with care. "What do you mean you didn't tell anyone?"

"Please, mister! I didn't. I didn't tell anyone. I'll do what you want. Please tell the chief. Tell him I didn't say a word."

I thought a minute. "The chief? You think we work for Chief Harris?"

"You do, don't you?" He paused, struggling to understand. He didn't understand.

"No, we're …" I stopped. "We're … ah, a … no, we're independent kidnappers."

"You don't work for the chief?" He wrestled with his thoughts. "If you don't work for the chief, who are you?"

"Adversaries," I said. "Look, it would take too much time to explain. Do you know what's going on down there?"

"Yes, but my family. I have a little boy and girl … a wife." He calmed but still was worried.

I turned to Dan. "Untie him. Give him your cell phone."

With a curious reluctance, Dan followed my orders.

"What's your name, son?" I spoke softly.

"Russ … Russell White … sir." He rubbed his wrists as Dan cut away at the tape restraints.

"Well, Russell, you don't have any reason to trust us, but if you think Chief Harris means harm to you or your family … we're here to help." I pushed my hat off my eyebrows.

"You don't understand. He has men, professional men … killers."

"Like Easton?" I interrupted.

My words shocked him. "You know Easton?"

"I killed him." Those words shocked Dan.

"Killed … dead?" The young officer pondered my words.

"Dead is the direct result of being killed," I answered. "Russell, may I call you Russell?" He nodded as Chewy and Dan helped him out of the trunk. "Russell, call your wife. Tell her there will be some men coming to your house. They will take her and your children to a safe place. Understand?"

I could see he was terrified. Who could he believe—his crooked boss or the guys that stole him off the street? I spoke again. "Look, I know. You have to trust me. Make the call before it's too late." He pressed the numbers. While he spoke to his wife, I told Chewy to have a couple of men go over to Russell's house and get his wife and children and take them to Dallas's office building. He nodded in understanding. I patted him on the shoulder. "Good job, but," I added, "you are *not* going to kidnap anyone else, is that clear? Neither will any of your men—got that? Repeat that order."

Chewy hung his head. "Yes, boss. No more kidnapping."

Russell was still on the phone with his wife. I spoke again. "Russell, you have to hurry. We have to go. Your boss snatched Jay Lee, one of his secretaries. I don't know if she is alive or dead."

Russell ended the call. "Ms. Lee is alive. I heard them talking."

We loaded up in Chewy's Cadillac and headed for Dallas's building. On the way, Russell filled us in. "I only started working at Wayfarer about two years ago. I had no idea what Chief Harris and his thugs were up to. You have to believe me. I just wanted to be a good cop. I discovered the smuggling operation purely by accident. When I went to the chief to report what I had found and turn over my evidence, I learned the chief and the city board were also involved. It was too late to go anywhere else. Chief had my evidence, and he had me. Damn!

"Harris threatened me with an ultimatum: I could either join them or be killed. He promised they would kill me, my family, even my parents. They had all my information, everything. They did an extensive preemployment background check."

"Harris's men, your fellow cops, would kill you?" I asked.

"No," Russell continued, "Chief Harris would have one of the gangs do it."

"What gangs?" I asked.

"The chief works with two gangs, ruthless gangs: the MSM and the Black Lord Demons. The MSM is a Chinese gang, and the Black Lords are primarily a black gang but they have a few Latinos. The way it works is the MSM provides the drugs and cash, and the BLD distributes the products. The operation runs the coast from Mexico to Vancouver. MSM brings the drugs, money, and whatever else on some old ships. The chief and his men go out and meet the ships with fast boats and pick up the drugs and money. Once the drugs and money are packaged as evidence, they make a run up the coast with our sixty-foot boat. They deliver to the BLD. Those people do the street sales and deliveries inland, taking most of the risk. We have actually arrested their people and prosecuted them as they were carrying drugs we sold them." Russell had to choke back tears. I saw the shame he was feeling in his eyes.

"What else?" I asked.

He struggled with his words and then answered between sobs of remorse, "Children, little children. The ship would bring in little children, and they were sold to the vilest men. God burn them in hell!"

"Well, Russell, we are trying our best to make sure God gets his chance with these guys, but we want the state of California to get them first," I replied and then asked, "How do you know that Jay Lee is still alive?"

"I think it would be easier to understand if I started at the beginning." Russell had composed himself. "Somehow she learned of the illegal activity and started keeping the chief's e-mails and recording his phone calls. She also copied his personal ledger. This ledger has all the names of his dealers and his contacts. When she found out the chief suspected her, she sent her copy of the ledger to someone she could trust."

"Smart girl."

"Yeah, but when the chief found out, he was furious; he had her picked up. I'm almost sure she is being held in an old four-story building controlled by the MSM gang. It's past the old warehouse district. I don't remember the street," he said, and I took the time to smile an "I was right" smile at Dan. Russell continued, "And as long as she doesn't tell them where her copy of the ledger is, they will keep her alive."

"Damn!" I said under my breath and then ordered Dan, in a voice filled with urgency, "Dan, we need to get some armed people over to my suite and to Bill Parker's, now! There are only two people this girl would have trusted: her sister Sky Lee and Bill Parker."

"Sure," Dan responded, and he immediately started working the keypad on his phone. As he dialed he asked, "Your suite?"

"Yeah, Jay's sister Sky is staying there," I answered. I think there was some condescension in Dan's shrug, but maybe it was just my guilty conscience.

"Russell, were you ever at this MSM gang house or warehouse?" I asked.

"No, no, sir," he answered.

Dan finished arranging for security and then called Dallas. He gave her the new information. She would meet us at her office. I smiled again at Dan. I liked being right. We finished the ride to Dallas's building in silence.

Dallas called the sheriff and the attorney general. She requested they send people over to her office to take Russell's statement. Her top criminal attorney would also be there to ensure Russell would not become the scapegoat in this situation. He would be granted immunity before giving his formal statement.

Dan and I were at Dallas's building only long enough for introductions; then we excused ourselves and left. We were running out of time. Russell was reunited with his family and would be staying in one of the executive suites under armed guard until this was over or Dallas moved them to the Taiwan Consulate.

Chapter 21

I didn't wish to bring any more of Dan's people directly into what I knew was going to happen next. I already regretted having dragged Dan and Chewy into this situation. I called the big twins, David and Darrell, and asked them if they wanted to participate in an operation that wasn't exactly legal. Their enthusiasm frightened me.

We went to Joshua's to pick up the van we had taken from the Chino Airport. Joshua spoke as I climbed into the van. "Hey, what do you think about sending the guys you kidnapped back to China when we're done with them?"

"How?" I asked, "We can't just buy them plane tickets and send them without losing control. I'm sure they would go to the police."

"Maybe."

"No, really."

"Okay, by private jet."

"Do you think they killed anyone, kidnapped anyone themselves?"

"No, strictly low level."

"Do they want to go back?"

"Oh, yeah."

I sighed. "Okay, when we get done with this mess. All right?"

"How long, Jack? How long before this is done?"

"Close, real close."

Joshua nodded. "Where are you going now?"

"I'm not sure you want to know."

"Try me."

"They took her, Joshua—Jay Lee, Sky Lee's sister. They have her, but we're going to get her back."

"Make room; we're going too," he volunteered without hesitation and waved for four of his people to get in the car and van. With some reservation, I accepted his offer, not knowing how much resistance I was going to face. There wasn't time for surveillance. He and two of his men rode with me. Dan and Chewy took the other two.

I watched Joshua carefully out of the corner of my eye. It made me nervous working this close to a gangster. My glances were noticed, but ignored. Joshua kept himself occupied by checking his handguns and looking out into the night.

I debated about turning over what I had to Detective Jim Collins and LA County, but I wasn't sure the statement of a kidnapped police officer would be enough for a search warrant, and of course, there was the problem of trying to explain the kidnapping of four low-level Chinese criminals. The kidnapped policeman was going to be Dallas's problem with the sheriff and the AG. Besides, we just hadn't the time to explain it all.

It was another simple plan: first, we placed our people like the pieces on a chessboard. Dan and Chewy would take a position on the roof of a taller building just across the street to the east, facing the front of the MSM building. Dan would be the sniper, and Chewy his spotter and our lookout. Darrell, David, and two of Joshua's men would wait across the street in the alley between the building where Dan and Chewy were and another warehouse to the south. Joshua, his other two men, and I would make our way to the back of the building on the west side.

When everyone was in their assigned locations, Darrell and David would launch the rigged, unmanned van from the alley, where it would cross the street and crash through the garage doors. As part of a larger distraction, the two would begin firing wildly at the building, as if they were attempting to gain entry to rob the place. The idea was to bring our adversaries to the front to prevent this supposed robbery.

Once the assault began on the front of the building, Joshua and I, along with his men, would gain entry through the back. We would find the girl and get out of there. I was hoping we could get in and out of the building without getting anyone shot—especially not any of my crew.

Field Marshall Helmuth von Moltker once said, "No battle plan ever survives first contact with the enemy." Truer words were never more aptly said. The van made its mark and hit the garage door as planned. However, unplanned, it bounced back into the middle of the street. The reason became very apparent as the lightweight roll-up garage door collapsed. Just inches beyond that door stood another door—a heavy metal inner door. Every other entryway was the same, reinforced with heavy steel. It shouldn't have been a surprise with the amount of money being shipped from here, but it was.

After the van hit, the gang inside the building began a barrage of bullets everywhere. Any shadow, any perceived movement, they fired at.

Joshua and I fell back across the street diagonally to the safety of another building. A thick fence made of bricks surrounded our cover building. We knelt down behind the fence and carefully peeked over the top to assess our circumstances. It became very clear that the MSM was prepared to take on intruders. Our people were pinned down under heavy fire. With all the gunfire, I was sure our robbery attempt ploy was working and the girl was safe for the moment.

"Well, General … you have any other great ideas?" Joshua asked over the top of his binoculars. "This needs to end quickly, or we need to get out of here."

I nodded. I searched the area and my mind for options. My heart was beating so hard, I thought it was going to explode through my chest. I found my other option: the excavator. I pointed at it, and before Joshua could respond, I ran back across the street and into the shadows. The shadows provided me concealment as I crept toward the machine.

I found it unlocked and the keys under the seat, a common practice in the construction industry. The giant machine thundered to life with a twist of the key. It took me a few seconds to familiarize myself with the controls.

I throttled it up and pressed the joystick forward. The tracks answered immediately, and I steered across the empty lots to the MSM building.

With the firefight going on in the front, my advance went unnoticed. The twins managed to move to the middle of the street and take cover behind the van. They switched from handguns to their shotguns with slugs. Their slugs shattered the bricks as they hit. They stopped a moment to watch my approach.

As I closed, I pulled the other joystick back, and the large steel boom arm reached out in the dark. I raised the bucket and raked the building's side. It tore through the old building with little effort. Bricks fell like rain in front of me. Blinding dust saturated the air in a cloud of dirt. The building shook; the sentries lost their footing and fell onto the roof. I pushed the controls forward, and the excavator tore at the floor joists, collapsing a section of the second floor.

Tearing the wall down did not go unnoticed. The two MSM sentries regained their footing and transferred their attention to me. The men on the inside divided efforts, and several gang members swiftly moved to prevent entry from the new opening torn in the south wall. They took turns firing at the track hoe through the huge gap. I reversed the excavator's direction. I wanted another hole. I needed another opening to separate the building's defenders again and force them to cover three possible entries. Bullets showered the machine. They were no longer firing a shot at a time. They had switched to full auto. The excavator cabin's glass exploded inward as I retreated. Small shards of glass stung my face.

I spun the hoe around on its tracks to evade the onslaught of gunfire. Track hoes spin quickly, but travel slowly on their tracks. A couple of gang members tried to approach the machine, but Dan's proficiency with a rifle kept the defenders inside the building and prevented them from running up on the machine. Every time one of the gang members started to crawl out of the hole, Dan fired, and his bullet would hit within an inch of the exiting gangster. Each time they would quickly retreat behind the safety of the wall. As I steered the machine to the rear of the building, we disappeared from Dan and Chewy's view. I lost my sniper support, but Joshua's men took up the task and continued to cover me with gunfire.

I made my way to the northwest corner of the old building to avoid the steel fire escape. I had to keep the stairs intact, so I could gain entry and egress. I raked the rear wall with the bucket. The hardened steel teeth penetrated the brick and gouged another hole. The dust and dirt covered the excavator. I backed up and aimed the track hoe to the center of the west wall. I rammed the throttle wide open and pushed the joystick forward. After I tied the seat belt around the joystick to keep the machine moving forward, I jumped from the machine and ran for cover. The tracks on an excavator are designed to displace weight, not for intense traction like on a bulldozer. The excavator stopped after crushing its way a few feet into the building, its tracks futilely spinning but refusing to give up.

Joshua's men providing cover fire had to run across the street over open ground to keep me safe. They fired aggressively as they charged. As one of our comrades got hit and fell, the other returned fire and hit two of the outlaws. I made my way over to Joshua's wounded man and dragged him out of the line of fire. It appeared to be a painful but not fatal injury.

Joshua made his way around the other side of the building and joined me. Together we made our way to his man at the rear opening. He was advancing at a good pace. David and Darrell were quicker. They had breached the south-side hole and were inside. One would fire as the other loaded, and they worked their shotguns in an orchestrated cover-and-move-forward technique.

They had the bad guys on the run. Two of the MSM gang members had dropped their empty guns and run out the front door into the street, leaving the front doors open. That gave us another option for ingress and egress, but there was nothing to stop the twins' volley of slugs that struck the walls around us as we crawled through the broken brick hole. We stepped into their line of fire, and I waved my arms to get the twins' attention. I failed. Another barrage of rounds exploded on the wall behind me. I picked up a loose brick and threw it. It landed near one of the two identical shotgunners. He frowned and gestured with his shotgun, directing my attention to the offices on the north side of the building—the only side not damaged. He held up three fingers. I nodded in understanding; there were at least three MSM members hidden inside those offices. I pointed at myself and then upward at the ceiling. Next, I pointed at the twins and then to the offices where the three gangsters were hiding. They nodded in understanding. Joshua and I were headed upstairs, and the twins were to deal with the three pinned down in the offices.

Joshua and I headed for the inner stairs, or what was left of them, as the twins directed their fire into the offices. Before we got halfway up the staircase, the three outlaws surrendered and ran out of the building. David and Darrell took posts on the openings, and one of Joshua's men took the front doors. His other man joined our ascent. We had secured the first floor.

I wasn't sure why we met no resistance in the staircase, which was the most vulnerable area for us and the easiest for the MSM to defend. The second floor was an open area, with bare steel bunk beds along the walls. Dirty mattresses and sleeping bags were piled everywhere. It was either used to hold trafficked victims or gang members. I saw movement in one of the filthy humps of bedding. Joshua covered me with his gun as I dug in the pile. It was a girl. It was Jay Lee. She was tied with wire that cut into her wrists and ankles. She looked beaten, but alive. I tore the tape from her mouth and pulled a dirty sock out. She gasped and inhaled a big breath.

Her scared glance bounced from Joshua to me. Her face was filled with terror, but her restraints were too painful for her to move. She attempted to speak. I put a gentle finger on her lips and spoke. "Don't try to talk. Jay, we are friends of your sister. We are here to get you. You're safe now, okay?" I smiled to reassure her.

The building began to yield to the force of the running track hoe. Cracks in the center supports began to expand. The floor buckled, and single boards started to snap upward. Joshua motioned his men to carry Jay Lee. We didn't have pliers to cut her restraints. The strongest one carefully took her into his arms. She winced with the movement. The wire cut deeper into her wounds.

Joshua turned to me as the floor rippled underneath us. "Do all your plans turn out this way?"

"Pretty much," I shrugged. "Jay, are there any more people being held here?"

She struggled with a nod and pointed up. "I think so, upstairs, maybe ten or twenty upstairs."

"Get her out of here," I instructed Joshua's men. "Grab the cash!" They looked confused. "In the vault! The cash—take it. Get the others to help." They nodded and made for the stairs.

I looked over at Joshua. His glare told me he wasn't going up the stairs of a collapsing building. "Come on … think what you might miss," I challenged him with a grin. It started to rain ceiling tiles.

"My kindness only extends to crazy Colorado sheriffs," he countered. I smiled again.

We were met by gunfire from the third-story stair landing. Joshua whispered, "Good thinking!"

I yelled up the stairs. "Hey! Upstairs! There is nothing left to save. Throw your guns down and get out of here while you can."

The third floor began to collapse as sagging floor joists broke. I yelled again, "You're going to get crushed or shot. Now, throw down the guns!"

Four handguns and a rifle landed at the bottom of the stairs. Four very scared men, with their hands in the air, slowly stepped down the shaking stairs. I resisted killing them. "Get the hell out of here! Now! Before I kill you, and I will kill you—all of you!"

Joshua rushed up the stairs. I followed. The third floor mirrored the second floor, with bunk beds and ragged bedding. Several young Asian women, frightened and confused, huddled behind some overturned beds. The building moaned and moved under our feet. I yelled at them to go … get out of here. They didn't move. I shouted again … nothing. A hundred years of settled dust filled the air. A shot rang out. Joshua returned fire. Another shot came from the shadows, and Joshua fired again. A man staggered to the middle of the room. Blood dripped from his hands to the floor. Fear consumed his face. He fell. I pointed frantically at the staircase.

Joshua yelled in Chinese. The women stirred and began to talk among themselves. Joshua yelled again. They all stood up and waited for Joshua's next instructions. He looked reluctant to leave me. We had another floor to clear. "Go; I'll be fine! Go! Damn it, go! Those girls need you!" I yelled over the sound of breaking glass, splintering wood, and falling bricks.

He glared at me in frustration. Left without a choice, he waved for the women to follow him. He directed them down the stairs. I climbed the last flight of stairs. Piles of empty boxes and junk covered the fourth floor. I crawled on my hands and knees. The floor was shaking too violently to stand. The piles of junk slowly yielded to gravity and began to slide to the center of the collapsing floor.

I stopped to clear my eyes of fine dust as I choked and coughed on the polluted air. Pieces of ceiling crashed painfully down on my back. I fought back my terror and panic. The excavator's engine went silent. Joshua must have ordered someone to shut it down. The building creaked under me as I moved forward. I wanted to run. I almost convinced myself there was no one else to save. Then came a cry! I followed the desperate sound.

I stood and moved some boxes. I uncovered another terrified face, another young woman hiding from the chaos created by our assault. Tears ran from her dark eyes. The stream of tears washed a trail down her cheeks. I smiled and reached for her. She cradled herself tighter. I smiled and spoke softly. "Are you alone?"

She just kept her arms locked around her legs and rocked in fear. I asked again. My words meant nothing to her. I reached again. "Look, I don't speak Chinese, and we don't have time to build trust. We have to go." I pulled her toward me, grabbed her into my arms, and rushed to the stairs. The stairs crashed down the stairwell, leaving an empty void with no escape. The young woman screamed in fear.

Aw, fuck! What do I do now? I was almost in a panic. My mind tricked me. My thoughts weren't of being crushed in a collapsing building or finding a way out, but being dug out by angry police and spending several lifetimes behind bars. I glanced around. I was so scared I was losing my breath.

The fire escape! I remembered. I pulled her along as I cleared a path on hands and knees through the maze of boxes and debris to the outside stairs. The undamaged wall was slowly surrendering its structural integrity. The top of the wall folded in under the unsupported weight. I shoved her out onto the fire escape and tried to shield her from the bricks raining down on us.

I grabbed the guardrails with both hands with the girl between my arms. I pulled my body against her and slid my feet toward the lower treads. The bolts inched their way out of the bricks with each step. The stairs dropped a couple of inches with a jolt. The girl yelped. She buried her face deep in my chest. I stepped again. We had made it to the middle of the steps when the stairs gave up their last tenuous grasp on the brick wall.

The fire escape spun around on its base and crashed to the ground. As the stairs folded, I lost my grasp and fell backward to the ground. The girl landed on my chest, knocking the wind from me. Dan and Joshua came rushing to our rescue. Once Joshua figured out I was all right, he started to laugh as he extended his hand and pulled me to my feet.

We had to get out of this nightmare. Even though we were in the middle of a forgotten, decomposing industrial area, the amount of gunfire and the destruction of a building would have attracted attention. David and Darrell attached the disabled van to Chewy's Cadillac with a chain. They loaded the women in the van and placed Jay Lee in the back of the car, along with Joshua's wounded man. We stuffed the last girl into the overcrowded van.

Chewy looked over at me. "Where are we going?"

My eyes appealed to Joshua.

Joshua looked at the needy faces of the displaced women and girls. He looked at his men and us, all of our eyes on him, waiting for him to make a decision. "Oh for God's sake! Take them to my place!"

It took some doing with bent wheels and the front tires rubbing on the fenders of our broken van, but we made it. Joshua called for a private doctor for his man and Jay Lee, while his staff took care of the women. They would be fed, allowed to clean up, and given new clothes. Joshua had to assure them several times that they were safe and would be treated with the utmost respect.

While they ate, several of the girls told Joshua their stories. The women were mostly recruited while they were at college. They had been told that they would have executive jobs, legal jobs, in America. They had to pay ten thousand US dollars for their new lives. The new life they were promised started with a thirty-day trip across the Pacific in an old ship with little food and water.

Once they had gotten close to American land, a police boat met the ship and took them ashore. The police confiscated their documents. If they asked questions or raised concerns, the police responded with quick retaliation by beatings or worse. They were moved to the warehouse and were waiting to be sold to massage parlors, garment manufacturers, or to work as live-in maids.

As Jay Lee's wounds were treated by Joshua's doctor, she gave her statement. Chief Harris suspected her of disclosing information about the illegal operation. He used her for a while to leak false information. When she learned he was using her, she recorded his calls and copied his ledger and e-mails. The ledger contained everything: times, dates, buyers of the counterfeit money, drugs, and the worst … the children. Her statement corroborated Officer Russell White's statement. We had them. But I wanted more: I wanted their statement, confessions, or admissions, and I would get it. I would get it at the truck stop exchange.

I called Dallas and made arrangements for Jay Lee to be transferred to Dallas's building. She would be interviewed by the sheriff. Thanks to Jay Lee and Russell White, we now had a case against the Wayfarer Police Department … a strong case. I called Sky and told her we had rescued her sister. Sky gushed with thank yous to God, to us, and to everyone. She hardly could speak more than a word at a time in her excitement and her relief.

"We grabbed well over a half million in cash," Dan announced with a hint of pride. "It's in the trunk of Chewy's car."

"Well, Sheriff, first kidnapping and now armed robbery, and you say I'm the gangster?" Joshua jumped into the conversation.

I pretended to ignore him and turned to Dan. "Divide the money between our men and the girls we found. Save some for Jay Lee as well—severance pay." Joshua nodded in approval. I checked my watch. There was no time for a victory celebration. We had more to do.

Chewy asked me if I was ready for another fast drive. My answer was a shrug. I actually dozed a minute or two while Chewy drove back into the city. Sometime while in my lapses of sleep, David and Darrell convinced Chewy to stop at a drive-through for some hamburgers and fries. I took the seat between them in the back of the old Cadillac. I thought being pinned between the large pandas was the safest seat in the car considering everything.

"Don't Stop Believing" by Journey was blaring from the back speakers. David and Darrell smacked their food over the music. Chewy and Dan were singing along out of key and with heavy accents. Darrell dropped a sack of hamburgers in my lap. "You got to eat, man." I unwrapped one and took a large bite. It tasted good. The old car roared as it flew down the dark road to our next destination. No, Asian Sin wasn't found in the building as I had fleetingly hoped, but it was a great moment to be alive.

Chapter 22

The trip across town to the storage units went fast in light traffic—five more hits from the eighties to be exact. Dan and Chewy joined in the singing of all five songs. Chewy turned off the street and drove down a short lane to a metal fence with vertical bars and a locked gate. He used his key to gain access to an electronic number pad. He pressed in his ten-digit number, and the gate slid out of our way.

With the press of the accelerator, Chewy drove the old Cadillac down the long line of identical storage units and slid to a stop in front of the one that matched the number on our key. Dan jumped out of the car and opened the two doors that hid our white van, filled with fake drugs and counterfeit money. I slid behind the wheel as Darrell and David loaded up in the back. Chewy took the passenger seat. Dan took off ahead of us in the old Cadillac. He was the forward scout. He would drive the route a few minutes ahead of us to make sure it was clear.

Before we got completely out of town, at the whining request of David and Darrell, we stopped one more time for food. Chewy used the time to sleep some. It would be close, but I would be there on time. I drove just a little above the speed limit, trying to avoid any attention. The exchange part would be over in a few hours, and I could turn this whole mess over to the authorities, and they would finish it.

Now, I have seen countless spy and cop movies. I have read numerous spy and cop novels, and in none of them, and I mean none of them, did their car die. I have been a part of numerous actual operations and never had a car or a piece of equipment fail me—until now. A little over an hour to the exchange point, the van just up and died. I tried everything I could think of, but it refused to start. I felt like exploding in a rage of cursing and throwing things, but there wasn't time.

After several attempts, I found a tow truck company that actually answered their phone. The dispatcher told me in an overly cheerful voice that a truck would be headed that way just as soon as I hung up. I paced while Chewy, David, and Darrell sat on the ground leaning up against the right side of the van, exchanging stories about the raid on the warehouse. Each story got a little larger and more exaggerated every time they repeated it.

I checked my watch with each about-face. Dan had called during my phone quest for a tow truck. He was worried we had been ambushed. He said that a SWAT vehicle was already at the exchange point.

"No, nothing as adventurous as an ambush. The damn van broke down." I let him hear my frustration and anger.

"Well, should I head back that way for you?"

"No, don't come back. A tow truck is on its way to haul us to the meeting spot," I told him. "I don't want to take the chance Harris would connect Chewy's old Cadillac with us if you drive by again."

"A tow truck? You're kidding, right?"

"Nope. If I were kidding, I'd say … oh, never mind."

"How's that going to look if you arrive with a tow truck in … tow? Or vice versa?"

"Not going to worry about that now. In fact, it might give us more credibility because he probably knows the van is a piece of junk." With that, I ended Dan's call.

Two hours later, the tow truck driver arrived and backed his truck up to the front of the van, got out of his cab, and grabbed a house broom from the back. The driver was a short man with a large stomach. He wore a cheap black wool cowboy hat, while his boots and leather belt were a scuffed and grimy white. His black vest had the tow company logo above the pocket and on the back. He knelt down and started shoving the broom under the van. I watched for a moment before impatiently asking him, "What the hell are you doing?"

After I got an answer that I couldn't understand, Chewy stepped in, and the two engaged in an animated conversation in Spanish with voices and hands. Finally, Chewy turned to me and with a shrug said, "He is checking for snakes." With the thousands of tow truck drivers and trucks in southern California, I had managed to find a driver that not only couldn't speak English, but was deathly afraid of snakes. Chewy explained, "Evidently, we have broken down right in the middle of snake country."

"Snakes? Oh for …" I handed Chewy my hat and crawled under the van's front bumper. "Have him hand me the chains." It took a little bit, but I finally got the van hooked up and crawled out from under it.

Looking at my watch, I told Chewy to make sure he knew we were in a big hurry. He nodded and gave the driver instructions. The driver talked fast and continuously as he finished hoisting the van; I wasn't sure if he were addressing Chewy or just talking. Chewy nodded in rhythm with the driver's diatribe.

Finally, the small truck pulled back onto the asphalt and headed down the road, the van in tow. I rode in the van with Darrell and David. Chewy rode in the tow truck with our snake-phobic driver. I had given Chewy very specific instructions on what I wanted to happen at the exchange. The driver was to pull the van to the south side of the old truck stop buildings, unhook, and leave.

I felt an uneasy nervousness building inside me. At least when I was driving, I wasn't thinking about all that could go wrong with this operation. The sun was well up in the sky when we drove past Harris and his six-man crew, three hours later than our original four thirty meet time. I was surprised they were there.

They were dressed in black fatigues, helmets, and bulletproof vests. All but Harris sported black, automatic carbines held at port arms. They stood in front of an armored, six-wheeled assault vehicle. Stenciled in large, light gray letters against the dark black hull was "Wayfarer Police SWAT." Smiling awkwardly, I waved as we slowed and turned into the dirt lot. Harris had a stunned expression of disbelief on his face. His SWAT team shared his look.

The tow truck driver followed Chewy's instructions and pulled between the tank farm and the buildings. We stopped about twenty-five yards to the north of Harris and his men. I didn't like that we were so close to them. I feared it would be too easy for them to discover the illusion being so close. I would have liked to have been another twenty-five yards farther away from him, but because of where they parked and where the buildings stood, it was impossible.

The SWAT team and the SWAT vehicle obviously unnerved our tow truck driver, as he stopped and then went forward a few more feet two different times. I could see Chewy trying to put the nervous little man at ease with pats on his shoulder. Finally, our driver jumped out and ran around the front of his truck and down the right side. Suddenly, he leaped on the back of his truck and started yelling. His screams filled me with fear, like ice water dumped down my back. He was about to get us all killed. I bailed out of the van. He was shrieking and jumping up and down, pointing down. I ran toward him, only to find a rattlesnake warming itself on the old concrete fuel island. By now, with all the shrieking and leaping, the rattlesnake was coiling for a fight. I grabbed the broom from the truck bed and jabbed at the snake, trying to convince it to leave. Harris and his men just gazed in confusion and curiosity.

Chewy negotiated with the terrified driver to at least operate the controls. I would have shot the snake, but the gunfire might have provoked Harris or one of his triggermen to shoot. The snake finally yielded and crawled off the concrete. It headed for the truck once, and the driver yelped. I steered it away with the broom. Chewy got him calmed down enough and convinced him he was safe on the truck bed. All he had to do was step over the boom and pull the lever.

The front of the van dropped to the ground with a bounce. I took a moment to make sure the rattler wasn't turning around before I crawled under the van to unhook the chains. The tow truck driver managed to climb from the back of his truck into the cab, cursing in Spanish, without stepping onto the ground. Chewy's role as a fake Wayfarer police hostage was compromised, and he had to leave with the driver. He would have Dan pick him up down the road. He whispered, "Good luck." The tow truck tires threw gravel into the air as the truck spun around in the dirt lot and headed off on the highway.

A sick feeling came over me as I watched the tow truck disappear and Harris's SWAT vehicle creep closer. Harris and two of his men walked along the left side by a large door that opened into the vehicle. The rest of his men must be in this six-wheeled monster. I stood there watching them approach. "What am I going to do?" I thought, just short of panic. "I'm short a man now. How am I going to do this?"

I put up my right hand. "Stop!"

Harris complied. I walked to the back of the van. "Sorry about the delay." I slapped the side of the van. "You just can't be too picky when you're stealing vans. You guys should consider better equipment."

I could see the anger on Harris's face as he spat, "Where's my men?"

"Don't worry; they're here." I slapped the van again. "How about my money and a talk?"

"Fuck your talk! Show me my men!"

I shrugged. "Okay." I opened the rear doors of the van. Darrell and David, with their faces covered, sat up from behind the fake drugs and money. "They're here! It's all here."

Harris asked, "Where's my third man?"

"You can count. Good for you."

"Well?" He trained his gun on me. "Where the fuck is he? I'm about to blow you to hell!"

I held up a box with several switches. "Now, Chief, slow down!" I bluffed. "He's safe. He is my insurance; he will be released with a phone call. What about my money?"

"Fuck you. That wasn't the deal."

"It is now."

"You're under arrest!" Two of his team members moved forward. I held up the switch box again. They stopped. I drew a gun with my left hand and fired a round into the van. Darrell and David jumped in surprise. I wasn't worried. I shot high enough to miss them.

"No, Chief, I'm not."

"Oh, really? I see a smuggler with two kidnapped officers and a bundle of drugs and money … counterfeit money." Confidence filled his voice.

I wasn't sure what to do. They inched closer. "Well, Chief, is this where I say, 'Make your play'?"

I stepped sideways away from the van. He spoke again. "Just surrender and give me that switch."

"If I blow this thing, you don't have much evidence."

"And kill two men just like that? Besides, I don't think you have any explosives … not even a firecracker." Harris was right. I didn't. It was a bluff, and I was called. He waved his armored car closer.

I fired again, only this time at his feet. "So, Harris, screw with me, and we all die! If you want to live, call your boss! Now!"

His two officers immediately raised their carbines and took aim at me. I was taking in deep breaths and slowly releasing them in an attempt to keep from trembling. Three more men exited the bulletproof vehicle and joined Harris.

"Boss? What boss? What the fuck are you talking about?" Harris growled. He gestured for his men to lower their guns. I had struck a nerve. All of a sudden he believed I had information, and he wanted to know just what all I knew.

"Yeah, the mayor. You wouldn't be here if you were the boss. You're just a stooge … a flunky. The real brain of your organization is comfortably at home, out of jeopardy." His anger visibly boiled. This professional killer was about to explode in a rage. I had him. I just needed to give him a little more of a push. "Call your mayor … I want to talk to the real man!"

He fired. The bullet cut into my leg, producing a sharp pain. I grabbed it as I went down. Damn! I hadn't figured on that. David and Darrell opened up on them with their handguns. The gunfire sent the SWAT members back toward the cover of the armored car. They returned fire at the two in the van as they retreated. For the moment, they forgot about me.

I rolled over on my back to test my leg and saw my solution: a high-pressure anhydrous ammonia tank on four wheels. I crawled over to it and pulled myself to a standing position. I leaned up against it and grabbed a heavy bar that rested on the steel cradle holding the giant tank. With all the force I could find, I swung the bar at the pressure gauge centered on the front of the tank. It sheared off, and the pressurized anhydrous ammonia spewed out as both a gas and a liquid. It showered Harris and his crew before they could run, and they fell immediately to the ground.

As the ammonia vapor filled the SWAT vehicle, the men trapped inside struggled to crawl out and onto the ground. The gas/liquid found their eyes, noses, mouths, and lungs--anything with moisture. I hit the ground and started to crawl away from the vehicle. I yelled for help. Darrell and David jumped from the back of the van. They pulled me several yards upwind and away from the emptying tank, and we watched from a safe distance in silence at the horror the evil men were experiencing. I looked at the twins. Their faces mirrored my own shock as these gruesome deaths unfolded before our eyes. Dan and Chewy came to a sliding stop by us. They had heard the shots while they waited. Neither said a word. As did the twins, they just watched.

Harris and his men thrashed on the dirt in complete agony. Their twisted faces screamed without sound. The fertilizer burned their larynxes as the poisonous fluid rushed to their lungs. The gas and liquid blinded them. They grabbed at their throats and gasped, trying to find air. They tore at their melting eyes and blistering faces until their lungs turned to scorched liquid. In minutes they were dead. I felt nothing for them, only for their victims. More ghosts with grievances could rest now … the *Yuan Gui* had obtained its justice.

We stood there a few minutes without saying a word. The twins, along with Dan and Chewy, tried to shake off what they had just witnessed. Sadly, I knew they would never forget it; it would haunt their dreams many, many times. In order to ensure we had evidence, I had to turn to Dan. "Get some pictures." He nodded, avoiding my eyes.

Darrell and David helped me get in the old Cadillac. Chewy taped my leg with some of his infamous duct tape. The second wrap stopped the bleeding. My wound was minor but painful. I asked Chewy, "So, how does it feel to use that tape on someone that you didn't just kidnap?" He shrugged.

Darrell and David kept apologizing for not stepping in quicker. I reassured them; they had done did the right thing. "I thought I could provoke Harris into confessing, not into shooting me. You were following my orders." I paused. "Sometimes following the orders and staying with a plan is considerably tougher than just winging it. You all did great. You would have just been killed or gotten me killed if you had moved sooner."

We headed back to town. The radio was off, and everyone was staring out into the desert trying to comprehend what had just happened. The silence served as a benediction to the recent events. Stuck between the twins, I fought pain and pressure as I dug my cell phone out of my front trouser pocket. I pressed in Dallas's number. After her hello, I spoke. "He's dead. Harris and his men are dead." I struggled for a moment to get my voice back under control. "Dallas, I failed."

She demanded harshly, "What happened?"

"They're dead."

"How?"

"Let's just leave it at 'They're dead.' It was ghastly," I answered. My body shook, reliving that moment.

"Did you get a confession or anything?" she asked.

"No."

"I have been in constant contact with the sheriff. She already has enough … she thinks she has plenty. I agree. The raid is on." Dallas softened and spoke in a reassuring voice. "Don't worry."

I asked her, "Can she do me a favor? Could she hold off on the mayor for a few minutes? I want to try something."

"Sure … why?"

"Just get me a few minutes." I winced as David switched his weight and pushed down on my leg. I didn't want to tell Dallas about my latest wound.

I called His Honor. "Mr. Mayor … we need to talk."

"Who are you? Talk about what?" he answered in a suspicious voice.

"Business, counterfeit money … drug business," I replied. "Your men are all dead … Harris, too."

"I don't know what you're talking about." He sounded nervous. "I'm hanging up now."

"Hold on a minute. I think it would be in your best interest to wait." I handed my phone to Dan, and he sent pictures of Harris and his men in the dirt, their eyes burned and white foam pouring from their bright red blistered mouths. "Do I have your attention now? Harris gave you up before he died. You want to hear the recording, or should I just send it to the press?"

"What do you want?" he asked, his quivering voice giving witness that the photos had been received.

"You know what I want … the five million. Harris was too busy dying to get it sent."

"I don't have the numbers," he pleaded.

"I think you do. After all, you were there when I made the deal with Harris … I'm checking the account in four minutes." I disconnected the call. I gleaned satisfaction that he hadn't denied my accusation.

We hadn't gone much farther when we met a small fleet of fire trucks and ambulances convoying toward the old truck stop. Apparently the bodies had been discovered.

It took only three minutes for Dan to confirm the transfer of five million dollars to the numbered account. We transferred it again with the help of Dallas's computer team. I called Dallas and told her that the mayor yielded and sent the five million.

"Dallas, tell the sheriff it was only a million dollars. Your people can bury the rest."

"My God, why on earth would I do that?" My request stunned her.

I continued, "Put the rest in Sara's account. If she's alive or dead, these guys need to pay for this … not her … not her daughters … not her son. If she doesn't need it or want it, she can give it to the women we have found. That will be up to her."

"None for you?" she asked.

"None," I answered.

It took her some time to answer. "You do know this isn't going to work. You need two miracles for canonization."

"What?"

"Sainthood. Regardless of what you do, you need two miracles to become a saint."

"I'm no saint. Just an ex-sheriff turned pirate with a sense of justice. I'll talk to you later."

I wasn't sure if it was the adrenaline crash, the lack of sleep, or just the hum of the tires, but I fell into a fitful sleep. I woke as the old Caddy slid into the hospital parking lot. Darrell and Dan stood me between them and walked me into the now-familiar ER. And there she was, hands on her hips and shaking her head, the cute ER doctor. "Mr. Conner! Surprise, surprise! You're back, and this time you're shot … how wonderful. Just when I thought you must have left the state."

"Not without saying bye to my favorite doc! I thought you were on nights," I gasped, trying not to struggle as the nurse scrubbed my new wound.

"Just rotated. Mr. Conner, have you thought of doing something else for a career? You don't really seem to be good at this one."

"What? You don't think I am good at being a professional target? Sorry."

"Oh, don't be. If you stay here much longer, I'll pay off my mortgage."

As far as gunshot wounds, this one hardly rated. It took only a couple of stitches, and she was able to remove the remaining staples that were left in for my deep cut. I was disappointed. I had managed to get through the last few days with just a few minor scratches and bumps, but yet, here I was again.

The doctor kept me until late evening. When I got back to my suite, Sky Lee was there. She smiled, grabbed me in a tight hug, and whispered, "Thanks," in my ear. Her tears fell on my cheek. "They got them, Jack ... all of them ... except Chief Harris and some of his SWAT guys. They were killed in a training accident or something."

"Training accident?" I thought to myself. I wondered if that was something Wayfarer came up with or the lady sheriff ... maybe even the feds.

"How's Jay?" I asked.

"Fine. She wanted to go home, but they didn't want her to go there for now. She will be staying at that office building apartment for a while."

"Good. I think you should go stay there with her for a while ... and no customers."

The defiance in her eyes told me everything. I was in for an argument. But it would have to wait. I needed sleep.

Dallas brought newspapers and champagne for an afternoon breakfast. She had a warm smile for me, but a suspicious and curious glare for Sky Lee. Sky Lee poured coffee for the three of us.

"Let's save the champagne. I'm not done yet." I cautioned.

Dallas saw that I wasn't ready for a celebration. She nodded and took it to the refrigerator.

I took the paper and read:

> *This morning at seven o'clock, deputies from the San Bernardino Sheriff's Office, along with agents from the DEA, FBI, and Federal Marshalls executed numerous search warrants and arrest warrants on the Wayfarer Police Department and Town Council. Arrests included several Wayfarer police officers and the Wayfarer mayor.*
>
> *Wayfarer Police Chief Blaine Harris and six members of the Wayfarer SWAT team were killed in an apparent training accident. It is unknown if the two incidents are related.*

The byline featured Bill Parker's name prominently. With Dallas's help, he had been invited along on the raid and had gotten the exclusive story. We owed him at least that much.

Dallas and Sky watched me read. Another article spoke of the destruction of a suspected gang house. Two gang members had been found dead in the rubble. Cause of death had not been established yet. It had been a busy night. A depressing night. In a moment of anger, I slammed the paper down on the table. "Damn it!"

Both women jumped. "What?" asked Dallas.

"Nothing, not a thing." I buried my head in my hands. "I have nothing new on Asian … Sara."

"Don't jump out a window yet." Dallas tossed a manila envelope on the table, and it slid in front of me. Her eyes were trained on mine as I opened it. "Your girl Jay and the officer you found were golden," she said, taking a sip of coffee.

It was all there. My eyebrows rose in surprise as I read each sentence, each page. She had e-mails, records of telephone conversations implicating Harris, his police force, and the city council in the kidnapping of Asian

Sin, the murder of Rock Hard, the smuggling of the money, drugs, and human trafficking. Harris's ledger named names, with contact information.

An e-mail confirmed that Rock Hard's murder was a mistake. The men they contracted were supposed to shake him down to find the police's stolen drugs. I understood. They were the same men who had been sent to warn me without touching me. "You need to get this to Jim Collins at the LA Sheriff's Office," I said, holding up the paper.

"Already done, and he was on the raid yesterday," Dallas answered proudly. "He wants to talk to you."

"I am sure he does." I sighed. There was the issue of a destroyed building with two dead in his jurisdiction to explain. I continued reading.

They took Asian, using the 9-1-1 call just like I had suspected, and put her on the ship to Hong Kong. The ship was diverted to Bangkok without an explanation of why the ship's course was changed.

Dallas pointed out, "We were on the right track. The Sheriff's Office determined the Hong Kong Police suspected the ship of something nefarious. All the information lacked detail, but with what they learned in their investigation, it was fairly easy to piece together most of the missing information. Proving it will be different."

"So, now what?" Dallas asked.

I leaned back in my chair and took a drink of coffee. "Bangkok."

CHAPTER 23

I had seventy-two hours before my Bangkok flight left. Dallas bought me a very expensive straw hat for the trip and to wear in the land of smiles. She explained the felt hat would never survive the humidity and heat. I took her word for it.

"About Keeley," Dallas started.

I tried to shake her off, but Dallas insisted on taking the time to remind me that she saw this possibility from the beginning. "I warned you that she has a lot of deep fears in her life that she needs to address and come to terms with before she can ever commit to anyone."

Dallas never asked me about Sky Lee nor why Sky had taken up residency in my suite. I was glad that she didn't, since I might have had to explain something I didn't quite understand myself.

Fourteen hours from Los Angeles to Bangkok allowed me time to think. To think about things I wasn't ready to or even wanted to think about. I should have been happy with the success of taking down the Wayfarer Police Department, but I wasn't. It frightened me. It changed me. I found myself swearing more … a disappointment. I shook my head, considering the person I had become, a person who in a short space of time had witnessed and/or been responsible for numerous deaths and criminal acts. Before stumbling on the mystery of Asian Sin's disappearance, I had been a man of law, who followed rules with very few exceptions.

This investigation had turned me into someone else. I thought back to the night when I killed Easton—not just the actual killing, but the fact that I did it so easily. Then the other events: the kidnappings, destroying a building, stealing money. They haunted me. A person should never think of his or her past crimes, even when done for a greater good. Whose greater good? The thing that brings a person to hate another is not how they are different, but how they are alike. I looked out the small window at the blue-gray sky.

My mind turned to Xiu Tang. I suppose she was my first real love, maybe my only true love. I can't remember a day when my thoughts didn't turn to her. How do I forget? Should I forget? I don't want to forget. I guess I wanted a place to put her in my mind that wouldn't cause pain, especially now that I knew she was lost to me forever by her death. She would have never wanted that for me. I want her to live in my mind, smiling and laughing while riding horses. Teasing me about being a capitalist as we rode together, exploring the endless dry creek beds on that Colorado ranch. I stopped. I felt tears coming.

Then there were Keeley, Dallas, Sky, and of course … the enigma that is Asian Sin. It was the first time I could really think about Keeley since the day she walked out. Things were happening so fast that all I could do was push my hurt deep somewhere inside of my mind. I had a job, a job that needed to be done and done quickly, a job that might have cost me my relationship with Keeley. But for right now, I had time to assess what had gone wrong. I think I pushed too hard. She felt like I was trying to trap her. I wish I would have just kept my mouth shut. I'd been here before. I begged another girl years ago … and had lost her, too.

I looked out the window at the clouds below. I watched the different shades of gray, white, and blue. The melding water vapors created shapes of wild animals, whales, and valentines. The heart-shaped cloud stayed for a moment before dissipating into the darkening blue. I opened my Thai guidebook to distract me from the obvious similarity of my love for Keeley and the fleeting of the heart-shaped cloud.

Dallas had wanted to send me on one of her private jets, but I didn't want to spend the money nor attract the attention. I had barely won that argument, but I lost the one about going alone. I was alone on this flight, but Dallas insisted that Dan and Chewy follow me in a day or so. I wondered if she had set me up from the beginning and allowed me to win the flying arrangements so she would get her way otherwise. She's that clever.

Dallas arranged for a private detective out of her Bangkok office to assist me. I would have her office and staff in Bangkok at my disposal. It was nice to have a rich, powerful ally, even though we struggled for who was going to run this investigation.

Upon landing, I retrieved my luggage and checked through customs without an issue. Politeness and smiles with each contact made my early morning arrival pleasant. I had slept some on the airplane, but I still was exhausted. Even with my heightened enervation, my excitement continued to build. Other than a couple of cruises and Mexican border towns, I had never been out of the country. It was just the airport, but I wanted to see everything.

Dallas's firm had arranged for a car and driver. The English signage and universal picture signs made it easy to find my way around the new airport. I found my driver with little effort. He stood in a black suit and tie, holding a sign with my name neatly printed on it. He folded the paper and stuck it in an inner jacket pocket and *wai*-ed with a large smile.

I returned the *wai*. I had read in the Thai guidebook that the wai, or clasping hands together and bowing slightly, was a polite greeting. The gesture, as handshaking, was developed to show greeting parties that they were unarmed. Many social rules governed the Thais in the proper use of the wai. I wasn't sure I would remember all of them.

The heat and humidity hit me as I followed my driver to the parking lot. The heat shocked me. I knew the weather would be warm, but in the middle of the night, I thought it would be cooler. My driver spoke English.

He started a conversation with me but never allowed a pause for me to answer or reply. He continued pointing out various temples and edifices as he drove. I think I got two yeses and a no in during the thirty-minute drive.

The Royal Suralay Hotel sat on the river, majestic and decorated in splendor. Suralay is one of many Thai words used to describe heaven. I learned that from a very ornate sign in the hotel lobby. "I could get used to this lifestyle I have been living," I thought as I entered the tall, gilded doors. Most important, I was relieved to find the hotel was air-conditioned. I checked in and followed the bellhop to the elevator and to my room. My luggage was unpacked and already neatly put away before my arrival. I tipped my uniformed escort and headed for the shower.

Before I went to bed, I looked down on the river and across the illuminated city. It was huge. Not only did the city span several miles, but it climbed to the skies as well. Scattered throughout the city, tall buildings monopolized the skyline, begging me to be a tourist. Even though I was enchanted by its beauty, I would have wait … maybe another trip.

I called Dallas before going to sleep. I followed my strict instructions to report every day. After the business was taken care of, we talked for a while. I enjoyed talking with her. I felt it made me closer to Keeley. I missed them both. Boy, do I know how to screw up a normal dull life.

Early the next morning, I met my contact in the hotel dining room, where buffet breakfast was being served. He introduced himself: Narong Khuenwang. He went by Luk. Unlike Dan, with his narrow-brimmed hat and flowered cotton shirts, Luk wore a dark three-piece suit. He was older than me and just recently retired from the Royal Thai Police, with the rank of detective sergeant. He spoke English as well as French, German, and Japanese. He assured me that he could have achieved higher ranks, but he liked the street and the work. His résumé included two degrees and several medals from the police as well as the army.

I felt undereducated and embarrassed. Other than knowing a few Latin words and how to order draft beer in Mexico, I knew nothing but English. I wasn't great with that. I didn't realize until now how much I didn't know. Even Sky Lee could speak French and Chinese. I felt cheated. But I had only myself to blame. There are many times I wish I would have learned more. This was one of them. I was a good cop, a mediocre mechanic, and a fair cowboy. I was a lousy international detective.

I ate a traditional American breakfast. Luk ate some fish, rice, and vegetables in soup. He was well-informed and well-briefed. "So, you're after Zhang-Fei? A bit ambitious, don't you think?" He stirred his soup.

"I'm after the girl, the woman. I don't care about Zhang-Fei or the MSM. I just want the woman," I answered.

"If he has the woman, then you are after him. We have tried for years to get him on something, but he has power and influence," Luk replied over his spoon before he took a sip.

"Can he stop bullets?"

Luk chuckled some. "You would have better luck in assassinating your American president."

"If he hurts her … I'll find a way." My threat sounded empty to him. I saw it in his eyes.

"I wish you good luck with that."

"Did you find anything out about the woman?" I asked. "What about Zhang-Fei?" I pushed.

"No … not yet." He pushed back his empty bowl. "There's a *farang* that runs a bar in Pat Pong. Tonight we will go see him. He is supposed to have a woman working in his bar that used to work for Zhang-Fei."

My guidebook informed me that *farang* was Thai slang for foreigner. I nodded. "Do you have any idea why Zhang-Fei diverted his boat from Hong Kong to here?"

He shook his head and stood. I stood. He spoke again. "I suggest you return to your room and get some more sleep. It will be a very long night."

With the air-conditioner going full blast and the TV on, I slept deeply. Darkness covered the city when I woke. I picked up a sealed envelope on the floor at the base of the door. It had been slid under the door during my nap. It was from Luk. He would pick me up around ten that night in the lobby of the hotel, which gave me three hours. I called room service and ordered an American hamburger and French fries before showering. As I ate, I stared out at the city while listening to an American news channel on the TV. It felt odd to hear morning news this time of night.

At precisely ten o'clock, the elevator door opened into the lobby, and I saw Luk. His dress was slightly more casual than this morning. He wore a light cream-colored jacket with matching trousers. We greeted each other with the customary *wai* and with a smile. As we walked out of the hotel and into a waiting taxi, Luk explained this would be easier than trying to find a parking space.

He said something about how fortunate it was the traffic was light. I looked out at the bumper-to-bumper cars with motorcycles and scooters weaving in and out of the openings between the cars. "Light?" I commented under my breath. I wasn't in a hurry. The creeping traffic allowed me to take in the strange brightly-colored three-wheeled motorcycles. They had rounded roofs, with cloth tassels hung along the roofline. The decorated storefronts and street vendors were busy putting out plastic seats and tables for the night.

The taxi driver asked Luk something in Thai from his right-hand driver's seat. Luk answered in Thai. Turning to me, he asked, "Have you ever been to Thailand before?"

I shook my head. "Never been anywhere … really."

"Maybe you can take some time to see it … if you live," Luk said in a remorseful tone.

I swallowed hard. It was time to change the subject. "Where are we headed again?"

"Pat Pong," he answered with a slight glare at my forgetfulness as he turned to give our driver some instructions. I remembered the name from my guidebook. Pat Pong was a nighttime entertainment center. It featured everything from key chain trinkets to women to men dressed like women. Market stalls filled the center of the alley, and nightclubs and bars lined the sides. The second floors had sex shows and brothels disguised as massage parlors. Adventurous pilgrims flocked here from around the world to become patrons of the shops and to visit the debauchery they wouldn't be caught dead in at their home cities.

Luk dismissed the driver with some money, and we took off on foot. He weaved in and out of the tourists thickly scattered along the market. We ignored and avoided eye contact with the hawkers trying to engage us in some transaction. "We are going to the Drunken Wallaby," Luk yelled over his shoulder. The noise roared. The sounds of the traffic blended with the bar music spilling out on the street. He cut through the crowd like a snowplow in a blizzard. "It is owned by an Australian."

I thought of a host of sarcastic remarks on the obvious correlation, but I remained politely silent. We covered about a third of a block. I was soaked in sweat, and my clothes stuck to me like glued wallpaper. I began to understand the practicality of wearing shorts, which in my case would never happen. Following Luk through two large glass-paned wooden doors, I welcomed the cool air and took in a deep breath. We sat at the bar.

A Thai woman, about forty, spoke to us. "What will you have, mates?" Her heavy Australian accent surprised me. A bright smile accompanied her question.

I looked around at the Australian memorabilia scattered on every flat surface and wall. A stuffed kangaroo stared at me from the whiskey bottles behind the bar. "Draft beer, if you please."

"A Yank, huh?" She smiled. "Well, welcome to Thailand."

"Thank you. Forgive me, but you don't sound Thai." Her dark face and Asian eyes smiled back at me.

"That's because she was raised in Australia." A large muscular man in a khaki shirt, neatly rolled and buttoned, and a matching bush hat spoke as he wrapped his large arms around her.

A tattoo of a crown centered in front of a rising sun flexed with his right bicep. Etched on a ribbon at the base of the crown were the words "Australian Commonwealth Military." She laughed as she escaped his grip. I looked up at a British .303 Lee Enfield that hung above the shelves of bottled alcohol, its bayonet fixed. A bandolier of .303 cartridges swung from the stock to the barrel. A bush hat with an ostrich plume hung under it.

"You're Australian Light Horse," I said.

He studied me a moment and looked over at Luk. The woman served me my beer and Luk his water. "Sergeant Major, 4th/19th Prince of Wales's Light Horse … Most Aussies that come in here don't know that." He became suspicious. "You a Vietnam vet, Yank?"

I shook my head. "Too young. I was never in the military."

"CIA?"

I laughed. "No, a retired sheriff's deputy, a detective."

"Sheriff, huh?" He was still guarded. His forehead wrinkled some with a slight frown. "How did you know?"

"The tattoo." I pointed over the bar. "The carbine … the hat with the ostrich plume … light horse."

He thought over my answer. He smiled. "Where you from, mate?"

"Colorado," I replied.

"I figured Texas with the hat."

"No … I've been there, but no, born and raised Coloradan." I took a sip of the beer.

He turned toward Luk. "What can I do for you, gentlemen?"

"I'm looking for a girl." I spoke before Luk had a chance to speak.

"A shy early, but they'll be about." He pointed at a couple of bar girls, wearing very short skirts, that found seats at the end of the bar. They joined the Aussie Thai woman in sharing a dish of shredded papaya covered in sugar and Thai chilies.

It took me a moment to understand. "No … no … not a *girl* … well, yes, a girl … what I'm trying to say is a kidnapped victim … a woman. She was taken from her home in California, and we think she ended up here aboard an old tramp steamer."

"You have an idea who absconded with her?"

"A hood that calls himself Zhang-Fei," I answered with another sip.

The Aussie looked over at Luk again. His face turned sour and reserved. He slowly wiped with the ragged towel. "A real shonky … not worth a zack." I didn't understand the Australian colloquialism. He saw it on my confused face. "Very bad man, mate." He shook his head slowly. "His gang, the MSM, owns interests in some bars here. Most people in the know stay the hell away." I nodded.

"I was informed that you have a woman working here that used to work for Zhang-Fei," Luk explained.

"You're talking about Nat."

"Yes, I believe that was the name. Do you know her?" Luk asked.

"She married a rich bloke from Sydney. He passed a few years ago. She doesn't work here. She just comes in here from time to time for something to do … to reminisce."

"Do you know how to get hold of her?" I asked.

He yelled over to the Aussie Thai woman, "Joy, do you know how to get hold of Nat?"

She shook her head.

"Does she speak English?" I took a big drink. The Aussie poured himself a drink … Irish whiskey, the same as Joshua drank.

"Sure, broken up a bit, but she does all right." He downed the shot. He put out his hand. "Mark Wallace." He wrapped his arm around the Aussie-speaking Thai woman again as she rejoined us. "This is my wife, Joy."

"Pleasure." I addressed her as I shook his hand. "Jack Conner."

"Irish, aye?" Wallace poured himself another and one for me. "To the Irish."

I raised the shot glass. "To the regiment."

"You're a good bloke. 'Tis a shame you're gonna get yourself kilt." He swallowed the shot.

My new friend grabbed up the bottle and a couple of clean glasses and pointed toward a table. I gladly made the move. I had grown tired of the stuffed marsupial watching my every move.

I sat in the corner. Luk sat to my right and Wallace to my left. We shared another toast. Before the night was over, we'd toasted everything from the invention of rolled toilet paper to the Magna Carta and everybody from the Queen of England to Richard Petty. Luk moved from water to pineapple juice with ice. I learned that Wallace and Joy married twenty-some years ago and had two sons, both in the military.

Both Wallace and Joy spoke Thai. Joy also spoke French, another "make me feel inferior moment." It was a slow night for the bar. The few customers left around midnight, and we were the only ones still seated. Joy took the last seat at our table. With a glare of disapproval, she looked at the empty bottle of whiskey that sat beside the one we just opened. We talked until dawn. Finally, Luk suggested that we try again tonight. I looked down at my watch. With a thirteen-hour time difference and a half bottle of Irish whiskey, I had no idea what time it was or what day it was.

Luk found a taxi. He wasn't happy that I was intoxicated. He reminded me that my friends were arriving sometime today. In a very serious Asian way, he chastised me. Because of my irresponsible actions, he would have to go to the airport and meet the arrivals. I thanked him.

Since Luk was upset and didn't want to engage in a conversation with a drunk American, I spent the short drive watching the street merchants cleaning their spots. Morning vendors replaced the prepared food stands with their woven baskets filled with fresh vegetables and fish containers of various shapes and sizes. I invited Luk in for breakfast, but he declined without looking at me. He told me he would return tonight … happier, I hoped.

CHAPTER 24

After I had slept the sleep of a drunk, I met with Dan and Chewy for dinner. They were both tired from the flight. I learned that Dan could speak Thai when he engaged in a short conversation with the waiter. I just stared at him with some envy.

"Why don't you guys get some more rest, since I know you are jet-lagged," I suggested. "But we should probably try to stay on the same sleep schedule since we will be working in the night here."

They agreed and took their leave to go to their rooms. "We will start tonight searching the river for Zhang-Fei's ship," Dan said as he exited.

I felt guilty and yet envious at the same time. Even though they might be slowly cooking in the evening heat, I pictured Dan and Chewy walking along the riverbank or navigating the river in some open-water taxi, taking in the sights and sounds of Bangkok. Meanwhile, Luk and I would be stuck inside the Drunken Wallaby. Of course, we would be enjoying its cool sanctuary, sitting at a table drinking cold beer and pineapple juice.

That evening, Luk's cold shoulder was colder than the air-conditioning when he picked me up for our return trip to the Wallaby. I was glad when both Mark Wallace and Joy invited themselves to sit with us, occasionally bouncing up to the bar to serve the random customer. Their customers were mostly disrespectful young Americans and Aussies that stopped for a quick drink and to check out the Drunken Wallaby's offering of bar girls.

Wallace and Joy allowed bar girls, but refused to collect bar fines and discouraged them from doing business in the bar. They thought of their bar as more of an escape and a place to relax—for girl and man alike. But the girls were warmly welcomed, and conversation was encouraged. If an occasional transaction occurred, it was overlooked.

"Most of these blokes travel to the kingdom in search of something, whether it's spiritual, love, or just getting high … looking for real answers to imaginary problems," Wallace explained. "Most of the time, they discover the problems they left, the problems they try to escape from, are themselves. They go home more discouraged than when they came; they return to their homes emptier and lonelier." We all sat there in silence after his malediction, contemplating those lost souls that Siam stole.

Wallace switched to telling war stories in an attempt to change the depressed mood that he had created. I only half listened. I wondered if I was one of those blokes, searching for answers to my own problems, real or imaginary. Was Asian Sin only an excuse to find myself … examine my own shortcomings? I rationalized that I hadn't chosen Thailand. Zhang-Fei had made the choice for me.

Suddenly the atmosphere changed for me. Nat entered the bar around eleven. She was a small, attractive woman. Her black hair was cut short and just off the collar of her bright orange shirt. From a distance, she looked to be around thirty. Closer, the lines that gathered in the corners of her eyes and around her mouth betrayed her. She was well over fifty. Wallace met her at the door and brought her to our table. He introduced us and then said, "They want to know about Zhang-Fei." Her eyes flashed, and she turned to walk away.

I spoke. "Please, wait. This is a matter of life and death."

She stopped and turned back. "Zhang-Fei only death … no life."

"Please."

She looked deep in my eyes. "What you need to know?"

"I'm looking for a woman," I said slowly, imploringly.

Before I could say more, she interrupted, "Look like many here." She looked around the bar and out on the street. Her well-trimmed and painted fingernails snapped open her purse. She dug deep into the handbag. A gold-clad cigarette box emerged in her fingertips. She opened it and pulled out an American cigarette. She offered everyone at the table one. All of us declined. She drew flame in the white tube from a gold lighter and then turned to blow a puff of smoke away from us.

Just as the night before, I explained I was not interested in a commercial girlfriend. Then I explained the situation with the kidnapping. Evidently, I needed to improve my word choice. Thailand was a world of literal assumptions.

She pondered a moment before she answered, "I very young when I know Zhang-Fei. Before I go to America. He very bad man."

It surprised me that she had been to America. I asked her about it. She had entered the United States illegally and worked in several massage parlors and escort services in several different states. After ten or eleven years, she returned to Southeast Asia, spending time in Hong Kong, Singapore, and Manila. She had earned enough money to buy a small farm for her widowed mother and a nice eight-unit apartment house for herself upon returning to Thailand.

She continued to support her family by working the bars in Bangkok. "I meet nice man here, and he marry me. We go live in Australia. We have two children. Then he die." Nat's eyes teared just a bit.

Wallace told us that both of the children were still in Australia. "Her husband left her with a sizable estate, which the kids manage for her."

"Nat, who kidnapped you and took you to America?" I asked gently.

She looked confused. "I not taken. I want to go to United States. I told if police got me, to tell police I trafficked. They take better care of you. They believe I trafficked. They want to believe I trafficked. They tell me they sorry and feed me. They give me visa to stay. Sometimes police don't believe I trafficked and fine me … make me pay money."

"Didn't you have a handler or pimp?" I prompted her.

"No, only pimp was US police. They take you to jail and make you give them money. I work harder to pay police and court … no good. Government worse than pimp."

Her analysis had merit, I admitted. "So, what about Zhang-Fei?"

"I know him long time ago. Not seen for many years. I know bar girls that work for Zhang-Fei now. He have bar here. I go to them … ask for you."

"Tell me or show me the bar and let me go ask," I replied.

Nat scolded me. "No, bad idea. He kill you, and maybe girl. I go." She repeated, "He very bad man. He poison."

"What about you?" I questioned. "I don't want you hurt or killed."

"Not worry. He not hurt me. He not dare to touch me." Nat blew a large puff of smoke. "Come back here tomorrow night after errevan." She got up to leave. All the males stood on my lead. With a *wai*, she left.

"Luk, can you have someone follow her? I don't want her hurt."

Luk reached in his jacket and made a call, after which he excused himself. "I will follow her myself until someone can replace me. See you tomorrow evening. Just meet me here." He nodded as he left.

"Don't worry about Nat. The streets of Bangkok raised her. She's tough and knows how to survive," Wallace interjected.

"She can be trusted, right?" I asked.

"Don't worry, mate. Her contempt and hate for that bastard is beyond anything you could imagine."

"Try me."

"All I know is what I heard. It was a long time ago. Zhang-Fei suspected one of his bar girls was stealing from him. He tied her to a doorway and skinned her alive in front of the other girls."

My blood ran cold, and I shivered taking in the horror. "You were right. I couldn't imagine that." I gulped my beer and ordered two more.

"The girl was Nat's sister. Hate—you have it. Trust—you have it."

I understood. We drank a few more beers, along with some scotch. I needed to drown Wallace's story out of my mind. It wasn't until I was almost to the point of passing out that I found a taxi and headed for the hotel. After Wallace's horrific revelation, I suddenly realized the caliber of the monster we were dealing with. I needed to pull myself together before meeting with Dan and Chewy.

When we finally met, it was in the dimly lit dining room the next morning. It wasn't quite six. A waitress served Dan and Chewy some tea and me some coffee as we talked and waited for breakfast. We were early; the cooks and other servers were still busy preparing for the breakfast crowd.

Dan and Chewy thought they might have found the ship. She lay about two miles downriver from the hotel and was tied off to another ship, moored to a rotting wood and bamboo dock. It was being repainted and undergoing some maintenance. Armed guards stood watch from the street, the dock, and both ships. Barbed wire and sharp pieces of steel covered the derelict ship closest to the bank, serving as a barrier and protection to whatever ship Zhang-Fei and his MSM tied to the derelict.

Attempting to board the *Yuan Liang* from the dock or from the river would result in a disaster. I really wasn't ready to start a shoot-out in another country, especially a country that fed their pretrial arrestees cockroaches and maybe some rice. That is, unless they decided to feed the pretrial arrestees to the crocodiles in the river.

Since we had never actually seen or known the ship, it was only a speculation that this ship was the *Yuan Liang*. She had no flag astern, and her markings were erased by grinders and new paint. We would have to inquire with at least three countries for any registration information and a ship description. That could take weeks. We also didn't know the most important thing: if Asian Sin was aboard.

We planned our next moves over the buffet breakfast. I would contact Luk and see if he could find out anything with his police sources about our mystery ship, and see what Nat was able to turn up. Dan and Chewy would go back down to the dock and work on contacting some sailors and dockworkers.

The pair finished their breakfast of fish, rice, and vegetables and headed upstairs to their rooms. I stayed at the table for another cup of coffee, trying to resist going to the twenty-four-hour convenience store and buying some cigars. I tipped the waitress, signed the tickets, and headed for my room.

I stepped into the elevator, and two well-dressed Asian men followed me. They flanked me on both sides. I really didn't think anything about them until I reached for the floor buttons with my right hand. The man on my right grabbed my wrist. The other shoved a gun in my left side. "Damn," I thought. "I didn't see that coming."

The guy on my right stuck an elevator key in the button board and twisted. We were heading for the penthouse. They weren't there to shoot me, or at least I didn't think so; however, the idea that they might be taking me to the roof to push me off did cross my mind. I thought of several clever remarks but remained silent. What would it accomplish? My callous escorts remained facing forward. Each of them kept the muzzles of their handguns dug into my sides to keep my attention.

Anticipation, apprehension, and some excitement built inside me during the short vertical ride. Maybe this was it. Maybe I was going to meet with the infamous Zhang-Fei. The large men marched me to the door of the penthouse. I thought of starting a marching cadence, but quickly relinquished that idea. Getting thrown off the roof was still in the front of my mind.

The giant to my right opened the door and entered in front of me. The one to my left went to my back as I stepped into the large living room. Once we were all inside, they flanked me once again. The room opened into a large garden and a private swimming pool. They directed me along a serpentine stone walkway past an artificial waterfall. It fed an illuminated pond. Footlong goldfish darted to the edge, expecting us to feed them as we passed. Large lily pads floated in the center of the blue-tinted water.

A short, stout man in a dark suit stood with his back to us. Gray streaked his meticulously groomed short black hair. He leaned on a stone fence looking out into the vastness of Bangkok. Additional armed men stood at his side. The sun was just above the horizon. I said nothing. I waited for the man to speak.

"Mr. Conner, with all the resources in the world at my fingertips, what makes you think you can find Sara Jones, when I can't … such arrogance." He spoke with little accent.

His question set me back. I thought a moment. If he wasn't Zhang-Fei, he must be the Korean, Keeley's natural father. I searched for words. The only sounds were from the falling water. I finally spoke. "It's not arrogance if I can back it up." I tried to make a step forward of my astute guards. They stopped my progress when they each placed an arm in front of me. I yielded.

"Mr. Conner, I am not in the mood for your pompous pretenses." His tone was harsh, but quietly spoken. "Mr. Conner, do you understand?"

"Sir, forgive me for my remarks." I tilted my head at his forbidding back. "You're hunting for Sara?"

"Yes."

"Again, forgive me; I thought you were Zhang-Fei." I stumbled with my words.

"Zhang-Fei is a pimp. Nothing more than a malicious pimp." His eyes filled with disdain. "I build factories and provide jobs. I pay respectable and fair wages. Zhang-Fei sells poison and steals women off the streets. Then he castigates the ideals of capitalism and free markets."

"So I heard."

"It's a façade." He continued staring out at the gigantic city before him. "His discourse keeps certain government officials in some countries from bothering him."

I paused a moment and then went on with a question: "Forgive me, but were you in LA a few weeks ago?" I couldn't say much more without selling out Sky Lee and the telephone conversation she overheard.

He turned around, looking puzzled. "No, I haven't been to the US in over a year. I would have to check my calendar to see when I was there last."

"Well, sir, someone has been using your name and implicating you in all sorts of things."

"That doesn't surprise me, and you already know who it was."

"Zhang-Fei," I said, not knowing myself if I were asking a question or making a statement. He nodded, looking back out at the city. I continued, "If you're not in with Zhang-Fei, then why the interest?"

He turned, and with a wave, he dismissed his guards. He waited until his men left the garden before he spoke. "Mr. Conner, I am an old man, and I have been very fortunate. I have twelve children by six different women, half of them with my current wives."

I didn't ask for him to expound on the word wives. "Okay …" I leaned back on the stone fence. I considered saying something about Dallas and Keeley but didn't. He already knew.

"Twelve children, but only one boy." He looked down at the stone walk as he spoke. "One son … my son to carry on my lineage, to carry on my work … my business."

"Aw, fuck," I said under my breath. I turned to him. "Asian Sin's … Sara Jones's son is your son."

"Yes."

Anger grew inside me. "He is more than just a son. You've learned of her heritage. Her son, your son … the emperor of China. This is more than your lineage … your business. It's about you. Your son … emperor. You first found Dallas and charmed her, a great niece, but then you learned of Sara, the emperor's granddaughter. You couldn't pass up the real deal. You just had to go for it. That's why she was gone for two years. She was with you. God damn! And you call me arrogant!"

"Mr. Conner, you don't understand. You don't understand the old ways … the history." His voice pleaded, but there was an underlying danger to his tone.

"I understand breeding stock. That's all she was to you. Imagine a Korean fathering the next emperor of China. Something you can take to the grave. Your last great conquest … the heir apparent. You need her in order to find the boy. That's your interest in her."

"Will you help me?"

"Go to hell," I snapped in contempt. "This whole thing is a battle between you and Zhang-Fei. He took her to get to you. God damn both of you."

I hit a nerve. I saw the pain in his eyes. Yes, he was an arrogant industrialist, a ruthless businessman, a pure son of a bitch, but at this moment, he was a vulnerable old man. My tough act folded, and I lowered my guilt-filled voice. "Look, when I find her—and I will find her—I will tell her about your desire to meet your son. Then it will be up to her and her son."

"You know, Mr. Conner"—his tired eyes surrounded by wrinkles looked through me—"if Zhang-Fei learns where the boy is … they are both dead."

I nodded. "Well, I will do my best to keep that from happening."

"You know, you are wrong. In my own way, I care deeply for Sara … Dallas, too. Please let me know if I can help."

I nodded again. I wasn't sure of his altruism.

"Thank you, Mr. Conner. I was told you were an honorable man. Thank you." His smile was gentle and real.

"You know, I know people, powerful people, who are afraid to speak your name. Why? You are just a man." I sighed. "I don't understand." I walked out of the garden and to the elevator, trying to make a dramatic exit. The elevator door opened and then closed behind me as I stepped in, only to remember … I needed a key.

The door reopened. He was standing with the key hanging from his finger. He didn't even try to hide his smirk. I returned a sheepish smile and bowed. He placed the key in my palm. He turned to walk away. "Sir," I conceded. Maybe it was because of his age or who he was or had been—I don't know. I bowed again. "It was an honor to meet you." He returned a slight bow and smile.

Later that day, Mark Wallace called and invited me to an Australian steak house. "You know, mate, American beef is shoe leather compared to Aussie premium beef!"

I agreed to the invitation. "But you do remember that at one time, I raised American shoe leather." Wallace laughed as he offered to come get me, but I told him I would just catch a cab.

A lesson learned. Just because your driver tells you he can speak English, it doesn't mean he really knows how to speak English. That doesn't mean he is lying either. What it means is that he knows how to say, "Yes, I speak English." After several miles and just short of an hour, I finally realized he had no clue where we were. I told him to stop. With a large thanks and a nod, I gave him a tip with the metered fee. He really had tried.

The next driver I found knew the place and took me right there. The short trip gave me the time to evaluate an important point. The miscommunication with the taxi driver drove the point home. I wasn't Asian. I didn't understand any of their cultures, cultures that can differ within a single province, let alone differ between countries.

But at least I now knew how much I didn't know. Before Xiu Tang, my only exposure to anything from the East was Godzilla and Mothra movies. We learned very little in school about the East, not that I would have taken the time to study anyway. I didn't know until now that even within the United States, these communities existed. They held their traditions, along with their superstitions, close, while embracing everything America offered—good and bad.

Mark Wallace was a nice guy. He went to war as a kid and never really left Southeast Asia. Oh, sure, he returned to Australia. He raised his children there, but his heart could never leave Southeast Asia. He told me it was the only place he could find peace. I understood a magic draw to this place, but that was all. There was no peace for me here.

I don't know if it was because it had been weeks since I had a steak or what, but it was a great steak. A short stab of pain hit me when I remembered that the last steak I had was when Keeley came back to me.

Wallace saw me fading to another place in my mind and intervened. "Jack, you're in for a fight … I wanted to tell you, without Joy around, that I'm up for it."

"Mark, I can't ask you, and I can't let you come along. You've done your duty. This is my fight; I couldn't face your wife if something happened."

His face dropped. "You know, there are worse things than death … like not stepping up when there's a good fight to be had."

I nodded. I understood. "Okay, you're in, but if you get yourself killed, you will have to explain it to Joy! Seriously, I'm not sure how much damn peace you can find with bullets flying around your head."

His smile went ear to ear. His massive hand took a glass up for a toast. "To the fight."

"To the regiment."

Later that night, Nat was prompt to the minute. She walked into Wallace's bar and took the same seat as the previous night. She lit the cigarette that hung from the corner of her mouth, and we all took our same seats at the table.

Nat had found out plenty. A bar girl took her to a Hong Kong sailor that had just come off the *Yuan Liang*. He told Nat that they had sailed from California and were supposed to answer a call at their home port, Hong Kong. Something went wrong. They got new orders and docked here.

"They have girl, woman. He saw her," Nat related. "He say ship had security *mock-mock* than before. The captain, he move his bed to keep captive."

"*Mock-mock?*" I questioned.

"More, a lot. The ship had more security," Wallace explained.

The captain's quarters. I thought about my scenario of her being tied somewhere deep in the bowels of the ship, baking in the heat and kicking off flesh-eating rats. I had to work on my scenarios and stereotypes. The sailor told Nat that there were always armed guards at the captain's door.

Nat continued to give her report in Thai to Wallace, who translated for me. One day the sailor was ordered to take food to the room. Because the guards weren't there, he just went in where he saw the woman. He was almost thrown overboard when the guards returned and found him. Even though he wasn't shipping out with them again, he was still afraid. They moved the girl off the ship in a speedboat just outside territorial waters just before they docked—a pattern that was apparently well-established, a technique they must have used around the world. The sailor didn't know where they took her.

Before going up the river into Bangkok, they were ordered to strip the name off the ship. The captain took the log with him when he disembarked. Nat added one more thing: the ship was getting ready to get underway … going back to Hong Kong.

"I work *mock-mock,*" she said as she stood to leave. "It be more easy if no put people to watch me." Wallace laughed, with a sly look at me.

I could tell Luk wanted to talk, but was reluctant to speak with Wallace at the table. "It's okay, Luk. Wallace has volunteered to help and is now part of our team."

With a look of misgiving at Wallace, Luk informed us that Nat's information was correct. The ship was indeed the *Yuan Liang* and was getting ready to embark. Luk added some somber insight. "We are making some people nervous in the police department with these inquires."

I sat back in my chair. "Will you be able to run interference with the locals?" I asked with caution. I understood that Zhang-Fei was a powerful man and had friends in governments all over the world. Hell, he owned a whole police department in California and a city council. "Is there someone in the police department that you could confide in … trust?"

"I will do what I can, but you understand I must proceed with caution. This could put my family in jeopardy as well." Luk excused himself. I got the feeling he didn't like me. He was a reserved man and a devout Buddhist. He didn't drink or smoke. Also, I think he resented the exploitation of his country. I could hardly blame him. From my little time here and from what I had seen, I had some resentment myself.

I spent the rest of the night with Wallace and his wife. We restricted ourselves to a couple of tall beers. This was carefully monitored by Joy. They showed me their photo albums. I heard stories of Australia, their children, and the life they made for themselves here. I surprised myself. I really listened and enjoyed the evening. Maybe I was growing up, after all.

Chapter 25

The morning meeting with Dan and Chewy went well, but nothing remarkable had turned up. I guess I was always a bit relieved that Chewy hadn't stolen anyone off the streets yet, but it had only been a couple days. It bothered me, and I reminded him several times during the course of meetings that there would be no more kidnappings, especially not in this country.

Dan gave a report concerning the ship's status. She stood tall in the water, which meant very little to me. I know very little about boats or ships, but I was sure a ninety-pound porn star would not change the waterline on a four-hundred-foot ship that could displace ten thousand tons. The nefarious crew would load the ship somewhere out of territorial waters if they had any illegal cargo. Before we left, I asked Dan if he could find the captain. He might be privy to the location of Asian Sin. He thought it would be a waste of time but reluctantly agreed.

Luk called early, wanting to meet with Dan, Chewy, and me before we headed out for the evening. He asked to meet in my room. I tried to find out why, but he insisted on telling me in my room. It was after eight when he arrived. He carried two large briefcases. I knew then. It was our guns. Dallas's Bangkok branch finally pushed through the Thai bureaucracy and got us our permits and weapons.

"You will still be accountable. You must use the guns only for self-defense," he warned us sternly. Luk was hesitant in handing over the weapons to us, but he put the cases on the bed and opened them, displaying a variety of handguns. "The government scrutinizes the use of guns very seriously."

I would agree if one of the parties were Thai, but I doubt they would have the same concern about foreigners shooting each other. I know I gave up on drug-dealing Mexican nationals killing each other after a couple of cases. It took me some time of really trying to solve a couple of these cases before I learned that not even the victims' families would help.

Luk gave us our permits written in both English and Thai. I selected a pair of 9mm semiautos. They were variants of the Colt 1911. I worked the actions, safeties, and triggers on both guns. They worked well. Dan and Chewy did the same with the guns they selected. I know Dan was disappointed there were no calibers above a .38 Special. He ignored my grin and selected a holster. I selected shoulder holsters that made the guns point down. It took me some time to get them adjusted. They were actually made for a smaller person. We thanked Luk, and Dan and Chewy left.

After Dan closed the door behind him, I turned to Luk. "I want you to go home. I'll meet Nat alone."

"I will go with you," Luk insisted.

"I know you are very worried about your family. I don't blame you. Look, we will go home after this is done. You will still be here. I don't want you to live in danger." I was trying to insulate him.

He seemed rather insulted by my comment. "I want to go. What is the difference between me and the Australian?"

His question hit home. "I'm sorry. I didn't even think of that. I was just worried about you, I guess." Okay, I hated myself now. Luc saw I was embarrassed and aggravated at myself. I then answered with some justification, "Wallace can send his wife to Australia, and his children don't live here."

"You don't think Zhang-Fei can reach him there?"

I had nothing. Luk saw my expression.

"I should thank you for your concerns." He attempted to allow me to save face. It cheered me up some. He spoke again. "If anytime I think things are too much, I will leave."

Nat was early. She had learned that Asian Sin was in Chinatown, along with Zhang-Fei, but they weren't together. She didn't know where either of them was. She explained that Zhang-Fei liked bar girls. Sometimes he called for four or five of them at a time. He never took them to the hotel where he was staying. He went to another hotel. Her expression filled with sorrow. She told us that Zhang-Fei was very cruel. It was a very painful visit for the girls. Sometimes they died.

I felt my anger boil. Maybe finding Asian Sin wasn't going to be enough. Wallace knew what I was thinking. "Settle down, mate. Remember this is the East. Things are different here."

"It shocks me you'd say that!" I snapped.

"Just trying to keep you alive." Wallace shrugged.

I smiled. He meant nothing by his remark. He was trying to keep me from doing something stupid. "I know things are different here, but maybe I can change this one thing this one time."

Chinatown was one of the oldest parts of Bangkok. It was a combination of new and old. It started with Chinese sea merchants and the hauling of goods by junks up the river. The crowded streets and intense heat gave me a feeling of claustrophobia. The fast pace added to my sensation of being trapped.

Luk, Wallace, and I worked up one street, while Chewy and Dan took another. We stopped at every food vendor and night merchant. By sunup we were beat and ready for bed. I was so discouraged. This was hunting for the proverbial needle. I needed a break.

Late the next afternoon, Luk called. His call brought more bad news. The *Yuan Liang* had shoved off this morning, heading for open waters. She left under a new name, registry, and captain.

"What about Asian? Is she on the ship?" I asked.

Luk answered, "I don't know—probably."

I jumped out of bed. I thought fast as I cleaned up, but I had no idea what to do. One thing I knew: I needed a boat. I called Wallace and shared the news. He had an idea. He told me to round up my crew and met him out front within the hour. I made the calls.

I called Luk back and gave him the option of staying or going with us. "Regardless, I am going after the *Yuan Liang*."

"I am going with you," he replied firmly.

I was ready in a few minutes. I opened the door only to run face-to-face into William Parker, who was about to knock on my door. "Bill, what the hell?"

"I hadn't heard from you for a while, so I thought I'd better come find out what's happening for myself."

"Look, I don't have time to explain right now. I've got to go. What room are you in? I'll get back with you." I stepped past him.

He picked up his camera bag and followed. "You're not going without me."

I stopped and turned. "Damn it, Bill! I don't have time for this."

"If I have to use a cab or bicycle, I'm going. I am either following or coming with you. You choose."

My mind raced. "All right! I don't have time to argue, but if you get yourself killed, don't blame me."

The rest of the crew was already on the street and waiting in the back of an old pickup when we got there. Joy was at the wheel. Wallace yelled for me to jump in, and I did, dragging along William Parker.

"Who is this, mate? Is he with you, or just trying to catch a ride?"

"I'll explain on the way. It is a long and convoluted story. Let's go!" I was still trying to find a place to sit when Wallace gave the order to Joy to go. She hit the accelerator, and I was flung to the back. I fell over Parker,

Luk, and Chewy on my way to losing my hat and hitting the tailgate with my head. Dan avoided being hit by bringing his knees up to his face. He started to laugh as he handed me my hat. The pickup screamed along the busy streets. As Joy darted around cars, motorcycles, and people, I crawled to the front and tapped on the glass.

"Where are we heading?" I yelled at Wallace.

He yelled back, "Rayong! Just south of Pattaya. Don't worry; just sit back and relax."

"What the hell is a Rayong? What the hell is a Pattaya?" I asked no one in particular as I turned over into a sitting position.

Luk explained, "They are both beach resorts, about three hours to the south by southeast from Bangkok."

I thought Dan was a terrifying driver, but Joy was far worse. The only redeeming thing about the ride was I was facing backward. I would never see it coming.

I must have been the only coward. Everyone else was talking over the squealing tires and honking horns. Parker introduced himself to Luk. He knew everyone else in the bed of the truck. I had no idea what Wallace had on his mind. I was along for the ride. I explored every option I could think of, and every option was the same. I was going to attempt boarding a vessel guarded by ten or fifteen men with automatic weapons. I had six men with a few handguns and one Lee Enfield—and no boat.

Joy made the three-hour trip in about two and a half hours. If she hadn't had to stop for tolls, I imagined she would have cut another fifteen minutes off her time. We rushed through the town, headed toward the water, and drove onto a pier. On the right side of the pickup was an old rusting boat about a hundred feet long and about twenty-five feet at the beam. She had been converted into a ferry. The old boat had a covered deck and could haul people, cars, or freight as the need dictated. An older Caucasian man stood on the top deck just in front of the wheelhouse. He held a pipe in his right hand and wore an old captain's cap. His clothes were ragged and dirty. His smile displayed only a few mismatched teeth. He was truly the last of a dying breed, the barefoot sailor.

Wallace jumped out. He walked around to the right side of the pickup and waved. The old man waved back. Wallace and Joy hugged and kissed as the rest of us piled out of the pickup bed. We had barely cleared the tailgate when she returned to the driver's seat, started the diesel pickup with a puff of black smoke, and squealed off.

Wallace spoke with a giant smile. "Gentlemen, this is Chester Blake … Captain Blake. He's one of you guys … a Yank. He's been sailing these waters since the war. He used to smuggle weapons in to the South Vietnamese for the Americans."

"Hello, gents." His voice was as ragged as his bell-bottom trousers. He tipped his hat. "Please get on board."

I followed Wallace onto the old boat. The deck creaked under our feet. "Are you sure of this?" I asked, lowering my voice so as not to insult our new captain.

"Sure; we'll be fine," Wallace bellowed. I saw the other three whispering to each other as they made their way on the lower deck. Parker followed, snapping pictures along the way and probably planning his next big headline.

"Will this thing go? Float?" I inquired in an unsure voice.

"She'll do twenty-four knots as sure as you're born," Chester bragged. He turned to his four crewmen and shouted an order in Thai. Three of them jumped to the pier and untied the boat. The fourth disappeared down some dark, oil-stained stairs to the engine room. Chester climbed up the stairs to the wheelhouse. The old two-stroke Detroit diesels whined to life with clouds of gray smoke. Captain Blake throttled them up, and we slowly pulled away from the dock. We were underway.

I walked forward on the rotting-wood planked deck. I tested the handrail for strength by pushing against it. It seemed solid enough. Gaining a little more confidence, I leaned forward on the rail. I let the mist kicked up by the forward keel wash the dried sweat off my face.

The water looked like ebony marble, with small waves of white. At least it would be smooth; I wasn't sure if the old boat would hold up even in light chop. "Okay," I thought, "I am here. Now what the hell am I going to do?"

As we headed south by southwest, I stood alone at the bow, trying to get my mind to concentrate on a plan. Dan, Chewy, and one of the sailors were cooking some food on the lower deck. With the smell of sweet and bitter curry, it had to be Thai.

Wallace joined me on the rail. "If she's heading to Hong Kong, we should intercept her in a few hours."

"Then what?" I asked, never moving. "I hope you have a plan, because I sure as hell don't."

"We'll follow her until dark, and then make our move," he answered.

"What move?"

"Chester tells me he can stop the *Yuan Liang*," Wallace answered with a little less than full confidence.

"Did I mention I haven't a clue how to swim?" I said, looking over the black expanse. A broad, ragged, burning reflection stretched across the water as the sun got lower on the horizon.

"Well, then, don't fall in, mate."

"Thanks."

Parker joined us and pulled a bottle of whiskey out of his camera bag. He took a drink and passed it. Wallace took a drink. I declined. I turned and leaned against the rail. "Wallace, meet Mr. Bill Parker, news reporter extraordinaire. Bill, you might wish you'd followed my advice and stayed in Bangkok. Your life expectancy would be longer."

"Maybe, but what a story—thanks, Jack … thank you a lot." Parker took another drink. "Glad to meet you, Wallace. We have some catching up to do, I have a feeling."

"What the hell for?" I grumbled.

"I'm a real journalist … a reporter with a real story. Got to have background on this story."

I shrugged. I didn't understand. He might rethink his position if we sink in the South China Sea. Wallace toasted Parker with Parker's bottle. He understood … or just wanted to drink. Wallace and Parker talked. I slid down to sit. I twisted away from them and let my legs hang over the deck and swing. I stared off at the water. There was a cool breeze coming off the sea. I think it was the first time I felt cool in the outdoors since I arrived here.

I hated this. I had no plan … no idea. My fate had been handed over to an old man, who was probably crazy, and we were going to attack a ship nine or ten times our size and maybe twenty times our weight. But even with all that, I had a hunch. Asian Sin was on that ship. I just knew it. Soon, it would all be over.

Dan appeared beside me with some stew … American beef stew. I smiled at him. "How?"

Dan returned the smile. "A can in the galley. I thought you might like a taste of home."

"Thanks."

Chewy and Luk brought up food for Parker and Wallace. They made a half circle, the four sailors joining them. They talked as they ate. I ate outside their circle. Wallace looked over at me with a warm expression. He nodded. He understood. I was in charge, the leader. It was my duty to stay outside their circle. The stew was warm, and Dan was right. It did taste of home, a Colorado ranch home.

After finishing my food, I went up the stairs to the wheelhouse and knocked. The captain yelled for me to enter. After I stepped in and shut the door, I took a place behind and to the side of the old man and watched him. He stood at the helm. His gray hair stuck out from the back of his cap. Deep wrinkles gathered in the corners of his steely eyes as he watched the water over his wheel. He occasionally dropped his eyes down to his instruments and compass, absentmindedly scratching the gray stubble on his cheeks. His radio played the Grateful Dead.

He hammered the ash out of his pipe on the window ledge. From the wear showing on the ledge, it looked like it was a ritual he had done for years. The ash fell to an overflowing trash can and onto a small pile of ash on the floor. He pulled an old leather tobacco pouch from his shirt, unzipped the pouch, and dipped his pipe. After carefully stuffing the tobacco into his worn pipe to his satisfaction, he used a matchstick to light it. He took a puff and then spoke. "So, Wallace tells me you're after Zhang-Fei."

I nodded.

"First-class son of a bitch," he added.

"I heard," I answered. "Can you really find his ship?"

"Lotsa water out there." He took another puff. "If she's heading to Hong Kong, I'll find her. The Bay of Thailand ain't very deep. The captain won't get too clever."

"What if she isn't headed to Hong Kong?"

"I don't know. I can try, but there's a lot of water to cover," he answered.

"Whatever it takes, and don't worry about the money. I'll get it covered."

He turned enough to look at me. "When Wallace told me you were going after Zhang-Fei, I told him I'd do it for nothing."

I listened to him talk for over an hour. He, too, came to Southeast Asia as a young man. He literally never left. There was nothing for him in America. It took some time, but he refound himself after the war. He mentioned a couple of wives in passing, and I didn't inquire further. His greatest enjoyment was talking about skippering his boat. He hauled goods and people all over Southeast Asia. His life was here on the water.

It was getting dark. I was on my second hour of listening to his war stories when he pointed to something off the port bow. A smile came across his face. "There she is!" I couldn't see it. He turned to port. "See! There!"

"Okay, I see it … I think." I smiled back at him. "Now what?"

"Simple. We get in her wake and follow until it's time." He turned the wheel some more.

"Time for what?"

"Just watch."

Chapter 26

The captain ordered no lights. I was concerned with the engine noise, but the captain wasn't worried. The *Yuan Liang* made a lot of noise; our Detroit diesels would never be heard. His concern was radar, but most captains didn't worry what was behind but rather what was in front of them. We closed the distance, and there was no reaction from the *Yuan Liang.*

We neared to the point where we could see armed guards on the deck. The captain left the wheelhouse to speak with his sailors. His men ran aft and uncovered two very high-powered fast boats. They pushed one of them off, jumped in it, and fired it up. From the stern of our ship, they took the end of a heavy cable from a spool. I could see hundreds of hooks on the cable that I assumed were used for salvaging large items from the sea.

The captain returned to the wheelhouse and throttled the engines up to full speed. He turned farther to port. The speedboat took off, unthreading the cable as it sped toward the *Yuan Liang.* The center of the ungreased spool squealed with each revolution. The captain moved his boat to the *Yuan Liang*'s port side. The fast boat headed around the rear of the ship and then up its starboard side. Its engines, though powerful, labored with the weight of the cable.

After what seemed an interminable time, the cable was dragged into the *Yuan Liang*'s screw. The propeller caught it, and it began to wrap around the propeller and the shaft. Once it caught and went taut, our sailors released it from the speedboat and headed back around to us. The cable spool began to spin faster until we heard a large bang from the *Yuan Liang*. She shuddered to a stop. The captain turned to me and said, "It's time for you to go."

I looked at the captain in bewilderment. So much for formulating a complex plan before having shit hit the proverbial fan. However, this was not so much proverbial as it was actual. "Go get your ship, Mr. Conner!"

My mind was spinning as I jumped to the deck and joined my crew. "Here's the plan, I think." I was plotting as I was talking. "Wallace, you stay here and be our sniper. Luk, you will be his spotter." I paused and looked for Dan and Chewy. "You two will go with me and two of our friends here." I nodded toward the two Thai sailors.

"Wait! You will need this!" The captain joined our circle and handed his old lever gun to Dan with a hearty slap on his shoulder. "Be sure you bring her back to me!"

As the second speedboat hit the water, I turned to Wallace and Luk. "Make sure that old Enfield does its job!" We then jumped into the idling fast boat; one of the Thai sailors throttled it up and steered toward the ship. About halfway there, he killed the engine. We sat with our backs against the boat's soft hull. "Dan, take the sailors and secure a safe position to cover Chewy and me."

The silent fast boat's momentum carried it to the bow of the large ship while a small crowd gathered aft searching for the trouble. Angry voices filled the air. We stealthily climbed the metal rungs on the bow, which reached from the waterline to the deck. The bow rocked up and down with the water. My finger cramped from gripping the small rungs. I inhaled and exhaled with concentrated purpose to prevent myself from shaking. As much as I love ships, I'm deathly afraid of water.

We all made it to the main deck without being noticed before a shot rang from the catwalk in front of the bridge. We ran for cover. I heard running footsteps and caught a glimpse of someone on the catwalk. The shooter fell off the walk a second before I heard Wallace's shot fired from our boat's wheelhouse. More steps, louder steps … I rose up from behind the steel hatch I was using for cover to see four or five men with AK-47s advancing toward our position. I fired. The first two fell. A shower of bullets hit the hatch I was hiding behind.

Wallace fired again. Another one fell. Dan shot from his position. He hit his mark and followed up with another shot. The last of the charging men dropped. I had counted six down. Since I didn't know how many there were total, I guess there wasn't much point in counting. But it kept me from running away in sheer terror.

More shots rained down on us as the shooters found positions atop the superstructure. A half wall of steel protected them. Wallace shot and missed. His target area was reduced from a full human body to a head, neck, and upper shoulders, a difficult shot even without the untimely pitching of two vessels at sea.

However, Wallace's shot drew the attention of the shooters. They opened up on the small boat's wheelhouse. The hail of bullets forced our captain, Wallace, and Luk from the wheelhouse. The sound of shattering glass echoed to the deck of the *Yuan Liang*. I hated that the assault had turned to Wallace, but it gave me the opportunity to dash to the front of the superstructure and gather up the dead men's auto carbines.

I slung two guns over each shoulder and carried the other two in my hands. I ran toward Dan's location behind one of the large anchor winch drums. I handed off all but one of the AKs. I whispered to Dan, "Drop the lifeboats." He looked at me like I was crazy. "Look, these guys are just sailors, and we have them trapped. If they have an escape route, they'll bail." I could tell Dan still wasn't sure. "Cut the damn boats," I repeated.

"Okay, boss."

"We'll cover you … Chewy." I looked for nods from both of them. "Fire."

Dan and one of the small mariners ran toward the starboard lifeboats. Chewy and I fired at the superstructure. Chewy was on full auto until I stopped him. We didn't have an endless supply of ammunition.

Dan and the sailor cut the first boat, but they didn't time their cuts. The bow dropped first, then the stern. It dropped like a powerless missile falling from orbit. It smashed into the sea and disappeared under the water. *Now they are going to think we are trying to trap them.* I glared at Dan; he was looking over to see if I saw his mistake. I raised my hands and rolled my eyes. He shrugged with a sheepish smile. I waved him on to the next. We opened fire again.

The second and third dropped to the water on their keels. I nodded in approval. Dan and his sidekick returned to their sanctuary. "Chewy, cover us. We are going to make for the superstructure … don't get trigger-happy." He nodded. We fired up at the bridge and half wall as we ran from the forward deck to the quarterdeck. I hated room-to-room searches, but it had to be done.

As we sprinted to the quarterdeck, the engineer and his shipmates emerged from below, ran across the deck, and bailed over the starboard side. Finally, an idea that worked! I stitched the deck with bullets behind them to keep them from changing their minds. Dan moved in and out of the rooms with great efficiency. He was well trained and practiced. I followed him into each room. He turned to the wall at the door and swept to the corner of the room and back down the wall. He checked every space, closet, or locker with professional caution and speed. I covered him and the other wall. Our two sailors were in charge of covering our backs.

We made it to the second floor and the captain's quarters. The door was locked. I nodded, and Dan returned the nod. I kicked the door, and we burst through, Dan leading with me at the rear. The room was searched quickly but meticulously. It was empty. We examined it again. It was the largest room we had explored. It was the cleanest, the most elegant room we had explored. It also was the only room with its own bathroom.

Dan slowly shook his head as he looked into my disappointed eyes. I took a long sigh and cursed under my breath. Dan stepped into my space and grabbed my shoulder. He squeezed. "Come on, boss. We got other rooms." I nodded. I stood and slammed the butt of my carbine into the large mirror framed in delicately carved walnut. The mirror shattered at my feet. I could see my angry eyes in a broken spatter of glass. I paused a moment.

I turned to Dan and smiled. "Let's finish this." He nodded. I had him grab the captain's log. We replenished our magazines with a box of ammo we found in the room. We searched it one more time for any evidence a woman had been there. We found nothing. All the clothes, the aftershave, and razor were all for a man.

We searched every room, every bunk, and every cubbyhole to the bridge. The bridge was abandoned. We could hear the remaining shooters above us. I thought about firing into the ceiling, but I wasn't sure if the 7.62 x 39mm rounds would penetrate the steel deckhead or ricochet around in the bridge until they hit one of us.

Dan yelled orders in Thai, Chinese, and English up the narrow stairway. The defending crew replied with gunfire. He tried until his voice went hoarse. Wallace managed to wound one of them during the exchange of words and bullets. We could hear the man thrash and scream until the shooters just threw him over the side.

Going up the steps would result in no more than suicide, and just shooting up the stairway was a waste of ammunition. Unknown to us, as Dan and I worked on a plan, Chewy had come up with his own. He and three of the Thai sailors crawled their way to the stern deck and hid behind the funnel.

Later, Chewy explained to us that he saw where he had the advantage, both in location and surprise. Using hand signals, Chewy had directed one of his sailors up the ladder on the smokestack. Chewy now controlled the highest point behind the shooters, who were too concerned about us on the bridge to notice the staging of an ambush. Chewy's other sailors flanked him. They were ready. The sailor on the exhaust tube had made a circle in the air with his stolen carbine, and Chewy attacked.

But at the time, Dan and I looked at each other in confusion. Who was shooting at whom? It took a few seconds, but then we figured out that Chewy had advanced from the rear and initiated an attack. We fired up the stairway a few times to remind the outlaws they were in a cross fire. After a couple of minutes, there was silence. Chewy and his crew must have captured the remaining crew of the *Yuan Liang* … or had killed them.

Chewy shouted down the stairway an all clear before he stepped into view. He cautiously stepped out where we could see him; he didn't want to get shot by friendly fire. Dan and I laughed, conflicted with tears. We had taken the *Yuan Liang*.

"Great job, guys!" we shouted as we made our way up the stairs to Chewy, who had made a bandana out of a rag he found and tied it around his head. "Who the hell you supposed to be?" I asked Chewy. I had a large smile when I asked. I looked over at the outlaw sailors with their hands in the air. Captain Blake's sailors stood over them. Each Thai sailor had a muzzle of their carbine pointed at the captives' heads. Only three remained, the last of a probable crew of twenty or thirty sailors and guards.

Chewy walked to the one wearing an officer's uniform and pointed the end of his rifle barrel at the man's head. He proudly announced to us, "This is the captain of this sorry tub of bolts."

I glared at the little man as I looked him over. He spit at my feet in defiance. I looked at Chewy. "Do you think you can find some duct tape now?"

No one could find an inch of tape on the entire ship. What we found in the hold were about forty girls and women ranging in age from six years old to their midtwenties. They were from Thailand, Cambodia, Laos, and Vietnam. Most had been stolen off the streets in their respective countries. A few were promised a new life for a price.

It took some doing with a few of the women and girls because of the language barrier, but we managed to talk them into transferring to Chester's boat. As we worked on moving them over, Luk found me and told me I needed to go with him. His grave tone and worried face earned him my full attention. I followed him down a rope gangway to Chester's boat.

We went to Chester's cabin. Bill Parker was on the bed. His stomach was covered in fresh blood. Wallace was standing over him, trying to stop the bleeding from two bullet wounds. He had been in the wheelhouse taking pictures when they fired at the wheelhouse. Wallace gave me a somber look and slowly shook his head.

I sat down on the corner of the bed. "Bill …"

"Jack, I ran into some bad luck." Parker struggled with his words and smiled.

I didn't know what to say. I thought about yelling, "Don't die on me, you SOB," but it sounded wrong. I leaned down to his ear and whispered, "Parker, you have a story to write. Somebody's got to tell this story. The world needs to know ... has to know."

He smiled, and blood trickled from the corners of his mouth. He gasped for air between words. "You might have to write this one." He fell unconscious.

I just sat there. Wallace walked over and grabbed me hard on the shoulder. "Mate, we gotta go. I'm sure they called for help. We don't want to be here when they show up. We gotta get out of here."

I stood. "Have we got everyone?"

Dan answered, "Chewy's bringing up the rear with the last of them."

I had to step through the women to get to the bow for some fresh air. Chester and Wallace were trying to get the wheelhouse back in operation. The old diesels labored with the additional load. I called for Dan and Chewy. They made their way to the bow.

I turned and ordered, "Bring me the captain and meet me on the upper deck."

Dan and Chewy carried the captain to the deck with the help of a couple of the Thai sailors. They threw him down at my feet. His feet and legs were bound with soft cotton rope. I tied one end of another rope to his legs and the other end to a steel corner upright. "Throw him overboard."

Dan ordered the two Thai sailors to carry out my request. Without hesitation they picked him up by the legs and shoulders, and on the Thai count of three, the *Yuan Liang*'s captain flew over the rail and splashed into the water.

I waited a full minute before I ordered him to be pulled aboard. They hung him upside down from the structure holding the deck cover. I knelt down and looked him in the face. Terror had replaced his defiant smirk.

"Does he speak English?" I asked over my shoulder.

Dan asked him in Chinese. The bound captain's answer sounded angry. Dan said, "No, boss, only Chinese and Thai."

"Tell him that I'm going to shoot him, cut him up, and put him in a bait box if he doesn't tell me where the woman that they stole from America is now."

Dan nodded and began to speak to him in Chinese. He screamed something back.

"What did he say?"

"Not good, boss."

With a thumb pointing to the water, I gave the order, "Pitch him!"

They untied my slipknot, and he dropped to the deck. The sailors started to pick him up. He started to yell at Dan. Dan put his open hand up to stop the sailors. They let him slip back to the deck. Dan started an interview. The interrogation lasted for several minutes.

Dan stepped over to me and whispered, "He said the woman is being held at the Blue Orchard Apartments. Apparently this Blue Orchard is some sort of fortress built to look like an apartment complex. It is well-guarded, with over a hundred armed men. They have closed-circuit TV and motion sensors along the concrete fence." Dan added, "The fence is a meter thick."

"She's still alive." I wasn't sure if I asked a question or made a statement.

Dan asked. Our large rope larva answered, and Dan smiled. "The last time he saw her, she was alive and well."

"Good. I'm going to go check on Parker."

"Boss." Dan stopped me. "What do we do with him?"

I looked down at the now-humbled captain. "Stow him belowdecks and feed him. Feed him what they fed the women on his ship." I wanted to just pitch him, but we might need him, and I was tired of killing.

Luk was watching over Bill. He stood when I entered the cabin. I asked if he was still alive. Luk answered, "Yes, barely. We have to get him to a hospital." I thought of another sarcastic remark, but refrained. Luk was good at stating the obvious. However, I could have hugged him when he added, "I already called for an ambulance. Do you have any idea what time we'll get back?"

I shook my head. "Luk, you're going to have to stay with these women and girls. We need to get them back to their families. Can you do it without involving the police?"

"I don't know. I'll try. That may be very difficult," he answered.

"I think it would be easier than trying to explain how we came up with these women in the first place."

"Perhaps you are correct," Luk replied.

"Call your firm. Maybe Dallas can help. I'm going to the wheelhouse."

Rayong's coastal lights were in view from the wheelhouse. Captain Blake held the wheel tight with both hands; his pipe burned with a red glow. Wallace was looking aft at the women sleeping on the top deck. Dan and Chewy were passing out food and some clothes we had taken from the ship. I had instructed them to take everything that they could carry. Add piracy to my list of misdeeds.

"We did a good thing here tonight." Wallace smiled at me.

I nodded. "I wish we could have done it without killing anyone."

"Aw, wouldn't worry much about that, mate. Some people just aren't worth keeping alive."

"Yeah, maybe, but who is to judge? Not me." I changed the subject. "How long until we get back to shore?"

"Couple of hours, maybe." He took a drink from Bill's bottle and swallowed hard. He tried to hand me the bottle, but I declined.

I wanted to be back on land before light. Light would bring the people out. The more people, the more curiosity. I didn't want or need a bunch of inquisitive people calling the police. I looked down at the water. It seemed we were barely moving. I stepped out of the wheelhouse and to the rail overlooking the bow and just watched the lights.

A scream followed by numerous screams and yelling in about four languages came from the main deck. Startled, I twisted around to find the source of the commotion. The *Yuan Liang* captain had escaped his ropes and made it to the bow on the main deck. He had a knife. I raised my handgun and shouted at him to stop. He turned, glared up at me, and screamed in Chinese. He grabbed one of the young women closest to him and used her as a shield. He put a knife to her throat and yelled again.

I aimed carefully and with hesitation began to press the trigger. I couldn't stop breathing hard. With the movement of the boat, I couldn't keep on my target. A shot rang out behind me. I jumped.

The man flung backward and off over the rail and disappeared under the boat.

Wallace came out of the wheelhouse and worked the bolt on his .303. He clicked the safety on and slung the rifle. He leaned on the rail beside me. "Well, another problem solved."

I glanced over at him and then back to the bow. "You know, I wanted to keep him around for a bit."

"Why?"

I sighed, "Damn! He sure didn't give us much of a choice, but I sure wanted to keep him.

Wallace replied, "Why, for God's sake?"

"I'm not sure now. Maybe a hostage we could have traded or maybe just some more information," I answered.

"Trade him?" Wallace chuckled. "You think Zhang-Fei would have traded for him? We couldn't get a one-legged roo fer him."

"Yeah, I suppose."

"Yes, sir."

I don't know if I was excited or anxious. I could see the outline of two large passenger buses waiting on the dock along with an ambulance. The eastern horizon glowed bright orange and red through the palm trees as we approached the dock.

Dan and Chewy helped Luk load the women on the buses while I assisted Wallace with Parker. Parker's breathing was shallow and slow. His skin was gray. Joy met Wallace at the ambulance with a hard hug and kiss. I turned away to give them a moment. I was a little envious; I wished I had a moment.

I watched Luk give each one of the women eight thousand Thai baht in an envelope as they boarded the bus. It wasn't much, about two hundred and fifty US dollars. But it was at least a month's wages here. The women didn't understand the generosity, but gladly took it with a grateful *wai* and smile. I smiled with them. It was nice to have such resources at my disposal, even if I had to pay it back. This charity wasn't exactly an approved expenditure.

Luk walked over and told me he would see me back in Bangkok. I nodded. "Be careful. Zhang-Fei might want his cargo back." Surprisingly, I received my first smile from him. He turned and climbed on board the bus. I sent Dan and Chewy with him.

I walked beside Chester and assessed the damage to the old boat. There wasn't one pane of glass left in the wheelhouse, which was well-ventilated with bullet holes. The same with the hull; it had taken a shower of bullets. "Skipper, work up a bill for the damage to your boat and for the ride. I'll make it good."

He nodded with an exhaled puff of pipe smoke. "Mr. Conner, I'll have to think about it. That was the best time I have had in years."

"I'm not sure I would consider what we just went through a great time, but thank you. Thank you very much. And, please, call me Jack."

"Jack." Chester extended his hand. "It was an honor. Thank you."

I nodded, shook his hand, and jumped in the bed of Joy's pickup. I had no fear or adrenalin left for Joy's driving. Surprisingly, she drove to the hospital without running one stop sign or being honked at by one horn.

Chapter 27

The hospital was a modern white stone building. Our clothes were covered in blood, so Joy left and returned with new shirts and trousers for her husband and me. She also brought some food and coffee for us. Wallace went to the bathroom first to clean up. I tried to thank Joy between bites of hot food and sips of coffee. She only nodded and avoided eye contact with me. She resented me for bringing her husband into this mess. I understood. I couldn't blame her, but I understood Wallace as well. We waited in the lobby for about six hours before the doctor came out to speak to us.

The young doctor wore dark blue scrubs, with his hair covered with a paper hospital hairnet. He looked tired. He spoke perfect English. I assumed he'd been educated in the West. He informed us that Bill Parker was in a coma and remained in critical condition. He said if they could get him stabilized, they would transfer him to Bangkok. With this somber assessment, he gave Bill less than a fifty-fifty chance.

Sometime, somewhere between yesterday and this morning, I had lost my hat. I avoided thinking of anything else on the ride back to Bangkok. With everything that had happened in the last twenty-four hours, the only thing I wanted to think about was my lost hat. It kept me from thinking about Bill Parker, Asian Sin, Dallas, Sky, and Keeley. It also kept me from thinking about how I was going to assault a fortress guarded by a hundred men.

Dan called, and everything went better than expected with the women. Dallas's firm was interviewing them for a possible lawsuit against several businesses owned by Zhang-Fei once my business with him was settled. Dan and Chewy were heading to Chinatown to find the Blue Orchid Apartments after they got some sleep. Luk was with Thai Immigration working on returning the women and girls taken from the surrounding countries. He assigned armed guards from his office to travel with them to ensure their safety.

It was late in the afternoon before I got back to my room. I wasn't sure when I had last slept. I couldn't remember. My sleep lasted all night and the better part of the next day. I woke with a sense of victory, but it was short-lived; disappointment and a feeling of failure filled my consciousness. I didn't call Dallas before my evening started. I failed to find Asian, and I wasn't up to explaining it to her. I wanted to be angry with myself for my failure to find Asian Sin, but I couldn't afford it. Not now.

I met with Dan at an exclusive Chinese restaurant in Chinatown. Chinatown was much like the rest of Bangkok, or at least what I had seen, except the nightlife wasn't dedicated to bar girls and alcohol. Shopping and food seemed to be its draw. The busy and crowded streets and sidewalks made me late. After searching the crowds for what seemed forever, I located Dan at a small round table at the back of the room. I sat down and ordered before letting Dan talk.

"Good news, boss. It wasn't hard to locate the Blue Orchid Apartments, and I managed to find us a hotel a few hundred yards from them." He paused to give me time to appreciate the fact. "And I got us a high room with a very good view of the building and the grounds. Chewy is already up there watching for anything."

"Wow." I was impressed. "Did you guys get any rest?"

Dan heard the discouragement in the tone of my words. "Yeah, we're fine. Maybe you need more rest. Why don't you take in the sights for the night? We have the watch for now; you can relieve us later."

"I will agree upon one condition," I insisted. "Take me to see the complex before I go do anything else."

He conceded and took me to the hotel. The Baodian Hotel was an older hotel and wasn't fancy, but it seemed clean and had a friendly staff. Dan explained Baodian was Chinese; it meant the King's Palace. I walked out on the balcony and looked down upon our target compound. From this vantage point, it appeared well-maintained and unassuming. Orange trees lined the driveway from the gates to the building's main entrance. I could see a series of sunken and raised water ponds, with various statues of mythical Asian beasts scattered across the well-manicured grass. Overall, the impression was of a peaceful retreat, rather than a forbidden danger zone.

The large building was a white four-story structure made of the same stone as the outer walls. It was designed to look like separate exclusive apartments on each floor. The ground floor had the least number of windows on the sides but the most windows on the front of any floor. The front and back had full covered balconies. It was a beautiful complex, even from our distance.

My agreement with Dan was to take the rest of thc night off, so when I left, I didn't tell him that I was going to the complex for a closer look. More or less I lied to him. But there I was, at the outer walls of the Blue Orchid Apartments, probably in the view of Dan and Chewy's binoculars.

The information that the captain of the *Yuan Liang* had reluctantly given us seemed to be correct. It was a fortress. The perimeter fence was at least eight feet tall and had spiked steel rods along the top. Two gated entries, one at the river and one at the street, provided the only visible access to the compound. There were alleys on either side.

I walked around the compound a couple of times, taking in everything I could without stopping. There wasn't much to take in from the street. Behind the heavy wrought iron gates, a second set of solid steel gates hung about a foot from the outer gates, a system much like the MSM building had in Los Angeles. The beauty and peace, however false, were invisible from the street.

Back in my room at the Royal Suralay, I called Dan one more time to have him call the hospital and check on Bill for me. I was too tired to try to navigate the language barrier that I knew I would run into. Dan didn't mention my lie; that was appreciated. A few minutes later, the phone rang. "There is no change in Bill, boss."

"Damn. Thanks for calling for me."

With a very deep sigh, I looked at the phone still in my hand. It was time to call Dallas and update her on the latest events, including telling her that William Parker had been shot.

After the international operator connected us, I managed to greet Dallas and fill her in on the most recent events before I broke down some, and my trepidations just spilled out. "Dallas, she has to be there. I know it!" I guess I needed to vent.

"How are you going to get in this place, this fortress?" she asked.

"Well, we are definitely too understaffed to assault this fortress head-on, and we can't go the police because of Luk's warning."

We both fell silent. Thinking out loud, I spoke again. "We can't use explosives or heavy equipment. Either of those ways would surely get Asian killed. In fact, I am lost on how to get in and get out without getting Asian killed … or ourselves, for that matter."

She reassured me, "Jack, you will think of something. Just give it time."

"Maybe."

"No, you will. Don't push it."

"Yeah, well, thanks. I wish I had the same confidence in me that you have," I answered, but I wanted to say more. I really wanted to talk, to ask her about Keeley and to tell her to talk to Keeley. I wanted her to convince Keeley that she needed me … but I just said good-bye and hung up the phone.

I sat on the edge of my bed and tried to concentrate, but it wasn't working. I was too restless. I finally decided to take a walk. Grabbing a couple of hotel address cards the hotel provided, I walked through the lobby and out into the humid evening heat. The cards in my hand were written in English and Thai and included a map. If a guest got lost, the guest could just flag down a taxi and give the driver the card. They would then return the lost guest home, even if the misplaced tourist were only a half block away from his destination.

The walk gave me a chance to get lost in the city and get lost in my mind. I went over every detail I could remember about the complex. The double drive-through gates built of steel had matching walk-through gates on either side of them and were trimmed with steel dragons and flowers. The alley walls were solid except for storm drains about every ten feet. They drained water from the alleys, which sloped to the river. One advantage I saw, or rather didn't see, was guards walking the outer perimeter or on top of the fence.

I walked down an alley and sat down on some abandoned steps. There were a couple of street dogs, *soi* dogs to the locals, digging in the trash for food. Feral cats watched the dogs root in the papers and cans. A cat would wait for a dog to find something edible, and while the other dogs were fighting for it, one of the mangy cats would steal it. I watched the drama repeat itself several times.

I felt better by the time I found my hotel and got to bed, but I couldn't sleep. I stared at the ceiling thinking of ideas. Then it came to me. I had it. My discouragement disappeared, and excitement replaced it. I had to find Nat.

I called Wallace. "Hey, Mark, is Nat there yet?"

"Naw, it is early yet." The bar must be busy tonight, because I could hardly hear him over the background noise.

"If Nat comes in tonight, ask her to wait for me, okay?"

"Sure, mate. What's up?" Hearing his boisterous voice made me feel even better.

"I will tell you about it when I get there. See you in a few."

I then called Luk. "I need you to get me four trucks with closed boxes tomorrow. We will need them at least until the end of the week."

He asked, "Why?" in his back-to-usual grumpy voice. I hung up without an explanation; there wasn't time right now. I headed down to the lobby and asked the desk to get me a taxi. I now had the beginning of a plan to work on with Wallace and Nat.

For the next three days, Dan, Chewy, and I divided up the surveillance on the complex. When Luk returned from obtaining the trucks, he joined the rotation, along another detective from Dallas's Bangkok branch. I worked on my plan when I wasn't on shift. On the second day, I had just eaten at the Suralay's restaurant and walked out into the lobby when I ran right into Joshua. He removed his sunglasses to greet me. Four large men followed him.

"Joshua, what the …?" I had to admit I was happy to see the gangster.

"Here." He handed me a new cowboy hat, identical to the one I had had wrenched from my head the night we took the ship. "My sister told me you lost yours. I was sent to deliver it."

I looked down at the hat and turned it by the brim with my fingers. Surprised at both the gift and his presence, I smiled. "I am not sure what to say. What are you doing here?"

He returned the smile, "Well, Sheriff, your posse is here!" I offered to buy him lunch in the restaurant before going to join up with the surveillance crew. While Joshua ate, I presented the plan to him. I wanted someone to hear it before I presented it to the group.

"You have thought this all out?" He sounded a little hesitant.

"Well, for the most part. Have I missed something?"

"Just all the things that could go wrong!" With reluctance he agreed with the plan. I understood his hesitancy; after all, he'd been on my operations before.

The next morning, I stood in front of the group. There were Dan, Chewy, Luk, Wallace, and Joshua with his four men; including me, we had a total of ten men. It was, at best, ten to one odds. Not the best odds, but it was what we had. The staff at the Suralay gave me the smallest of their conference rooms for my meeting. I sketched out the Blue Orchid on the chalkboard and began to outline my plan.

Wallace and Luk once again would serve as sniper and lookout, this time from the hotel balcony. Joshua handed Wallace a high-grade Remington sniper rifle with a long-range scope. He had been here less than a day and had already managed to obtain the weapon. The scope alone would cost over a thousand dollars at home. It was probably twice that much here.

Joshua and his men would arrive by boat and take the gates on the river side. Dan, Chewy, and I would take the street gates. Once Joshua's men forced entrance through their gate, they would retreat and join us at the street side. I was pinning my hopes on the chance that we were dealing with untrained personnel, not skilled professional soldiers. I wanted to drive them out, not kill them. I had no idea how to explain to the Royal Thai Police a hundred dead or wounded men in the middle of Bangkok. The idea of spending even one night in Bangkok's infamous Bangkwang Prison haunted me.

With Dan's help I passed out the carbines and other equipment we had liberated from the *Yuan Liang*. Dallas's firm purchased some small two-way radios with boom mics and earpieces, and Luk brought them to the meeting. Luk was visibly nervous and seemed to be in deep thought concerning something. I think he didn't like the idea of having a bunch of automatic carbines on the streets of his city. At one time he had taken an oath to protect his people from such. I understood his misgivings; I had been in his place before.

"Are there any questions?" All of them looked at me in silence. Either they all thought I was crazy, or I had given a good briefing. Judging from their "deer in the headlight" looks, I was leaning toward the former. Before we broke up for the day, we destroyed our notes to erase any and all evidence of the conspiracy. We would hit the complex tonight after midnight.

Chapter 28

The remainder of the day was dedicated to rest and sleep. I doubted that anyone would actually sleep; I knew it was going to be impossible for me. But I tried. About sundown, I went to the hotel restaurant for a light dinner. I nibbled at my food, but I worried too much. Finally I gave up on the food and caught a cab to the Baodian Hotel to check on Luk and Wallace.

When I walked in, Wallace was working the action and dry firing the Remington. I studied the complex from our balcony. It looked quiet. From what I could see from my position, the yard was empty. The far side of the complex was my vulnerable area. I had no one on that side, so I would try to avoid it. All that was left to do was wait.

Shortly before midnight, Nat arrived with Luk's trucks—right on time. She sat on the passenger seat in the first truck. The four trucks drove slowly down the empty street. The convoy stopped about a half block from the complex. I turned and faced Luk and Wallace. "Well, there are your trucks." I *wai*-ed to Luk and shook Wallace's hand.

"Don't worry, mate." Wallace smiled. "I got yer back." I returned the smile, slung my rifle, and walked out the door.

Nat yelled at the drivers in Thai, and they jumped from their cabs and ran to the rear of each truck. As the drivers dropped the tailgates, twenty or so bar girls dropped protest signs and sacks of vegetables, raw meat, and fish to the street before jumping down themselves.

Under Nat's orders, the girls assembled on the sidewalk by the trucks. Covering their faces with scarves and masks, they picked up their signs. I had no idea what was written on the signs since they were in Thai script. Nat gave the cue, and the girls began to march and chant in Thai. As Nat's column moved to the side of the complex, they began throwing the produce and meat over the stone wall.

I met up with Dan and Chewy, and we hid around the corner of the stone wall and waited. I wanted to see, but it was impossible. The yard light came on, and we heard running in the compound. In my earpiece, I heard Wallace warn, "Be on guard, mate. They're a'coming!"

Two of the guards rushed out one of the walk-through gates to confront the protesters. As I had hoped when formulating my plan, they left the gate open. When the guards rounded the corner, Chewy grabbed the first guard by his shoulders and threw him onto the sidewalk. Dan kicked the second in the throat, and as he fell, I grabbed him. We stripped their black blazers off them and secured them with heavy plastic zip ties as Chewy gleefully duct-taped their mouths. We loaded them into the back of one of the trucks. Dan and Chewy put on the jackets and walked in the compound through the iron threshold without encountering any hostility.

They were far enough away and it was dark enough not to be discovered as intruders. I followed behind them, stooped over. They passed on by the guardhouse, and I entered it. It was dark. I searched the walls with my fingertips. The control box hung beside the breaker boxes on the back wall. With the flip of a couple of switches, the gates that guarded the driveway slowly swung open; I heard the quiet hum of electric motors.

My fingers found the breaker switches. I just went down the switches flipping all the breakers off. I hoped I had managed to kill the power to the control boxes. I didn't want to be electrocuted. I dropped my carbine off my shoulder and raised it to the gate control box. With all the force I had, I struck the short rifle's butt to the box; it tore from the wall and hung by the wires. I pulled my knife and cut the wires. The box hit the ground, and I stomped it into pieces. I wanted to make sure the solid steel gates couldn't close.

The first shots were fired as Joshua and his men tried to open the river gate. They couldn't get the gate to open. Zhang-Fei's people discovered us quicker than I had anticipated. Joshua had to withdraw; the incoming fire was too great. Dan and Chewy began to shoot to draw fire off Joshua. Shattered glass drenched me as bullets struck the guardhouse. Nat yelled, and her girls retreated in a sprint to the back of the trucks. Once the last girl got in, the trucks sped off.

Three days ago I had convinced Nat to recruit the girls with the promise of a hundred dollars each to stage a protest. They exceeded my expectations. I watched to make sure they were well away before I ran for better cover.

Some of Zhang-Fei's men gathered on the rooftop of the compound and began shooting at us. They positioned two snipers kitty-corner on the roof. But they didn't own the high ground—we did, at least on the one side, the side I wanted to own.

Dan and Chewy got pinned down behind a raised water pond about fifty yards from the building. The gunfire came from shooters in the windows at the front of the complex. A sniper on the front corner kept me down behind a short half wall about twenty yards behind Dan and Chewy. He was good. His bullets hit the bricks just above my head; I couldn't move. I looked up at the hotel, hoping for relief. I wasn't sure how long the old bricks would hold out under the persistence of the sniper's high-caliber rifle.

The sniper jerked and fell back. Then I heard the report of Wallace's rifle. Wallace had joined the fight. Before anyone on the roof reacted, Wallace got the second sniper. He turned on the other shooters; two more fell as they evacuated the roof. I slammed my head against my rifle's forestock in anger and disappointment. I didn't want another gunfight.

Zhang-Fei's snipers were dead. With the roof clear, Joshua and his men entered through the street gate and advanced without being molested. They ran past me and took refuge behind a couple of dragon statues in line with Dan and Chewy. We had enough firepower to push back the shooters at the windows.

The ones that escaped Wallace's first volley and fled the roof were now taking positions in the second-, third-, and fourth-story windows. But Wallace had a great view of these windows. It only took a few shots before the guards surrendered these platforms.

I moved forward cautiously, half crawling and half running. I joined the others. I took cover at the same dragon statue protecting Joshua. He glared at me as he switched magazines in his rifle. "No shooting, huh?" He replenished the empty magazine with cartridges from his jacket pocket. "That sounded a lot like gunfire to me." I just shrugged.

Chewy and Dan kept firing at the windows until there were no return shots. I signaled Joshua that I was moving to the covered porch. He followed me up the steps and leaned tightly against the outer wall. I pointed to the window. He nodded. I glanced carefully inside the window. Zhang-Fei's men had abandoned their positions. I dropped through the window and landed on my back. I rolled up on my knees, then to my feet, and scurried to unlock the door. Joshua followed before I got the door unlocked. His entry lacked the drama of mine. He just stepped through the opening one foot at a time.

Dan and Chewy, along with Joshua's men, ran to the door and into the building. Two of Joshua's men took guard at the door. The first floor was part of the façade. It had a customer counter, a staircase, and a long, wide hallway to the back door. Joshua waved at the last of his men to cover the back door. It appeared we controlled the first floor. I was anxious. I didn't know where the fleeing guards had gone. I felt we were heading for disaster. I didn't have enough men for this type of room-to-room, floor-to-floor operation.

Four evenly spaced doors opened to the hallway. It was time for the room-to-room search. Dan and Chewy took the lead. Joshua and I followed. I didn't have to worry about the hallway. We were well covered by Joshua's men.

The first door opened to a sleeping room. It was a large room filled with bunk beds in a military barracks fashion. The beds were tightly made, and the room smelled strongly of disinfectant. This was the barracks of well-trained soldiers, not tattooed gangbangers. We searched everything. I found three military ammo boxes stuffed with cartridges. It was a great find. We needed bullets.

We decided to search the room on the same side of the hall. It was a supply room. Boxes of clothes, dry food, and support equipment. Unlike the MSM house in Los Angeles, this one was very clean and organized. Our search turned up nothing.

We took the next door across the hall. When Dan jerked the door open, gunfire filled the air. Dan slammed it closed. Apparently I didn't own the first floor after all. I fell back against the hallway wall in frustration. We had no smoke, no flashbang grenades … no way to make a safe entry. I couldn't just go in shooting. Not only was it suicide; it was possible Asian Sin was in there. I didn't want her shot.

I felt everyone's eyes scrutinizing me. They waited for orders. I didn't have any. Then I remembered. In the storage room, there were several large boxes of fireworks stacked against the wall. I waved Chewy over and whispered for him to follow. We returned to the storage room. I grabbed one of the boxes, took it to the hall, and handed it to Joshua. He smiled. I almost knocked Chewy over when I ran back into the supply room for another box.

Dan readied himself to open the door. We tore the firecracker boxes open. Another problem—I didn't have a match. I don't know why, but I searched myself for matches in a vain act. Dan, Chewy, and Joshua were in the same situation … no matches. I shook my head. Joshua yelled to one of his men at the end of the hallway in Chinese. He nodded and ran to us, pulling a cigarette lighter out of his pocket. He handed it to an impatient Joshua.

Joshua lit one of the strings of large firecrackers from the box Chewy was holding. He dropped the burning string back into the box, and with a nod, Dan flung the door open, and Chewy threw the box into the room through a hail of bullets. We repeated the act two more times.

We heard bangs and whistles as the firecrackers and small rockets detonated behind the door. We were about to attempt entry when the door exploded in the hall. The blast slammed us to the floor, and black smoke started to fill the hall. There must have been either some large mortars or gunpowder in one or two of the boxes.

I recovered from the blast and stood shakily back to my feet, pulling Dan up to his feet. I swung my head around to see if anyone got hurt. Other than a few cuts and Chewy's nosebleed, everyone survived. There was no gunfire. Joshua stood with the help of the wall and whispered as he dusted himself off, "Tell me, Jack, have you ever had a plan that worked?"

"None that comes to mind lately."

"I wondered."

"Well, maybe next time … if we live through this one." I sighed. I had a discouraged look on my face.

Joshua asked, "What?"

"I hope all of this didn't just get her killed." I leaned on the wall. The smell and taste of burned gunpowder filled my nose and mouth. I coughed. I worried that if she were here, I had just gotten her killed, and I worried that if she weren't here, this was another failed attempt.

Joshua broke into my self-defeating thoughts. "Maybe, but she'll have died knowing someone cared enough to try to save her. Now, let's do this." I nodded.

We rushed the smoke-filled room and found two guards dead. There were four other guards seriously injured, stunned, or both. The percussion caused them to bleed from their noses and ears. As the smoke cleared, we saw the stainless steel counters and cupboards. An eight-burner stove divided the counters. A giant oven with a large lower door and two small top doors stood at the end of the counter. Beside it was an industrial mixer. This was the kitchen.

We zip-tied the guards to the uprights on the counter. Dan and I both tried to get them to talk, but they refused. I looked around the kitchen while the others searched. I felt the kitchen looked too small compared to the outside of the building. Dan came out of one of the very large coolers, and I stepped inside it. Pork and poultry carcasses hung from metal rails.

Prepared food and feedstock filled the shelves. Even with the lights on in the insulated room, it was dim.

I studied the cooler carefully. There was something there. I walked between the carcasses and shelves. I moved to the back of the cooler. A dot of light hit my shoe. I stepped back, and it was there again. I took a closer look at the back wall to find the source of the light. I moved the frozen boxes. A small hole was just above where the wall met the floor. It was a false wall.

I called for help. We stacked the boxes on the floor. Now emptied, the shelves folded so the wall could open. We searched the wall for a latch or switch. We didn't find one. I was about to resort to taking out my frustration on the wall with my gun butt when Chewy found a hidden switch behind the light control box outside the cooler. He tried it. He had found it accidentally, but a find is a find. The door began to open. We took positions in case of resistance. There was none. Inside were stacks and stacks of kilos of drugs wrapped in plastic. Dan read the Chinese markings aloud in English. There were cocaine, methamphetamine, and heroin.

We headed to the next cooler. It had the same system. When the hidden door opened, we found stacks of cash, but still no Asian Sin. Anxiety washed over me. I had to keep my emotions in check. We had one more door to open.

When we opened it, we walked into a hotel-style room. It had a bathroom, a bed, a dresser, and a desk. If the dimensions we had found in the two coolers held true, this back wall was also fake. This time, we found the switch with ease. I flipped it. This back wall slid open instead of folding. Another door appeared as the wall disappeared inside itself. Joshua opened it with little effort.

I stepped in the doorway, swinging my carbine from left to right. I stopped and let the muzzle of my gun drop. There, huddled on the corner of the bed, she sat … Asian Sin. I smiled and stared in disbelief. I couldn't speak. I had rehearsed this moment a thousand times, but my words didn't come. With a gasp, Joshua pushed past me. When she saw him, she jumped up and ran into his arms.

He squeezed her tightly. He turned with her in his arms and smiled. We stepped into the kitchen, where everyone let out a relieved cheer. Asian … Sara was still too shocked to say anything. I cut the celebration short. We still had to get out of there.

We then moved as a group out into the main hall, moving toward Joshua's men at the river side of the building. "Mark, how are we looking from your point?"

"Not good, mate. We can see some fifty or sixty of Zhang-Fei's men standing at the perimeter walls. We also saw some move into the windows and the balcony at the front of the building." He was breathing hard. I heard some gunfire as Wallace attempted to force Zhang-Fei's men to take cover at the same ponds and statues we had used. "I am going to guess that it looks about as treacherous on the back side as it does on the front. They must have been ready for us." Wallace punctuated his sentences with additional shots.

They had set a trap. They used Asian Sin for bait, and I went for it. That was why we were able to take the first floor of the complex so easily. I knew it—if I had just thought about it. They controlled the space in front of us, behind us, and on top of us, but they hadn't moved yet. Why? They had us. All they had to do was move in on top of us. I thought a moment and again remembered the large cache of fireworks in the storage room. Maybe it wasn't over yet.

I motioned for Chewy and Dan to follow me. The three of us went back to the storage room and started carrying boxes of fireworks to the back door. As we carried out the boxes, the others emptied them and scattered the fireworks out as far as they could. We created a path between the piles of fireworks. Next, we went to the kitchen and found some cans of stove fuel and some empty pop bottles.

We filled the pop bottles with fuel and stuffed rags in the top of them. When everyone was ready, Joshua lit the rags, and we began throwing the improvised Molotov cocktails. Joshua's men tossed some up over the balcony railings as we chucked some at the piles of fireworks. The first ones to hit their target were the ones thrown onto the balcony. They burst into large balls of flames as they shattered, forcing the guards back into the building away from the blaze.

The secondary volley did the same, only they ignited the fireworks. As the firecrackers exploded and rockets flew in all directions, we opened up with the carbines and ran for the rear guardhouse. We had to open the gate. The fastest of the men volunteered to go first. He made it under fire from the guards at the south wall. We covered his movement with the carbines as he ran. The guards were in the open and unprotected, but moving fast toward the complex. They would easily overpower us with their numbers. The guards on the street side were moving back to the complex as well. They had pushed Joshua's men back to the first doors in the hallway. We threw fire bottles down the hall and into the entrance room to give them a chance to join us.

As the gate opened, men dressed in black uniforms with their faces covered ran into the compound, taking cover and then engaging the charging guards. Suddenly I recognized them, or at least their style. I had seen them before … on the beach in Wayfarer under much the same circumstances—rescuing my butt as before.

"Move, everyone!" I screamed. My crew hesitated before the oncoming reinforcements. "Go! They are with us!" More in trust than in certainty, they ran through the fireworks, bottle rockets, and fires. Anyone with unused cocktails added them to the fray as we eluded our adversaries. We made it to the back gate, and everyone scrambled onto the waiting boat. Joshua fired up the boat as I jumped back to the dock and untied it, tossing the rope onto the deck. "Go! Get out of here!" I ordered as I turned back toward the compound.

"What the hell are you doing?" Joshua shouted.

"Get her out of here!" I yelled back.

"Come on!" Dan and Chewy screamed together, reaching for me.

"I'm going after Zhang-Fei!" I ran back to the gates.

Joshua motioned for one of his men to take the throttle tiller. He jumped back on the bank. "For Christ's sake," he cursed as he joined me at the gate. We watched the boat disappear down the river before we went back into the compound. With the guards engaged with the mystery men, we made it back to the complex without much effort.

Police and fire truck sirens echoed up the street. We weren't alone. An older man was on the covered porch at the rear of the building. He was encircled by a group of bodyguards. He broke out of his circle of protection by violently pushing past his personal guards. They continued firing at us. We were forced to retreat back to the outer walls. Joshua and I each managed to hit one of the guards.

The mystery men shot ropes over the fence and escaped over the stone wall as the police began to fill the front of the compound. They had never been there to confront the police. The old man ordered his men to drop their guns. He was going to surrender to the police.

I walked past the gate. "Zhang-Fei!" I shouted, my voice full of hatred.

"Yes," he answered, turning back to me. I didn't know what to think. He was a small man in a light gray suit. I wasn't sure what I had expected. I dropped my rifle to my side. He spoke again. His voice filled with rage and disdain. "I don't know who you are, but you're dead." He raised a pistol.

Joshua yelled, "Move!" I hadn't realized that Zhang-Fei had placed himself between the police and me; he was walking toward me, and the Thai police were running in our direction. If I raised my gun, they would think I was bringing it to bear on them. Zhang-Fei repeated as he took aim, "You are dead, you meddling bastard!"

The side of his head exploded; he fell facedown on the pavement. I heard the report … Wallace. The police ran for cover, with a new threat behind them. Wallace's shot stopped the police from advancing. Joshua seized the moment. He saw we had a small window of opportunity to escape ourselves. Joshua grabbed my shoulder, looking down at the corpse. "Now, can we get the hell out of here?" I dropped the carbine, and we ran for the river. We glanced back long enough to see more police and firemen swarm the compound before hiding ourselves in the river vegetation.

We treaded sticky mud as we walked along the bank of the river. Each step was taken with care, knowing that Thailand hosted many venomous snakes. After a half hour of walking, Joshua asked as he swatted at biting insects, "I got to know. When you jumped from the boat, did you think about how you were going to get back to the hotel?"

"Nope."

"A second boat would have been nice."

"Yep."

Chapter 29

We walked another mile before we made it up to the streets and at least another mile on the street before we found a cab to take us to the hotel. Dan, Chewy, Luk, and Wallace were in the bar. They were drinking coffee. It was too early in the morning to buy alcohol. Before we arrived, they had taken Asian Sin to Joshua's room, where they had set Joshua's men to guard her.

They poured me a cup. They were wired. Joshua found a seat at the table, but I remained standing. I raised the cup for a toast. "We did it!"

"That's it?" Joshua questioned my speech. "'We did it'?"

"How do I find words for what you guys did? How do I express my gratitude? There are no words for what you did." I raised my cup again. "To all of you."

They raised their cups and touched them together. Wallace invited us down to his place tonight for a celebration. "I will close to the public for the night. The Drunken Wallaby will be just for us tonight!"

"Hear, hear!" the rest of the table chimed in. We agreed to meet at Wallace's after we got some sleep. It had been a long day.

I slept like the dead that Zhang-Fei had tried to make me. Dan's phone call woke me. He had good news. Parker had been moved to Bangkok and was awake and talking. He was going to make it. I was in the process of just finishing dressing when a knock came at my door. I opened it. It was Asian Sin.

"Please, come in." I shut the door behind her. This was the first time I had really gotten to see her. I had been too busy at the compound for even an introduction. She wore a robe. I was taken back by how much she looked like Dallas. They could be twins. She appeared more hardened, more streetwise, but the fire in her eyes and the intense smile I saw in her movies were still there. They intimidated me.

She walked over to the edge of the bed and sat down. She studied me before she spoke. "Sorry about the robe. I don't have any clothes. Joshua went to buy me some."

"Of course." There she was, Asian Sin, Sara Jones. *But who is she?* I wondered to myself. *A porn star, a mother, a queen-empress, who?* As much as I had read about her and studied her life, I didn't have an answer as to who she was.

She looked down and then back up at me. "Joshua told me everything. I can't believe there are people who would do so much for someone they don't know … for a stranger."

"It was the least we could do for an empress," I answered in a soft voice.

"Please; you didn't know that when you started to look for me, I know." Her soft reply was tinged with an oriental accent not apparent in her movies.

"Joshua has a big mouth," I answered.

"Then, why?" she asked.

I thought a moment. "I'm not sure I understand."

"Were you a fan?"

"No … sorry. Actually, I had never heard of you nor seen you until I read a newspaper about your being missing. Then I started the case, my investigation." I still couldn't explain it to myself. How was I going to explain it to her?

"So, then why?" she asked again.

"Sometimes you must travel paths you don't choose." I shrugged.

She laughed. "You talked to Dallas."

"Indeed." I looked away for a moment.

"What?"

"Well, maybe I did it for me, for me and an old friend." I smiled. Her brow wrinkled with confusion. "Look, I don't expect you to understand. Sometime, ask Dallas."

She stood up and closed into my space, wrapping her arms around me. She kissed me gently on the cheek. She stepped back and smiled. "There is nothing I can do; there is nothing I can give you to repay you."

"I'm not asking for anything." We looked at each other in silence. In that moment, I learned who she was: a person, albeit a remarkable person. Suddenly my look darkened.

"What's wrong?" she asked.

"William Parker. Do you remember him?" I answered with a question. After everything she had been through, I wasn't sure she was ready for anything else.

"Of course … why?"

"You know, he loves you … I mean, I know it from just listening to his voice when he talks about you. Would you go see him for me?"

"Love? Loves me?"

I nodded.

"Dallas told me you were a romantic sap."

"Christ, does your family have any secrets?" I felt myself blush.

She laughed again. I enjoyed hearing her laugh. "A few." She stood and went to the door. "Mr. Conner … I don't know what to say or do."

I returned her smile. "You already did it … Empress." It was her turn to blush. "Miss Jones …" I hesitated. "There's another matter."

She came back and sat down. "What?"

I wanted a drink, but I didn't have one. "The Korean, the father of your son. He's here."

"Here in Bangkok?" She sounded shocked.

"Here in the hotel … the penthouse, in fact," I answered.

"Now? Here now?" She sounded trapped.

"Don't worry."

She thought a minute. "A diametrical paradox."

"Excuse me?" I asked.

"Of all the things I've done, the one thing I regret the most is my relationship with him. But at the same time, he gave me my son." She stopped. "He pursued me over a year before I even agreed to see him. The flowers, the gifts, the attention—he wore me down. You know, I seriously thought about marrying him. But besides being insanely jealous, he was completely obsessed with our unborn child. He went into these tirades that his son would be rightful successor to the throne … to an empire. A Korean would be emperor of China. It got worse after our son was born; he frightened me.

"Then to make matters worse, his brother went after me. So, I fled, and to protect my son, I followed the course of my real mother, and we arranged for an American couple to adopt him. I was so afraid of the brother and what might happen that I haven't seen my son since we fled."

I was stuck on her statement. "His brother?"

She looked up at me. "Zhang-Fei … Zhang-Fei was his brother. I thought you knew."

Stunned, I sat back on the writing desk. "No … I didn't know."

"I'm not sure Dallas or Joshua ever knew," she answered and then explained, "He and Zhang-Fei were business partners at one time. Fei used the family name then. But while my son's father was working eighteen or twenty hours a day, Zhang-Fei was out drinking and chasing girls. The partnership ended when Zhang-Fei stole a considerable amount of money from their company. The Korean dissolved his partnership with his brother. It almost killed him, but at the same time, it fed his drive and fire. Fei turned into this criminal, with the façade of being a devout communist. Zhang-Fei hated everything the Korean stood for and worked for."

I sat on the edge of the small desk, looking down, taking in all she was telling me. I found it strange that even she never said his name. I had met him; he wasn't God. I wanted to ask, but didn't. I finally spoke. "I told him that I would ask you if you would be willing to meet with him … you and the boy. He won't try to contact you. Don't worry."

"Never! He never cared for me! He wanted my lineage, not me! This lineage I hate." Sara stood, looking as if she were about to bolt out of the room. "This great secret for years was kept from me. It wasn't until I went to college that I learned of my heritage. My own mother was a secret to me, but I was forced to learn to speak Chinese, to learn Chinese history, everything Chinese. I never asked to be this nor did my son, but this thing, this heritage forced me to send him away. Do you have any idea? I'm not a princess. I'm not an empress. I'm me." She fought back tears as she finished. "Don't you understand?"

"Don't ask me. I'm a commoner." I smiled with my answer. She laughed. "I don't understand anything about your family," I added. "But, Sara, he tried to find you. He even offered his assistance to help me. He's an old man now. I guess I feel sorry for him a little."

"Did you take his assistance?" she asked. She was thinking about it.

"No," I said. "I felt sorry for him. I never said I trusted him." My eyebrows rose with my reply.

"You do understand then."

"Maybe," I answered with a sigh. "I'm not insisting that you go see him. That's up to you. But would you go see Bill?"

"Of course, I'll go see Bill." She walked to the door and stepped into the hall. She smiled wistfully at me one more time before closing the door.

We had our celebration at the Drunken Wallaby. I stood at the bar and watched everybody interact. After a beer, I sat down with Wallace and Joy and said, "There is nothing I can say."

"Then don't try," Wallace answered from behind his beer.

"Thank you, both of you."

Joy chimed in, "Well, thank you for bringing my husband back to me alive."

I looked in the eyes of Wallace and then Joy and said, "I don't want to say good-bye."

Joy asked, her gentle voice reassuring, "Do you know the American writer Theodor Geisel?"

"Yes, Dr. Seuss."

He is attributed to having said, "Don't cry because it's over. Smile because it happened.'" She smiled.

We clanged our glasses together. I gave the toast: "To the regiment."

Before I started to tear up, I left their table and sat down with Nat and Luk. Luk was trying to convince Nat to keep some of the money for herself and not just give it to the girls. "She won't take it," Luk said with frustration in his voice.

"Why not?" I asked her.

"I got money. Girls do not have."

"Okay, I understand. Nat, would you have a drink with me?"

She nodded. I had another beer while she ordered something in Thai. Before I could thank her, she declared, "Thailand better. The world better today. It good he dead."

"Maybe for a little bit, but there will be others."

"Maybe. Not today." She smiled up at me.

"Nat, thank you very much. Please thank the girls, too."

She nodded.

I could see Luk wanted to say something. I asked, "Luk?"

He held out his open hands. In his palms lay a gold mandala: a Buddha in the center, suspended by a gold chain. "Mr. Conner, this is for you. For everything you did."

"Luk, I can't." I could see it was very expensive. "Luk, it was us—it was everyone here."

"Please."

I was afraid I would offend him if I didn't take it. I gathered it into my hand and *wai*-ed as I said, "Thank you."

I went out into the heat and sat down in a chair just outside the entrance. There was sadness deep in my heart. Asian Sin had given me something very special: the opportunity to bring together a group of people with a common cause. We had fought a hard fight, but because of their courage and heart, we had won. I toasted Asian Sin for the last time … and saluted Sara Jones with heartfelt admiration.

Chapter 30

There was some trouble getting travel documents for Sara, since she was brought to Thailand without a passport, visa, or any type of ID. Everyone returned to Los Angeles on Dallas's private jet except me. Her jet was full, so I volunteered to fly back alone commercially.

I wanted time to think anyway. I read the English version of a Bangkok newspaper for the first part of the flight. The lead story had officials describing the firefight at the Blue Orchid Apartments as a drug war between rival gangs. A major drug lord was killed in the incident. I had wondered how they were going to explain it. I also wondered how much Dallas's firm helped with the explanation.

Would Keeley meet me at the plane? I even rehearsed my lines. I selfishly craved a moment like Wallace and Joy had after we returned from taking the ship. But it didn't happen. Instead, I was met by sheriff's deputies. Detective Jim Collins had questions for me, questions that had several lifetimes of jeopardy attached to the answers. I never lied, but I did leave a lot out. He didn't press; he was thankful we solved the murder of the senator's son. Then, with just a few days left in California before going home, I was hoping every minute that Keeley would come see me or call. She never did.

Dallas had another party to celebrate Sara Jones's homecoming. After the party ended, I would be leaving to go home the next day. I wasn't sure

I wanted to go home, but where would I go? I spent the night with Dallas. I know, I know …

During the party, Joshua had volunteered to drive me to the airport. I accepted. Dallas wanted to go, but her work got in the way. Joshua and his driver picked me up at the hotel. We drove a few blocks before he spoke. "Jack, I don't know what to say. You saved my cousin's life. How does it feel to be the man that saved the empress of China?"

I chuckled as I answered, "First off, *we* saved her. Second, I still don't believe all that."

"Then why did the secret Imperial Guard show up in Wayfarer and in Chinatown to help you?" he asked with a clever tone, and then added, "Actually, they saved your ass."

"Imperial Guard?" I said, confused. "The guys in the black uniforms and covered faces?"

He nodded. He wore a smirk.

"You know, I never told you about Wayfarer. You know, you being a crook and all," I added. Joshua said nothing. He only looked forward with a large grin.

"How *did* you know?" I thought for a minute. "You couldn't have known … that is, unless you're one of them." He didn't answer. "I should have figured. You're not a gangster at all, are you? Let me ask you since you have an inside track, why didn't these guys just investigate Sara's disappearance themselves? They appeared to be highly trained professionals." I was still trying to wrap my mind around the whole royal thing.

"Simple," he answered. "They're trained soldiers … guards sworn to protect the royal family, and to do it in secrecy. They're not investigators, Jack. They can't attract that kind of attention."

I gave a cynical, slow nod. "I'm sorry, but I'm still having a real tough time with all this."

Joshua only continued to grin.

Sara stood outside the terminal on the sidewalk to greet us and say her good-byes. We sat and had a great lighthearted visit in an airport coffee shop before I left. I still couldn't get over how Sara looked like Dallas. Last night at the party, I had watched them together. If it wasn't for the different hairstyles, I couldn't have told them apart. I shook Joshua's hand at the coffee shop, and we said our good-byes. Sara wanted to walk me to the security gate alone. She ran her arm through mine as we walked.

"You never asked me why," she asked.

I switched from reading directions and gate signs to looking at her from the corner of my eyes. "Asked you why … what?"

"About my profession. You never asked me why I got into the porn business," Sara answered.

I buried my hands deep in my pockets as we walked; her hand was still at my elbow. "It was none of my business."

"Dallas told me you never judged me. You never asked."

"I wondered some … I guess." I led her out of the foot traffic, and I leaned on the wall. She took the lead, and I followed her to an empty section of chairs.

Before she began her explanation, I told her, "You don't have to explain … not to me."

"I want to. I need to."

I smiled and nodded. "Okay."

"I don't know what you've been told about me or how I learned about my heritage. But I'm going to tell you. When I graduated from high school, my real mother and my adopted mother sat me down and explained it to me. There were people in the Chinese government that found out I existed. I didn't know until then that my real mother was alive. Not only was she alive; she was my au pair. She used to tell me when I did something wrong, 'That's no way for a princess to act.' I thought it was a nickname. You see, Jack, my whole life was a lie. I don't know. I guess I wanted to just be me. This princess is someone else." She started to tear up, but refrained.

I took both her hands and squeezed. "They did it for you. To protect you."

She smiled. "I know that now, but then ..."

"I understand."

"I can't undo my life ... my choices." There was regret in her voice.

"You thanked me for not judging you. Don't judge yourself, Sara. You are a remarkable woman. I'm proud to know you. Don't be so hard on yourself. There is nothing to forgive, but if you really, really think there is, then just do it and move on." I looked down. I was afraid I had said too much.

"How?"

I looked into those enchanting eyes and smiled. "I don't know. I think each person has to figure that out for themselves. You'll have to figure that out ... If you do, tell me, okay?"

"Jack, when I asked you why ... why you came after me, you told me maybe it was for an old friend."

"Yeah?"

"I don't know what you think you did, but maybe it's time for you to forgive yourself as well. What do you think?"

I didn't say a word—only nodded.

"Thank you, Jack." With a confused smile, she stood. She kissed me on the cheek, and we walked to security in silence.

Once on the plane, I tried to convince myself I was happy it was over, but deep inside, the sadness was still there. I would miss them all ... especially Keeley. I had even tried to call her a couple more times. And I was returning to Colorado a different person. This had changed me. The stolen girls, the drugs ... it was hard to believe the biggest case in my life came after I had retired. I fell asleep with the hope my dreams would let me relive the good and forget the bad.

I called both of my girls to see if either of them was available to pick me up at the airport, but neither was available. I was strangely disappointed. I had hoped to reconnect in some manner with the two girls that reluctantly called me Dad. Dallas, however, came through again. She had already arranged a car for me. It was a lonely drive home. The sadness continued to build inside me to the point that I wasn't sure I was ready to go home. But go where? To California? To Thailand? I didn't have an answer.

When I walked into my house, I don't know if I first smelled or heard the bacon and sausage frying in my kitchen. It surprised me and confused me. Before I could think, Keeley came around the corner and wrapped herself around me.

"Hi, Conner! Are you hungry?" she asked but didn't wait for an answer. Instead, she brought her lips to mine.

"I thought you ..."

She interrupted, "Thought what?"

I felt tears well up as my laughter grew. My heart was going a hundred miles an hour. I couldn't speak.

"Conner, we are getting married this afternoon, so hurry and go get cleaned up. Your food will be ready by then."

"Married? What?"

"Yes, Conner. You wouldn't want me to raise our baby by myself, would you? Now hurry!" She returned to the kitchen.

"Baby?" I followed her.

"Congratulations, Conner! You're going to be a father. So, you are going to marry me, right?" She turned the bacon and sausage. "That thing about cowboys and honor?"

"Yeah ... I guess ... yes, of course ... I think ... sure!"

She cracked the eggs on the side of the skillet and turned. "Conner, go shower! Mother will beat us to the church."

"Mother? Dallas?" That would be for sure an awkward moment for me. I left it at that and turned to go to the bathroom.

"Conner!" she yelled.

I turned back to face her. "Yes?"

She stood in the doorway. Her smile was soft, and her eyes shone with passion and excitement. Her words poured out slowly and softly. "Conner, I love you."

Chapter 31

Who could have imagined that a young woman from a land so far away could affect so many lives? Even after her death and the over three decades since we had met, she fulfilled her dream. Xiu Tang's life dream was to save and care for her people. Indirectly, she did so in ways she couldn't have imagined. Her chance meeting with a cowboy at a small Old West fair had started so many changes for many others as well. After all, it was because of her that I had followed this path to find Sara Jones.

In the four years after finding and returning Sara Jones to the United States, the lives of all involved were changed forever. In one of the happier outcomes of the entire quest, William Parker and Sara Jones were married. After a painful year of recovery, he was released from the hospital on their wedding day. Sara had spent every day by his side at the hospital. Together, they closed the strip club and remodeled it. It is now a dinner playhouse, which features different dance, food, and plays from all over the world. They feature a different country or culture each month. They tell me it is doing very well. It must be; they paved the parking lots and put in new sidewalks and gutters. They also run a halfway house and rescue shelter for trafficked women and children. Parker still runs his little weekly newspaper and is writing a book. His same employees still work for him; they just have different jobs.

Sara gave her house to her groundskeeper and housekeeper. In turn, they hired another retired porn couple to replace themselves. Sara's oldest daughter is working for Dallas's firm as an intern. The Korean passed away about two years ago, but Sara had relented and taken her son over to meet him before he died. She also forgave him.

Dallas probably surprised me the most after our adventure. This highly successful businesswoman adopted the three children we recovered on the beach that night in Wayfarer. She is retired from the day-to-day business of her empire, but she keeps her position as president, as well as her personal private office there. She spends most of her retirement with her new children and her grandchildren, spoiling them unmercifully. We have never once spoken about our encounters, but every now and then we share a look and smile. She also calls me from time to time to look into something that she doesn't want her regular detectives to work, which means work that may lead to me having to do something illegal.

Keeley and I occasionally have coffee together with Sky Lee and her husband, a rich businessman from Colorado. She leaves me with the same French phrase when we part. Someday I'm either going to look it up or just ask her what it means. She is expecting her first child. In another turn of events, her sister married a sheriff's deputy in California.

Wallace and Joy call about once every other month, giving us all the latest news from Thailand. Luk lost his wife to cancer about a year after we left. He and Nat have been keeping company and are going to marry in the near future. Wallace took over the bars that were under the control of Zhang-Fei and the MSM. Nat is going to operate them for him.

Keeley has started a part-time law practice. She and I have two daughters. After their births, my two older daughters began coming around and visiting with us. There is nothing like the allure of a sweet baby to heal old wounds. Keeley still calls me Conner, and under the threat of death or worse, I am never to refer to Dallas as "granny" or "grandma." The girls, even my older daughters, call her Grandmother, sometimes in English and sometimes in Chinese.

A few weeks ago, Dallas called, inviting my family to journey to China with her. It was more of an order than a request. In the true oriental inimitable way, she told me I had one more thing to do. Plying her to give me more information was ineffective. It was not until we arrived in northern China that her directive became clear.

Epilogue

And there I was on my knees at a simple stone monument outside a small village near the Tibetan border. Tears came to my eyes as I knelt at the monument. Dallas, Keeley, and the five girls stood behind me. The script was in English and Chinese. It gave the years she lived and the words, *"She cared for the sick and injured. She gave everything."* Above the words, engraved in the stone, were the caduceus, a pair of spurs, and a cowboy hat. In my hand, I tightly grasped her hairpin.

An elderly man with thinning gray hair came and stood over me. "May I help you?" he asked. He spoke English with little accent.

I stood to greet him. "No … thank you." He looked over at Keeley and Dallas. "My wife and my mother-in-law." My four-year-old ran over and grabbed my leg before I could introduce the children.

"Sorry." I apologized to the old man for her actions. "This is my daughter Xiu."

"Xiu?" His smile was gentle. "That was my daughter's name."

"I know."

"Did you know my daughter Xiu Tang?"

"Yes … yes, I did, a long time ago." I wiped away the tears.

"You are her young man from America." The statement was made with a quiet confidence.

I nodded. I hadn't heard "young man" in a sentence describing me in a while, and had never heard myself referred to as "her young man."

"She talked of you often. She was very fond of you." His smile grew as he remembered.

I reached out and opened my hand. "Here; I think you should have this."

He looked at the hairpin. He closed my hand back around it. "Please, wait here."

Xiu tugged on my pant leg and asked, "Daddy, what's this?" She touched the doctor's symbol.

"That means this person was a medical doctor," I explained to her.

Xiu announced with the pride of a four-year-old, "I'm going to be a doctor when I grow up." More tears came; I couldn't help it. I wiped them away, almost angry that they betrayed me. "What's wrong, Daddy?"

Keeley stepped over and took Xiu by the hand. "Nothing, honey." Keeley had tears as well. The old man returned. He opened my hand and took the pin. He placed it with the other pins from her set.

He asked, "May I?" I nodded in confusion. He knelt down to be face-to-face with Xiu. He presented the set of pins to her. "How are you, daughter?"

She looked up at me for approval. I smiled and nodded.

He said, "A gift from my daughter to your daughter … a gift from my daughter to our daughter." He stood again.

I was really bewildered.

He smiled. "Do you think life is all about biology and chemistry? Look around you. Life is everywhere. The spirit lives in us and around us." He stopped and looked at me. "She knew you loved her. It wasn't to be. Now it's time for redemption … you need to forgive yourself for whatever you believe you should have done or for whatever you are blaming yourself for. Things happened the way they should have." He knelt again and took Xiu's hand. "Promise to come back and see me."

She looked up at me again. I nodded approval. She struggled out of Keeley's grasp and hugged the old man around the neck. "I promise."

"Thank you … thank you very much." He stood and walked back to his home. I think he was crying.

Everyone was asleep on the trip back to the States. I couldn't let the old man's words go. I looked over at the girls and Keeley. I will never forget Xiu Tang. I will always remember the love and the special bond we had shared that one Colorado summer long ago, and I will never forget her father's words.

The few months we had together—a gift, a treasure. A young woman that changed my life forever, and maybe this was how it was supposed to be. I never considered what we did as a sin. Perhaps we had broken humans' rules regarding religion and politics at the time, but so what? Our love was under the approval of a higher authority.

"Don't cry because it's over. Smile because it happened."

Printed in the United States
By Bookmasters